VICTORIAN CRIME,
MADNESS AND SENSATION

Victorian Crime, Madness and Sensation

Edited by

ANDREW MAUNDER
University of Hertfordshire, UK

GRACE MOORE
University of Melbourne, Australia

LONDON AND NEW YORK

First published 2004 by Ashgate Publishing

Published 2016 by Routledge
2 Park Square, Milton Park, Abingdon, Oxfordshire OX14 4RN
711 Third Avenue, New York, NY 10017, USA

First issued in paperback 2016

Routledge is an imprint of the Taylor & Francis Group, an informa business

British Library Cataloguing in Publication Data
Victorian crime, madness and sensation. – (The nineteenth century series)
1. English fiction – 19th century – History and criticism 2. Penny dreadfuls – History – 19th century 3. Crime in literature 4. Criminals in literature 5. Scandals in literature 6. Mental illness in literature 7. Crime and the press – Great Britain – History – 19th century
I. Maunder, Andrew II. Moore, Grace
823.8'093556

Library of Congress Cataloging-in-Publication Data
Victorian crime, madness and sensation / [edited by] Andrew Maunder, Grace Moore.
p. cm. – (The nineteenth century series)
Includes bibliographical references and index.

1. English fiction – 19th century – History and criticism. 2. Crime in literature. 3. Crime – Great Britain – History – 19th century – Historiography. 4. Great Britain – Social conditions – 19th century – Historiography. 5. Great Britain – History – Victoria, 1837-1901 – Historiography. 6. English prose literature – 19th century – History and criticism. 7. Detective and mystery stories, English – History and criticism. 8. Sensationalism in literature. 9. Mentally ill in literature. 10. Criminals in literature. I. Maunder, Andrew. II. Moore, Grace, 1974- III. Series: Nineteenth century (Aldershot, England).

PR878.C74V53 2004
820.9'3556—dc22

2004004237

ISBN 13: 978-1-138-24666-9 (pbk)
ISBN 13: 978-0-7546-4060-8 (hbk)

Contents

The Nineteenth Century Series
General Editors' Preface

The aim of the series is to reflect, develop and extend the great burgeoning of interest in the nineteenth century that has been an inevitable feature of recent years, as that former epoch has come more sharply into focus as a locus for our understanding not only of the past but of the contours of our modernity. It centres primarily upon major authors and subjects within Romantic and Victorian literature. It also includes studies of other British writers and issues, where these are matters of current debate: for example, biography and autobiography, journalism, periodical literature, travel writing, book production, gender and non-canonical writing. We are dedicated principally to publishing original monographs and symposia; our policy is to embrace a broad scope in chronology, approach and range of concern, and both to recognize and cut innovatively across such parameters as those suggested by the designations 'Romantic' and 'Victorian'. We welcome new ideas and theories, while valuing traditional scholarship. It is hoped that the world which predates yet so forcibly predicts and engages our own will emerge in parts, in the wider sweep, and in the lively streams of disputation and change that are so manifest an aspect of its intellectual, artistic and social landscape.

Vincent Newey
Joanne Shattock
University of Leicester

List of Illustrations

Notes on Contributors

Maria K. Bachman is an Assistant Professor of English at Coastal Carolina University. She is presently co-editing a volume of essays on Wilkie Collins to be published by the University of Tennessee Press. She is also co-editing a critical edition of Wilkie Collins's novel, *Blind Love*, to be published by Broadview Press.

Máire ní Fhlathúin lectures in the School of English, University of Nottingham, and researches Irish and Indian postcolonial literature and history. Recent publications include 'The Irish Oscar Wilde: Appropriations of the Artist', *Irish Studies Review* 7.3 (1999); 'The Location of Childhood: *Great Expectations* in Postcolonial London', *Kunapipi* 21.2 (1999); 'The Anti-Colonial Modernism of Patrick Pearse', in *Modernism and Empire*, eds. Howard J. Booth and Nigel Rigby, Manchester, 2000; 'The Travels of M. de Thévenot through the Thug Archive', forthcoming in the *Journal of the Royal Asiatic Society*.

Christopher E. Forth is a senior lecturer in history at the Australian National University. He is the author of *Zarathustra in Paris: The Nietzsche Vogue in France, 1891-1918* (Dekalb, IL: Northern Illinois University Press, 2001) and *The Dreyfus Affair and the Crisis of French Manhood* (Baltimore: Johns Hopkins University Press, 2004). He is currently writing a history of the male body in the Western world.

Nicholas Freeman teaches English at the University of the West of England. His research interests are essentially grounded in English literature and society during the late Victorian era, but he has also written on film, popular culture and twentieth-century fiction. He is, at present, researching a study of London at the turn of the twentieth century.

Dallas Liddle is Assistant Professor of English at Augsburg College in Minneapolis, Minnesota. He has published articles on Victorian press anonymity, the development of the leading article, and the journalism of George Eliot. He is currently writing a study of the cultural work of genre in nineteenth-century periodicals.

Andrew Maunder is lecturer in English at the University of Hertfordshire. His research interests include Victorian and Edwardian fiction, the periodical press and reception histories. He has published articles in a range of journals including *Etudes Anglaises, Trollopiana,* and the *Victorian Periodicals Review.* He has contributed essays to the *New Dictionary of National Biography* and to *British*

Women Writers (Greenwood Press: 2000) and is General Editor of the series *Varieties of Women's Sensation Fiction* (2004).

Leslie Ann Minot is a freelance writer and journalist. She obtained her PhD from UCLA. Since graduating she has published widely on a variety of topics.

Dafydd Moore is a lecturer in the School of Humanities and Cultural Studies at the University of Plymouth. He has published articles in The Scottish Literary Journal and the British Society for Eighteenth-Century Studies Journal. He is currently working on a study of nineteenth-century appropriations of the Ossianic legends.

Grace Moore is lecturer in Literary Studies at the University of Melbourne, Australia. She has published articles on Dickens, Robert Louis Stevenson, Peter Carey, Bernhard Schlink, and Virginia Woolf. Her book, *Dickens and Empire*, will be published by Ashgate in 2004. She is at work on a new book, provisionally entitled *Victorian Silhouettes*, which will examine twentieth-century re-workings of the Victorian novel, and she is also working on an edited collection on Victorian piracy.

Karen Odden obtained her PhD in English from New York University. Her dissertation, entitled *Broken Trains of Thought: The Railway Crash, Trauma and Narrative in British Fiction, 1848-1910* examines a group of novels and short stories in which a mechanical or financial railway crash figures importantly and situates these fictional texts with respect to Victorian medico-legal discourse. She has published essays on Matthew Arnold, Robert Browning and Eavan Boland; short pieces have appeared in *The New York Times* and women's magazines. She is at present an independent scholar.

Barbara Onslow *teaches at the University of Reading. She is the author of* Women of the Press in Nineteenth-Century Britain *(Macmillan 2000) and has published extensively on both Victorian journalism and science.*

John Plunkett is a lecturer in English at the University of Exeter. He won the 1999 Pevsner Prize for his work on Queen Victoria's funeral and is at present working on a book entitled *Death and Dominion*, along with a popular print culture reader. His book *Queen Victoria: First Media Monarch* was published by Oxford University Press in 2003.

Sally Powell has recently completed her doctoral research at Oxford University. Her thesis, *Cadaverous Narratives: The Displaced Corpse in Victorian Fiction* examines the role of the displaced cadaver in the period's most popular genres and reveals the extent to which the image is employed as an expression of social anxiety and cultural disquiet in relation to a broad range of contemporary issues.

She is currently working on an anthology of selections from nineteenth-century penny fiction.

June Sturrock's edition of *Mansfield Park* appeared in 2001 as part of the Broadview Texts series. Recent publications include *"Heaven and Home": Charlotte Yonge's Domestic Fiction and the Victorian Debate on Women* (Victoria, BC: University of Victoria, 1995). Her many articles usually concern either women's writings, or the late poems of William Blake, which, diverse as they are, constitute her two main interests. She is currently working on a critical book to be entitled, *Home Renovations: British Women's Domestic Fiction, 1808-1883.*

Gita Panjabi Trelease teaches on the Princeton Writing Program and works on criminal anthropology and nineteenth-century mystery narratives.

Acknowledgements

The editors would like to express their gratitude to all of the contributors to this volume. We are extremely grateful to Ann Donahue and Erika Gaffney of Ashgate, both of whom have been model editors at every stage of this project. We would also like to thank the series editors for their help and advice.

The VICTORIA list administered by Patrick Leary has, as ever, been a superb resource and we thank all those who dealt with queries during this project's development. Thanks must also go to staff at Bristol University's Arts and Social Sciences Library, the University of British Columbia's Rare Books and Special Collections Library, the British Library, the Beinecke Library at Yale University, the University of Idaho Library, and Washington State University Library. Brigitte Istim of the Punch Archive in London has also been especially helpful. Thanks are long overdue to Andrew Robinson for his patient assistance with formatting and other many other queries.

USEFUL SUNDAY LITERATURE FOR THE MASSES;

OR, MURDER MADE FAMILIAR.

Father of a Family (*reads*). "The wretched Murderer is supposed to have cut the throats of his three eldest Children, and then to have killed the Baby by beating it repeatedly with a Poker. * * * * * In person he is of a rather bloated appearance, with a bull neck, small eyes, broad large nose, and coarse vulgar mouth. His dress was a light blue coat, with brass buttons, elegant yellow summer vest, and pepper-and-salt trowsers. When at the Station House he expressed himself as being rather 'peckish,' and said he should like a Black Pudding, which, with a Cup of Coffee, was immediately procured for him."

Punch, Useful Sunday Literature for the Masses; or Murder Made Familiar (1849).

Introduction

Andrew Maunder and Grace Moore

> "The public want novels, and novels must be made—so many yards of printed stuff, sensation-pattern, to be ready by the beginning of the season".[1]

A dynamic period of social, economic and political transition; the nineteenth century saw a change not only in the scope and perception of crime, but also in its representation. The rise of both a police force in 1829 and the detective police in 1842 focused attention on issues of law enforcement and the tracking, capture and taxonomy of the criminal. Reforms to the law and its codification in the 1820s, along with the rise of inexpensive mass print culture and an expansion in readership, led to a growing public fascination with crime and punishment, as criminals made their way from the pages of the newspaper into the novel and short story. Debates swiftly arose regarding the crossover between fact and fiction, with fiction frequently taking the blame for a decline in national (and primarily working-class) morals. Harriet Martineau warned grimly in 1865 against affordable, blood-drenched tales of murder, commenting that, "love, crime, madness, suicide, wherever they may be got in print, are powerful in preparing the young for convict life".[2] Later in the century an anonymous writer for the *Edinburgh Review* remarked:

> There is now such a verifiable mountain of pernicious trash, mostly in paper covers, and all 'Price One Penny': so-called novelettes, romances, tales, stories of adventure, mystery and crime; pictures of school life hideously unlike the reality; exploits of pirates, robbers, cut-throats, prostitutes, and rogues, that, but for its actual presence, it would seem incredible.[3]

As John Springhall has suggested, 'penny bloods' and their successors the 'penny dreadfuls' were turned into scapegoats for working-class crime.[4] Such arguments were not, however, solely restricted to working-class reading matter, and concerns also arose about the moral well-being of middle-class readers of sensation fiction, along with the increasingly sensationalized rhetoric that began to trickle into newspaper accounts of crimes and trials.

This collection follows the nineteenth-century reformulation of attitudes to crime, and examines how the boundaries of the new criminal system were delineated and transgressed throughout the Victorian period. By surveying a diverse range of crimes, criminals, detectives, modes of detection and reportage, we chart the development of crime writing as a genre and the growing dialogue between fact and fiction throughout Victoria's reign. John Plunkett begins this examination by concentrating on several cases from the Queen's earliest days on the throne. In his chapter on the royal stalkers and would-be assassins who came to be known as "The Queen's Lovers", Plunkett probes the discourses of insanity invoked by the news media to discuss the young monarch's pursuers. He also considers how these treasonous outbursts were dealt with in the work of popular novelists like G.M.W. Reynolds. In the case of "The Queen's Lovers" the stalkers' regicidal attempts are reduced to expressions of insanity, rather than acts of discontent at the state of the nation during the "Hungry Forties". However, for the fictitious counterparts of these men, the characters in G.M.W. Reynolds' *The Mysteries of London*, the links between assassination attempts and radical politics are made explicit.

The rapidly growing cities that came with industrialism were, owing to poor living conditions and the sheer numbers of people migrating from the country to the city, hotbeds of radicalism and vice. In spite of Sherlock Holmes's late-century proclamation that "the lowest and vilest alleys in London do not present a more dreadful record of sin than does the smiling and beautiful countryside", the anonymity offered by the urban centre allowed whole communities of criminals to cluster in slum areas.[5] In 1891 the Reverend William Douglas Morrison referred to the cities as "the nurseries of modern crime", and Morrison's words neatly encapsulate the wealth of opportunities offered by the sheer enormity of the city to the would-be offender.[6] To suggest that the city was a magnet for those with an innate propensity toward crime is a gross simplification, and Morrison points to the way in which the poverty engendered by the metropolis nurtured criminal tendencies within its underclass. A prime example of such a group would be those who belonged to the overcrowded and notoriously exploitative "governess trade", as Barbara Onslow outlines in Chapter 7. Many of those who migrated to urban areas—and governesses were far from unique in this respect—moved in search of improved conditions and were horrified by the reality of unemployment or exploitation that awaited them there. In an over-crowded profession, a large proportion of governesses were compelled to resort to either occasional or professional prostitution as a means of supporting themselves, although they were certainly not the only social group compelled to resort to crime in order to survive.

One of Henry Mayhew's commentators, the Reverend William Tuckniss pointed to the relationship between urban poverty and crime when he stated with a tone of despair:

> We have been dealing with effects rather than with first causes, and in our zeal to absorb, divert, or diminish the former, the latter have generally escaped detection. When too late, we have discovered that mere palliatives will not suffice, and that they are powerless to resist the steady growth of crime in all its subtle developments.[7]

Tuckniss was all too aware here of the need for widespread social reform as a means of quelling the disease-like spread of crime which had come to pervade the city. In Chapter 3, Sally Powell presents us with a London that is quite literally dripping with pestilence of the kind that mid-century reformers like Tuckniss, Mayhew and Edwin Chadwick sought to highlight. Powell tracks the threat of growing urbanization and the forces of industrialism in her essay on the "penny blood"—an immediate successor to the Newgate Novel—exploring the criminality of a capitalist economy grounded in exploitation and the individual petty criminal's response to this state. Just as Reynolds deployed his *Mysteries of London* to highlight class tensions and poor living conditions in the capital, so Powell reads the Victorian obsession with displaced, robbed or violated corpses as a trope for the slave labour economy that quite literally took possession of the body of the living worker. Considering the adulteration of mass-produced food, the foetid slum areas of the city and the threat that consumerism posed to individual working-class identity, Powell shows how the trade in "resurrected" corpses which followed the 1832 Anatomy Act may be read as a wider allegory for a trade in bodily waste and bodily parts of all kinds. She examines the lack of sanctity accorded to the urban corpse, alongside the more particular threats posed to the female body, in addition to considering capitalist society's willful refusal to probe the unpleasant stories of sweated labour and adulterated products lurking behind a veneer of prosperity and efficiency. Powell effectively captures the dangers inherent in mass manufacture when she states "with the burgeoning city offering a seemingly ever-expanding captive market for stories that effectively evoked the gothic flavour of city life or offered a means of imaginative escape in the form of sensational romance for weary working-class urbanites". Her examination of the *Sweeney Todd* story draws particular attention to both fictitious and factual discourses of cannibalism and ingestion—or consumerism—in the heart of the city.

As Georg Simmel suggested in his 1903 essay "The Metropolis and Mental Life", the urban experience fostered a new form of mentality that was distinct from that of the country-dweller. According to Simmel, the urbanite was forced, out of basic self-preservation, to develop a "negative type of social conduct" by filtering out a large number of extraneous influences and stimuli that, if fully absorbed, would completely overwhelm the city dweller:

> If the unceasing external contact of numbers of persons should be met by the same number of inner reactions as in the small town, in which one knows almost every person he meets and to each of whom he has a positive relationship, one would be completely atomized internally and would fall into an unthinkable mental condition.[8]

In his chapter on James Thomson's much-neglected polyphonic poem of the metropolis, Dafydd Moore details the sheer despair induced by the trauma of city life and looks back to the Blakean city of the damned to demonstrate how industrialism irrevocably altered the consciousness of both the flâneur and the people of the street. Moore considers the difficulties the metropolis posed to the man of letters, and the problems that urban chaos presented to those, like Thomson, hoping to read the city. The tension described by Sally Powell in her essay on living amongst urban detritus surfaces again in Moore's essay which analyses the "geometry of delirium" which was both cause and effect of city life. Moore focuses on what he describes as the "partial insanity" of the city dweller in relation to broader nineteenth-century debates on the boundaries of madness and sanity.

The Victorians were, as Máire ní Fhlathúin notes, completely fascinated with the "other", whether that other was the imperial subject in a far-off colony, the revolting emaciated inhabitant of the slum dwelling or the newly demonized criminal. After the appearance of *The Origin of Species* in 1859, greater attempts were made to biologize crime, and the later work of Nordau and Lombroso attempted to link crime to the perpetrator's genetic history.[9] This deduction downplayed the impact of the social inequalities that led to criminal acts like theft or prostitution and thus relieved the ruling classes of the responsibility for improving basic living conditions. Crime was figured as a kind of national malady, and the logical extension of such studies were the late nineteenth and early twentieth-century eugenicists' calls for the regulation of the known criminal's reproduction.[10] Another result of attempts to uncover the physical causes of crime was an increased attention on the individual body.

This policing of gender also brought about a re-coding of sexuality and a policing of the individual body, as Foucault puts it, "Sexuality was carefully confined; it moved into the home. The conjugal family took custody of it and absorbed it into the serious function of reproduction".[11] Foucault argues that with the post-industrial valorization of the heterosexual couple came the persecution and criminalization of alternative sexualities. He cites the nineteenth century as the period when "sexual transgression"—namely any deviation from monogamous heterosexuality—was persecuted and criminalized.[12]

Homosexuality was far from being the only clandestine sexual practice that took on the appearance of a vice to be policed, this time by concerned parents, doctors and quacks. Grace Moore's chapter on *Dr. Jekyll and Mr. Hyde* takes issue with Elaine Showalter's assertion that Robert Louis Stevenson's novella is a tale of *fin-de-siècle* homosexual panic and observing Henry Jekyll's near-constant state of solitude, argues instead that the text is concerned with regulating the body of the masturbator. By juxtaposing Stevenson's descriptions of the respectable Jekyll's tortured metamorphosis into Hyde with late-Victorian works like Joseph Howe's *Excessive Venery*, Moore demonstrates the persecution of the so-called "self-polluter". Chapter 10 particularly highlights how a process of self-exploration and self-satisfaction came to be viewed as a crime against the self, society and even an economy that valorized the heterosexual family unit. Robert Mighall has, in an examination of *Dr. Jekyll and Mr Hyde*, drawn attention to the growing convergence between the roles of the doctor and the policeman. He argues that: "[A] certain esoteria surrounds the medical expert on masturbatory disorders, whose methods and strategies often resemble those of the fictional detective...or even the ghost-hunter or vampire-slayer of horror fiction".[13] Moore probes the late-Victorian "secret life" through examining case studies of "disorders" alongside quack pamphlets offering "cures", and she also addresses the ways in which discourses of crime were invoked to regulate gender and sexuality.

It was not simply sexuality that the Victorians sought to regulate; reading practices also came under scrutiny with the advent of mass literacy. Emerging in the 1850s the "Sensation novel" was a title originally bestowed upon Wilkie

Collins's serial *The Woman in White* (1859-1860). However, as writers like Ellen [Mrs Henry] Wood, Mary Elizabeth Braddon, Charles Reade and Collins himself produced more and more works of murder, adultery, bigamy, poisoning and mistaken identity, the decade came to be referred to as the "age of sensation". Although today the term is a useful shorthand, for the Victorian reader and critic, the term "sensational" was often a loaded one. In an article critiquing a number of sensation novels, H.L. Mansel complained at the taint of trade that was, for him, one of several factors to mar his enjoyment of the works:

> A commercial atmosphere floats around works of this class, redolent of the manufactory and the shop. The public wants novels, and novels must be made—so many yards of printed stuff, sensation-pattern, to be ready by the beginning of the season.[14]

Mansel was far from alone in his criticism of the blatant commercialism of the genre, and a number of periodicals entered into lively debate about the dubious quality of plot-driven novels that played so directly upon the senses and that were so clearly manufactured for a mass audience. The form was seen to be symptomatic of the degeneration, not only of literature, but also of moral values, and there were very real concerns that readers—particularly female readers—would be adversely influenced by the amoral characters to be found in these works. To appreciate this anxiety in full, one must remember that in the post-Darwinian climate fears regarding any form of cultural descent ran high. The craving for sensation fiction was hence perceived as a form of cultural malaise; addictive, debilitating and self-indulgent. Jenny Bourne Taylor describes the novel's incipient danger superbly and in terms that recall the nineteenth-century anti-masturbation tract:

> The sensation novel was seen as a collective cultural nervous disorder, a morbid addiction within the middle class that worked directly on the body of the reader and as an infection from outside, continually threatening to pollute and undermine its boundaries through this process of metaphoric transference and analogy.[15]

Not only did the sensation novel depict atavistic modes of conduct, it also had the power to debilitate and degenerate the reader herself. Nevertheless, the reading of sensation fiction remained a highly popular form of diversion and its techniques soon came to be employed by journalists seeking to increase the circulation of daily newspapers.

Although herself the epitome of bourgeois respectability, Mrs. Henry Wood's 1861 work *East Lynne* contained all the elements of scandal that made for the perfect sensation novel. Drawing upon Wood's novel, Andrew Maunder considers mid-century anxieties surrounding an inherited propensity towards crime in his discussion of the degenerate aristocrat, Lady Isabel Vane. By reading *East Lynne* though the work of contemporary experts like Henry Maudsley, Maunder addresses the middle-class author's assertion of moral superiority over the self-indulgent aristocrat, lacking in both self discipline and a sense of responsibility.

Whilst Ellen Wood's narrator was explicitly condemnatory of Lady Isabel's conduct, the novel nevertheless excited controversy and debate. Margaret Oliphant may have condemned the novel's immorality, but she was willing to concede that the act of elopement made the adulterous Lady Isabel a far more interesting protagonist than any of the virtuous middle-class characters who surrounded her. Oliphant expresses her reluctant attraction to the heroine when she observes:

> From first to last it is she alone in whom the reader feels any interest. The Magdalen herself, who is only moderately interesting while she is good, becomes, as soon as she is a Magdalen, doubly a heroine. It is evident that nohow, except by her wickedness and sufferings, could she have gained so strong a hold upon our sympathies. This is dangerous and foolish work, as well as false, both to Art and Nature. Nothing can be more wrong and fatal than to represent the flames of vice as a purifying fiery ordeal, through which the penitent is to come elevated and sublimed.[16]

Charismatic though Isabel may be, Oliphant is unequivocal in her condemnation, and her words encapsulate the wider concerns expressed by many critics about the sensation novel's potential impact on public mores. Debates of this type, questioning the quality and morality of mass culture continued throughout the century and not only in Britain (as Christopher Forth shows in Chapter 11, they also spread to France).

The periodical press played an important role in feeding a seemingly insatiable public demand for crime stories like the early "shilling shockers", sensation novels and the later "penny dreadfuls", all of which were serialized in journals of varying degrees of respectability. The public was not simply interested in fiction, though, and many journals, following the lead of Dickens's extremely successful "Inspector Field" articles in *Household Words* presented readers with what became highly popular stories of true crime and real-life feats of detection. The key to the successful "true crime" story was, for many journalists, to be sure that it contained all the ingredients of a sensation novel. Dallas Liddle points to this "uneasy intermeshing of public and private—the family chronicle as sensation novel, domestic drama as national news" in Chapter 6, with his examination of the 1868 "nine days' wonder" surrounding the disappearance of the Reverend Benjamin Speke. Himself adopting the role of detective, Liddle reconstructs the compelling true story of Speke's disappearance and subsequent re-emergence to demonstrate the dialogue between sensation fiction and the news media by drawing on reports from *The Leader* and *The Times*. Speke's apparently missing body became a space onto which journalists projected a whole range of anxieties surrounding the perceived dangers of the metropolis, from secret societies to paid assassins, all of which could have been culled from the most popular sensation novels of the day. Speke later appeared unharmed in the somewhat unlikely guise of a Cornish cattle drover, and Liddle uses the story's anti-climax to demonstrate how the sensation genre tempted the reporter to theorize the mundane and ultimately reveals how the case may be seen to have posed a challenge to the newspaper's narrative authority, by carefully examining how the sensational rhetoric and speculation that characterized accounts of the disappearance had been directly imported from the works of writers like Wilkie Collins or Mary Elizabeth Braddon.

This interplay between fiction and reality was, though, by no means a one-way process, as H.L. Mansel commented in 1863:

> If a scandal of more than usual piquancy occurs in high life, or a crime of extraordinary horror figures among our causes célèbres, the sensationist is immediately at hand to weave the incident into a thrilling tale...The sensation novel, be it mere trash or something worse, is usually a tale of our own times. Proximity is, indeed, one great element of sensation. It is necessary to be near a mine to be blown up by its explosion; and a tale which aims at electrifying the nerves of the reader is never thoroughly effective unless the scene be laid in our own days and among the people we are in the habit of meeting.[17]

In her chapter on the Kent murder of 1860, June Sturrock looks at three such tales of the times and explores the sensation decade's responses to what was initially regarded as the unfounded accusation of Constance Kent of her younger brother's murder. Drawing on Charlotte M. Yonge's *The Trial,* Mrs Oliphant's *Salem Chapel* and Mary Elizabeth Braddon's *Lady Audley's Secret*, Chapter 5 addresses mid-century constructions of bourgeois womanhood and femininity by examining the female murder suspect. Sturrock contrasts newspaper narratives of the 1860s with contemporary fiction to ask just why female novelists could not conceive of middle-class womanhood on trial for murder, in spite of the public's clear fascination for the Kent case. By examining the discrepancy between the bourgeois myth of "the angel in the house" and the frustration, anger and feelings of entrapment experienced by many women, she considers parallels between Constance Kent and Leonard Ward, the protagonist of Yonge's *The Trial.* Sturrock points out that "Yonge's traditionalist and hierarchical Tractarian views of family and gender roles [meant that] in order to be acceptable, a 'sensation' plot necessarily...involves a male rather than a female protagonist" and goes on to consider mid-Victorian discomfort at the prospect of middle-class women, and middle-class secrets being exposed to the public gaze. Sturrock remarks that while the reading public was fascinated with the minutiae of the Kent investigation and eventual trial, novelists like Braddon, Oliphant and Yonge were highly reluctant to permit female characters to take the stand. Citing *Lady Audley's Secret* as an exemplar, Sturrock reminds us of the overwhelming anxieties felt by both the declining aristocracy and the arriviste middle classes at the prospect of losing respect and status. It is for this reason that the fictitious Audley family—and indeed, Braddon herself—choose to incarcerate the scheming Lady Audley in an asylum, rather than subject the family honour to public scrutiny.

Such feelings of vulnerability were not, for the middle classes, simply a question of respectability. The bourgeoisie, having only recently arrived at a position of economic and political power, often felt anxious that both its wealth and political power might be fleeting, since they were founded upon finance capital, rather than rooted in the land like that of the aristocracy. Fortunes, as the railway crashes of the 1840s showed, could be lost even more swiftly than they were gained. Stephen Knight has remarked that one explanation for the Victorian fascination with mystery and crime stories is the apparent transience of middle-class power and capital.[18] Suspicion and speculation surrounded the mysterious origins of self-made individuals who seemed to appear from nowhere and lacked connections. The rapidly accrued and often unexplained wealth of figures like Dickens's financier Mr. Merdle, or Trollope's swindler, Augustus Melmotte aroused immense conjecture, not to mention debates about the distinctions between inherited wealth and breeding and the alleged vulgarity of "new" money and the social ostracism of its trade-tainted holders. In her chapter on railway investment fraud in Trollope's *The Way We Live Now*, Karen Odden addresses the mysterious new wealth of railway barons, and the rise of white collar crime as a distinctly nineteenth-century phenomenon. She also reappraises some of the ways in which scams like Trollope's Vera Cruz railway venture, or the real-life corruption of the "railway king" George Hudson, altered the Victorian conception of crime itself. Franco Moretti has observed that "the perfect crime—the nightmare of detective fiction—is the featureless, deindividualized crime that anyone could have committed" and few crimes could be more featureless than the railway frauds that ruined thousands.[19] Reading the railway entrepreneur's deeds and promissory notes as little more than waste paper, Odden assesses Trollope's own sense that the author who writes for money is, like the desperate hack Lady Carbury, a cheat akin to the capitalist railway barons. This reading is complicated by the fact that Trollope himself wrote to earn a living, and Odden draws upon his autobiography to make connections between Trollope and his characters. In *The Way We Live Now* hack writing, is represented as mere puffery that, like the railway shares smacks of trade and can never deliver on its promises. Through its sheer clumsiness, poor writing is ultimately, for Trollope, nothing less than a crime.

Barbara Onslow goes beyond concerns with the perpetration and detection of crime to look instead at the captured criminal and the growing public interest in punishment and rehabilitation in her chapter, "The Inside Story: Crime, Convicts and Careers for Women". In addition to considering such pioneers of the periodical article on prison conditions as Charles Dickens, Onslow examines the paradoxical manner in which the prison became a liberating force for the middle-class woman. Onslow points out that early campaigns for penal reform had, by the middle of the nineteenth century, been taken up by female journalists and campaigners for women's rights like Barbara Bodichon, Harriet Martineau and Bessie Parkes. Onslow highlights these women's commitment to addressing the causes of crime and the ways in which these proto-feminists used the issue of prison reform (especially for female prisoners) to acquire a public political platform. In addition to advancing calls for women's rights, these women also sought to alleviate prostitution, often the last resort of the desperate woman of both the middle and working classes, by finding employment for those females who could not be incorporated conveniently within the normative two-parent family.

As Thomas Hood's humorous poem "I'm Going to Bombay" (1832) reminds us, the British Empire seemed to offer opportunities, not only for those women without a mate whom George Gissing was later to dub the "Odd Women", but also for those hoping to improve their prospects.[20] With the conquest of territories in

India and later Africa the Victorians were faced with the need to subordinate and police local indigenous populations, often involving innovative detection practices. Hence, there arose multifarious connections between the policing and detection of crime in the mother country, and the British Empire, the latter often serving as a locus for experimentation and discovery of new techniques. In narrative terms, Britain's imperial holdings offered an exotic backdrop and even more outlandish crimes for both the reporter and novelist, and stories like Philip Meadows Taylor's sensationalist *Confessions of a Thug* (1839) or John Lang's articles in *Household Words* were eagerly devoured by a fascinated reading public. Máire ní Fhlathúin examines the expansion and narrative embellishment of the British war against the ritualistic "Thug" murders in India from the 1830s until the 1870s. Chapter 2 traces the assimilation of the Thuggee narrative into European crime writing, focusing particularly on the works of Eugène Sue and Jules Verne. Drawing attention to the many links between British India and metropolitan France, Fhlathúin considers the rise of the master criminal as a nineteenth-century phenomenon—beginning with Vidocq's somewhat questionable memoirs—and examines the role that Thug narratives played in the construction of omnipotent "Napoleons of crime" like Sue's "Faranghea" or Verne's "Feringhea". Fhlathúin traces the demonization of the original Feringhea by novelists, the media, and colonial administrators, considering the many changes in discourses of criminality that occurred in the second half of the nineteenth century. She also considers the growing necessity for the figure of the master criminal as a focus for public concerns and as a scapegoat for crimes that could not be stamped out.

The "convergence of the exotic and the domestic" was definitely not limited to the depiction of ever more powerful criminals who posed increasingly formidable challenges to the police detective. The overseas territories played a significant role in both the detection and the punishment of crime, initially North America and then later Australia and Van Diemen's Land. Up until 1867 when the last convict ship sailed, criminals were regularly exported to Britain's overseas territories, rather than being offered rehabilitation in the mother country. Indeed, more than 160,000 men, women and children were shipped to Australia as prisoners of the Crown between 1787 and 1868.[21] The empire's role in upholding the forces of law and order was not restricted to shipping convicts shipped overseas to face a type of Darwinian struggle against often-hostile climates and terrains. Ronald Thomas has astutely observed that in many ways, the colonies "served as the laboratory in which criminological theories and techniques were discovered, developed, and tested for eventual application on the common criminal back home".[22] One excellent example of this process of experimentation is the "discovery" and appropriation of fingerprinting in India by Sir William Herschel in 1860. Originally used by Indians as an indisputable form of identification, the process was adopted, or rather appropriated, by Herschel. Having tested the technique in the district of Hooghly, Herschel initially published his results in 1880, and they were later popularized by Francis Galton in his 1892 work *Finger Prints*.

Like Máire ní Fhlathúin, Gita Panjabi Trelease demonstrates the importance of India to European crime writing and criminology—this time in relation to detection and prevention—in her chapter on crime management and technologies of detection in the years following the Indian "Mutiny" of 1857. Offering an analysis of fingerprinting's growing significance in the detective narrative from Twain's *Pudd'nhead Wilson* in 1894, Trelease returns to Herschel's oft-neglected work to chart the origins of dactyloscopy and the role that its emergence played. Reading the Victorian period's most famous detective, Sherlock Holmes, as not simply a scientist, but also an orderer and assembler of narratives, Trelease points to a crucial disjunction between the police detective and his fictional counterpart. It would seem that for the true-life detective, the fingerprint became a form of irrefutable evidence that reduced the need for police officers to construct narratives in order to prove a criminal's guilt. In his typically contrary fashion, Holmes demonstrates that the detective should be wary of relegating himself to the desk, and shows in the case of "The Norwood Builder" that even the apparently incontestable proof of identity signaled by the fingerprint may not always be a secure foundation on which to rest a case.

Maria Bachman considers a colony much closer to mainland Britain in her chapter on Wilkie Collins's last novel, *Blind Love*, in which she examines Collins's depiction of the Mephistophelean criminal Lord Harry in relation to contemporary concerns with insanity and imperial rule. Bachman addresses Collins's politicization of madness through his depiction of an amoral, insane Irish peer—a portrait that drew upon popular stereotypes of Irish impulsiveness, vulnerability and evolutionary regression. Furthermore, Bachman puts forward a compelling case for a psycho-sexual reading of Anglo-Irish relations by examining the "blind love" of the quintessentially English woman Iris Henley for the demonic Lord Harry. Reading Iris's fascination with Harry as analogous to the sympathetic stance taken by some of the English public to the Irish Question, Bachman suggests that Collins sought to expose the ultimate disappointment that would ensure from this fatal attraction between nations.

Race is an important factor in the essays by Christopher Forth and Nicholas Freeman, both of which focus on notorious criminal trials of the late nineteenth century, and both of which examine the role taken by the popular press in fashioning criminal identity. Forth's essay focuses on one of the most infamous criminal trials of the nineteenth century: the 1894 trial for treason of Alfred Dreyfus, a Jewish officer in the French army. In "The Novelization of the Dreyfus Affair", Forth examines how—as with the Speke and Kent cases in Britain—the Dreyfus affair prompted both an outpouring of imaginative literature and its own trial by media. In addition to considering the French public's attempts trying to make sense of the accusations and counter-accusations thrown backward and forward by Dreyfus's supporters and detractors, Forth also considers a number of *fin-de-siècle* anxieties. He considers the investigation of "deviant" sexuality and crises of masculinity, concerns with racial decline and degeneration, along with the notion of the courtroom as a place of public theatre. As Forth makes plain from the outset, criminality in France, as a label and instrument of discipline, drew on many of the same fears as it did in Britain.

Nicholas Freeman explores another real-life case—this time from *fin-de-siècle*

London—that of the greatly-reviled serial poisoner and Ripper suspect, George Chapman. The Chapman case had all the classic ingredients of a successful penny dreadful: murder, bigamy and a shadowy foreign assailant. As with the Speke case and the Kent murder, Chapman's crimes—he murdered three women, each of whom he had married bigamously—excited widespread public interest and tapped into a number of late Victorian and early Edwardian cultural anxieties. This Polish poisoner of English womanhood was, like Stoker's *Dracula*, an Eastern European immigrant whose criminality played upon *fin-de-siècle* fears of reverse colonization from the East. As with the Dreyfus case, these concerns were inextricably bound up with anxieties regarding miscegenation, degeneration and the future of the race. As Stephen D. Arata has said in his discussion of *Dracula*, the East was, in the 1880s and 1890s, "first and foremost the site, not of superstition and Gothic romance, but of political turbulence and racial strife.[23] Freeman pieces together the story of Chapman's poisonings and his subsequent trial, focusing particularly upon accounts of the criminal's "otherness" and his bizarre charisma. Freeman probes the public interest in this serial criminal and the way in which this case, like the Dreyfus affair, tapped into so many late Victorian and early Edwardian cultural anxieties.

Leslie Ann Minot considers another narrative of a deadly, but alluring Easterner in her chapter, "Vamping the Children". By reading Bram Stoker's *Dracula* alongside W.T. Stead's famous exposé of child prostitution, "The Maiden Tribute of the Modern Babylon", Minot reads Dracula's voluptuous first victim, Lucy Westenra as a sexual menace to young children. Downplaying the usual focus on the evil Count, Minot examines the growing emphasis on child protection at the end of the nineteenth century and also looks at the ways in which Stead's controversial articles over-emphasized the role of women in corrupting young girls. Like Judith Walkowitz, Minot focuses on the dangers the sprawling city of London posed to young women and presents us with a picture of a labyrinth of crime. Highlighting the friendship between Stoker and Stead, Minot reads *Dracula* alongside legislation on child protection in the 1880s and 1890s, flagging up Lucy's role as a public danger, rather than an innocent victim.

As these essays demonstrate, the shift in the boundaries of criminality and the growth of a mass readership completely re-defined the crime story genre. In real life, as well as in fiction, crimes became increasingly intricate as the newly-emerging master-criminal sought to out-wit the detective and, in cases like the Sherlock Holmes stories, to elevate crime to a high art. This collection explores a wide variety of transgressions, from the mainstream to the neglected, encompassing cases as diverse as child abduction, bigamy, infanticide, poisoning, sex crimes and crimes against property. Each essay sheds light on nineteenth-century moral and social values, the construction and perpetration of new forms of crime, and the developing sciences of criminology and detection. It is fitting that this collection should end with a study of George Chapman (aka Severin Antoniovich Klosowski), who was, on his arraignment in 1903, put forward by Inspector Frederick Abberline as the *real* Jack the Ripper.[24] As a brutal serial killer, Jack the Ripper has often been referred to as the first criminal of the twentieth century. We shall probably never know the true identity of the man who menaced the East End of London in 1888, disemboweling five prostitutes. George Chapman's more subtle poisonings could, then, be regarded as marking the end of an era. Although Sherlock Holmes referred specifically to the coming of the Great War when he warned Watson of a "cold and bitter" east wind that was to sweep across England, his words could equally be read as a premonition of the many alarming and horrific crimes that have characterized the post-Victorian world.[25] This collection brings together a number of quintessentially Victorian transgressions to chart the ways in which not simply murder, but many other forms of crime fiction and reportage were, as the nineteenth century progressed, elevated to a fine art.

Notes

1. Henry Mansel. "Sensation Novels", *The Quarterly Review* 113 (April 1863) 483-4.
2. Harriet Martineau. "Life in the Criminal Classes", *The Edinburgh Review* 122 (1865)
3. Quoted in John Springhall. "'Pernicious Reading'? 'The Penny Dreadful' as Scapegoat for Late-Victorian Juvenile Crime". *Victorian Periodicals Review*, 27, 1994.
4. Springhall. 337.
5. Arthur Conan Doyle. "The Adventure of the Beryl Coronet". *The Penguin Complete Sherlock Holmes*. Penguin: Middlesex, 1981. 323.
6. Quoted in Clive Emsley. "The Criminal Past: Crime in Nineteenth-Century Britain". *History Today*. Volume 38, April 1988. 41-48.
7. Henry Mayhew. *London Labour and the London Poor. Volume IV: Those That Will Not Work, comprising Prostitutes, Thieves, Swindlers and Beggars, by several contributors*. Introduction by John D. Rosenberg. New York: Dover Publications, 1968. xii.
8. Georg Simmel. "The Metropolis and Mental Life". In Georg Simmel. *On Individuality and Social Forms*. Chicago: University of Chicago Press, 1971. 331
9. See Lombroso-Ferrero, Gina. *Criminal man, according to the classification of Cesare Lombroso, briefly summarised by his daughter Gina Lombroso-Ferrero*. New York: Putnam, 1911, first published in Italian, 1876. Also Nordau, Max. *Degeneration*. 1895. Transl. George L. Mosse. Lincoln & London: University of Nebraska Press, 1993.
10. For further reading on nineteenth-century eugenics see Angelique Richardson. *Love and Eugenics Among the Late Victorians*. Oxford: Oxford University Press, 2003, Johanna M. Smith "Degeneration and Eugenics: Late-Victorian Discourses of the Ending of the Race". *Australasian Victorian Studies Journal*. Volume 4, December 1998. 55-66.
11. Michel Foucault. *The History of Sexuality. Volume One: The Will to Knowledge*. 1976. Transl. Robert Hurley. Harmondsworth, Middlesex: Penguin, 1990. 3.
12. Foucault rather overstates his case against the Victorians and their "repression". See Michael Mason. *The Making of Victorian Sexuality*. 1994. Oxford: Oxford University Press, 1995. Also Matthew Sweet. *Inventing the Victorians*. London: Faber & Faber, 2001.
13. Robert Mighall. *A Geography of Victorian Gothic Fiction: Mapping History's Nightmares*. Oxford: Oxford University Press, 1999. 180.
14. H.L. Mansel. *Quarterly Review*, volume 113, April 1863, 495-6.
15. Jenny Bourne Taylor. *In the Secret Theatre of Home: Wilkie Collins, Sensation Narrative, and Nineteenth-Century Psychology*. London & New York: Routledge, 1988. 4.
16. Margaret Oliphant "Sensation Novels". *Blackwood's Magazine*. Volume 91, 1862. 567.
17. "Sensation Novels". *The Quarterly Review*. Volume 113, 1863.

18. Stephen Knight. "Radical Thrillers" in *Watching the Detectives: Essays on Crime Fiction*. Eds. Ian A. Bell & Graham Daldry. Basingstoke: Macmillan, 1990
19. Franco Moretti. *Signs Taken for Wonders: Essays in the Sociology of Literary Forms*. Trans. Susan Fischer, David Forgacs & David Miller. London: Verso, 1983.
20. See Chris Brooks and Peter Faulkner (eds). *The White Man's Burdens: An Anthology of British Poetry of the Empire*. Exeter: University of Exeter Press, 1996. 157-159. The protagonist of Hood's poem is a not-so-young woman on the point of embarking for Bombay in order to procure a suitably affluent husband.
21. Robert Hughes. *The Fatal Shore: A History of the Transportation of Convicts to Australia, 1787-1868*. London: Harvill Press, 1996. 2.
22. Ronald R. Thomas. *Detective Fiction and the Rise of Forensic Science*. Cambridge: Cambridge University Press, 1999. 217.
23. Stephen D. Arata. "The Occidental Tourist: *Dracula* and the Anxiety of Reverse Colonization". *Victorian Studies*. Volume 33, number 4, Summer 1990. 627.
24. Given the fact that Chapman/Klosowski would have been a mere twenty-three years of age at the time of the Whitechapel prostitute murders (eye-witness accounts suggested the murderer to be in his late forties), Abberline's accusations seem to have been a desperate attempt to finally close a case that had baffled him in the late 1880s.
25. Sir Arthur Conan Doyle. *The Penguin Complete Sherlock Holmes*. Middlesex: Penguin, 1981. 980.

Chapter 1

Regicide and Reginamania: G.W.M. Reynolds and *The Mysteries of London*

John Plunkett

> "The rage is begun. Bedlam is certainly let loose. We are all going stark staring mad. Nothing is heard or thought of but doves and cupids, triumphal arches and whit favours, and last, but not least, variegated lamps and general illuminations". *Satirist*, 9 February 1840.[1]

Queen Victoria acceded to the British throne on June 20, 1837, less than a month after her eighteenth birthday and the attainment of her legal majority. Circumstances contrived to maximize the promise of the new reign. With the end of the seven-year rule of William IV and with the reactionary Duke of Cumberland succeeding to the throne of Hanover—Victoria being debarred by Salic law—her enthronement ended the long and uninspiring affiliation with the throne by the sons of George III. Young, female, attractive, politically innocent, yet with decidedly Whiggish views, the new Queen seemed far removed from the excesses of her aged Hanoverian uncles. Laetitia Landon described the accession as the advent of a "spring-like reign".[2] Scores of poems, prints and street ballads were produced, all effusively idealizing Victoria. *Figaro in London*, a popular, if ephemeral, satirical journal, claimed that John Bull was so pleased at the idea of being governed by a girl, he would cut off his ears if her little Majesty required them.[3] Victoria basked in the tangible freshness of a revivified royal populism, comparable in the magnitude of its sentiment to that aroused by Queen Caroline in 1820: only this time it was in support of the monarchy.

The trope of an individual and collective madness was frequently used to describe the sensation engendered by Victoria. In January 1838, the *Spectator* bemoaned the malady of "Reginamania" that prevailed to such an extent that coverage vered from the mundane to the ridiculous: "dwelling constantly on the beauty not only of the Queen's face and features, but of her feet and even of her slippers".[4] By June 1838 the affliction had reached epidemic proportions. John Bull was said to have gone "coronation mad" with the only possible cause being Queen-worship.[5] Mrs Stevenson, the wife of the American ambassador, similarly wrote that everybody was "running about mad with loyalty to the young Queen. Even the Americans here are infected. In all societies, nothing is talked about but her wisdom, her goodness and self-possession".[6] This chapter examines why the excess of affect was cast as madness, and the role of the publishing industry in encouraging this emotional link between Victoria and her people. The obsession with Victoria also had potentially criminal consequences because it encouraged intrusion into the intimacies of palace life, whether on the part of individuals or specific publications. In G.W.M. Reynolds's *The Mysteries of London*, one of the most popular fictional series of the 1840s, a mad infatuation with Victoria even fed into the ultimate crime of attempted regicide.

The figuring of excessive affect as madness was keyed into longstanding tropes regarding the nature of popular politics. James Vernon has argued that the language of Old Corruption derided "a mass popular politics without virtue, whose only salvation was the possession of reason".[7] The pervasiveness of this discourse is reflected in the way radical critiques of Victoria's Coronation appropriated the Enlightenment values that were used to deride popular politics. Chartists and other utilitarian critics turned the idiom against its dominant usage. The *Northern Star* dwelt on the Coronation's feudal barbarity, the irrationality of its aristocratic mummery, and the infantile nature of its tawdry attraction. The *Spectator* was typical in describing the event as an occasion exploiting that superstitious "love of noise and tinsel which barbarism and children are understood to share".[8] Similar criticisms characterized the radical response to those newspapers and periodicals that were most ebullient and toadying in their support for Victoria.

One of the most striking elements of the initial sentiment surrounding Victoria is that it was widely believed to stem from the ubiquitous dissemination of her image. Victoria's face was available via a diverse assortment of media, ranging from dioramas to street ballads, from commemorative pottery to expensive steel-engraved portraits. The British monarchy was one of the most notable beneficiaries of the burgeoning print and visual culture of the 1830s and 1840s. The 1840s, for example, saw the commencement of popular weekly newspapers like the *News of the World*, *Weekly Times* and *Lloyd's Weekly Newspaper*. Lithography, along with wood and steel engraving, also became increasingly prominent, resulting in a large number of cheap portraits of Victoria that promoted her as a desirable Court Beauty. Wood-engraving was utilized to create the graphic reportage of the *Illustrated London News* and the *Pictorial Times*, which began publication in 1842 and 1843 respectively. Illustrated journals and cheap Sunday newspapers gave fulsome coverage to Victoria and Albert's many civic tours and visits, as well as their domestic activities.[9] Whipping up royal fervour nevertheless rendered the press liable to charges of irrationalism. It undermined their enthusiastic support for the monarchy and, more generally, cast doubt on the enlightening role of print media. Attacks on the sensation around Victoria were part of a wider conflict concerning the interaction between popular politics and print media.

The remarkable cathexis of desire around Victoria's fetishized figure in the first years of her reign can best be understood through a group that became collectively known as "the Queen's lovers". Until her marriage, Victoria was frequently stalked, physically intruded upon and bombarded with letters from subjects, whose sole declared intent was to gain the Queen's hand in marriage. Acting under the conviction that they each were destined to be the chosen Consort, the criminal behaviour of the three men was widely reported and their conduct usually resulted in a committal to Bedlam or similar institutions.[10]

Foremost amongst the Queen's lovers was the case of one Captain Goode. He began to follow Victoria when she was a Princess at Kensington. Every evening Goode would watch for Victoria's carriage emerging from her private road in Kensington Gardens. He would then follow the carriage wherever it went. Captain Goode believed himself to be a son of George IV and rightful heir to the throne, an honour he pronounced himself willing to forego so long as Victoria consented to be his wife. Having been imprisoned several times for his harassing behaviour, he was eventually examined and committed in November 1837.[11] Goode was far from alone, though. Another suitor managed to obtain admission to the Chapel Royal, wherein he proceeded to bow and kiss his hand to Victoria.[12] Then there was Tom Flower, who was arrested after trying to gain entrance to Westminster Abbey during the Coronation.[13] He was well known for his attempts to gain Victoria's hand in marriage. He had twice been bound over to keep the peace after similar incidents, including an attempt to gain entrance to the Queen's box when she was at the opera. Flower was removed to Tothill Fields House of Correction for his troubles. Ned Hayward, another unfortunate, was also committed for stopping the Queen's horse in Hyde Park and attempting to give Victoria a letter. He had in the past written numerous missives to the Home Office wondering whether Victoria would consent to marry him.[14] Next, in October 1839, came an unknown Scottish admirer. Having persuaded himself that he was the object of Victoria's affections, he made a pilgrimage to see her at Windsor. At one of the Queen's appearances on the Windsor terrace, the extravagance of his behaviour rendered police intervention necessary. In January 1840, there was the case of Thomas Richard Evans, who declared his undying passion for Victoria in numerous letters written to Lord John Russell, begging him to intercede on his behalf and prevent the marriage to Prince Albert.[15] Perhaps the most famous case of all was that of Edward Jones, who even acquired the famous sobriquet of the "Boy Jones". A youthful intruder who was caught inside Buckingham Palace several times, Jones was eventually put to ship for his escapades, having claimed to have spent weeks living inside Buckingham Palace unobserved by the palace staff.

I have given only the bare facts of these individual cases, yet each event gripped the public imagination. In its early years, *Punch* frequently regaled its readers with mock reports from the "Boy Jones". Dickens, too, drew upon the Queen's lovers in a joke with John Forster and Daniel Maclise which involved the trio pretending that they were all hopelessly in love with the Queen. In a letter written three days after Victoria's wedding, Dickens imagined a journey down to Windsor on the day after the event:

> On Tuesday we sallied down to Windsor, prowled about the Castle, saw the corridor and their private rooms—nay, the very bedchamber (which we know from having been there twice) lighted up with such a ruddy, homely, brilliant glow—bespeaking so much bliss and happiness—that I, your humble servant, lay down in the mud at the top of the long walk, and refused all comfort—to the immeasurable astonishment of a few straggling passengers who had survived the drunkenness of the previous night. After

> perpetrating sundry other extravagances we returned home at Midnight in a Post Chaise and now we wear marriage medals next to our hearts and go about with pockets full of portraits which we weep over in secret.[16]

Dickens's letter clearly plays upon the behaviour of the Queen's lovers. He also links their devotion with the affect invested in the commemoratives of the occasion. In Dickens's somewhat risqué imaginative excursion into the Queen's honeymoon chamber, Victoria's attraction creates an obsessive charting of her every movement.

The Queen's lovers were thus transformed into a discursive entity. As individuals, they were profitable news stories. However, as the Queen's lovers they were taken up as a trope to demonstrate the collective ardour surrounding Victoria. Those who were literally insane became symptomatic of a more general condition of madness through excessive loyalty. The Queen's lovers were part of a fascination with trying to understand how Victoria was perceived, and why she seemed to dominate both the imagined and imaginary lives of her subjects. Over a period of six months, for example, the *Penny Satirist* printed a series of fictional letters under the heading "The Queen's Lover".[17] First appearing in July 1839, the periodical claimed that for several months the editor had been receiving letters filled with rapturous poetry:

> I find it hard to love a Queen. I see her lovely features so often in picture-shops, and her name is too often mentioned to effect a speedy cure. I must find some retreat, where no journals come, where no picture-shops are, and where her name is never, or seldom, heard. I must find some Cave, and live like a hermit, and write about her till I die, or make a perfect cure...Could I only respect her as my Queen, then I should do; but her sweet lips, her pure bosom, and her lovely eyes, are eternally before me, and I speak to her as if she were my equal.[18]

The Queen's lover is infatuated to the extent that Victoria pervades his everyday experience. His inability to regard Victoria as the Queen, with all the corresponding implications of social and personal distance, is intrinsic to his fetishizing. The distance between them has been compressed into an affective and sensual intimacy, and this is explicitly linked to the impact of the numerous royal prints, newspaper stories and street ballads. The Queen's Lover is not a subject of Victoria. Rather, he is a consumer of her image.

The Queen's Lovers were also taken up as part of a wider attack on the newspapers and journals that were most exuberant in their support for the monarchy. Individual acts of obsessive loyalty were equated with the fawning language that characterized reportage of royal occasions. Over the next four decades, attacks on the extensive and gushing royal coverage of the press were a common feature in anti-monarchist publications like *Reynolds's Weekly Newspaper*. Royal reportage was also frequently mocked by satirical journals like *Punch*. In one mocking exposé, Douglas Jerrold pounced upon a comment made by the editor of the *Athenaeum* over the birth of the Prince of Wales. The editor claimed that he had spent at least half the day in fancy at the palace taking his turn of loyal watch by the royal cradle.[19] Jerrold gleefully took the editor at his word and dramatized the literal results by imagining himself to be beside the cradle for at least twelve hours of the day. Taken literally, his absorption is quickly distorted into fanatical delusion. The editor's housemaid is dandled up and down like a baby; the printer's devil is force-fed with the ink for the presses; the tax-gatherer who knocks at his door is treated to a rendition of "Ride-a-cock-horse to Banbury Cross". Jerrold questions whether the editor should be prevented from carrying on his working activities by such "beautiful evidences of an absorbing loyalty".[20] In its most solemn of tones, a tongue-in-cheek *Punch* declares the question to be one of the greatest importance. An end to all individual liberty is threatened if the enthusiasm of loyalty was rendered as madness.[21] Jerrold mockingly claimed to fully believe the editor's profession of his loyalty in that it was comparable to similar statements made by other public figures. Nevertheless, harking back to the Queen's Lovers, he warned that many men had been deprived of their freedom for much less fanciful feelings toward Victoria.

Through eliding the distinction between the extravagant newspaper pronouncements about Victoria and the actions of the Queen's lovers, Jerrold sought to attack the unrestrained avowals of loyalty circulated by the press. *Punch* desired forbearance in the newspaper mania surrounding Victoria, otherwise, like the editor of the *Athenaeum*, the public risked moving from metaphorical insanity to being quite literally mad about Victoria:

> If, however, he and other influential wizards of the broad-sheet, succeed in making loyalty not a rational principle, but a mania—if, day by day, and week by week, they insist on deifying poor, infirm humanity, exalting themselves in their own conceit, in their very self-abasement—they may escape an individual accusation in the general folly. When we are all mad alike—when we all, with the editor of the *Athenaeum*, take our half-day's watch at the side of the little Prince's cradle—when every man and woman throughout her empire believe themselves making royal pap and airing royal baby-linen—then, whatever fortune we may have, we may be safe from the fate of Poor Weekes...who, we repeat, is most unjustly confined for his notions of royalty, seeing that many of our contemporaries are still at liberty to write and publish.[22]

Jerrold acerbically evokes the prominence that Victoria was made to occupy in the lives of her subjects. For Jerrold, like Dickens and the letter-writer in the *Penny Satirist*, such absorption was directly linked to the pervasive and deferential media attention devoted to the young Queen.

The Mysteries of London

Dickens and the *Penny Satirist* reworked the story of the "Queen's Lovers" in a way that critically played upon, but added to, Victoria's reputed attractiveness. This media-constructed sensation around Victoria was also the subject of G.W.M. Reynolds's retelling of the "Boy Jones" stories in his famous series, *The Mysteries of London* (1844-48). Along with the "penny dreadfuls" of Edward Lloyd, the

A STRANGER IN HER MAJESTY'S BEDROOM.

THE BOY JONES AGAIN!

"What will Mrs. Grundy say—Mrs. Lilley?"

On Wednesday, shortly after 12 o'clock, the inmates of Buckingham Palace were aroused by an alarm being given that a stranger had been discovered under the sofa in her Majesty's dressing-room. The domestics and officers of the household were immediately in motion, and it was soon ascertained that the alarm was not without foundation. The daring intruder was immediately secured, and safely handed over to the custody of the police.

The inquiry into this mysterious circumstance has created the most intense interest at Buckingham Palace and the west-end of the of the town, where the report spread with the rapidity of lightning. At first it was not generally believed, but when it was known that the prisoner was under examination at the Home Office public curiosity was at its height, and inquiries into the most minute particulars were made in every place where it was likely to obtain information respecting an event which might, under present circumstances, have been attended with most dangerous effects to the health of our beloved Queen.

Shortly after 12 o'clock one of her Majesty's pages, attended by other domestics of the royal household, went into her Majesty's dressing-room, which adjoins the bed-chamber in which the Queen's accouchement took place. Whilst there they imagined that they heard a noise. A strict search was commenced, and under the sofa on which her Majesty had been sitting only about two hours before they discovered a dirty, ill-looking fellow, who was immediately dragged from his hiding-place, and given into the custody of Inspector Stead, then on duty at the Palace. The prisoner immediately underwent a strict search, but no weapon of any dangerous nature was found on his person. He was afterwards conveyed to the station in Gardener's Lane, and handed over to Inspector Haining, of the A division of police, with instructions to keep him in safe custody until he received further orders from the Home Office. We understand that as soon as the prisoner was handed over to the police he was immediately recognised as the same person who effected such an extraordinary entrance into Buckingham Palace about two years since, for which offence he was tried at the Westminster Sessions and acquitted, the jury being of opinion that he was not right in his mind. It may here be stated that the name of the daring intruder into the abode of royalty is Edward Jones; he is 17 years of age. In person the prisoner is very short of his age, and has a most repulsive appearance; he was very meanly dressed, but affected an air of great consequence; he repeatedly requested the police to address him in a becoming manner, and to behave towards him as they ought to do to a gentleman who was anxious to make a noise in the world.

At 12 o'clock on Thursday the prisoner was brought in custody of the police to the Home Office, and shortly afterwards taken before the Council, when, we understand, he was interrogated as to his motives for such extraordinary conduct, and particularly as to the mode by which he obtained an entrance into the Palace. He (the prisoner) told their lordships that he was willing to point out to the police the way he effected an entrance, and to state all particulars. Their lordships, on this statement, directed the police immediately to convey Jones to Buckingham Palace, and obtain the information he promised to give, and adjourned the inquiry until half past two o'clock.

The prisoner was taken to the Palace, and brought back again to the Home Office at two o'clock. At half-past two the Council re-assembled, when we understand the prisoner made the following extraordinary statement:—

On Monday night he scaled the wall of Buckingham Palace garden, about half-way up Constitution Hill; he then proceeded to the Palace and effected an entrance through one of the windows. He had not, however, been there long before he considered it unsafe for him to stay, as so many people were moving about, and he left by the same mode as he entered. The next day he again effected an entrance in the same manner as on the previous night; and he went on to state that he remained in the Palace the whole of Tuesday night, the whole day on Wednesday, and up till one o'clock on Thursday morning, when he was discovered under a sofa in her Majesty's dressing-room, as above described. The prisoner pointed out all the passages and places he had gone through previous to his arrival at the room in which he was discovered, and there appears no reason to doubt his statement. The hiding place of the intruder was first discovered by one of her Majesty's pages, and when he was asked what brought him there, he replied, that he wanted to see what was going forward in the Palace, that he might write about it, and if he was discovered he should be as well off as Oxford, who fared better in Bedlam than he (prisoner) did out of it. He was also asked if, during the time he was in the Palace, he saw the Queen or the infant Princess, and he replied that he did not, but that he had heard a noise, which he thought came from her Majesty's room.

Her Majesty's page, who discovered the prisoner, and the constable who took him to the station-house, were then examined.

The Council came to the decision that, as no property or dangerous weapon was found on the prisoner, it would be better to inflict a summary punishment; and a warrant was accordingly made out, and signed by Mr. Hall, committing the prisoner to the House of Correction, Tothill Street, as a rogue and vagabond, for three months.

The prisoner was immediately afterwards conveyed in a cab to Tothill Street.

LATEST PARTICULARS.

The sensation caused by the late mysterious entrance of the boy Jones into Buckingham Palace, appears to be even greater than that produced by his apprehension in the same place in December, 1838. The object which prompted so daring a proceeding is still involved in the utmost doubt; but it was not probable that it was his intention to do any personal injury to her Majesty, for had such been his purpose abundant opportunities of carrying it into effect presented themselves during his concealment in the chamber where he was secured. From a well informed source, we have heard the sofa under which Jones was found is in the ante-room in which the Princess Royal and Mrs. Lilley, her Royal Highness's nurse, repose. On the night in question the latter had not long retired to rest ere she fancied she heard a noise similar to that likely to be caused by a person who was endeavouring to prevent his presence from being discovered, and was moving in a stealthy manner. Mrs. Lilley at first treated the matter as of no moment, thinking probably that the noise might have been imaginary. Its renewal, however, created an alarm, and she instantly summoned those of the attendants who were on guard in the adjoining ante-chamber. On their arrival the offender was quickly discovered and drawn from his place of hiding. The statement then goes on to say that her Majesty, who but three hours previously had been sitting on this particular sofa, having been disturbed by the confusion to which the event had given rise, called out and desired to be informed as to its cause. As an apprehension was, however, entertained that the sudden communication of the occurrence might be attended with an unfavourable effect on her Majesty, the attendants gave an evasive answer. The Queen repeated her command, and then the fact of the boy's concealment and subsequent apprehension were made known to her.

The circumstances at that time appeared not to produce any very visible effect on her Majesty, but on Thursday symptoms of other than a satisfactory character were apparent. It affords us the highest gratification to be able to add that a few hours of quietude tended to the restoration of her Majesty.

It would appear that there is now no doubt but that the account given by Jones as to his having effected his entrance into the Palace by scaling the garden wall from Constitution Hill is correct. Upon being asked whether he had not met some of the attendants in the course of his progress along the corridor and staircase, he replied, "Yes," but that, when he saw any one coming in his direction, he hid himself behind the pillars, or behind any piece of furniture which happened to be near. Hitherto he has been silent as to the motive which induced him to take so extraordinary a step as that of forcing his way a second time into the royal apartments, and when asked on Friday morning, after he had been upon the tread-wheel, how he liked his punishment, his answer was to the effect that he had got into the scrape, and must do the best he could.

There does not appear to be the slightest ground for the rumour that he is insane.

Many circumstances have transpired to show that Jones was in the Palace the whole of Wednesday. The delinquent states that during the day he secreted himself under different beds and in cupboards, until at last he obtained an entrance into the room in which he was discovered. Not much reliance can be placed in his statements, but, as such general curiosity exists on the subject, we may state that, in answer to interrogatories, he said, "that he had sat upon the throne, that he saw the Queen, and heard the Princess Royal cry."

Prince Albert was in the room with her Majesty taking leave for the night when the miscreant was discovered under the sofa.

The fellow's shoes were found in one of the rooms of the ground-floor. The sofa under which the boy was discovered, we understand, is one of most costly and magnificent material and workmanship, and ordered expressly for the accommodation of the royal and illustrious visitors who call to pay their respects to her Majesty.

1.1 "A Stranger in Her Majesty's Bedroom" in John Ashton (ed). *Curiosities of Street Literature*. London: Reeves & Turner, 1871.

1.2 "The Queen and Prince Albert" from G.W.M. Reynolds *The Mysteries of London* (1844-1848).

1.3 "Holford's Attack" from G.W.M. Reynolds *The Mysteries of London* (1844-1848).

success of *The Mysteries of London* epitomizes the expansion in popular publishing in the 1840s, particularly for a newly literate urban working-class readership. From the work's commencement in October 1844, Reynolds's weekly penny numbers were enormously popular. Sales of 30,000 to 40,000 copies were soon reported. Significantly, though, Reynolds's commercial success existed alongside, and because of, his outspoken republican politics. As Trefor Thomas has pointed out, *The Mysteries of London* is a mixture of radical politics, Gothic sensation, melodrama, and urban horror.[23] Its juxtaposition of urban deprivation alongside aristocratic libertines merged the traditional targets of Old Corruption with the new concerns of Chartism and the Condition-of-England question. For a brief period Reynolds combined an active political career with numerous publishing activities. He spoke on several mass platforms during the Chartist agitation in 1848, while continuing to write *The Mysteries of the Court of London* (1847-56), which portrayed the debauched decadence of the Regency Court. In May 1850, he launched *Reynolds's Weekly News*, which became one of the most significant and popular of the working-class Sunday newspapers. *Reynolds's Weekly News* was also notorious for its virulent attacks on the monarchy and aristocracy.

Three chapters from the first series of *The Mysteries of London*, and, in the repetition of an obviously successful formula, four similar chapters from the second series, focus on Victoria and Albert. Reynolds's treatment of the monarchy illustrates some of the contradictory pressure attendant upon his synthesis of commercial success and radical politics. As Anne Humpherys has neatly argued, Reynolds's success stemmed from his ability to "absorb the contradictory impulses and desires of the populace without making any "irritable" effort at resolution".[24] Despite Reynolds's notorious anti-monarchism, *The Mysteries of London* draws upon the actions of the Boy Jones and the Queen's Lovers to allow the reader to experience Victoria's attractions. In so doing, Reynolds comes close to embodying the type of fetishization derided by Jerrold. Through exemplifying the fascination of Victoria within its narrative, the appeal of its royal chapters is premised upon the reader enjoying the frisson of intruding into Victoria's life. *The Mysteries of London* enacts the excess of infatuation through the actions of its characters, and consequently draws the reader into its melodramatic potency. The portrayal of Victoria's attractiveness nevertheless exists in tandem with a strident anti-monarchism. Reginamania is shown to lead to regicide as Reynolds reworks the assassination attempt of Edward Oxford in the same way as the Boy Jones stories. In June 1840, Oxford fired two pistols at Victoria and Albert when they were driving up Constitution Hill. The dramatization of the attempted regicide of a reigning monarch, even if the readership were already aware of its failure, embodies Reynolds's inssurectionary impulse.

The Mysteries of London is keyed into the general fascination exerted by a royal private sphere. One of the most frequent claims made of Victoria and Albert was that the security of the monarchy rested with the unimpeachable domesticity of their private lives. Adulation of royal propriety was clearly a product of the increasing ideological value attached to the family. However, the affect attached to the portrayal of Victoria's palace life was also a consequence of the weight of attention devoted to her. The royal hearth was the place where the "real" Victoria could be uncovered, anterior to any mediation, thereby offering a more authentic experience for the reader or viewer. Nevertheless, there remained an inherent structural contradiction between the self-enclosure of the private sphere and the communicative function of the print and graphic media. Any overt intrusion into palace life was heavily censured. Royal privacy was caught inextricably between fascination and distaste.

Desire for an intimate insight into the Queen's pastimes can be found within publications that reached a broad variety of audiences. Periodicals like the *Illustrated London News* were wholly reverential towards Victoria's private life, yet they were consequently equally concerned with providing coverage of her domesticity. One of the very first engravings of Victoria in the *Illustrated London News,* showed her dandling the infant Prince of Wales and noted that although the journal did not wish to intrude, it could not "be prevented following her in thought...into the retreat of domestic felicity".[25] Reynolds himself was not immune from the attractions of royal family life. In December 1846, *Reynolds's Miscellany* published a wholesome engraving of Victoria, Albert, and their children, grouped happily around a Christmas tree. Reynolds's engraving predates a similar engraving in the *Illustrated London News* by two years, the latter of which is often credited with helping to introduce the tradition of the Christmas tree to the Victorian home.

Reynolds's depiction of the royal couple underlines his debt to the aural, printed and visual coverage of royalty in the early and mid 1840s. He combines a through-the-keyhole account of Buckingham Palace—a titillating revelation of Victoria and Albert's most intimate conversations—with a condemnation of the luxury enjoyed by the court. The narrative conflates an exotic exposé of aristocratic high life, with an intrusion into, and acknowledgement of, the royal couple's domesticity. The demythologizing and radical impact of literally turning royal lives into a melodramatic fiction is emphasized by the way Reynolds uses the same technique in *The Mysteries of Court of London.* His sequel to *The Mysteries of London* dramatizes events around the Prince of Wales's Court, including George's first meeting with Queen Caroline, his drunkenness on their wedding night, and numerous subsequent tête-à-têtes with mistresses in various states of undress. Reynolds's intrusion into palace life in this series is about reducing royalty to the lowest common appetites: greed, desire, deceit, and selfishness.

The Mysteries of London nevertheless saturates its radical politics with royal melodrama and romance. It is firmly implicated—albeit more sensationally than periodicals like the *Illustrated London News*—in the much broader construction of Victoria's feminine appeal. The use of melodramatic tropes was clearly politically enabling and successful (as Anna Clark has argued of the Queen Caroline affair), yet its use arguably also disabled Reynolds's political approach. He attacks the court and the iniquities of aristocratic wealth but does so only through encouraging sympathy for and empathy with Victoria.[26] The Queen's relationship with Albert is portrayed as stifled by the court formality to which the couple are forced to adhere.

Reynolds comments of aristocratic etiquette that "even the best and most tender feelings of the heart are to a certain extent subdued and oppressed by that chilling influence".[27] The melodramatic treatment of Victoria is thus both radical and populist: it throws into relief the gilded insensitivity of the Court while forestalling any political attacks on the Queen. Victoria is treated as the innocent victim of the Court rather than the fount of its very existence. The divisiveness of class conflict is fused with the connective empathy of a human-interest drama.

The central protagonist of Reynolds's chapters is neither Victoria nor Albert, but one Henry Holford, a pot-boy-cum-burglar who begins by breaking into Buckingham Palace and ends by attempting regicide after he has been ejected from its splendours. Reynolds's narrative is clearly dramatizing the "Boy Jones" story, much as his *Pickwick Abroad* (1838) exploited Dickens's success. Victoria was also subject to several assassination attempts in the early 1840s, and Reynolds utilizes his audience's familiarity with the sensation of such events. From *Punch* to the *Penny Satirist*, the "Boy Jones" story had been frequently re-worked and by 1844 *The Mysteries of London* was reproducing what was virtually a narrative trope for symbolizing the magnetism of Victoria's private life.[28] In *London Labour and the London Poor*, Mayhew's interviews with street-patterers and ballad-singers emphasize that this episode had become very much part of street lore. One running-patterer interviewed commented that "The Boy Jones in the Palace wasn't much of an affair for the running-patterers; the ballad singers—or street screamers as we calls 'em—had the pull out of that. The patter wouldn't take; they had read it all in the newspapers before. Oxford and Francis, and Bean, were a little better, but nothing to crack about".[29] Disseminated through newspapers, ballad sheets and patterers, Reynolds recycled what was already a familiar narrative in print and in working-class aural culture. The tropes of his story were already profitably established. In choosing to amalgamate the "Boy Jones" incident and the assassination attempts of Oxford, Francis and Bean, Reynolds was using the street stories about Victoria that had been most widely circulated because of their sensational value.

The "Boy Jones" achieved his notoriety through his claim to have repeatedly entered the palace—to have explored its corridors undiscovered and overheard the conversations of all the royal servants. *The Mysteries of London* similarly described Holford's adventures around the palace. Its principal attraction is the thrill of being a voyeur on the intimacies of Victoria and her household. The first chapter begins with a diatribe against the extreme contrast between rich and poor, yet the luxury Holford sees once inside the palace is experienced with unbounded wonder and delight. Rooms are described in all their finery and Holford hides beneath a sofa, upon which the Queen herself is sitting, enthralled with admiration at all the opulence of a royal ball. He is captivated by the "brilliant uniforms of several military officers of high rank",[30] the "blaze of light in which the room was bathed",[31] and describes the diamond tiara, stomacher and earrings worn by Victoria. In keeping with this admiration, Victoria herself is praised for her pleasing countenance, good figure and "fantastic bust". The Queen portrayed by Reynolds is more of a maiden monarch than a matriarch. Victoria is also benevolently described as having the true condition of her subjects concealed from her through only being given newspapers that are favourable to the Whig ministry. Holford, whose standpoint the reader is asked to share, is enchanted by his encounter with the Queen, feeling "an unknown and unaccountable species of happiness in recalling to mind and pondering upon all that had fallen from her lips".[32] Inspiring deference rather than disloyalty, *The Mysteries of London* revels in following Holford around the palace, including a visit to the throne room and a brief but revolutionary occupancy of the throne itself.

Holford's visit does not simply comprise a physical exploration of the rooms. He prolongs his stay because of a desire to see Victoria again. Overhearing two Court ladies gossiping over the imminent arrival of Prince Albert and the rumours of her Majesty's expected betrothal (the chapter is set in 1839), Reynolds's narrative shifts from illegal intrusion to romantic melodrama. Added to the sentiment is a dark hint—alluded to in whispers by two courtiers—that the scrofula that afflicted George III was an hereditary illness. Victoria is reportedly haunted by fears of her own potential madness. However, this suggestion of hidden secrets merely augments the melodrama, stressing as it does the pitfalls rather than the fortunes of Victoria's royal birthright. On the arrival of Prince Albert, Holford, from his vantage point beneath a couch, overhears a *tête-à-tête* between the royal couple. Reynolds piously observes, "We shall not record any portion of their discourse",[33] before immediately then noting that "for a short time they seemed to forget their high rank, and to throw aside the trammels of court etiquette, in order to give vent to those natural feelings which the sovereign has in common with the peasant".[34] The accompanying engraving emphasizes the intimacy of the encounter, with the couple posed confidentially together and Victoria affectionately giving her hand to Albert.

Through Holford's voyeurism, Reynolds's narrative is predicated upon the transgressive affect of intruding into Victoria's private sphere and looking upon the virtues of the young Queen and the decadence of her courtiers. The fascination with disclosing royal domestic life was such that Reynolds, via Holford, returned surreptitiously to Buckingham Palace in the second volume of *The Mysteries of London*. He again overhears the gossiping of the court ladies on the licentious proclivities of George IV, the inequity of the Queen Caroline affair, the Duke of Cumberland's alleged murder of his servant, and Victoria's own increasing tendency to bouts of melancholy over the anticipated onset of the hereditary madness. All of the most widely circulated episodes of recent royal scandal are uninhibitedly ranged over. The narrator, without any irony towards his own role in communicating their discussions, critically notes that "no-where are scandal and tittle-tattle more extensively indulged in, than amongst the members of that circle of courtiers and female sycophants who crowd about the sovereign".[35] In Reynolds's narrative, Holford's intrusion can be overlooked, and the court gossip of a prurient aristocracy can be disapproved of, while the reader is simultaneously left free to enjoy his or her participation in the self-same scandal.

The second set of chapters reproduces the same motifs as the first, with Holford watching Victoria and Albert breakfasting alone—every detail of their conversation being recounted. Appropriately enough, Holford hears them discussing the reports in the daily newspapers of the distress in the country, with the couple refusing to believe in the extent of working-class distress. Victoria recounts how her ministers have told her that the nation is prosperous and that the newspaper reporters should not be believed because journalists are remunerated according to quantity and therefore amplify the details as much as possible. She cites with approval an editorial in the *Morning Post*, a newspaper notorious for its high Tory standpoint. The *Morning Post* devoted much attention to royalty and aristocracy, to the extent that *Punch* christened it the "*Fawning Post*". Victoria notes the devotion of her subjects as described in the *Morning Post*, only to be questioned by Albert as to why the report should be any more truthful than the newspapers that she has already dismissed. Victoria and Albert are sceptical readers within the text, and Reynolds assumes a similar scepticism on the part of his readers towards the standpoint of the *Morning Post*. Yet his own chapters are notable for the immediate and transparent relationship they assume between reader and text. The sentiments of the *Morning Post* can be dismissed while those propounded by Reynolds remain unquestioned.

Holford is eventually discovered by none other than Prince Albert, but is ejected from the Palace without arrest, owing to the Prince's magnanimity. Nevertheless, because Albert is responsible for removing him from the Queen who has filled his imagination, Holford is driven to despair and hatred. Contemplating regicide, Holford spends an entire chapter studying the assassinations of earlier monarchs, including Louis XIV of France. Through the very seductive attractiveness of palace life, and "the ineffable delight in contemplating the person of his sovereign",[36] Holford is forced to feel his own class inferiority and experiences what Althusser would label his interpellation into the social order. He is overwhelmed by self-disgust, repulsion, and abasement, "how little, how contemptible did he feel himself to be".[37] Victoria's appeal remains as strong as ever, but the growing sensation of his inferiority leads to murderous resentment. His experiences as a voyeur of the royal couple's private life were claimed to be "as necessary to Holford's mental happiness as tobacco, opium, snuff, or strong liquors are to many millions of people".[38] Holford's planned attack on Victoria and Albert stems not from republican principles; it is caused by his expulsion from the charms of royalty. Reynolds suggests that Holford's actions are the result of the inequity in wealth between the Court and the majority of the population: the very difference in their conditions causes his fetishistic attraction to Victoria.

Holford is also driven by the fame and notoriety he would enjoy by committing regicide. He dreams of himself as another Jack Shepherd, a popular legend created through the excessive attention criminals received by different print and dramatic media:

> The curiosity [towards criminals] passes all legitimate bounds. The newspapers, with a natural attention to pecuniary interests, obey the cravings of that feeling by serving up the most highly seasoned food to suit that particular appetite. Portraits of the guilty one are exhibited in each picture shop. Apposite allusions are introduced into dramatic

> representations; and even the presiding genius of a 'Punch and Judy' show mingles the subject with his humorous outpourings.[39]

The cumulative coverage in various media seemingly offers Holford the chance to become a fetishized figure in the same way that curiosity was created around Victoria. The narratives surrounding Holford and Victoria are linked as much by a drive for sensation as by an overarching anti-monarchism. Moreover, in the same way that Reynolds denies his own agency in narrating a palace exposé, his account of Holford's failed regicide conveniently ignores the fact that his own narrative is itself a melodramatic spin-off from several assassination attempts.

Holford's intra-textual narrative is interesting because it replicates the relationship between Reynolds and the implied reader. Initially the reader is asked to share the appeal of the adventures around the palace and the expose of Victoria's luxurious home life. Readers are asked to share Holford's realization of immense imbalances in the distribution of wealth, before then condemning his failed attack upon the Queen. *The Mysteries of London* is both predicated on and a representation of the potency of Victoria's domesticity. Holford's obsession exemplifies the interest it aroused and the prominent role it played in the figuring of Victoria for a broad range of audiences. Conversely, Holford's intrusion into the confines of Buckingham Palace and the crime of his attempted regicide are two episodes that demonstrate the anti-monarchism and lack of deference of *The Mysteries of London*. It is the very open-endedness of Reynolds' royal chapters, their multiple standpoints towards the Queen, which makes *The Mysteries of London* so successful and such a compelling read.

The Boy Jones and the Queen's Lovers were figures used to express the novel media attention surrounding Victoria and Albert. The multiple remaking of their stories exemplifies the process by which Victoria became an intimate yet ubiquitous presence in the day-to-day lives of the public. Although references to the Boy Jones and the Queen's Lovers disappear after the mid 1840s, royal revelations continued to exert a high degree of fascination, while the allure of palace life also continued to encourage criminal intrusion. During the 1840s, *Punch* often attacked journalists following Victoria for seeking the same degree of intimacy as Henry Holford. In 1848, Albert took out several injunctions against a publisher, William Strange, who was trying to organize an exhibition of etchings stolen from Windsor Castle.[40] The etchings had been executed by Victoria and Albert and showed scenes from the royal nursery. Similarly, when *carte-de-visite* photographs of the royal family became widely available in the early 1860s an enormous number of illegal copies entered into circulation. Several photographers were prosecuted for infringement of copyright. These prosecutions, however, existed alongside the widespread belief in the political value of making Victoria's image and, ultimately, her life, available to her subjects. Her position meant that intrusion into her activities was more permissible and excusable than the celebration of her domesticity would suggest. When she famously published her own Highland journal in 1868, the *Athenaeum* noted the "great and legitimate public curiosity" it would arouse.[41] *Blackwood's Edinburgh Magazine* knew it would appeal because "Her Majesty is of herself interesting to everybody".[42] Yet the enthusiasm towards Victoria's domestic life could never be wholly reconciled with the physical intrusions that such acclaim indirectly assisted. Royal privacy remained intractably caught in the ideology of its own making.

Notes

1. "London, February 9, 1840", *Satirist* 9 February 1840. 2.
2. Laetitia Landon "To Victoria", *Flowers of Loveliness; Twelve Groups of female figures, emblematic of flowers: Designed by Various Artists; With Poetical Illustrations by L.E.L.* (London: Ackermann & Co., 1838) n.pag.
3. "The Queen Riding the Bull", *Figaro in London* 20 January 1838. 9. *Figaro in London* (1831-1839) was a small satirical journal, illustrated with one woodcut on the front page. Best known as one of the forerunners to *Punch*, its writers included Douglas Jerrold, Gilbert A'Beckett and Henry Mayhew.
4. "Postscript; the Reginamania". *Spectator*, 6 January 1838. 8.
5. "The Coronation", *Spectator* 28 June 1838. 600.
6. Quoted in Giles St. Aubyn, *Queen Victoria: A Portrait* (1991; London: Scepter, 1992). 87.
7. James Vernon, *Politics and the People: A Study in English Political Culture, c. 1815-1867* (Cambridge: Cambridge UP, 1993). 105.
8. "Topics of the Day: A New Game for Children", *Spectator* 28 June 1838: 609.
9. See Celina Fox, *Graphic Journalism In England during the 1830s and 1840s* (New York: Garland, 1988). Richard Altick, *The English Common Reader: A Social History of the Mass Reading Public 1800-1900* (1957; Columbus: Ohio State University Press, 1998). Louis James, *Print and the People* 1819-1851 (London: Allen Lane, 1976).
10. See Agnes Strickland, *Queen Victoria: From her Birth to her Bridal* vol. 2 (London: Henry Colburn, 1840). 82.
11. "The Late Outrage to Her Majesty. Final Examination and Committal of Capt. Goode", *The Times* 13 November 1837: 5. "The Gross Outrage Towards Her Majesty", *The Times* 7 November 1837. 3. "Captain Goode". *The Times* 24 November 1838: 2.
12. Strickland 84.
13. "Police". *The Times* 29 June 1838: 8. "Police". *The Times* 5 June 1838: 7.
14. "Edmund Hayward". *The Times* 10 August 1839: 7. 21 August 1839: 7.
15. "Another Suitor to Her Majesty". *The Sun* 8 January 1840: 2.
16. Charles Dickens, *The Letters of Charles Dickens 1840-41*, ed. M. House and G. Storey, vol. 2 (Clarendon Press: Oxford, 1969) 25.
17. The *Penny Satirist* was reportedly one of the first penny broadsheets produced after the reduction of the Stamp Duty in 1836. Subtitled "A Cheap Substitute for a weekly newspaper", it contained a mixture of news commentary as well as a large woodcut by C.J. Grant. Moderately radical in its politics, its circulation in June 1837 has been claimed at 15,000. W. Anderson Smith, *Shepherd Smith the Universalist* (London: Sampson Low, Master & Co., 1892) 164.
18. " The Queen's Lover". *Penny Satirist* 6 July 1839: 2.
19. Douglas Jerrold, "Loyalty and Insanity". *Punch* 1 (1841): 258.
20. Jerrold 258.
21. Jerrold 258.
22. Jerrold 258.

23. Trefor Thomas, intro. George W.M. Reynolds *The Mysteries of London* ed. Trefor Thomas (Keele: Keele University Press, 1996) vii.
24. Anne Humpherys, "G.W.M. Reynolds: Popular Literature and Politics", in Joel Weiner (ed.) *Innovators and Preachers: The Role of the Editor in Victorian England* (Westport, Conn., Greenwood Press, 1985) 13. See also Ian Haywood, "George W.M. Reynolds and the Radicalization of Victorian Serial Fiction", *Media History* 4.2 (1998) 121-136.
25. "A Scene in the Nursery at Claremont". *ILN* 1 (28 May 1842) 40.
26. Thomas Lacquer, "The Queen Caroline Affair: Politics as Art in the Reign of George IV". *Journal of Modern History* 54 (1982) 417-466. However, Anna Clark has disputed Lacquer's claims, arguing that the melodramatic representation of Queen Caroline helped to make a radical mass movement possible. Anna Clark, "Queen Caroline and the Sexual Politics of Popular Culture in London, 1820" *Representations* 31 (Summer 1990) 47-68.
27. Reynolds 281.
28. The narrative of the "Boy Jones" was still being referred to in *Punch* as late as vol. 7, "The Boy Jones and the Boy Joinville" 35. For ballads see Charles Hindley, *Curiosities of Street Literature* (London: Reeves and Turner, 1871)
29. Henry Mayhew, *Life and Labour of the London Poor* (New York: Dover, 1968) vol. 1, 223.
30. Reynolds 97.
31. Reynolds 97.
32. Reynolds 99.
33. Reynolds 105.
34. Reynolds 105.
35. George Reynolds, *The Mysteries of London* vol 1. (London: George Vickers, 1846) 196.
36. Reynolds 279.
37. Reynolds, *The Mysteries of London* vol 2, 182.
38. Reynolds, *The Mysteries of London,* 1846, 247.
39. Reynolds, *The Mysteries of London*, 1849, 249.
40. "Prince Albert *v* Strange", *The Times* 7 November 1848. 6; 11 December 1848. 7; 14 December 1848. 6; 15 December 1848. 6; 17 January 1849. 6; 27 January 1849. 6; 27 January 1849. 6; 29 January 1849. 6; 30 January 1849. 7; 21 January 1849. 6; 23 May 1849. 7; 2 June 1849. 7; 4 June 1849. 7.
41. "Leaves from the Journal of Our life in the Highlands", *Athenaeum* 11 January 1868: 47. For more details, see John Plunkett, *Queen Victoria: First Media Monarch* (Oxford: Oxford University Press, 2003)
42. "The Queen of the Highlands", *Blackwood's Edinburgh Magazine* 103 (1868) 243.

Chapter 2

The Making of a Master Criminal: The 'Chief of the Thugs' in Victorian Writings on Crime

Máire ní Fhlathúin

In *Around the World in Eighty Days*, Jules Verne takes his protagonist Phileas Fogg to India, and remarks in passing that the countryside through which he is travelling is "under the sway of Feringhea, the chief of the Thugs, the king of the Stranglers".[1] The brief reference is part of the establishing of India as "other", the exotic location for Fogg's acquisition of his beloved Aouda. Her rescue from her husband's funeral pyre is an enactment of a nineteenth-century narrative of the colonial salvation of India for which the outlawing of *sati* became a sign, given a sardonic twist by the Frenchman Verne, who makes Fogg's servant Passepartout the true hero of the affair. The invocation of the "chief of the Thugs" recollects another version of the same narrative: thuggee, the robbery and ritual strangulation of victims, was the companion-piece to *sati* in the reforms that characterized Lord William Bentinck's governor-generalship (1828-35) in the history of British India. In Verne's novel (as in many adventure fictions), the "moment" of the defeat of evil is recovered from the past and re-enacted in the contemporary present: though the novel is set in 1872, the rite of *sati* is there to offer the European party their chance at bravery. Similarly, the narrator says, though the British have "found means to effect a considerable reduction in the numbers of these murders [by thugs], ... the dread association still exists".[2]

While *sati* provides one of the main plot-engines in *Around the World*, thuggee is alluded to only in passing. The mention of Feringhea, however, encapsulates a narrative of crime and criminality that pervades the popular culture of the nineteenth century. Although his moment on Verne's stage is a brief one, he plays a part in many other historical and literary works, in the process coming to embody the Victorian fascination with the "other", which is also, of course, an aspect of the "self". He is the ultimate alien figure, the Indian murderer; but is consistently linked to the British. This chapter will examine the constitution of this figure, who embodies many elements of the discourses on crime evolving throughout the nineteenth century, the merging of the categories of "fact" and "fiction", the classification of the criminal as "other" in terms of race, class or gender; and the perennial narrative of the restoration of order in the confrontation of the detective and the criminal.

The accounts of the British authorities' classification of and actions against thuggee in the 1830s form a readily identifiable category of the discourses of crime mentioned above. Starting as what purport to be wholly factual narratives of the discovery and eradication of a long-established association of religiously-motivated murderers, they are, in the course of the nineteenth century, incorporated into most of the genres of fiction, as well as popular sermons. William Butcher, editing *Around the World in Eighty Days*, suggests that the name and character of Feringhea were taken from Eugène Sue's earlier work, *The Wandering Jew*, which features one "Faranghea" as "one of the most redoubtable chiefs of the stranglers".[3] A far more likely source is René de Pont-Jest's *Le Procès des Thugs*, serialized in a Paris newspaper in 1866; the "Feringhea" of this text, unlike Sue's, provides both spelling and location for Verne's reference. All three derive ultimately from the work of W.H. Sleeman, the first "General Superintendent" of the campaign against the thugs, whose series of reports on thug practices and history and on the operations of his department against them provided almost the entire body of knowledge on thuggee available during the nineteenth century, and the material for all the fictional and semi-fictional versions outlined above.[4]

The "real" Feringhea, as described in the records of the East India Company, was one of the leaders of a gang of criminals who robbed and murdered travellers on the roads of central and northern India in the early decades of the nineteenth century. He was captured in December 1830, was admitted as a government "approver", or informer, gave evidence over the next few years against many of his former associates, and then disappears from the records. He would have been transferred, once his use as an informer had been exhausted, to a Sagar or Jabalpur jail, where the rate of prisoner mortality was such that he was unlikely to have lived long. In all these respects, his career mirrored those of hundreds of other informers, and thousands who were not admitted as informers, but convicted and executed or transported overseas. His transformation into a master criminal whose name became synonymous with thuggee in the nineteenth century was not owing to any special characteristic of his own, so much as to the demands of the Anglo-Indian political and administrative context of the time; and later to the evolving Western discourse on criminality within which thuggee was constituted.

The fore-grounding of individual criminals who were given special attention was, in the beginning, a consequence of the policing and prosecution techniques in use in early nineteenth-century India. The need to secure convictions for crimes which, by their nature, left no witnesses meant that officials relied almost exclusively on approvers' evidence against their former associates. These approvers were most often gang leaders or long-standing criminals—those best placed to inform against the greatest number of others. Held apart from other prisoners, questioned over and over about the details of thugs' lives and practices, they frequently became the object of fascination for the officials who interrogated them.[5] It was in their interests, of course, to represent themselves in the blackest possible light, as having been present at the greatest number of murders, because this increased their value as informers. The result may be seen in the reports and tallies of the East India Company officials, whose accounts of "the best approvers" are often accompanied by league tables of those approvers highlighting the most successful murderers.[6]

Already, therefore, the conditions are such that certain criminals are singled out, and their stories given special attention in the reports written by the officials of the Thuggee Department (TD). Feringhea is one of these—an amorphous figure whose attributes vary according to the context in which he is described. In the reports of his capture and interrogation, the impression is given that he alone can offer the key testimony with which the entire conspiracy of thuggee may be laid open. He claims knowledge, in his evidence, of many prisoners unknown to the other approvers.[7] But he was not the first approver to give evidence; nor was he a supreme leader—the success of Sleeman's operations at Sagar depended largely on the presence in the area of at least two rival gangs, the members of each willing to inform against the members of others.[8] The five hundred rupees paid in reward for his capture was no more than was offered for many others.[9] Feringhea is described by Sleeman as a "tall stout and handsome young man", his age estimated variously as twenty-five or thirty-five.[10] This would have made him, at most, fifteen years old "in the cold season of 1814", when Sleeman describes him as one of the "principal leaders" of a gang of 200 Thugs.[11] Some scepticism appears to be called for, but Feringhea seems to have excelled at making the most of his experiences: his depositions against his associates culminate in his own confession, where he claims that his family had been thugs for eleven generations, his father and grandfather were noted thugs, and that "no one knows so much of the Thugs as I do".[12]

Feringhea's own wish to present himself as a kingpin was fortuitously in tune with Sleeman's wish to find a kingpin to capture. The taking of Feringhea happened at a crucial period in Sleeman's career, when he (with his immediate superior, F.C. Smith) had devised a plan to set up a separate Department for the Suppression of Thuggee. In their correspondence with government on this topic, the publicity value of capturing an important criminal figure is made the most of.[13] Sleeman was never reluctant to talk up the work he was doing, stressing the "most dreadful and extraordinary system" of the thugs.[14] The advantage of a named and formidable enemy is clear: his seizure can be advertised as a success for Sleeman, and the assurances of his value can justify the questionable means used to take him, and later others (The act of holding his wife and family hostage was something even Smith found at first sight "repugnant" to Englishmen).[15] "Feringea[16] the great Thug" could also be used to promise further success, by the information he would volunteer on his former colleagues.[17] Whatever his practical value, his capture was unquestionably presented as a publicity coup.

In the fore-grounding of approvers' testimony, in Sleeman's wish to publicize his work, and in the value of Feringhea's evidence as proof of his success, the "master criminal" of the later years begins to be formed. The process is visible in the dialogues of the first volume of *Ramseeana*, where Feringhea, among others, gives information in reply to Sleeman's questions about thug beliefs; in the sensational and seminal episode where Feringhea points out bodies buried under the campsite where Sleeman's tents were placed (a literal unearthing of a criminal underworld); and in the narrative of detection that accompanies his capture.[18] The sense of triumph in this last account is unmistakable, and the tone of the piece is the more remarkable by contrast with the detached, summary narrative voice of Sleeman's usual writing. His various reports of arrests are presented always in the past tense, and in the passive voice ("They were all soon apprehended and brought to Saugor"),[19] but the taking of Feringhea is a personal matter: Sleeman describes how he "ascertained precisely Feringeea's residence in the Jhansee territory", sent a guard for him, and, when he escaped, held his family hostage. He continues:

> I knew Feringeea would not go far while links so dear to him were in my hands; and I sent off a second guard to Jhansee... [S]upposing the house to be surrounded by soldiers, he suffered himself to be bound without resistance by those two boys, both of whom he was strong enough to have strangled...[20]

In this rare instance of personal narrative may be found a relationship that fits into one of the dominant narrative patterns of the nineteenth century: the confrontation between the criminal and the detective. On the surface, this account of the criminal's capture displays Sleeman as a figure of ultimate control, sharing something like the "marvellous calm efficiency, all-knowing and all-powerful" that Ian Ousby attributes to Dickens's detectives.[21] There is also, unspoken but present, the other aspect of the relationship, the uneasy symbiosis between the detective and the criminal.

Feringhea, in Sleeman's reports, is cast as his greatest enemy; later he comes to stand for the alienness and evil of the Indian character that thuggee represented in the British mind. However, he is never completely "other"—he cannot be divorced or distanced from the British presence in India. The narrative of his capture foregrounds the "English blunderbuss and pistol" that were his weapons of choice;[22] and his former career in the service of Sir David Ochterlony, the Resident in Malwa and Rajputana, made the government reluctant to allow him the status of approver.[23] Even his name reflects the role of the British in his making: his mother's village is "assaulted and burnt" by a "Regiment under Blake Sahib" for nonpayment of taxes; "in her flight [she] gave birth to Feringeea, and he got his name from that event—Feringeea, from the attack of the Feringies".[24] In this, he is exceptional, but he is also, on a metaphorical level, representative—the spectre of British responsibility for, or even complicity in, the thugs' activities, haunted those who dealt with them and wrote about them. One of the problems of the government's dealing with them was identified by F.C. Smith as a complicated system of ransoming and seeking security from captured thugs, which had as its end result their being allowed to go free and resume their careers of crime with a view to repaying fines incurred for past transgressions. "Without intending it", he said, "the British authorities ... have made themselves accessories to the subsequent thuggies, which the liberated thugs committed to pay for their ransom".[25] The approver system also lent itself to this kind of abuse, including some instances where criminals used government badges and marks of identity, passing themselves off as officials. The Court of Directors of the East India Company wrote to the Bengal government:

> [W]e fear that ... these people have been enabled to turn to the purposes of their horrible occupation the opportunities afforded by public employment. It is proved that the head of the gang who perpetrated the Lucknadoon, and so many other murders, was a police officer, who was actually sent in search of a thug who had broken prison, and took that occasion of going himself on a thug expedition. On his first apprehension he obtained his release and that of the whole gang by exhibiting to Mr. Molony his warrant, and other proofs of his identity as a police officer. Two other police officers of inferior rank formed part of the same gang".[26]

While such activity is literally threatening to the stability of the British administration, tending to discredit that administration's servants and institutions, it represents also an insidious "mimicry" (in Homi Bhabha's sense) whereby a criminal establishment mirrors (a police officer is also a thug leader) and perverts the structures of the colonial state. While exposing the wrong-doings of thugs, the officers of the TD were simultaneously highlighting the weakness and corruption of their own organization. This recurrent thread of anxiety forms an uneasy counterpoint to the rhetoric of protection and salvation more usually produced by the officials responsible for the campaign against thugs. Nor was it groundless concern: modern scholarship tends to highlight the indirect cause-and-effect relationship between the British presence in India and the activities of predatory criminals, accounting for the appearance of "thugs" in the early nineteenth century by reference to the instability of the contemporary political and economic landscape. The lives and livelihoods of many were disrupted; some of these turned to crime and were conveniently categorized as "extraordinary" criminals–thugs–in order to facilitate the sanctioning of harsh legal and political moves against them.[27] Such arguments were unthinkable–or at least unvoiceable–in the nineteenth century, where the defeat of the thugs was given a prominent part in the narrative of British "progress" and civilization of India.[28] Yet in fiction, and in the sensational "reportage" of the popular press, the link between the colonial authority and its criminal enemies is always present: British (and French) men and women are found to be thugs; thugs are relocated from India to Paris or London; Indian thug leaders speak English and French, even share aspects of "Western" physiognomy.[29] The continual and repeated invocation of Feringhea, the original "hybrid" thug, is a frequent accompaniment to this narrative of complicity.[30]

Eugène Sue's "Faranghea" is a notable example of such a portrait. He is described as a literal hybrid, "a mongrel",[31] though the narrator later refers to him as "an Indian by birth" (124). Like his original, he is "one of the most redoubtable chiefs of the stranglers" (42), and "remarkable for his intelligence and sagacity" (124). Sue, however, makes literal the original's "Western" aspects, giving him the ability to speak English and French "tolerably well", and presenting him as "clothed like a European" (42). He also embodies one of Sue's Western targets, as he allies himself to the Jesuits. "Rome and Bohwanie [or Kali, supposed to be the goddess of thugs] are sisters", he claims, because the Order of Jesuits seeks to kill "man's desires" (125). His career culminates in his becoming servant to a Cardinal, as Sue makes explicit the comparison between thuggee and Catholicism: "Bohwanie makes dead bodies which rot, and the holy Society dead bodies that walk" (296). In creating this character, Sue makes maximum use of the intersection of the alien and the familiar to further his anti-clerical agenda: the Catholic church is demonized by association with thuggee—the thugs "try everywhere to make proselytes by preaching in the night their abominable doctrines" (41)—while, as a probably unintended consequence, thuggee is correspondingly domesticated. This incidental use of thuggee as a motif is not confined to Sue; it surfaces in the works of others as a convenient analogy for whatever aspect of contemporary life is being considered.[32] But thuggee as a system, and the thug lore collected (or created) in the process of TD investigations, were also being incorporated into the mainstream of European writings on crime, and being subject to the same process of transformation that gave rise to Sue's westernized Faranghea.

Sleeman's reports were published in very small editions, and circulated mainly among officials of government in India, but they rapidly made their way overseas, as other writers saw the potential for public interest in these melodramatic events. Sleeman's *Ramaseeana* was revised to produce Edward Thornton's *Illustrations of the History and Practices of the Thugs*, published in London in 1837; a pirated edition was published two years later in the USA and Philip Meadows Taylor reviewed *Depredations* (and highlighted the episode of Feringhea's capture) in 1843.[33] These revised versions focused mainly on the more sensational elements of the narratives, and the accounts of thug practices, their criminal adventures and their defeat by the forces of the British state made their way into the cultural landscape of Europe and America. By the 1840s, the campaign against thugs had been proclaimed a success–thuggee was effectively defeated, and the TD turned its attention to dacoits and other criminals.[34] Popular interest in the topic did not fade, however. Both in Europe and in India, the thug narratives were re-visited and often re-enacted–either literally, in the form of repeat performances by thug approvers, or in the incorporation of thug narratives, figures and motifs into the fictional and semi-fictional crime writings of the later nineteenth century.

Once popular interest in thuggee had been awakened, the imprisoned approvers and their families became a focus of attention outside the legal process. Sleeman attributes his decision to publish his conversations with approvers to the presence during his interrogations of "different European gentlemen who happened to call in", and who manifested "a good deal of interest" in the proceedings.[35] In 1837, the thug jails in Oudh were a tourist attraction for the men of Emily and Fanny Eden's party, and the prisoners demonstrated their techniques for the benefit of the British visitors, as they were to do for many others.[36] John Lang, whose articles from India were featured in Dickens's *Household Words*, describes such a visit in an account highlighting the "stage" nature of the demonstrations: to him, he writes, the sight is a play or a tragedy, but "to these domesticated demons it was a mere farce". An old man trains children in their performance, and the boys go through the ritual, "much in the same spirit that an actor and actress would go through the strangling scene in *Othello*, to please a fastidious manager".[37] For those who could not get to India, the published accounts of thug practices were supplemented by exhibited models of thugs at work, some of which figured in the 1851 Exhibition as well as in the British Museum's Ethnological room.[38] The re-enactment of the moment of killing by thugs safely corralled within prison walls (and metaphorically within the stabilizing discourse of the British-authored reports of their narratives, or yet more securely contained as figurines in an exhibition, with the carpet of their own weaving hanging nearby as the sign of their domestication) serves the same function as the eternal triumph of the adventure hero, or the repeated drama of the *sati* rescue. It foregrounds, for the benefit of the British observers, the justification for the thugs' defeat, and the fact of their powerlessness—repeating in miniature the moral and practical rationale for colonialism itself.

The accounts of these re-enactments also show the increasingly sensational nature of the discourse on thuggee, as more "shocking" elements–such as the involvement of women and children in the act of murder–are introduced into the performances. This is evident in John Lang's articles in particular. He describes or alludes to several women thug prisoners, one of whom claims to have murdered twenty-one victims, and who re-enacts the drama of strangling for his benefit.[39] This version of events appears to contradict the accounts earlier produced by the TD, where a single female thug is alluded to as an extraordinary exception to the general rule that thugs "never allow their women to accompany them or take any part in their murders".[40] Several explanations could be offered for these tensions: it might be the case that the TD was mistaken in its gendering of murder, or that the families of male prisoners found it expedient to create their own parts in these performances, or that Lang himself had an eye to what his readers would find interesting. In any case, the salient point is the expansion and sensationalizing of the earlier "official" discourse on thuggee.

This turn towards the sensational also took place on a more general level, as the deeds of thug criminals were translated from their original context in the East India Company's administrative records into the burgeoning field of writings on crime. Thuggee was in many ways ideally suited to this new context, in which fiction and fact were becoming increasingly interwoven into a discourse on crime which, like the TD's dealings with its prisoners, foregrounded both extraordinary criminals and the investigative powers of those who pursued them.

Interest in the "true confessions" genre of criminal narratives was already of long standing,[41] and exacerbated in the first half of the nineteenth century by the institution of new police forces and the publicity given to their activities. Marie-Christine Leps notes the increase in "factual reports" of crime in the 1820s, with the circulation of such texts as the fictionalized memoirs of the French detective Vidocq, and the role of these publications as models for fictional crime stories.[42] The detective story proper was also developing, and again synthesizing fiction and fact in works like Edgar Allan Poe's "Mystery of Marie Rogêt", based on the real-life disappearance of Mary Celia Rogers of New York. Later in the century, the phenomenon of mass journalism saw "factual" accounts of crime using increasingly fictional techniques, as crimes were regularly presented as "the daring exploits of master criminals", in a style which transcended the division between fiction and fact, so that comparisons were regularly made between "real" and fictional villains.[43] The structure of the thug narratives lent themselves to these techniques, as the question-and-answer format of interrogations became the confessional narrative of Ameer Ali in *Confessions of a Thug* (1839), the first and most famous of the thug stories, where "real" episodes and motifs from Sleeman's reports are the basis for the picaresque adventures of a fictional anti-hero.[44] The novel immediately made its way into the tradition of "real" data on thugs (it is cited, for example, by T.D. Landon, whose *Narrative of a Journey through India* includes the account of a visit to the "Thug Institute" in Jabalpur, in 1851, where he claims to have found Ameer Ali, "chief of Thugs"; the reader is referred to Taylor's *Confessions* for his story).[45] Equally significantly, it popularized both the subject of thuggee, and the handling of that subject by the focus on one representative criminal.[46]

By the mid-nineteenth century, then, the discourse on thuggee was well established as part of popular culture, sharing with other varieties of crime-writing a semi-fictional, semi-factual status; as well as a tendency to foreground a "master criminal" possessing attributes of both hero and villain. The treatment of this criminal, in the texts produced after Taylor's work, shows a distinct pattern emerging, influenced both by the original colonial context for thuggee, and by the specifically Western concerns of the writers who used it as a motif. It can be summarized as a pattern of convergence of the exotic and the domestic. The anxious distancing of the colonial state from its thug enemies in the TD's reports is replaced by a portrait of the thug which incorporates elements of both west and east (as with Sue's Faranghea, discussed above), while the accounts of thugs and their practices are revised to consider themes unrelated to the Indian context, but of great concern to contemporary British and French writers.

The intersection of colonial and domestic discourses on crime is best exemplified in the work of one of Sue's successors, René de Pont-Jest, whose *Le Procès des Thugs* was serialized in *Le Petit journal* during 1866. *Le Petit journal* was the first and most successful exponent of popular journalism in Paris from its beginnings in 1863, and its contents featured especially crime reportage and crime fiction.[47] The presentation of *Le Procès des Thugs* had aspects of both. It was published at a time when thugs were "la fureur du jour", as an unrelated item in the same paper pointed out,[48] and heralded by a series of advertisements run during the days before the appearance of the first instalment: these promised the "complete account" of the "appalling trial" of "Feringhea, great leader of the stranglers", before the "supreme courts of Calcutta and Madras".[49] The story is structured as a courtroom drama, with each section offering a different witness's "evidence"; this allows Pont-Jest to use the question-and-answer format of the TD reports, which provide in addition many of the names and incidental details of his narrative. Consequently, it also mirrors the contemporary press coverage of criminal cases, which were frequently presented through metaphors of the theatre.[50] In a further blurring of the dividing-line, the story is immediately preceded by a letter to the paper's star columnist, "Timothée Trimm", purporting to be from a "former apprentice strangler", an Englishman named "Robinson".[51] As well as Feringhea himself, the story features many other real-life participants, including Sleeman and some of his assistants, and, as presiding judge of the courtroom, "Lord William Bentick" [*sic*].[52]

Though there is no formal plot, the principal movement of the story is from the beginning of the trial to the thugs' conviction and execution, with a succession of "proofs" of their guilt emerging from the courtroom confrontation between Lord Bentick and the accused, most notably Feringhea. In this respect, *Le Procès des Thugs* sustains and heightens the role of thuggee in the discourse of colonial India, as Pont-Jest relocates the action from the small, widely-scattered locations of the original trials to the "central court" of Calcutta, and replaces the many trials before different judges with one trial held by the supreme authority, the Governor-General. Its successful outcome thus becomes an emblematic triumph of the British restoration of order–the final vignette is set on the Ganges, among the charred bodies of the executed thugs, while "European society celebrated their deliverance, and the punishment of the followers of Kali".[53] All the sensational aspects of thuggee are made much of, and others added; these include an element of human sacrifice in thugs' initiation rites, the kidnapping for ritual murder of white women, and several gruesome killings where the agents of death are rats, snakes, wild pigs, boiling silver, etc.[54] These elements were doubtless added by Pont-Jest in deference to the tastes of his audience, but the effect, again, is to establish the thugs–and by extension India–as savage and barbaric, and the British as the representatives of order and civilization.

The undercurrent of anxiety over colonial complicity with thuggee, which accompanies the main plot of the establishment of distance and control in the TD's narratives, is also represented in Pont-Jest's work, perhaps the more so since he was explicitly describing British (as opposed to French) colonial authority.[55] The thugs of his story are persistently aided by Europeans at every level, from the comic Irishman "Paddy Turnlboat" of the parish of St Patrick, through the respectable Sir Gordon, to the very centre of power, where Lord Bentick's valet turns out to have been for years forging his master's signature to decoy victims into the thugs' grasp. Feringhea himself, as in Sue's work, is given European attributes: a "Greek countenance", and features that seem "as if taken from a bronze coin". He claims the status of a "descendant of a royal race".[56] But while these connections between Feringhea and Western "civilization" underline the narrative of complicity Pont-Jest constructs, they also serve to mitigate the longstanding failure of the colonial state against the thugs, with the implication that it was so defeated only by rogue elements within itself. Feringhea's success is further explained by his almost supernatural powers, which again set him apart from his associates; he is described as "comme un génie infernel", and Bentick comments on how the other accused "tremble before him, lowering their eyes before his gaze".[57] In the end, these qualities make his defeat and the accompanying triumph of the restoration of order that much more spectacular. And, as in Sleeman's accounts, Feringhea's fate remains indeterminate, the narrative leaving open the question of whether he died in prison, or made a deal with the authorities, or caused the locks of his cell to open through supernatural powers.[58] Like the thug prisoners in their performances, he is forever capable of resurrection for another enactment of the narrative of the establishment of colonial order, so that Jules Verne can lead his intrepid heroes, on their way to rescue their damsel in distress, through the vaguely menacing countryside of the "king of the Stranglers".[59]

Less obviously, the themes and structures of *Le Procès des Thugs* can be seen as part of a discourse on contemporary crime in Western societies, as well as a reprise of the adventure hero's triumph over exotic and alien forces of evil. The location of crime among the lower classes, and the portrayal of women as by nature more inclined to criminality (both commonplaces of contemporary ideas on crime) are mirrored exactly in Pont-Jest's narrative. The only British man not of the lower classes revealed as Feringhea's associate, Sir Gordon, proves to be of Irish birth and motivated by anti-English feeling. The women display stereotypically feminine characteristics, like Miss Clary Trévor, a woman of low morals who gets Feringhea to kill her lover. Their treachery can be exploited for sensational ends without implicating society as a whole, and attributed to the various weaknesses of character natural to their class or gender, as with the French woman thug whose last word at her death is Feringhea's name.[60] Criminal acts and inclinations, in this framework, can have no dimension other than the personal. The focus on individual character obscures any possibility of the thugs' crimes, or those of their European associates, having a basis in any inequality of resources or opportunities, or in the instability associated with the colonial conquest of India. The message is emphasized by Pont-Jest's continual reiteration of the thugs' fondness for torture and imaginatively horrible killings (never present in the original records), acts attributable only to personal evil rather than to a rational motive of robbery for gain. Crime is explained by reference to the naturally base tendencies of those outside the state of respectable normality, or to the extraordinary qualities of the "master criminal" who transcends any moral or social norms.

The transformation of the original reports on thuggee into Pont-Jest's sensational fiction makes apparent the changes and innovations in the discourses of criminality between the first and second halves of the nineteenth century, between British India and metropolitan France. At the same time, the same basic themes persist throughout the thug narratives in all their incarnations. Crime is perforce recognized as both exotic and domestic, European and Indian, made possible by the complicity of the society that should be controlling it. The concluding scene of judgement is only the final element in a process of narrative resolution involving not only the discovery and punishment of criminals but also their definition as "other" to the society against which they have offended. Because the narratives focus on the criminals, leaving unexamined the underlying economic and political structures of their societies, they typically fail to register the necessity or even desirability of any change in the conditions that produced them. The master criminal, created at the intersection between an instance of "wrong-doing" and its public presentation, has to be continually re-invoked and reinvented to explain the persistence of criminality.

Notes

1. Jules Verne, *Around the World in Eighty Days* (1873), ed. William Butcher (Oxford: OUP, 1995). 50.
2. Verne, *Around the World.* 50.
3. Eugène Sue, *The Wandering Jew* (London, 1845). 42.
4. W.H. Sleeman, *Ramaseeana*, 2 vols, (Calcutta, 1836); and *Depredations Committed by the Thug Gangs* (Calcutta, 1840).
5. Fanny Eden comments that "all the Europeans who have had much to do with their examinations view them in a most romantic light". *Tigers, Durbars and Kings: Fanny Eden's Indian Journals*, ed. Janet Dunbar (London: John Murray, 1988). 120.
6. See James Paton's narratives of thug interrogations, and his map, reprinted in Sleeman, *Depredations*, chapter 8.
7. See Bengal Political Consultations (hereafter BPC) 19 August 1831, nos 19, 21, BL.
8. See BPC 17 June 1831, no. 78, BL.
9. See Sleeman, *Depredations.* 124.
10. BPC 18 March 1831, no. 11, BL; Board's Collections F/4/1568 64220, 266, BL.
11. Sleeman, *Depredations.* vi-vii.
12. BPC 19 August 1831, no. 19, BL
13. See BPC 18 March 1831, nos. 11-19, BL; BPC 25 February 1831, no. 27, BL.
14. Board's Collections F/4/1566 64217, 148, BL.
15 F.C. Smith, 20 January 1831, in BPC 18 March 1831, no. 11, BL.
16. The spelling varies; I have standardized except where quoting directly from texts.
17. W.H. Sleeman, 7 January 1831, in BPC 18 March 1831, no. 11, BL.
18. Sleeman, *Ramaseeana.* i.32-3.
19. Sleeman, *Depredations.* 73.
20. Sleeman, *Depredations.* 67-8.
21. Ian Ousby, *Bloodhounds of Heaven: The Detective in English Fiction from Godwin to Doyle* (London & Cambridge, Mass.: Harvard University Press, 1976). 88.
22. Sleeman, *Depredations.* 67-8.
23. See the Court of Directors of the East India Company to the Bengal Government, 28 November 1832, in *The Correspondence of Lord William Cavendish Bentinck*, 2 vols. ed. C.H. Philips (Oxford: OUP, 1977). ii.954.
24. Sleeman, *Ramaseeana.* i.175.
25. F.C. Smith, 20 June 1832, in *Bentinck Correspondence.* ii.840.
26. 28 November 1832, in *Bentinck Correspondence.* ii.954-5.
27. See Sandria B. Freitag, "Crime in the Social Order of Colonial North India", *Modern Asian Studies* 25.2 (1991). 227-61; Stewart N. Gordon, "Scarf and Sword: Thugs, Marauders, and State-formation in 18th Century Malwa", *Indian Economic and Social History Review* vi.4 (1969). 403-29 (rpr. in Stewart Gordon, *Marathas, Marauders, and State Formation in Eighteenth-Century India* (Delhi: UP,1994)); Hiralal Gupta, "A Critical Study of the Thugs and their Activities", *Journal of*

Indian History 37 (1959). 167-77; and Radhika Singha, *A Despotism of Law: Crime and Justice in Early Colonial India* (Delhi: OUP, 1998).

28. See, for example, John William Kaye, *The Administration of the East India Company: A History of Indian Progress* (London, 1853), whose illustrations of British success in India include two chapters devoted to the suppression of thuggee and dacoity (353-416).

29. See, for example, James DeMille's *Cord and Creese* (New York, 1869), where John Potts proclaims himself "the only Englishman that ever joined the Thugs" (137); the evidence of popular fiction would suggest that, on the contrary, he should have had many compatriots among his criminal associates.

30. Alongside the narratives of crime discussed in this chapter, the invocation of Feringhea is continued in other texts, where he similarly embodies both alienness and complicity. See, for example, his characterization in Mark Twain's meditations on thuggee in *Following the Equator* (1897), where his image – "across this abyssmal [*sic*] gulf of time we still see Feringhea's lips uncover his teeth, and through the dim haze we catch the incandescent glimmer of his smile" – is counterpointed to Twain's remark that "the joy of killing" and of "seeing killing done" are "traits of the human race at large. We white people are merely modified Thugs" (*Following the Equator and Anti-imperialist Essays* (New York & Oxford: OUP, 1996). 434-7).

31. Sue, 42. Further page references are incorporated into the text.

32. See, for example, Digby Hussy de Burgh, *Western Thugs; or, Ireland and the English Speaking World* (c. 1920s), which attributes the parlous state of Ireland (ie, Anglo-Ireland) to a combination of Catholicism, communism and stupidity: "The readers of this book ought to know by this time what the Catholic Conspiracy is. It is Thuggee, and the Socialist Conspiracy is Thuggee also…" (117).

33. [W.H. Sleeman], *The Thugs or Phansigars of India* (Philadelphia: Cary & Hart, 1839). Philip Meadows Taylor's review of *Depredations Committed by the Thug Gangs* follows Feringhea's story with his own comment: "Feringhea is now an approver, and one of the best that has ever been admitted; his active and daring habits, and prudent caution in conducting expeditions, had made him a successful leader…" ("State of Thuggee in India", *British and Foreign Review* 15.29 (1843). 253-4).

34. This claim is open to some doubt; as Sandria Freitag points out: "thugs [were] after 1840 relabelled as dacoits–just as dacoits after 1870 were frequently recast as criminal tribes" ("Collective Crime and Authority in North India", in *Crime and Criminality in British India*, ed. Anand A. Yang (Tucson: University of Arizona Press, 1985), 186).

35. *Ramaseeana*. i.65-6.

36. Eden, 104.

37. [John Lang], "Wanderings in India", *Household Words* 16.399 (14 November 1857). 457.

38. Edward P. Eddrup, *The Thugs; or, Secret Murderers of India* (London, 1853). 6-8.

39. Lang, "Wanderings in India", 457-8. See also his "Wedding Bells", where a child bride "falls victim to a woman Thug". *Household Words* 6, No. 152 (19 February 1853). 552.

40. Sleeman, *Ramaseeana.* ii.359.
41. Ousby. 44.
42. Marie-Christine Leps, *Apprehending the Criminal: The Production of Deviance in Nineteenth-Century Discourse* (Durham and London: Duke University Press, 1992). 84.
43. Leps. 107-8.
44. Philip Meadows Taylor, *Confessions of a Thug*, ed. Patrick Brantlinger (Oxford: OUP, 1998). While Taylor was an officer in the service of the Nizam of Hyderabad, and played up his association with the thuggee police, claiming his story as a true-life account, the novel is often self-consciously literary, and draws heavily on Sleeman's work. See Javed Majeed, "Meadows Taylor's *Confessions of a Thug*: The Anglo-Indian novel as a genre in the making", in *Writing India 1757-1990*, ed. Bart Moore-Gilbert (Manchester: MUP, 1996); and David Finkelstein, "A Study of the Works of Philip Meadows Taylor", PhD thesis (University of Edinburgh, 1990), 14-19, 33-68.
45. T.D.L., *Narrative of a Journey through India* (Westminster: Thomas Brettell, 1857). 67-8.
46. According to Taylor's own account, "not only did the London papers and periodicals take it [*Confessions*] up but the provincial press teemed with flattering reviews and long extracts from it". *Story of My Life* (1878), intro. Dennis Walder (London: Pluto, 1989). 108.
47. See Leps. 87.
48. "Les Thugs de Paris", *Le Petit Journal*, 7 September 1866. 2.
49. See *Le Petit journal*, 12 September 1866, 3. Translations are mine; *Le Procès des Thugs* has never, to my knowledge, appeared in English.
50. Leps. 110-12.
51. *Le Petit journal*, 26 August 1866. 1.
52. Bentinck was Governor-General of India at the inception of the campaign against thuggee. The persistent mis-spelling of his name, as well as Pont-Jest's uncertain grasp of the details of British honourifics and courtroom etiquette, occasionally engenders a comic effect unintended by the author.
53. René de Pont-Jest, *Le Procès des Thugs*, chapter LXII. The text was serialized daily in *Le Petit journal* from 27 August to 15 October 1866, and "Le Procés" was later published with its two sequels, "L'avatar" and "L'héritage de Satan" in book form as *Le Procés des Thugs* (Paris: Bunel, 1877). My references are to the serialization.
54. Pont-Jest, chapters XXV, XXXV, XXXVII.
55. Martine van Wœrkens identifies as a theme in the later parts of the novel the idea that "les Anglais ne méritaient pas l'Inde" (*Le Voyageur Étranglé* (Paris: Albin Michel, 1995), 332-3).
56. Pont-Jest, chapter I.
57. Pont-Jest, chapters LII, LVIII.
58. Pont-Jest, chapter LXI. Though Feringhea never re-appears in Pont-Jest's work, his son Nadir is the protagonist of the two sequels, which trace his progress from a thug leader to an Indian nationalist who finally renounces violence and devotes himself to working for his people (Van Wœrkens, 327).

59. The most recent version of this resurrection is the Merchant-Ivory film *The Deceivers* (1988), where Feringhea appears as a gang-leader, "a very well-respected man". Once again, the narrative of colonial order is juxtaposed with instances of British complicity with the criminals, as Feringhea's pact with the renegade official George Angelsmith allows him to operate freely in Angelsmith's district, in return for Angelsmith's sharing in his plunder. (Neither of these elements appears in the novel by John Masters (1951) on which the film is based.) *The Deceivers* also reverses the drama of the *sati* rescue, as the British hero William Savage not only fails, ultimately, to prevent a *sati* but is himself the killer of the woman's husband.

60. Pont-Jest, chapter XXXIV.

Chapter 3

Black Markets and Cadaverous Pies: The Corpse, Urban Trade and Industrial Consumption in the Penny Blood

Sally Powell

When Tim Roper and Ben Bandy decide to turn their hands to resurrection in Henry Thornley's penny blood serial *Life in London* (1846), Roper reveals the shocking extent to which the resurrected and dissected corpse is commodified and secreted into the marketplace. When surgeons have finished with the corpse, declares Roper, "human flesh is frequently converted into a hadipose substance, not unlike spermaceti ... [which] is sometimes burnt as candles and at others it's used as soap".[1] One dissectionist, he reveals, "used to sell the skulls as nail boxes, soap trays, and handles of knives".[2] Whether such practices actually occurred in mid-century Victorian England remains obscure, but it is clearly evident that the penny blood exhibits a persistent preoccupation with the displaced corpse and with its black market commodification.

Within the urban landscape of the mid-century penny blood, the figure of the displaced corpse constitutes a palpable and thrilling presence. Secreted in sewers, sealed up in cellars, left to corrupt in tumble-down houses, unearthed fragment-by-sensational-fragment in overcrowded cemeteries, butchered and sold in pies, emitting noxious gases, even causing explosions in the penny blood, the displaced urban corpse is at once a highly sensational and deeply anxious entity. Within the genre, such cadaverous narratives not only explicitly reflect the corporeal actuality of the sights and smells of the Victorian urban experience, but more implicitly constitute an articulation of the threat posed by city commercialism to the sanctity and survival of the working-class individual.

Published in weekly parts, the penny blood specialized in drawn-out melodramatic tales of crime, adventure and romance, often including shocking exposés of low-life degradation and underground deviancy. With its antecedents in the street ballad, the gothic novel and the *Newgate Calendar*, the penny blood enjoyed popularity among the urban working classes throughout the 1840s.[3] Technological advancement and improved levels of literacy amongst the poorer classes resulted in a mid-century explosion in the publication of popular fiction with the burgeoning city offering a seemingly ever-expanding captive market for stories that effectively evoked the gothic flavour of city life or offered a means of imaginative escape in the form of sensational romance for weary working-class urbanites.

Narratives in which bodies are "burked", scavenged, disinterred, traded and dissected were entirely in keeping with the penny blood's sensationalist mission and regularly featured in its pages. Such fictions afforded the writer full scope to dramatize and exploit the corporeal horror of the cadaver for the titillation of the common reader. Yet they are also suggestive of an expression of profound social anxiety, most simply to do with the sanctity of the corpse in the face of the demand created by the anatomist, but also related to the growing perception that the sanctity of selfhood is threatened by the aggressive commercial forces generated by the industrial city.

Few low-life penny narratives are without at least one episode of body-snatching and many revel in the brutality and callousness of the crime. Experience in the field of cadaverous trading appears to be an essential qualification for the hardened penny-blood villain. In G.W.M. Reynolds' *The Mysteries of London* (1844-1848), the Resurrection Man is placed at the centre of the fiction's criminal underworld; in Thomas Prest's *The Old House of West Street* (1846), the old house is revealed as a resurrectionist's hide-out and a burker's den; in *The Wild Boys of London* (1866)—an example of a later juvenile sub-genre—the penny dreadful, the criminal outsiders who encroach upon the Wild Boys' underground territory scavenge a murdered body from the river and deal with professional body-snatchers.

Indeed, at mid-century many of London's working-class penny blood readers would have been familiar with the sight of the river's dredger-men, fishing primarily for saleable material debris but ever in hope of snaring a potentially profitable corpse.[4] However, cadaverous trading presented itself as most pertinent to the working-class reader given that, since the late eighteenth century, when trading in corpses had begun in earnest, it was the bodies of the poor that were most likely to fall prey to the burker and the body-snatcher.[5] The destitute often died alone, without the protection of family or friends, and were buried in shallow graves in easily accessible coffins. With the introduction of the Anatomy Act in 1832, which sanctioned the dissection of the "friendless" bodies remaining unclaimed in the nation's institutions, the threat posed by the anatomist's scalpel to the body of the poor became further entrenched in the working-class consciousness.

It is, therefore, not surprising that working-class popular fiction persistently sensationalizes and exploits the threat of resurrection, given the vulnerability of the working-class corpse to trade and dissection. *The Wild Boys*, for example, features the vivisection of a man whilst he is still alive. In *The Mysteries of London*, the "polished marble limbs" of the corpse are "rudely grasped by the sacrilegious hands of the body snatchers".[6] The body is stripped naked, its neck and heels tied together by means of strong cord, before it is thrust into a large sack. There is also a persistent suggestion in penny fiction that the snatching and dissection of the female corpse constitutes a rape. The salvaging of the dead female body in *The Wild Boys* is highly eroticized. The boys remove the dead woman's dress and their eyes fall upon "the rounded breasts nestling amid the damp but snowy white lace, and the soft arms and the softer outlines of those glorious limbs which were lavishly displayed".[7] It is only, we are assured, that they are used to seeing in their horrid business "the undraped form of beautiful girls, warm with the glow of ripe maidenhood", that they were not "moved to something more than business".[8] Whilst the illustration depicting the body once it has been handed over to the professional snatchers shows it fully clothed—for the text is consistently able to overstep the boundaries of decorum in a way that is denied the more blatant illustration—the image supports the suggestion that the body will be sexually ravaged: a dark figure, holding a knife, stands by as if ready to pounce greedily, whilst a dandified "business man" looks on [See figure 3.1]. Once delivered to the surgeon, it becomes evident that the woman is not actually dead and the doctor claims her as his mistress, carrying out an invasive and sexualized examination that proves she has "loved before" and is therefore "no shy virgin who would be alarmed by his advances".[9] The representation of the dissection of the female body as rape is also present in *The Mysteries of London*. In "The Body-Snatching Song", the corpse of the beautiful virgin is disinterred and the process to which it is subjected figured as a sexual despoiling. The body is laid out "on the dark black mould, / That the pale moonbeam may kiss its brow!", whilst "the student doth his knife prepare / To hack all over this form so fair, / And sever the virgin limb from limb".[10]

Such a preoccupation with resurrection and cadaverous trading is metonymic of the existence of a mid-century urban retail environment that was distinctly corporeal in nature. Penny fiction writers followed the example of social commentators and were keen to evoke in their sensational urban expositions the sights and smells of the human and animal body that pervaded the buying and selling in slum areas. As Henry Mayhew reveals the importance of bodily waste to the economic survival of many of London's working-classes (such as the night-soil men and the pure-finders who collect and sell dog excrement to the city's tanneries), so *Life in London* features a woman who deals in cat-skin and dogs' teeth, knocking the latter out of the heads of dead dogs she finds in the road. It is revealed that Barker—so named for her tendency to bark like a dog whilst faking seizure in the street—secretes the corporeal material of her gruesome trade in the cellar of her home. In the decomposed matter and animal intestines that constitute the ground of her cellar, she keeps "an immense number of dead cats", all of which have been buried alive with their heads downwards.[11]

The presence of the relatively large-scale marketing and slaughtering of livestock continued to take place within the confines of the burgeoning urban landscape and forced itself upon the sensitivities of the city inhabitants. In *Oliver Twist* (1837), Charles Dickens declares that it is "covered, nearly ankle-deep, with filth and mire" and that "a thick steam, perpetually rising from the reeking bodies of the cattle, and mingling with the fog, which seemed to rest upon the chimney-tops, hung heavily above".[12] And in Dickens's *Great Expectations* (1860-61), Pip discovers that Smithfield Market is a "shameful place … all asmear with filth and fat and blood and foam".[13] In *Ragged London in 1861*, John Hollingshead comments on the nuisance arising from cattle being kept in the heart of the city—at least two hundred and eight different stations in as many streets—and the "sanitary difficulty" caused by the presence of slaughterhouses "belonging to small, struggling butchers, in the closest part of the neighbourhood".[14] It is this London, sickened by the insistent presence of corporeal trade, that is revealed in the penny blood.

The Mysteries of London begins with a youth amidst the "labyrinth of narrow and dirty streets" in the immediate vicinity of the "foul and filthy arena of Smithfield Market".[15] The surrounding area is described as choked by the "foetid and sickening odour" from the knackers'-yards of Cow Cross and the establishments in Castle Street where horse-flesh is boiled down to supply food for the dogs and cats of the metropolis.[16] Here, the eye is as offended by the sight of the animal bones hung in the windows to bleach, as the nerves are repulsed by the stench of the horse-meat that, if left unsold, speedily becomes putrid, and pervades the entire neighbourhood.

Both legitimate and black market trading in corporeal goods constituted a palpable presence in the most densely over-inhabited areas of the city and—possibly in response to such an urban tumult of living bodies, bodily waste and animal trade—penny fiction writers responded anxiously to the relationship between the sanctity of the individual and the economics of the Victorian city, by suggesting that the commodification of the human body was integrated into its commercialism. In *Life in London*, a seasoned resurrectionist outrageously suggests that corpses, like other commodities, are priced in relation to their quality and yardage, claiming that "The surgeons pay for every adult corpse, perwided it's neither green nor putrid, two guineas and a crown; and for minors, six bob for the first foot, and a tanner and a-half per inch for all above it".[17] This representation of the human corpse as product stands as testimony to the existence of mid-century working-class anxiety in relation to retail, production and consumption, an anxiety explicitly played out in the genre's most notorious narrative, Thomas Prest's tale of Sweeney Todd, the Demon Barber. Published in 1846 by Edward Lloyd under the deceptively romantic title *The String of Pearls; or A Sailor's Gift*, the tale features Sweeney Todd, the murderous barber, Mrs Lovett, a successful pie manufacturer, and a captive worker, Mark Ingestrie, who is forced by Todd and Lovett to produce the pies.[18] The unpalatable "secret" at the centre of the narrative is, of course, that the meat used in the pies is the human flesh of the barber's victims.

At mid century, when issues of *The String of Pearls* were selling as quickly as Mrs Lovett's pies, the question of food adulteration was at its most publicized point. In an account of an early dramatized version of the serial, Thomas W. Erle declares that:

> The uncomfortable atmosphere of suspicion and distrust which already envelops the rations of opaque slime and gristle conventionally known as mutton pies is amply sufficient of itself, without the addition of any further unpleasant misgivings which might be suggested by *The Barber Fiend*, to discourage one from partaking of those ambiguous delicacies.[19]

Given a consumer confidence shaken by "suspicion and distrust", it may well have taken no great leap of faith for the audience to readily accept the playbill's declaration that the drama was indeed "Founded On Fact!"

The quality of fresh meat sold in the city was a particular and legitimate cause of anxiety. Hollingshead reports that the medical officer of health for one London district reported that from the area's markets and slaughterhouses his officers had seized nearly two-and-three-quarter tons of diseased meat in one week.[20] Given the poverty of the urban slum and the profit-driven commercialism of the city, a market could always be found for poor quality, cheap meat. Sharp's Alley in the City, reveals Hollingshead, "was once famous for making common sausage of refuse meat, known in the slang of the district as 'blood-worms'".[21] The notion that the quality of urban meat-produce is highly suspect is frequently evident in penny fiction and often plays an important part in the genre's attempts to offer a sensational representation of the city's commercial underworld. In *The Mysteries of London*, a knackerman claims that of all the horse-flesh boiled in the city slaughter-houses, the healthy meat is sold to sausage-makers—the knackerman asserting that there is not a sausage shop in London that does not use it—or is marketed as "hung-beef" to boarding-schools and work-houses, whilst horse-tongues are salted and pickled and passed off as ox-tongue. Diseased meat, reveals the knackerman, is rubbed over with fresh suet and fat in order to give it a brighter appearance and a better smell.[22] In *Life in London*, Barker sells cat fur to a marine store that displays the sign: "No questions axed", but she melts the animals' fat down and sells it to the poor as dripping, grinds the bones for bread and sets the flesh aside for "to-morrow's dinner".[23] Pies and sausages were the food products at the centre of most adulteration scares and Barker's trading practices echo a contemporaneous concern that cat-meat often found its way into them.[24]

During the decades in which the working-class reading public and London theatre-goers were riveted by a narrative in which pies are adulterated with human matter, there was a growing awareness that the city's food shops presented a particular health problem. It was customary for such businesses to trade on the ground floor and to prepare the products in the basement in which soil-pipes were sited. There was a distinct possibility, therefore, that food products could become contaminated with human waste-matter leaking from old and ill-maintained sewage pipes. In his report to the Sanitary Commission in 1847—the year in which the first publication of *The String of Pearls* concluded—Dr. William Guy submitted the following findings:

> ... [in] a decent-looking shop, in a respectable neighbourhood, I found the soil-pipe within a foot of the trough in which the bread is made; the pipe in a very unsound state, and the floor in some danger of being moistened by its contents. Indeed, I was assured by a baker who accompanied me, that he had himself seen the sewage flowing into the trough.[25]

Moreover, it was not just urban foodstuff that was vulnerable to such corporeal contamination. At a time when Henry Mayhew declared that 278,000 tons of sewage was being emptied daily into the Thames, of the nine separate private water companies supplying London, seven drew their supplies from the central stretch of the Thames or nearby tributaries and only six claimed to filter it. Slum inhabitants, for whom there was limited or no piped water supply, collected drinking-water directly from the open sewers, but even the supply of water to which all other Londoners were subject was proven to contain a significant amount of corporeal matter.

The notion that London's drinking water contained "body" was further heightened by Arthur Hill Hassall's published illustrations of his microscopic analysis of Thames water, illustrations that were satirized by *Punch* to shocking effect [See figures 3.2 and 3.3]. "What are those infinitesimal semblances of humanity which have thus been detected in London water?" asks the writer.[26] "They are only found in the well-water of cities, whose inhabitants bury the dead among the living", he concludes.[27] That many city-dwellers living in close proximity to London's overcrowded cemeteries experienced the tainting of their food and drink, further supports the suggestion that Prest's narrative of cadaverous food adulteration exploits mid-century urban anxiety in relation to the integrity of supply and consumption. In Edwin Chadwick's report on the practice of interment in towns in 1843, one medical practitioner claimed that a glass of water offered to him whilst staying at a London hotel "presented a peculiar film on its surface" and, after numerous inquiries, became satisfied that the contamination "arose from the coffins in a churchyard immediately adjoining the well where the water had been drawn".[28] Reynolds records the problem of such corporeal seepage in *The Mysteries of London*. He describes the houses surrounding the Globe Lane cemetery as being penetrated by the odour of the rotting cadaver, that it is present in "every room and every inhabited nook or corner", and that the inmates' food comes to taste of the damp grave.[29]

As E.S. Turner mockingly suggests, "a psychologist could be found to assert that the macabre relish with which successive generations have devoured the stories … of Sweeney Todd, the Demon Barber, springs from a desire deep down in every man's heart to know what his neighbour tastes like".[30] Yet a study of the social context in which the tale has its genesis and in which it was repeatedly reproduced, demonstrates that within the mid nineteenth-century industrialized city, such tales exploited a growing fear that in the commodities consumed, urbanites were already savouring the corporeal flavour of their fellow citizens.[31] Cannibalism presented itself to penny blood writers as a suitably sensational topic, but beyond the obvious appeal of such outrageous subject matter, the popularity of the tale of Sweeney Todd testifies to the existence of a mid-century working-class perception that in a newly industrialized urban economy there existed not only a literal but a metaphoric relationship between the consumption of goods and a cannibalistic feeding upon one's fellow urbanites. Thus, *The String of Pearls* focuses on the relationship between the greedy profiteer and the ravenous consumer. Prest recognizes that it is not simply the aggressive agents of manufacture and retail who invest the commodity with an invasive vitality, but the consumer's appetite for the commodity itself. Whilst Todd and Lovett are both highly threatening characters who represent the immoral capitalist ready to exploit the vulnerable and the ignorant, it is made clear that their gruesome trading activity is propelled by market demand.

In 1846, a cartoon by George Cruikshank appeared in *Our Own Times*, depicting a huge grinding machine into which women workers are forced in their bid to make a living.[32] Whilst a satanic Todd-like character turns the handle, the bodies of these women are ground-up in the machine and processed into cheap products and bags of profit [See figure 3.4]. The customers on the other side of the curtain are shown to be unthinking and uncaring of the "tremendous sacrifice" of those whose exploitation has ensured the cheapness of the garments they purchase. Published in the same year as the first issue of *The String of Pearls*, the cartoon supports the suggestion that at this time representations of the pulverized and processed body speak implicitly of the exploitation of the worker, the inhumane demands of the employer, and the blind appetite of the consumer for the desirable and affordable product.

In *The String of Pearls*, Prest exposes Lovett's customers as remaining wilfully ignorant of the nature or source of the product they consume. So thoroughly seduced are they by the "magic" of an industry that delivers hundreds of delicious and affordable pies, so happy are they to fulfil their desire for the commodity, that they do not wish to question the product's origin or the integrity of its production. When Lovett is asked on which farm she raises her swine and cattle, she replies: "Really, sir, you want to know too much", and her other customers chime in that they "don't know anything about it" and "don't care", for "Sufficient for the day is the pie thereof".[33] Given that by the 1840s industrialism had realized mass production, the success enjoyed by the tale of Lovett's pies suggests a growing awareness of the probability that food, like other products, would be further subject to mass manufacture and that in consuming such a product, the customer would be required to make an increasingly significant leap of faith in relation to its integrity.

Prest's depiction of Lovett's pie factory suggests that the products are mass-produced by industrialized means. The cellar beneath Fleet Street houses an "immense manufactory" for the production of "what, at first sight, would appear such a trivial article".[34] Whilst the imprisoned sailor, Ingestrie, has a hand in the making of the hundreds of pies that emerge daily from Lovett's cellar, the place in which he slaves is no antiquated kitchen, but a factory equipped with up-to-date machinery that enables mass production.[35] Lovett demonstrates:

> … [H]ow a piece of meat thrown into a machine [is] finely minced up, by merely turning a handle; and then how flour and water and lard [are] mixed up together, to make the crusts of the pies, by another machine, which [throws] out the paste thus manufactured in small pieces, each just large enough for a pie.[36]

The narrator is quick to comment upon the remarkable labour-to-production ratio, to explain the automated nature of the manufacturing process, and to lament the misery of the worker enslaved and alienated within:

> It seems astonishing that such a man, even with the assistance of Mrs Lovett, could make so many pies as are required in a day; but then, system does wonders, and in those cellars there are various mechanical contrivances for kneading the dough, chopping up the meat, &c., which greatly [reduces] the labour. But what a miserable object is that man–what a sad and soul-stricken wretch he looks![37]

Like many Victorian industrial workers, Ingestrie's entire existence is subsumed by his employment. He is literally imprisoned by his work, experiencing nothing beyond the manufacture of the goods he has been engaged to produce and that he is forced to ingest—as his name implies. His mind wanders longingly to the days of his youth, to a pastoral landscape—a village green, a bubbling stream—and a pre-industrial, even feudal, age—"the ancient mill, and the old mansion-house, with its tall turrets, and its air of silent grandeur".[38]

Ingestrie wonders if he is to grow old and grey as nothing more than a "mere pie machine"—surely a lament to echo those of the many who sweated contemporaneously in appalling conditions, "hidden" in the midst of the city, driven into such slavery by the threat of abject poverty and destitution. "Is it possible", he wonders, "that even in the heart of London, I am a prisoner, and without the means of resisting the most frightful threats that are uttered against me?"[39] Many of Prest's working-class readers may well have agreed that indeed it was. Moreover, Todd's voice, emanating from the darkness of the underground factory, is that of the exploitative manufacturer eager to rationalize his methods:

> Make pies ... eat them, and be happy. How many a man would envy your position–withdrawn from all the struggles of existence, amply provided with board and lodging, and engaged in a pleasant and delightful occupation; it is astonishing how you can be dissatisfied![40]

Having instated Ingestrie, his employers distance themselves from any responsibility for his welfare. They remain wholly alienated from him, ensuring his compliance by means of a threat communicated in a note that informs him that he must work or die, that as long as he continues to make pies he will be safe but, should he refuse, his throat will be cut in his sleep.

The relationship between the physical sanctity of the worker and the profit of the industrialist is central to the discourse surrounding mid-century calls for legislation that would ensure the safety of those men, women and children working on, or in the vicinity of, factory machinery. Reports and articles, such as that written by Henry Morley in 1854 for Dickens's journal, *Household Words*, sought to reveal the extent of the physical dangers to which industrial workers were exposed and to argue the need for enforcing the implementation of safety measures. Morley details the nature of the accidents taking place in the country's factories; fatal incidents in which hands are wrenched off at the wrist, arms torn from the shoulder joints, legs cut off. Commenting upon one man's industrial mutilation, Morley concludes that he was "rent asunder, not perhaps for his own good; but, as a sacrifice to the commercial prosperity of Great Britain" and, having calculated the number of lives lost and bodies deformed in the preceding three years, wonders "how much cash saved to the purses of the manufacturers is a satisfactory and proper off-set to this expenditure of life and limb and this crushing of bone in the persons of their work-people".[41] Opposing the tenets of *laissez-faire*, Morley exposes the extent to which the mutilation of the worker is regarded by manufacturers as just another quantifiable cost of mass production. His rhetoric fully exploits the notion that the brutality of modern commercialism is literally inscribed upon the body of the worker, a suggestion that offers up the severed body as both empirical evidence and symbolizes the alienation of the dispassionate industrialist from the welfare of the worker. Thus, within the context of the Todd/Lovett manufacturing enterprise, the threatened mutilation of Ingestrie and the butchered human flesh with which he is forced to work, constitutes an articulation of the threat posed to the physical sanctity of the worker by the profit-driven industrialist "master".

Ingestrie's place on the pie production line also ensures that he is alienated from the product itself. He is put to work purely on the assembly of the pies and is kept entirely ignorant of the nature of the meat and the means by which it is acquired. When he asks how it arrives in the cellar, he is told: "That's no business of yours; so long as you are supplied with it, that is sufficient for you".[42] In its portrayal of Todd, Lovett and Ingestrie as manufacturers of products, *The String of Pearls* is clearly troubled by the moral alienation of the producer from the nature of the product. This sense of the horrifying amorality of commercialism and the dispassionate relationship between the profiteer and the abject product is evident in other penny blood tales. Often the woman, the conventional touchstone of affection and human feeling, is shockingly revealed to be the most dispassionate "producer" of all. In *Life in London*, Barker skins her cats with professional dexterity and callousness; in *The Mysteries of London*, the Resurrection Man's mother is unmoved by "the revolting spectacle of a corpse putrid with decomposition", considering it only as "an article of commerce", handling her wares "as a trader does his merchandize", caring no more for its sickly and foetid aroma "than the tanner does for the smell of the tan-yard, or the scourer for the fumes of his bleaching-liquid".[43] Whilst it is unclear whether or not Lovett plays an active role in the butchering of the human flesh that ends up in her pies, her ability to knowingly and ruthlessly market the final product is seen to undermine her womanly nature. Whilst some of her customers are enamoured with her, others suspect that the smile "upon her lips" has "no place in her heart".[44]

For penny blood writers in general, an exploration of the dark underside of urban commercialism anxiously reveals the moral alienation of the producer or retailer from the integrity of the product—a relationship most evident in the estrangement of the resurrectionist/dissectionist from the humanity of the corpse. Yet, unlike most penny blood villains, Prest's Todd and Lovett do not belong to the urban criminal classes, but are established traders in a respectable marketplace. By allowing them a degree of respectability and at once revealing that they are morally alienated from the humanity of the cadaverous meat and the labour from which they profit, Prest goes further than many of his contemporaries and looks beyond the moral morass of the urban underworld to question the fundamental

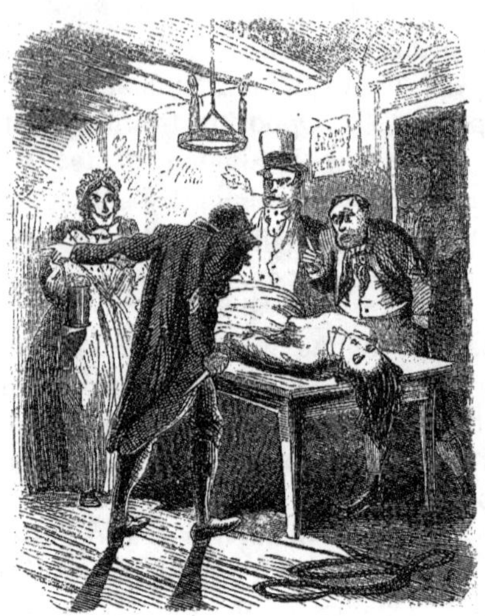

3.1 "Margaret in the Hands of Body-Snatchers" in *The Wild Boys of London.*

3.2 "East London Water: Microscopic Analysis of Thames Water as revealed by Arthur Hill Hassall in *A Microscopic Examination of the Water Supplied to the Inhabitants of London and the Suburban Districts* (1850).

A DROP OF LONDON WATER.

3.3 "A Drop of London Water: Revealed, infinitesimal semblances of humanity".

TREMENDOUS SACRIFICE!

3.4 "Tremendous Sacrifice". George Cruikshank's Todd pulverizes the body of the worker in *Our Own Times* (1846).

morality underlying the "legitimate" practice of mass manufacture and retail.

As Peter Haining concludes of Sweeney Todd's popular success, "there was very definitely something 'in the air' at this time which attracted the public to such a story".[45] Indeed, the significance of the displaced, commodified and consumed corpse in mid-century Victorian popular literature could be said to have been literally "in the air", for to breathe Victorian city air was potentially to ingest the miasma of rotting corpses, the effluvia of poorly sanitized overcrowded housing and the air-born debris of industrial activity. The air contained the very stuff of the modern metropolis, of aggressive consumption and production, of disease and disorder, of "improvement" and progress; a context in which at mid-century the displaced "dreadful" corpse spoke of a profound anxiety relating to the working-class experience of an increasingly complex and threatening urbanization.

Notes

1. Henry Thornley, *Life in London*, (London: E. Dipple, 1846). 70.
2. Thornley, 70.
3. For the publishing history of penny fiction, see Louis James, *Fiction for the Working Man 1830-1850*, (London: Oxford University Press, 1963). 28-44.
4. Mayhew's dredger-man claims that whilst only a shilling is paid out in inquest money for bodies handed in at Deptford, Rotherhithe pays out 5s. 6d. Henry Mayhew, *London Labour and the London Poor*, (London: Frank Cass & Co., 1851). Vol. II, 150.
5. All sixteen of Burke and Hare's victims were poor vagrants or street folk. "By 1827-1828 (if not before) the position had been reached at which the bodies of the poor had become worth more dead than alive". Ruth Richardson, *Death, Dissection and the Destitute*, (London and New York: Routledge & Kegan Paul, 1987). 132.
6. G.W.M. Reynolds, *The Mysteries of London*, (London: George Vickers, 1845). Vol. I, 127.
7. *The Wild Boys of London; or, The Children of Night*, (London: Newsagents' Publishing Co., 1866). Vol. II, 28.
8. *Wild Boys*, II, 29.
9. *Wild Boys*, II, 32.
10. Reynolds, I, 125.
11. Thornley, 13.
12. Charles Dickens, *Oliver Twist* (1837), ed. Kathleen Tillotson, (Oxford: Clarendon Press, 1966). 136.
13. Charles Dickens, *Great Expectations* (1860-1861), ed. Margaret Caldwell, (Oxford: Clarendon Press, 1993). 163.
14. John Hollingshead, *Ragged London in 1861*, (London: Smith Elder, 1861). 126.
15. Reynolds, I, 3.
16. Reynolds, I, 43. Hollingshead also comments that the pollution beating down upon the poor from neighbouring factories is punctuated by the smell generated by cat meat preparers who "boil their cauldrons amongst them without fear". (Hollingshead, 88.)
17. Thornley, 70.
18. Owing to the rarity of the 1846 edition, I refer here to a later 1850 extended reprint, re-titled *Sweeney Todd or, The Barber of Fleet Street.*
19. Thomas W. Erle, *Letters From a Theatrical Scene-Painter* (1880), cited in Peter Haining, *The Mystery and Horrible Murders of Sweeney Todd, The Demon Barber of Fleet Street*, (London: Frederick Muller, 1979). 86.
20. Hollingshead, 19.
21. Hollingshead, 19.
22. Sarah Freeman confirms the actuality of this practice, known as "polishing" after the practice of rubbing off the fat with hot cloths. Sarah Freeman, *Mutton and Oysters: The Victorians and their Food*, (London: Victor Gollancz, 1989). 27.
23. Thornley, 13.

24. The Wild Boys play a prank on a street pie-man in which they place a dead cat in his broiler. Accusing him of using cat meat in his pies, the boys then insist that he reveals the nature of what he is cooking, which he does to the horror and outrage of his regular customers. However, Sarah Freeman contends that there is no evidence to suggest that cat meat was used on any scale in sausages and pies, and if it was, that the custom had certainly ceased by mid century. Freeman, 27.
25. *Parliamentary papers* 1847-1848, Vol. LI, "Copy of the Evidence given by Dr Guy before the Sanitary Commission in reference to the Persons Employed in the Baking Trade". 367. Cited in Freeman, 77.
26. *Punch*, 8, 1850, 189.
27. *Punch*, 8, 1850, 189.
28. Edwin Chadwick, *A Supplementary Report on the Results of a Special Inquiry into the Practice of Interment in Towns*, London: W. Clowes, 1843. 29-30.
29. In *Bleak House*, Jo points out the pile of bones in the churchyard that lay "close to that there kitchinwinder!". Charles Dickens, *Bleak House* (1852-53), (London: Penguin, 1994). 207.
30. E.S. Turner, *Boys Will Be Boys: The Story of Sweeney Todd, Deadwood Dick, Sexton Blake Billy Bunter, et al*, (London: Michael Joseph, 1948, rev. 1975). 34.
31. "Well-water, percolating the earth of churchyards", points out *Punch*, "must needs contain alderman,deputy, and similar bodies in solution". *Punch*, 8, 1850. 189.
32. Helen Rogers uses this cartoon to illustrate her article "The Good Are Not Always Powerful, Nor The Powerful Always Good", *Victorian Studies*, 40, (4), 1997. 489-623.
33. Prest, 331.
34. Prest, 58.
35. The first machine capable of mass producing bread had been introduced in c.1840 and consisted of a combined sifter and mixer that ran on four engines and had a capacity of approximately 2,000 loaves per day. See Freeman, 23.
36. Prest, 60.
37. Prest, 58.
38. Prest, 59.
39. Prest, 110.
40. Prest, 111.
41. Morley, *Household Words*, April 22, 1854, 224, 225.
42. Prest, 60.
43. Reynolds, I, 125.
44. Prest, 18
45. Haining, 123.

Chapter 4

"Stepchildren of Nature": *East Lynne* and the Spectre of Female Degeneracy, 1860-1861

Andrew Maunder

> Lady-wife-mother! Should you ever be tempted to abandon your home...pray for patience; pray for strength to resist the demon that would urge you so to escape; bear unto death rather than forfeit your fair name and your good conscience; for be assured that the alternative, if you rush on to it, will be found far worse than death![1]

East Lynne (1860-1861), Ellen Wood's sensational novel of adultery, desertion and divorce announces itself loudly as a "story of modern life". Wood presents the reader with a series of warnings against the "voluptuary" disease affecting apparently respectable women (261). Through her creation of the "brute" aristocrat, Lady Isabel Vane (later Carlyle), brought low by an adulterous liaison, Wood brought a host of contemporary moral, social and scientific anxieties to the fore. The fear that civilization might be nothing more than a thin veneer, and that civilized man (or, even more alarmingly, woman) might regress, was widely prophesized in the years following the evolutionary debates of the 1850s.

In 1861, just as *East Lynne*'s serialization in Harrison Ainsworth's *New Monthly Magazine* drew to a close, *The Times* was just one of many voices raised against a "state of things that is truly alarming", predicting that England was moving towards a condition of "degeneracy worthy of Hogarth's pencil".[2] *The Times* was certainly not alone in its warnings; in 1860 *The Lancet* had diagnosed England as "a literal breeding ground of decay".[3] The nation's superficial success was, it would seem, a veneer that hid both "mental alienation" and immorality. The young Henry Maudsley warned, later in the decade, against the sexual degeneracy and "naked lust" exhibited by apparently respectable but "ill-constituted" women.[4] The *Saturday Review* of 1862 had also expressed fears that the whole of the country seemed to wreak of "moral sewerage [which] is neither deodorised nor floated out to sea, but remains in the midst of us polluting and poisoning our air".[5] It is this "hideous dream"[6] of moral contamination, of the wife and mother gone mad with uncontrolled sexual longing, that Ellen Wood takes up in the pages of *East Lynne*, as both a threat to the individual family unit and the broader morality of the nation as a whole.

As R.B. Kershner has suggested, British fears of degeneration became a sort of "negative national rallying point" and a source of recurrent panic to middle-class Victorians.[7] "Notions of progress", as Jenny Bourne Taylor puts it, "began to transmute into degeneration".[8] A new Condition of England was envisaged, characterized, as John Ruskin suggests, by "progress and decline...strangely mixed".[9] Others noted that modern living and its many pollutants, both literal and figurative, was making the population progressively more susceptible to disease—the knock-on effect being an inability to resist the lure of sensualism and crime.[10] "We seem to be going back to the morality of the last century", complained one *Times* correspondent, "illicit connexion is no longer called adultery, but 'temporary engagement'...robbery is called 'defalcation'".[11] Meanwhile, *The Lancet* looked beyond mere semantics and saw "a world with a population such as the imagination of Dante figured with horror in the dark abodes of his 'inferno'".[12] Alcoholism, pollution, prostitution, physical debility, adultery, hysteria, consumerism, the new Divorce Court and the Road Murder, were all, as *Fraser's Magazine* pointed out, "frightful evidence" that society had indeed retrograded, and anxieties ran high.[13]

Descent, decay and disease all pervade Ellen Wood's *East Lynne* and draw attention to how the trope of degeneration had, by 1861, begun to permeate reading matter. The craze for sensation fiction and Wood's own immense popularity operated, as Susan David Bernstein reminds us, as "telltale sign(s) of a degenerative culture of boundless desire.[14] The *Christian Remembrancer* certainly viewed Wood as responsible for spreading moral disease and in 1863 it accused her of "drugging thought and reason...stimulating the attention through the lower and more animal instincts...tampering with things evil and infringing more or less on the confines of wrong".[15] Sensation fiction was, then, not simply a symptom of degeneration, but rather an agent of contamination, which, in the words of Robert Buchanan, worked by "enfeebling the minds of men and women, making flabby the fibre of their bodies, and undermining the vigour of nations".[16] Such fears of disorderly conduct were never far from view when hostile critics discussed the sensation novel, not least because the want of restraint attributed to its writers and readers seemed to mark a dangerous falling away from the norms of bourgeois self-control. In an 1861 review of *East Lynne*, Richard Holt Hutton referred explicitly to one of the most influential texts for mid-Victorian degeneration theorists, Benedict Morel's *Treatise on the Degeneration of the Human Species.*[17] Hutton described *East Lynne*'s atmosphere of excess as "morbid" and "repulsive", and criticized Wood for being "led far astray from the ordinary current of human life".[18] It is not apparent whether Hutton, or, more importantly, Wood herself, actually read either Morel or Maudsley. Nevertheless, the concerns raised by theorists of descent were debated in drawing rooms across the nation, and Mrs. Henry Wood was certainly, as noted by *The Spectator*, "familiar with medical lore".[19]

East Lynne certainly invoked the discourse of degeneration and contemporary angst concerning the "brute" natures of the excitable women of modern life and those classes that were on a downward trajectory. Wood's novel tells the story of the aristocratic and beautiful Lady Isabel Vane. Left penniless by her profligate father's early death, Isabel is rescued from her penury through a pragmatic marriage with the hard-working bourgeois lawyer, Archibald Carlyle. Once married Isabel, a sickly woman who exists in a state of (possibly hereditary) nervous weakness, struggles to resist her attraction to an earlier admirer, the debauched aristocrat, Francis Levison. Persuaded by the "serpent"-like Levison's suggestions that her husband is in love with a neighbour, Barbara Hare (296), Isabel succumbs to temptation and self-pity, eloping with Levison. Once abroad, Isabel is woefully neglected by Levison and faces a life of exile, penury and stigma until she is involved in a railway accident which kills her illegitimate child and leaves her apparently dead, but actually only severely disfigured. With uncharacteristic resolution and strength, Isabel seizes the opportunity offered by reports of her death and returns, in disguise, to East Lynne, where she serves as governess to the children she deserted. By this time, Isabel has been replaced as Mrs. Carlyle by Barbara, whose patient, but restrained and silent adoration of Carlyle has now been rewarded with marriage. Prematurely aged by the traumas of her life Isabel—like her mother before her, and her younger son—who seems to have inherited his mother's weakened constitution—succumbs to a wasting disease and is buried in an unmarked grave.

While many feminist considerations of *East Lynne* have argued that the novel is subversive in its portrayal of an adulterous wife and mother, Wood's labelling of her heroine as "mad" and "brute" is singularly lacking in irony.[20] At a time when anxieties about women were loudly constituted as questions of sexual and social health, there are implicit connections between Wood's sermonizing of her adulterous wife and mother brought low through uncontrolled desires and the national context in which she embeds her "phantoms" of female failing. Of course some contemporary critics like the reviewer in the *Christian Remembrancer* saw Wood's novel as symptomatic of a wider cultural malaise, a part of the degenerate aesthetics that marked the sensation genre. However, *East Lynne* can also be understood as a polemical literary text engaging with both the degeneration debate and the accompanying surveillance; policing and punishment deemed necessary to keep women's sexual appetites in check.

Michel Foucault has described how the discourses of law, medicine and social science were manipulated to transform the unruly (female) body into a docile, passive one. He argues that the principles of traditional law and authority engage with other discursive fields, like the degeneration trope, to establish modes of normalization, which in turn become part of the transition towards a disciplinary society.[21] In the foreword to *The Novel and the Police*, D.A. Miller observes that

> [T]he most noticeable reticence in Foucault's work (on disciplinary power) concerns precisely the reading of literary texts and literary institutions, which though often suggestively cited in passing, are never given a role to play within the disciplining process under consideration.

Miller goes on to question how the novel "systematically participate[s] in a general economy of policing power".[22] He draws attention to the realist novel's function as a guidebook to impressionable young women or would-be transgressors, by showing within the narrative, the unequivocal consequences of deviating from prescribed codes of conduct, whether these pertain to sexuality or to wider concerns with crime and punishment. Miller's question is crucial to our study of *East Lynne* and to the works of nineteenth-century degeneracy theorists and middle-class ideologues like Morel, Maudsley and Herbert Spencer, all of whom participate in this economy of policing power.

Whether the subject under scrutiny is an "idiot", a "fallen" woman, or a dissolute aristocrat, the middle-class writer, like Wood, encourages the reader's eye to collaborate with the interpolating policing (and censuring) gaze. Few mid-Victorian novelists were more respectable that Mrs. Henry Wood who, in spite of those critics who wished to hold her personally responsible for the climate of degeneration, was celebrated by the *Pall Mall Gazette* as a "good Englishwoman of strong domestic tastes", thus marking her out as a bastion of middle-class mores. Indeed, Wood's devoted son Charles hit back at his mother's critics, asserting that Mrs. Wood's aim in writing *East Lynne* had been to counter what he described as a "vicious tendency". According to this version of Wood, then, the reader's moral position should shift abruptly from Lady Isabel in the wake of her transgression, and align itself instead with the morally upright, devoted, and obviously middle-class second wife, Barbara Hare.

That the aristocratic Isabel Carlyle's moral and physical degeneration is central to the novel can scarcely be contended, for her every mistake, however excusable, is met with a near-deafening chorus of condemnation, in which the loudest voice is that of the narrator herself. In the first third of the novel, Wood's commentary restricts itself to gentle reminders that Isabel's failings as a middle-class wife stem from her immersion in a completely different mode of behaviour, having been raised as an aristocrat in an economically and physically degenerate family unit. As a consequence Isabel is completely ignorant in matters of domestic management, and stands as a direct contrast to her tough sister-in-law Cornelia, who is ruled by the account ledger and displays all the values held dear by the mid-Victorian self-made family.

Wood's comments are also evidence of how degeneration theory and the biological determinism that it espoused could be turned to ideological advancement: namely the lack of racial vigour of the aristocratic wife who finds it impossible to adapt to bourgeois codes of domestic, economic and moral behaviour. Wood initially conceals this inability to adapt and survive by endowing Isabel with saintly qualities—most notably a deep love for her children, compared to Barbara Hare's resolution to always place her husband first. Later, however, after Isabel's elopement, the narrator, perhaps afraid that the "fallen" Isabel has gained in charisma, becomes more outspoken and overtly moralistic. Isabel's crime against the institution of the family—her "mad act"—is accompanied by a condemnation on the part of the narrator that has seemed to many critics, reading the novel in three-volume format, staggeringly excessive. Wood's narrator declares: "Every taunt cast upon her by the world, every slight that would henceforth be her portion, for she had earned it, must tell too heavily on her crushed spirit" (335). And again, rather melodramatically, "Her whole future existence, whether spent with that man [Levison] or without him, would be one dark course of gnawing, never-ending retribution" (335). Isabel is undeniably rendered "criminal" in these extracts. Indeed, she would seem to correspond to the predictions of the author of "Manners and Morals as Affected by Civilisation" in the September 1861 issue of *Fraser's Magazine* in which the author shudderingly predicted a future English race where, "the mothers will be the fast girls, the pretty Amazons of the modern Rotten Row; whose fathers will be men who have learned to talk of feminine purity as a myth".[23] Isabel was certainly cast as this type of "thoroughly bad woman" by the anonymous critic of the *Christian Remembrancer* (718).

Once she has taken her "blind leap in a moment of wild passion", she is metamorphosed by the narrative into a hideous abomination and finds herself "plunged into an abyss of horror from which there was never any more escape; never, never more" (237). The echo from Poe's raven here reinforces the extent to which Isabel is doomed, whilst the references to the abyss illustrate the depths to which the narrator believes she has descended. Thus the transgressing Isabel is cast as "morally insane" a central element of degeneration, since the moral faculties were considered to represent the high point of the evolutionary process, "the refined and complex emotions of the highest civilisation".[24] Hence, these sensibilities would be the first faculty to be lost during the downward slide. Sexual "depravity" among women in particular—including any sexual interest outside of marriage—was regarded as a sign of nymphomania or lunacy, but also as regression or degeneration: a horrible fall from woman's place near the top of the evolutionary, moral and social trees. Thus, in a rush to throw off the mundane middle-class frugality and domesticity prescribed by Miss Cornelia, and to gratify her sexual proclivities, Isabel becomes an inversion of nature, destined for punishment. Paradoxically, then, her natural sexual desires are rendered unnatural by the codes that guard bourgeois morality and keep "good" women firmly in their places.

As a tale of identity for the newly affluent middle classes, *East Lynne* draws upon the discourses of degeneration to reinforce both bourgeois (moral) hegemony and notions of aristocratic decline. Most obviously, there is the question of bloodline; Isabel's debauched patrimony has been imprinted in both her behavioural patterns and her lack of physical vigour so as to make her fall almost inevitable. Wood inserts on the very first page of the story, clues to a latent, inherited degeneracy from which Isabel cannot escape. Like his daughter, the Earl, "whose once attractive face bore the unmistakable look of dissipation" (41) is incapable of finding a "sober" or "steady" approach to life. He descends from a promising legal career to a "gamester above all gamesters", corrupted by "fast" aristocratic society and then to the (sexual) excesses hinted at in "a gay man outstripping the gay" (42). His elopement with his future wife, an act that kills her father, represents a turning away from the family, while his alcoholism puts the seal on a career of vice.

As Kelly Hurley has noted, a key part of Benedict Morel's theory of progressive degeneration centred on the probability of the sins of the parents being visited upon their children. Morel, like Wood, wrote in a "highly coloured" melodramatic style of "organic degradation", a vicious circle of cause and effect, in which a poisonous environment could infect the susceptible individual. The individual would then pass the infection onto her/his offspring who would in turn contaminate society once again.[25] Wood's narrator refers on several occasions to the "sins bequeathed by the fall of Adam", yet it is clear that for Wood some sectors of society are more susceptible to the effects of original sin than others.[26] As a declining aristocrat, Isabel carries a weakness not only in moral fibre, but also in her blood.

Both Wood and Morel employ the trope of the weak-willed alcoholic parent and their miserable descendants, characterized in varying degrees not only by "dementia", but also by the "abolition of the moral sentiments". These were people who in Morel's words "have sacrificed to their frenzied desires all which they out to have held most dear".[27] An addiction to drink ensures that Isabel's father leaves her penniless and ill-educated, with the bourgeois lawyer, Carlyle asserting a symbolic economic (and moral) dominance over the waning aristocracy by acquiring East Lynne and its daughter almost in one swoop. In its representation of the novel's men, *East Lynne* portrays, as Deborah Wynne has noted, "a contest to prove the 'fittest'", a contest which Carlyle indisputably wins.[28] In fact, the novel's women are also participants in this genetic contest. Whilst her father is indubitably a gouty "spendthrift among spendthrifts" (42), Isabel herself takes her inheritance of debauchery to such extremes that the narrator informs us that, "Could the fate that was to overtake [Isabel] have been foreseen by the earl, he would have struck her down to death, in his love, as she stood before him, rather than suffer her to enter upon it" (51). The aristocracy is for Wood a species in decline, which can only save itself by a Darwinian process of adaptation to the new economic and moral climate, namely through a process of bourgeoisification. Too much given to idleness and frivolity, it is Isabel's lack of activity—a marked contrast to the almost manic busyness of Carlyle's sister—that gives her the time to imagine an intrigue between Mr. Carlyle and Barbara.

The delicate Isabel is juxtaposed with her imagined rival, the sturdy, fair-haired Barbara Hare, who rather than acting upon *her* feelings of desire articulates them but once in a secret conversation with Carlyle, and then represses them. So immersed is Isabel in the world of the senses that she fails to understand that the "quiet calmness into which her husband's once passionate love had subsided" is by no means a sign of disloyalty or attraction to Barbara, but rather the form that love takes in everyday life (248). Unlike the dignified, but impulsive Barbara, the two aristocrats Isabel and Levison gratify their desires physically, although it is fair to say that Levison's degeneration is at a more advanced state of degradation than that of Isabel. The "faint flickering" of liking that Isabel feels for Carlyle is snuffed out under the force of her animal desire for Levison, whose own "shallow pated" skull provides the reader with clues to his inherent depravity—a mark of the atavistic criminal.

One of Wood's basic assumptions in *East Lynne* is that in every woman there are two natures struggling for dominance; the higher self and the brute animal. Henry Maudsley wrote later in the 1860s of the "highest effort of mental evolution", according to which the higher self stands for chastity, self-restraint, responsibility and hard work; the lower is steeped in sensual gratification.[29] One of the most earnest messages of *East Lynne* is that what woman must learn to rule is this passionate side to her nature, which threatens to destroy "all that reticence that woman loves to observe...as to her inward feelings" (511).

Lady Isabel Vane is, then, an embodiment of the worst fears of degeneration. Her too comfortable life—and that of her forebears—has destroyed all energy, intelligence and strength; instead she is vapid, idle and effete. During her marriage, Isabel's regressive animal nature gradually manifests itself via three tell-tale signs: sexual desire, self-indulgence and apathy. She is not only, according to middle-class criteria, an unsatisfactory wife, her sexual jealousy also makes her easy prey for Levison's seduction. Her elopement appears as a pathological rejection of the rules of bourgeois existence, a retreat from responsibility into emotionalism and self-absorption. As Margaret Oliphant put it, Isabel is literally a woman "driven wild with love".[30] A further aspect of this degenerative process is the terrifying speed at which Isabel changes from a state of "surpassing beauty" (49) to a "broken-down woman" (446) or "shattered wreck" as Henry Maudsley labelled fallen women.[31] Isabel suffers a prolonged illness when she is in exile, which is partly attributed to pregnancy, but also to her overriding state of "misery [which] marks the countenance far more than sickness" (336). "If you thought she looked ill when she took that voyage over the water with Mr. Carlyle, you should have seen her now", trumpets the narrator, "Her face was white and worn, her hands were thin, her eyes were sunken and surrounded by a black circle; care was digging hollows for them" (336).

The direct connections between Isabel's "piercing stings of guilt" (352) and her bodily weaknesses are repeatedly marked. When she believes that her husband has tracked her down in France, sensations flood in. We learn that, "every pulse within Lady Isabel's body throbbed rebelliously: her heart bounded until it seemed about to burst her side and she turned sick with excitement" (354). When she discovers that it is not Carlyle, but the new Earl of Mount Severn, she reacts immediately and physically, gasping for breath and "flung her hands over her burning cheeks of shame" (354). She suffers a "depressing illness" (350), the symptoms of which are those conventionally associated with "hysteria"; throbbing head, intense restlessness, and disordered thoughts. For weeks after the birth of her illegitimate child Isabel is "restless" (373), both her mind and body are "diseased" (353). Her physical degeneration is completed by the railway accident, after which she is left limping and hunched, no longer able to pass herself off as an upright Englishwoman. Isabel's tortured and disfigured body thus becomes both the site of punishment for her transgression and a marker of her wrong-doing, as both nervous malady and fate intervene to undermine her weak constitution still further. She suffers the kind of nemesis which, as William Greenslade has noted, obsessed degeneracy theorists like Maudsley and which, it was claimed, would inevitably follow the violation of "natural law". Such "disobedience", Maudsley wrote, "...whether physical or moral is avenged inexorably in its consequences on earth, either upon the individual himself, or more often, perhaps upon others".[32] So it is that when the disfigured and ghostly Isabel returns to her children as Madame Vine she can only be re-united with her family through proximity. Her broken body ensures that she remain unrecognized, signifying the gravity of the crime which debars her from resuming the roles she now yearns for as lady, wife and mother.

After Isabel's return to East Lynne in disguise, much of the novel's melodrama revolves around motherhood. By the early 1860s, the unsettling figure of the deviant or reluctant mother had outraged medical men; she had also long been a source of concern for the writers of advice manuals, and other idealogues. Addressing mothers in *The Women of England* (1838), Sarah Stickney Ellis had been outspoken in her condemnation of "the sickly sensibilities, the feeble frames, and the useless habits of the rising generation", which were undermining the "nation's moral wealth".[33] So, too, was *The Lancet*, when it spoke of "the enfeebled, and the incapable [wives], who inflict and burden the nation".[34] In 1861, adopting the familiar (middle-class) language of the cash register, Herbert Spencer addressed the "evil consequences" of those more energetic women who wanted to disrupt the workings of separate spheres by demanding opportunities beyond marriage and motherhood. Spencer reminded them that "an exertion of the brain beyond the normal amount...is sure to entail a slowly accumulating degeneracy of physique". He went on to assert, "[n]ature is a strict accountant; and if you demand of her in one direction more than she is prepared to lay out, she balances the account by making a deduction elsewhere". "Nature", in Spencer's terminology, was the process of reproduction—women's "natural" role. Excessive activity in any other form produced a damaging "tax" on the female system. As Spencer argued: "assuming the preservation of the race to be a desideratum, there results certain kinds of obligation to pay this tax and submit to this sacrifice".[35] Although there was a good deal of diversity of opinion about what should be done, the keynotes resounding in professional advice to the bourgeois mother were ordered living, moderation and willpower. A regime of healthy living and moral sobriety was essential if they were to produce sound offspring and thereby transmit their personal reputation, property, legitimacy and life to the next generation.[36]

For Ellen Wood, the capacity to be a good mother was identified with womanliness, health and sexual purity. In *East Lynne* these widespread expressions of concern for the responsibilities of motherhood and the healthy family are reflected in Wood's description of the Carlyle household when the staunchly middle-class Barbara assumes the reins of power following Isabel's flight. On her return, the disguised Isabel is met with a "flood of golden light" as the front door is thrown open; the "neat" servants conduct her to her rooms, where "cheerful" fires always burn. In this "picture of home peace" (393) Wood offers comfortable and ordered views of a family life from which Isabel is deservedly excluded. As the new Mrs. Carlyle, ensconced within this ideal of a stable home,

Barbara is introduced as a paragon of good health, biological performance and middle-class vigour, not to mention an upholder of domestic values. While Isabel's appearance has degenerated, Barbara is the epitome of the physically and morally robust bourgeois wife and mother, "Inexpressibly more beautiful looked Barbara than Lady Isabel had ever seen her...Her pretty features were attractive as ever, her cheeks were flushed, her blue eyes sparkled, and her light hair was rich and abundant. A contrast, her hair, to that of the worn woman opposite to her" (461-2). If we accept the mid-Victorian equation of women's hair with their sexuality, Barbara's hair, then, reflects the healthy channelling of her sexuality within the confines of her marriage, whilst Isabel's "worn" hair is yet another marker of her decline.[37] Barbara's children, according to the laws of heredity, share her physical and moral robustness, but Barbara is, unlike her predecessor, able to delineate clear boundaries between the duties of the mother and those of the wife. Thus, Barbara keeps her children and step-children at a "healthy" distance, and rather than indulging their every whim she is also very clearly a moral manager for the family. Her adoption of this role becomes ironically clear when Barbara asks Isabel/Madame Vine to ensure that Isabel the younger (re-named "Miss Lucy" in a bid to blot out her mother's moral stain), is kept from a "like fate" (463). Later in the conversation Barbara outlines her moral mission explicitly when she lectures the new governess: " I hope I shall never fail to gather my children round me daily at stated periods for higher purposes", she announces, "to instill into them Christian and moral duties; to strive to teach them how best to fulfil life's obligations. *This* is a mother's task..." (464-5).

East Lynne's condemnation of crimes against the family, coupled with its celebration of well-regulated motherhood, families and "healthy stock" has, as Sally Shuttleworth has shown, a good deal in common with the sentiments expressed in popular domestic manuals and medical guides.[38] However, it is also possible to see in Barbara's rational version of motherhood, traces of Herbert Spencer's *Education* (1861), a significant text for *East Lynne* and another important guidebook for the Victorian middle classes. As Spencer explains, it is in the family that the most advanced stage of human development can be observed. Spencer urges his readers:

> Morally you must keep in constant exercise your higher feelings and restrain your lower...It is a truth yet remaining to be recognised that the last stage in the mental development of each man and woman is to be reached only through the proper discharge of the parental duties...That it cannot be realised by the impulsive, the unsympathetic and the short sighted, but demands the higher attributes of human nature, they will see to be evidence of fitness for the more advanced states of humanity. Though it calls for much labour and self-sacrifice, they will see that it promises an abundant return of happiness, immediate and remote.[39]

Spencer could almost be describing the disparities between Isabel and Barbara here, with Isabel failing to adhere to Spencer's doctrine of restraint, altruism and proper parenting. In *East Lynne*, Wood seems to suggest that successful and rewarding mothering is only for the more deserving members of humanity. It is only by controlling (as far as she is ever able to) the "impulsive" and "lower" instincts and taking on the middle-class virtues of "labour and self-sacrifice" that Isabel herself can be reunited with her children. The reconciliation is, of course, incomplete as Wood emphasizes in her handling of the famous scene (made more famous by its theatrical dramatization) where Isabel is forced to watch while her eldest son, William, dies of consumption. Wood stresses Isabel's misery while reminding the reader of her treacherous double crime of abandonment and infidelity. Wood also takes the opportunity to remind the reader that Isabel's degenerate endowment is partly to blame for her son's early death:

> She leaned over him, laying her forehead upon his wasted arm; she burst into a flood of impassioned tears. "You will know her [his "dead" mother, once he is in heaven]; never fear, William, she has not forgotten you".
>
> "But how can we be sure that she will be there?" debated William, after a pause of thought. "You know"—sinking his voice, and speaking with hesitation—"she was not quite good. She was not good to papa or to us. Sometimes I think, suppose she did not grow good, and did not ask God to forgive her?"
>
> "Oh, William", sobbed the unhappy lady, "her whole life, after she left you, was one long scene of repentance, of seeking forgiveness. Her repentance, her sorrow was greater than she could bear..." (642)

The exchanges between mother and son here place all responsibility for wrongdoing on the unfaithful wife, who is meant, as the writers of medical handbooks constantly told their readers, to be the moral safeguard of the family (and hence, by extension, the state) and her children's protector. Once she breaks that sacred trust she must be punished and reaps the fruits of her sin, in Isabel's case, the death of her child. Lady Isabel's "dreadful misery" (652) and self-torment arises from her own feeling that "If I had not done as I did—how different would it have been now!" (652). Rather than acknowledge that both her husband and seducer were at least partially at fault, she blames herself in a series of self-castigating internal monologues: "*She* had brought it forth. Not Mr. Carlyle; not Barbara; she alone" (652). Isabel's lamentations for her previous conduct resonate with Morel's suggestion that a degenerate is one who "has...sacrificed to their frenzied desires all which they ought to have held most dear".[40] Isabel tortures herself because she realizes what she has lost.

One of the reasons that later in the century *East Lynne* came to appear on lists of recommended reading for young Victorian girls stems from Wood's ability to capture what Laurie Langbauer has labelled the "consolations of gender".[41] It is not sufficient to show Isabel (or indeed Barbara Hare) acquiescing to the middle-class woman's prescribed role; she must come to want and honour this role as passionately as she once disgraced it. Isabel's sense of longing and misery when she loses home, caste and children must therefore resonate. In her delirium she imagines that she was indeed "a proud mother, an honoured wife" (352). It is this form of simple moralism that helped give *East Lynne* a special place on the Victorian reading list. The novel carries the symbolic weight of wifely duty, implicitly aligning those who would criticize matrimonial responsibilities with the degenerate Isabel. As *The Reader* expressed it in 1864, the "intense conservatism of Mrs. Wood's principle" shines through.[42]

Although Elaine Showalter has read *East Lynne* as a subversive proto-feminist text, it is difficult to read the novel in this light when faced with the remorseless disciplining that Wood metes out to the transgressive wife.[43] One early critic believed that the "pure morality" of Ellen Wood's novel rendered it "particularly valuable at the present time...when the sanctities of domestic life are threatened...It is a matter of no small importance that the follies...the vices of society should be so ably portrayed and so thrillingly denounced as we see them in *East Lynne*".[44] Indeed, as Lyn Pykett has suggested, the tale is a sensational "story of the feminine and a feminine story".[45] The collection of alienating adjectives that Wood bestows on her (anti-)heroine in *East Lynne*—"mad" and "criminal" to name two of the more muted—reflect a highly topical concern with the need to distinguish good and bad women, along with a related attempt to re-invest middle-class women with a sense of their duties as mothers of the race.

Wood's narrative of female failing, discipline and punishment thus presents Lady Isabel Vane as an object lesson, whose degeneration is enacted and condemned, rather than explicitly theorized. The novel affirms William Greenslade's recent assertion that the degeneration debate was an "enabling strategy", which allowed the eminently respectable middle classes to "justify and articulate their hostility to the deviant, the diseased and the subversive".[46] *East Lynne* must therefore be read as a text that concerns itself with policing and othering degenerate women. Indeed, by 1861 any moderately well-read woman or man would have understood the basic tenets of the degeneration debate and would have condemned Isabel's lack of self control accordingly. Thus, Mrs. Henry Wood must herself be re-evaluated as a guardian of bourgeois propriety and the moral health of the nation.

Notes

1. Ellen Wood. *East Lynne*. Ed. Andrew Maunder. (Peterborough, Ontario: Broadview Press, 2000). All further references to this edition will be given parenthetically within the body of the text.
2. *The Times*. 2 July 1861. 8.
3. K. Corbett. "The Degeneration of the Race". *The Lancet*, August 1861. 170. In Daniel Pick. *Faces of Degeneration: A European Disorder, c.1848-c.1918*. (Cambridge: Cambridge University Press, 1989). 190.
4. Henry Maudsley. *The Physiology of Mind*. Second edition. (London: Macmillan, 1868). 356.
5. Unsigned article. "The Garrotting Panic". *Saturday Review*. 1862. 241.
6. Henry Maudsley. *The Physiology of Mind*. 356.
7. R.B. Kershner. "Degeneration: The Explanatory Nightmare". *Georgian Review*. 40, 1986. 424.
8. Jenny Bourne Taylor. *In the Secret Theatre of Home: Wilkie Collins, Sensation Narrative and Nineteenth-Century Psychology*. (London: Routledge, 1988). 135.
9. John Ruskin. *Modern Painters*. In Jerome Buckley. *Triumph of Time*. Cambridge, Mass: Harvard University Press, 1966). 58.
10. See William Greenslade. *Degeneration, Culture and the Novel, 1880-1940*. (Cambridge: Cambridge University Press, 1994). 20.
11. *The Times*. 29 June 1861. 12.
12. "The Degeneration of the Race". *The Lancet*. 22 December 1860. 620.
13. Unsigned article. "Manners and Morals as Affected by Civilisation". *Fraser's Magazine*. September 1861. 365.
14. Susan David Bernstein. "Dirty Reading: Sensation Fiction, Women and Primitivism". *Criticism*. 36, Spring 1994. 216.
15. Unsigned article. "Our Female Sensation Novelists". The *Christian Remembrancer*. 46, 1863. 210.
16. Unsigned article. "The Vice of Reading". *Temple Bar*. 42, 1874. 251. In Pamela Gilbert. *Disease, Desire and the Body in Victorian Women's Popular Novels*. (Cambridge: Cambridge University Press, 1997). 22.
17. Richard Holt Hutton. "East Lynne". *The Spectator*. 28 September 1861. 1068-9. Morel's *Treatise* had been serialized in *The Medical Circular* in 1857.
18. Richard Holt Hutton. *The Spectator*. 1068-9
19. Unsigned review. "Madness in Novels". *The Spectator*. 3 February 1866. 135.
20. See, for example, Elaine Showalter's analysis of the novel's "subversive" potential in *A Literature of Their Own: British Women Novelists from Brontë to Lessing*. (Princeton, New Jersey: Princeton University Press, 1977). 158-61. See also Sally Mitchell, introduction to *East Lynne*. (New Brunswick: Rutgers University Press, 1984). xiii.
21. Michel Foucault. *The Birth of the Clinic: An Archaeology of Medical Perception*. Trans A.M. Sheridan Smith. (New York: Vintage, 1975). 41. See William Greenslade, *Degeneration* 1-4 for more on Foucault and degeneration.
22. D.A. Miller. *The Novel and the Police*. (Berkeley and Los Angeles: University of California Press, 1988). viii & 2.

23. [Unsigned article]. "Manners and Morals as Affected by Civilisation". *Fraser's Magazine*. 64, September 1861. 309.
24. Henry Maudsley. *The Physiology of Mind*. 366.
25. Kelly Hurley, *The Gothic Body: Sexuality, Materialism and Degeneration at the Fin de Siècle* (Cambridge: Cambridge University Press, 1996): 66-67.
26. Ellen Wood. *East Lynne*. *New Monthly Magazine*. 119, May 1860. 91. NB the phrase does not appear in the three-volume version of the novel.
27. Benedict Morel. *Treatise on the Degeneration of the Human Species*. 109. In Hurley. *The Gothic Body*. 71.
28. Deborah Wynne. *The Sensation Novel and the Victorian Family Magazine*. (London: Palgrave, 2001). 67.
29. Henry Maudsley. *The Physiology of Mind*. 361.
30. Margaret Oliphant. "Novels". *Blackwood's Magazine*. 102, 1867. 259.
31. Henry Maudsley. *The Physiology of Mind*. 407.
32. Henry Maudsley. "Materialism and its Lessons". *Fortnightly Review*. 26, 1879. 244-60. In William Greenslade. *Degeneration*. 27.
33. Sarah Stickney Ellis. T*he Women of England, their Social Duties and Domestic Habits*. (London: Fisher, Son & Co. 1838). In Sally Shuttleworth, "Demonic Mothers". 35.
34. Unsigned article. "The Degeneration of the Race". *The Lancet*. 22 December 1860. 620.
35. Herbert Spencer. *Education: Intellectual, Moral and Physical*. (London: G. Manwaring, 1861). 184, 179.
36. See Lynda Nead. *Myths of Sexuality*. (Oxford: Blackwell, 1988) 80. See also Carol Smart, "Disruptive Bodies and Unruly Sex" in Carol Smart (ed.). *Regulating Womanhood: Historical Essays on Marriage, Motherhood and Sexuality*. (London: Routledge, 1993). 28.
37. See Elisabeth G. Gitter. "The Power of Hair in the Victorian Imagination". *PMLA*. 99, 5, October 1984. *936-954*.
38. Sally Shuttleworth. "Demonic Mothers: Ideologies of Bourgeois Motherhood in the Mid-Victorian Era". In Linda M. Shires. *Rewriting the Victorians: Theory, History and the Politics of Gender*. (New York: Routledge, 1992).
39. Herbert Spencer. *Education: Intellectual, Moral and Physical*. (London: G. Manwaring, 1861). 142-3.
40. Benedict Morel. *Treatise*. 109. Cited in Hurley, *The Gothic Body*. 71.
41. Laurie Langbauer. *Women and Romance: The Consolations of Gender in the English Novel*. (Ithaca: Cornell University Press, 1990). 9.
42. Unsigned article. *The Reader*. 16 January 1864. 70.
43. See Showalter. *A Literature of Their Own*. 158-61.
44. Cited in Charles Wood. *The Memorials of Mrs. Henry Wood*. (London: Bentley & Son, 1894). 254.
45. Lyn Pykett. *"The Improper Feminine": The Woman's Sensation Novel and the New Woman Writing*. (London: Routledge, 1992). 118.
46. William Greenslade. *Degeneration*. 2.

Chapter 5

Murder, Gender, and Popular Fiction by Women in the 1860s: Braddon, Oliphant, Yonge

June Sturrock

In 1860, in the village of Road in Somerset, Constance Kent, aged sixteen, was arrested for the murder of her three-year-old half-brother, who had been found in a privy in the garden with his throat cut. Later that year, the charges against her were dismissed, and the case remained unsolved, until in 1865 she confessed to an Anglican priest.[1] Kent was condemned to death, but her sentence was commuted to life imprisonment. The Victorian taste for murders is well-documented; but the especially "tremendous pother" about this notorious case—*The Great Crime of 1860*, as the title of a book published in 1861 asserts—arose from the accusation of a violent family crime against a young and middle-class woman.[2] Moreover, as Anthea Trodd has demonstrated, the British public was outraged at police intrusion into the Kent family's privacy.[3]

Cultural anxieties concerning gender, privacy, and transgression in the early 1860s are implicit in the three popular novels published by women between the exculpation of Kent and her subsequent conviction. These years, 1860-1865, are notoriously the early years of the "sensation decade", and one of these three novels is that quintessential sensation novel, *Lady Audley's Secret* (1861). The other two, less well-known nowadays, are also both evidently affected by the sensation market: Margaret Oliphant's *Salem Chapel* (1863) involves both a woman accused of murder and another woman actually guilty of attempted murder, while Charlotte Yonge's *The Trial* (1863), which I discuss at greater length, involves an unjust conviction for violent murder. The exhaustive and excited newspaper coverage of the Kent murder contrasts sharply with the silences and avoidances regarding similar material in these novels, which nevertheless undeniably exploit its dramatic potential.[4] This contrast between the narratives in newspaper reports and in fiction suggests not only the uncertain boundaries between what could be represented as news and what could be represented as fiction, but also the unease arising from a clash between the ideal and the reality of the domestic woman—between the ideal of the middle-class woman as inevitably sheltered in the privacy of her own home and the less sheltered reality experienced by actual women.

Linda Colley, addressing this clash in relation to a slightly earlier period, speaks of "separate spheres rhetoric" as arising in part over "apprehension about the roles of the sexes", asserting that "the literature of separate spheres was more didactic than descriptive".[5] Philippa Levine argues on similar lines,[6] while Amanda Vickery reminds us that "where historians have researched the activities of particular individuals rather than the contemporary theories that allegedly hobbled them, Victorian women emerge as no less spirited, capable and, most importantly, diverse a crew as in any other century".[7]

The anxieties over women's changing roles which Colley describes are certainly evident in the early 1860s. The periodical press of all political shades constantly debated in these years such issues as the employment of women. Also, the Society for Promoting the Employment of Women was in its early days, as was the feminist *English Woman's Journal.* The sensation novel—and such quasi-sensation novels as Oliphant's and Yonge's—must therefore be understood in the context of this extreme sensitivity concerning women's public roles. That most threatening representation of the public woman, the violent woman on trial for her life, could be represented and sensationalized by newspapers because their narratives on such cases as the Kent case, or that of Madeleine Smith, were based on "fact".[8] The fictional narratives of these three women novelists, on the other hand, deal with such representations as nightmares. It is their hesitations and avoidances that are examined in the following pages.

In the early 1860s, when Braddon, Oliphant and Yonge were writing the novels discussed here, Constance Kent was generally regarded as a virtuous young woman, wrongfully accused of a hideous and notorious crime, and cruelly exposed to public scrutiny. The excitement aroused by such cases provides one context for these narratives of murder and attempted murder. In particular, the parallels between the Kent case and Yonge's *The Trial* merit some comment. *The Trial*, after being ignored for decades, has recently been reissued, an important publishing event for the history of Victorian popular fiction as this novel shows the effects of changing literary markets, being a quasi-sensation novel written as a sequel to a purely domestic novel, Yonge's great success of 1856, *The Daisy Chain.*[9] In *The Trial*, Yonge presents obvious echoes of the Kent case in the narrative of Leonard Ward. Like Constance Kent, Leonard Ward is represented as the child of parents of rather dubious social standing who nevertheless insist on expensive display.[10] Both are very young—barely old enough to be regarded as responsible people—Leonard is 17, Kent was 16. They are both of good character: Kent won a good conduct prize at school, and Leonard is represented as earning "general affection and esteem".[11] Both, moreover, have a past episode that strengthens suspicions against them: Constance Kent had run away from home and Leonard had thrown a stone at his brother in a fit of temper. The circumstantial evidence against both is strong. Similarly, in each case the crime is the brutal murder of an especially vulnerable family member: Leonard's old, feeble, and half-senile uncle is battered to death and Kent's sleeping infant brother has his throat cut. The press interest and consequent public interest in both factual and fictional cases is intense, an important feature which I shall return to later. And both young people—or so the assumption was when Yonge was writing—were completely innocent of the crimes of which they are accused. However, all the numerous resemblances between the real-life scandal—the *cause célèbre* of its period—and the novel might well be overlooked because of the obvious difference between the two accused: the difference in gender.

While it is interesting that, like Wilkie Collins later in *The Moonstone* (1868), Yonge apparently weaves episodes from the Kent case into her own crime novel, my point is not so much that she uses this notorious case as that in using it she masculinizes it. The rationale for such a change must be considered.[12] The unjust accusation of a violent crime made against a sheltered and virtuous young person provides the basis of a good plot. The amount of press coverage given to the Kent story—like the Madeleine Smith case before it—indicates that such an accusation, when made against a very young woman, creates an even better story. Yet the spectacle of a woman publicly accused of murder removes middle-class femininity from the private sphere with a violence that Yonge—a devout Tractarian—was not prepared to countenance as an acceptable fictional device. Presenting a middle-class woman as an accused criminal would undermine the concepts of femininity Yonge develops and debates in most of her fiction. So, while retaining as a female centre of consciousness Ethel May, the heroine of *The Daisy Chain*, Yonge chooses the murder of a man by a man for the typically 1860s sensation plot of the sequel. In *The Trial* her genre demands dramatic action and emotional response. Reluctant to address commonplace female fictional delinquency (bigamy, adultery), Yonge turns to violent crime, and keeps herself in the current market with a brutal murder, since in the Britain of the 1860s, according to Oliphant, "murder is our *cheval de Bataille*".[13] But Yonge's murder plot, though arguably based on the Kent case, is wholly concerned with male actors, and the glare of publicity surrounding the murder trial is associated with the male rather than the female characters. Yonge carefully avoids writing directly of the intrusions into domestic spaces notoriously associated with the sensation novel.[14]

Thus *The Trial*, the sensational sequel, contrasts strongly with *The Daisy Chain*, its domestic originating text, in its insistence on public as well as private life. The various differences between the features of the sensation novel that Yonge chose to exploit and those she avoided provide an interesting commentary on anxieties concerning gender in a period of rapid and highly self-conscious development in popular fiction.[15] Eight years earlier *The Daisy Chain* had vindicated its heroine, Ethel May, through her activity within the domestic sphere. *The Trial*, on the other hand, through its generic modifications, allows Ethel to be vindicated beyond the confines of the domestic, indeed beyond the confines of England. However, this enlarged sphere comes not through extended independent action but through "feminine influence"—her power over a male protagonist. Furthermore the "feminine", ahistoric, pastoral, domestic world of *The Daisy Chain* is firmly placed in the context of contemporary history in its sequel, through the role in the plot of "masculine" public events, such as the 1859-60 invasion scare in England, the consequent volunteer movement, the American Civil War, and the settlement of the Mid-West. Yonge's work moves with the current of the time from the secluded tranquillity of the domestic novel to the wider-ranging excitements of the plot-driven novel.

The Daisy Chain announces on its title page both its moral pretensions and its literary sub-genre: its full title is *The Daisy Chain or Aspirations: A Family Chronicle.* Its limited and private dimensions are reiterated in the preface to its first edition, which insists that the novel should "be considered merely as what it calls itself, *a Family Chronicle—a domestic record of home events, large and small*" (my emphasis).[16] *The Daisy Chain*, that is, proclaims itself as more domestic than the domestic novel and thus as the quintessence of the most popular genre of its period. As Oliphant points out eleven years later, with a certain sardonic nostalgia, "the last wave but one of female novelists [the *Daisy Chain* wave, that is] was very feminine. Their stories were all family stories, their troubles domestic, their women womanly to the last degree, and their men not much less so".[17] The sub-title of *The Trial*, eight years later, is *More Links in The Daisy Chain. The Trial* thus proclaims itself immediately as a sequel to this family chronicle. Not until almost halfway through the novel does it become apparent that the sequel is in fact generically different from its originating text, and that its narrative focus is not on the various quiet histories of the May family, the central characters in *The Daisy Chain*, but rather on the more dramatic life of their young friend, Leonard Ward. In chapter twelve, Leonard disappears, his rich old uncle is found dead, with his head battered in, and Leonard's rifle is discovered with blood and white hairs on its stock. From this point onwards the novel centres on the murder and its consequences—Leonard's arrest, his trial, conviction, and imprisonment, and his eventual vindication when the real murderer is discovered, dying horribly after a Parisian brawl. After chapter twelve, that is, *The Trial* moves beyond the private realm of the family chronicle to take on many of the horrific, extreme, and mysterious trappings of the sensation novel, the new vogue in popular fiction.[18]

While *The Trial* may not be a fully-fledged product of the "present school of fiction", which Yonge condemns as "feverish" and "offensive" (*The Trial*, 52), all the same it employs many of the essential elements of the sensation novels she deplores—violence, injustice, madness, and mystery, all set against a carefully contemporary background. Yonge moves from the domestic novel, *The Daisy Chain,* to the novel of plot, *The Trial*, to re-confirm that novel's exploration of appropriate forms of feminine behaviour. In doing so, however, she faces the problem that her idea of appropriate feminine behaviour clashes with the demands of a sensation plot in a market beginning to be dominated by sensation fiction. So feminine action, which was direct, though restricted, in the domestic novel, functions more extensively but indirectly through the masculine in the sensation sequel.

At the beginning of *The Daisy Chain* the heroine of both novels, Ethel (Etheldred) May, is fifteen, intellectual, brilliant, vigorous, plain, clumsy, tactless, indifferent both to her personal appearance and to household details—unfeminine in short. As the novel progresses she acquires slowly, painfully and conscientiously a gender identity. So effectively does she learn her lessons in femininity that she becomes the centre of the household, taking her dead mother's place as her father's beloved companion and the teacher and protector of the younger children. Her considerable energies are by no means strictly confined to the home. However, as a woman she is represented as still essentially confined to the private sphere, and her family avoid any public acknowledgment of her intellectual and charitable achievements as being either "very painful, or very hurtful to her"—as leading, that is, either to embarrassment or conceit. (*Daisy Chain*, 643) For all her remarkable qualities, Ethel must remain at home and without a formal public role.

In *The Trial* Ethel retains her central position, but she functions in the public world through Leonard, achieving a much more dramatic vindication, but through precept rather than through direct action. Her power over Leonard (ten years her junior), his "chivalrous devotion" (*The Trial*, 302) to her and her teaching, motivate him to survive a wrongful conviction for murder, penal servitude and near-madness, and to succeed in his dream (implanted by her) of becoming a missionary in the South Pacific. His last words in the novel are addressed to her: "If ever I come to any good [as, of course, he does] I owe it to you" (*The Trial*, 372). Ethel's virtues act through Leonard, so that the feminine domestic narrative can develop into the public sensation plot. Given Yonge's traditionalist and hierarchical Tractarian views of family and gender roles, in order to be acceptable, a "sensation" plot necessarily for Yonge involves a male rather than a female protagonist.

Now although the combination of the feminine and the public commonly produced anxiety, few novelists of the period shared Yonge's especially sensitive scruples about gender and public action. Eneas Sweetland Dallas, writing in 1866 at the height of the sensation trend, acknowledges the problem of combining action and the feminine, but implies that few novelists solve it as Yonge does:

> The first object of the novelist is to get personages in whom we can be interested; the next is to put them in action. But when women are the chief characters, how are you to set them in motion? The life of women cannot well be described as a life of action. When women are thus put forward to lead the action of a plot, they must be urged into a false position. To get vigorous action they are described as rushing into crime and doing masculine deeds...the novelist finds that to make an effect he has to give up his heroine to bigamy, to murder, to child-bearing by stealth in the Tyrol, and all sorts of adventures which can only signify her fall. The very prominence of the position which women occupy in recent fiction leads by a natural process to their appearing in a light which is not good. This is what is called sensation. It is not wrong to make a sensation; but if the novelist depends for his sensation upon the action of a woman, the chances are that he will attain his end by unnatural means.[19]

Dallas's observations, despite his "impersonal" masculine pronouns, apply mostly to women sensation novelists and provide an interesting footnote to Oliphant's well-known diatribe of 1867 against the women writers and readers of sensation novels and their "nasty thoughts, ugly suggestions" and "imagination which prefers the unclean".[20] Their strictures may be applied to Braddon's Lady Audley, for example. She may not resort to secret child-bearing in the Tyrol, but she does, of course, commit bigamy, attempt murder twice, and organize very skilfully a complete change of identity.[21] Unlike Braddon, Yonge held the views of gender and nature suggested by Oliphant and Dallas, and in an extreme version. Her gender code and her stated purpose in writing as "a sort of instrument for popularizing Church Views"[22] debarred her from presenting transgressive women.[23] The bigamy, fornication, and adultery that were staples of many sensation novels—and one critic complained that eight of the twenty-four novels he reviewed in 1863 were "bigamy stories"[24]—were not viable plot elements for one so schooled, and nor was female violence. When market considerations drove her towards what Dallas calls "the novel of plot" as opposed to "the novel of character",[25] she refused to depend for her "sensation upon the action of a woman" and instead chose a male for both passive and active (and both positive and negative) public roles, transforming the well-known Constance Kent plot into the Leonard Ward plot.

In *The Trial*, Yonge foregrounds the shift to the public realm associated with the masculine from the private realm associated with the feminine—two realms that are kept unusually separate in this novel, as I shall show. Structurally the complete contrast between the earlier and purely domestic chapters of the novel and the later focus on crime and punishment has this effect, and so does the almost literally central role of the murder trial. The protracted (fifteen-page) description of Leonard Ward's trial is described in the same terms of catharsis and mass emotion—extreme "sensation"—used in newspaper accounts of the Constance Kent hearings. The fictional crowds of spectators are occasionally reduced *en masse* to "a universal weeping and sobbing" (*The Trial*, 181) and individually to fainting and hysterics. The *Wiltshire and Somerset Journal* in 1860 describing the Kent hearing as "powerfully affecting", similarly stresses somatic effects: it informs us that "when the poor creature who was accused of so dreadful a crime fell into her father's arms and kissed him a sensation was produced that had a marked effect on the crowd for the whole day".[26] Furthermore, in 1865 when Constance Kent, after confessing to the crime, was condemned to death the same newspaper reports that "the greater part of the public as well as the jury were in tears" and that furthermore "when the learned judge had proceeded about halfway through the awful sentence he broke down literally [sic] from excessive emotion".[27]

The public excitement surrounding Leonard's ordeal is further underlined by references to ghoulish sightseers and "curiosity hunters" (*The Trial*, 193) who resemble those "fashionably dressed young ladies" who visited the Kent house "seeking to learn every particular and view every spot connected with the murder", according to the local newspaper.[28] The crowd of crime reporters brought in by such a murder transform the local spectacle of the trial into national entertainment. In the fictional case "Murder of an Uncle by his Nephew", headlines figured everywhere in the largest type; newsboys on the railway shouted "To-day's paper—account of inquest", and the illustrated press sent down artists (*The Trial*, 166). In the actual case, at Constance Kent's hearing in 1860 "three rows of reporters stretched across the room", while for the 1865 hearing, when crush barriers had to be erected, the building was thronged with "London reporters and special correspondents and a whole host of representatives of the provincial press".[29] At a period when the power of the press was perceived to be growing rapidly, crime journalism itself was becoming increasingly newsworthy; in the Kent case one notes reporters reporting on reporters, as they would later do in the O.J. Simpson trial reports. London papers such as *The Times,* and especially *The Daily Telegraph*, as well as provincial and county newspapers, vied with each other over the fullness and immediacy of the details of their crime stories, stories that, like sensation fiction, were expected to awaken both terror and pathos. To "do the Police in different voices"[30] might indeed add zest to reading aloud these newspapers. Patrick Brantlinger writes of "the direct relation between the sensation novel and sensation journalism" (9) and contemporaries rapidly perceived this connection.[31] Fiction and newspapers alike combined a powerfully emotive narrative of exceptionally dramatic events with an insistently contemporary background, just as Yonge does here.

The sense of the uneasy intermeshing of public and private—family chronicle as sensation novel, domestic drama as national news—is intensified by the careful historical placing of *The Trial*. In *The Daisy Chain*, Yonge had created a timeless domestic idyll with few overt signs of its period. However, in sensation novels "proximity of time is deemed indispensable to the effect that they are intended to create", as the *Temple Bar* critic Alfred Austin observed in 1870.[32] Winifred Hughes writes of "the sensation paradox"—its combination of melodrama and "the same solidity of physical detail characteristic of nineteenth-century realism".[33] *The Trial*, accordingly, like a contemporary newspaper, juxtaposes sensational crime with both the national and international events of the day, so that virtually all its events can be precisely dated. The murder weapon itself is acquired in order to enable Leonard to join the local Volunteer Corps, a fictitious branch of an actual organization that was set up in 1859-60 all over the country in response to a scare over a possible French invasion. After the murder trial Leonard's family, in order to escape public humiliation, leave England for the United States and become directly involved in both the hardships of the settler's life in Indiana and the anguish of the American Civil War, which was being fought as Yonge wrote.[34]

The Trial constantly and minutely juxtaposes fact and fiction, insisting on the ways in which public events affect private lives: the provincial town where the action is set acquires public baths as a memorial to the Prince Consort (who died in 1861), and its drainage system as a celebration of the Prince of Wales's marriage in 1863 (*The Trial*, 288). Moreover the novel is placed as contemporary not only through public events but also through repeated references to current fashions in dress and behaviour, to the skirts spread over "a mountain of mohair and scarlet petticoat...upborne by an over-grown steel mouse-trap" (*The Trial*, 22), which encumber the female characters, and to the hanging sleeves that knock everything over. Fashionable pastimes of the day like illuminating and fossil-collecting also touch on the plot (Leonard throws a pointed belemnite at his brother). Even the weather is dated: "though it was the year 1860", a summer apparently notorious for incessant rain, the sun shines for the Volunteers' parade (*The Trial*, 97).[35] The idyllic and generalized domesticity of *The Daisy Chain* has become emphatically and disturbingly the here and now.[36]

Yonge thus juxtaposes the public world of national and international events and the national publicity involved in uncovering a mystery. Publicity is represented as distasteful and even destructive, but it is a necessary part of Leonard's eventual exculpation and vindication. Yet while she is prepared to write of public accusation and condemnation, Yonge refuses to present a middle-class woman as the accused. When such women appear in the courtroom, as they do in her other novels of the 1860s, they are not defendants but witnesses, and their courtroom performances operate as public confirmations of the novel's position on their gender correctness—or lack of it. That is, they appear as the quintessence of the "sustained social performance" which constitutes "gender reality", according to Judith Butler.[37] The presence of an audience, watching and judging, is essential to these scenes. To Yonge, as to other women writers, the essence of a trial was the public gaze. Women witnesses, and more especially women defendants, became temporarily "public women". In *Hopes and Fears* (1860), the virtuous Phoebe, who has saved her brother's life during an armed robbery, is, when under oath as a witness, "too much occupied with the act before God and her neighbour to be self-conscious or to think of *the multitude eagerly watching her young simple face, or listening to her grave clear tones*" (my emphasis).[38] Conversely, Rachel, the "unfeminine" title character of *The Clever Woman of the Family*, who has been duped by a confidence-trickster, feels as a witness at his trial, "as though all eyes were looking in triumph at that object of general scorn and aversion, a woman who had stepped out of her place".[39] During her subsequent illness she is haunted by this memory, finding her eyelids "as it were, lined with tiers of gazing faces and curious looks turned on her" (*CW*, 362). Her suffering is described in terms of shame at her public exposure rather than guilt over her foolish behaviour: "the crush of public censure was not at the moment so overwhelming as the strange morbid effect of having been the focus of those many, many glances" (*CW*, 262). In repeated nightmares she experiences "the world of gazing faces, feverishly magnified, multiplied and pressing closer and closer on her", or "the whole morbid sense of eyes staring at her" (*CW*, 262, 284). She constantly wears "the same bewildered distressed look that had been as it were stamped on her by the gaze of the many unfriendly eyes at the Quarter Sessions" (*CW*, 268). She has offended against gender codes and is punished in a peculiarly feminine way—through her sense of outrage and humiliation at a public exposure. Yet, although in this novel a former maidservant is tried for cruelty to children, Yonge carefully avoids presenting a middle-class woman as an accused criminal.

In presenting in nightmare terms the combination of the middle-class woman and the trial, Yonge resembles other women writers of popular fiction in the early 1860s. Mary Elizabeth Braddon in *Lady Audley's Secret* (1862), despite her entirely different attitude to fiction-writing and to many issues of gender, is like Yonge in representing the trial as nightmare, though here she represents it as a family rather than a personal nightmare. Indeed, part of the calculated emotional impact of this novel arises from the conflicts of Braddon's detective figure, Robert Audley, the heir of the Audley estate. Suspecting his uncle's wife of murder and bigamy, he is both bound as a friend of the victim to uncover the crime and yet equally bound as an Audley male, devoted to his "jolly old prince" of an uncle, to conceal it.[40] Although he feels compelled to uncover the truth, he dreads the publicity of a murder trial, the exposure of an Audley woman to public humiliation and the public gaze.[41] He wakes in an "agony of shame" from nightmares of "a crowded courthouse, and his uncle's wife, in a criminal dock, hemmed in on every side by a sea of eager faces" (*LAS*, 377).

Lady Audley intelligently exploits this weakness in her adversary: "*I* am not in a criminal dock, Mr. Audley, and I do not choose to do anything but laugh at your ridiculous folly", she says, knowing that "he could do no more without bringing everlasting disgrace upon the name he venerated"—the Audley name (*LAS*, 273, 372). "God forbid", Robert Audley says to Sir Michael, his uncle and Lady Audley's husband, "that the lightest shadow of dishonour should ever fall upon your honoured head—least of all through any agency of mine" (*LAS*, 129). Even in the *maison de santé* she reminds Robert Audley, "it would kill your uncle to see me in a criminal dock" (*LAS*, 373, 394). As Jonathan Loesberg notes, "sensation novels evoke their most typical moments of sensation response from images of a loss of class identity" (*LAS*, 17). Male honour—male social status—is vulnerable through the public exposure of female relations. To avoid dishonour—loss of status—Robert Audley must avoid publicity and hence the law. He speaks of his greatest fear as being "any exposure—any disgrace" (*LAS*, 380). Lady Audley's secret has to remain a secret, "a solemn confidence to be violated under no circumstances", as Robert Audley warns the specialist in mental disorders whom he consults (LAS, 375). As D.A. Miller argues, the "double-talk" of this doctor is necessary to establish "two contradictory propositions: 1) Lady Audley is a criminal in the sense that her crimes must be punished and 2) Lady Audley is not a criminal in that neither her crimes nor her punishment must be made public in a male order of things". Miller goes on to point out that though her acts "qualify as crimes" they are more conveniently treated as madness.[42] Jill Matus indeed regards the very discourse of madness itself in this novel and elsewhere as a cover-up, allowing "historically specific issues of class and power to be represented instead as timeless and universal matters of female biology".[43] Certainly Lady Audley's immuring in the *maison de santé* ensures finally that in fact "whatever secrets she may have will be secrets forever" (*LAS*, 381). Here her guilt is obliterated and she herself is rapidly obliterated too—"Buried Alive", according to Braddon's Dickensian chapter title. The Audley nightmare of an Audley woman on trial remains only a nightmare.[44] Lady Audley ends not in the public gaze but in the more sinister and absolute privacy of her asylum. Moreover, both her murder attempts fail, for this sensational narrative finally shies away from presenting either a woman as murderer or a woman on trial for her life.

Among the most articulate and intelligent of the many critics of the "sensation school",[45] of which *Lady Audley's Secret* was a notable example, was Margaret Oliphant, whose *Blackwood's Magazine* articles in the 1860s express some admiration, some patronizing amusement but finally overwhelming contempt for the vogue.[46] All the same, like Yonge (a less vocal but equally staunch opponent of the trend), Oliphant deliberately exploits the sensation vein in her own fiction of the early 1860s, and like Yonge she moves from humdrum realism to melodrama.[47]

The tensions and humours of the nonconformist congregation in the early chapters give way to a tale of violence and insanity. In *Salem Chapel* (1863) Oliphant employs, like Braddon, the trope of family terror at the prospect of a woman on trial for murder. Her narrative includes a young girl, Susan Vincent, who is suspected of killing the married man to whom she had supposed herself to be engaged, maddened by outrage at an attempt on her virtue. Oliphant presents the visual spectacle of Susan's own grief as she lies delirious and near death. Indeed, Tamar Heller discusses this novel as a "hitherto neglected example of the plot of woman as spectacle".[48] However, the agonies that are articulated are not hers but those of her mother and brother, who are as much concerned with her shame—and theirs—as with her sufferings.

Again, as with Robert Audley, a woman's guilt is represented as significant mainly as it represents loss of social status for her male relations. Oliphant establishes in the early pages of the novel that Arthur Vincent, Susan's clergyman brother, is extremely sensitive about his uncertain class position within Carlingford; even his passion for Lady Western is affected by his concerns about status. Immediately after Susan's story becomes public, he feels that "his innocent honourable name was already sullied by the breath of the crowd".[49] His first reaction at the realization that his sister is a murder suspect explicitly concerns not her guilt, nor the possibility of capital punishment, but disgrace:

> The horror of this accusation had come home to Vincent's mind at last. He saw, as if by a sudden flash of instant enlightenment, not guilt indeed, or its awful punishment, but open shame—the disgrace of publicity—the horrible suspicions which were of themselves more than enough to kill the unhappy girl (*SC*, 281).

The outcome he most fears, the ultimate degradation for himself and his sister, is the trial, in his eyes a fate worse than death: "the very thought of it drove her unhappy brother desperate. Would it not be better if she died and escaped that crowning misery which must kill her anyhow if she survived to bear it?" (*SC*, 290). After Susan is cleared of the charges, her mother is still agonized that her name should be publicly spoken, even in exculpation, "before the magistrates!...But, thank God, it is not here...you must not let your sister's name be talked of among the people" (*SC*, 329). Like Braddon, Oliphant avoids representing a woman as guilty of murder. Not only is Susan completely innocent but the murder attempt (by another outraged woman) also turns out to be a failure. The excitement of the Susan Vincent episode of *Salem Chapel*—an excitement that brought Oliphant considerable success—depends largely on the potential of shame, on the possibility of a woman publicly disgraced. But like Braddon, Oliphant uses this possibility to titillate and to represent anxiety over the possibility of woman as spectacle, while avoiding actually representing a woman in the criminal dock for murder.

Yonge's victim is less fortunate than those of Braddon and Oliphant. While these novelists write of family dread at the possibility of a woman brought to trial, and avoid representing actual murders and real trials, Yonge's narrative includes both murder and trial. Yet although she exploits the details of an actual case of a woman accused of murder—the Kent case—she tacitly rejects the connection between guilt and the middle-class woman in her quasi-sensation novel by using a male as her accused murderer. Rather than following the female sensation novelists and, as Lyn Pykett has suggested, "both implicitly and explicitly...rais[ing] questions about gender identity", Yonge in *The Trial* is concerned to affirm traditional ideals of the feminine.[50] Her later novels show the complexity of issues of gender identity, especially in the explicit anti-feminism and studied conservatism of *The Clever Woman of the Family* (1865) and *The Three Brides* (1876). However, feminine roles in the family are as unchallenged in *The Trial* as in *The Daisy Chain*—more so, in fact, for the women characters are exceptionally blameless in this novel, where the very worst extreme of feminine behaviour represented is excessive harmonium-playing in church (*The Trial*, 74). Yonge scrupulously avoids any possible contamination from the sexual and gender implications of the popular sensation genre. Even Oliphant, in *Salem Chapel*, allows her female characters to be abducted, threatened with seduction, temporarily insane, and murderous in intent, but Yonge's quasi-sensation novel carefully dissociates itself from the sub-genre's concern with feminine dissidence. Violence, madness, and treachery are essential to its plot, as they are to Braddon's and to Oliphant's, but here they are scrupulously removed from any direct connection with the female characters.[51]

The popular fiction of this period increasingly comes to represent the home not as a place of refuge but as a place of threat. As Trodd writes, "the sensation novel promoted a belief that there was something inherently suspect about the privacy of the middle-class home, and formulated those suspicions by displaying the home as a place where secret crimes flourished".[52] What she calls "the guilty home" certainly plays its part in Yonge's murder mystery. But while in *Salem Chapel* and *Lady Audley's Secret*—and a dozen other sensation novels—domestic tensions focus on female characters, in *The Trial* the tensions are expressed almost entirely through male interactions. Leonard's violent rejection of his elder brother's patriarchal authority after the family is orphaned causes him to be sent away to live with the old uncle who is the murder victim, and doubly strengthens the case against him, while the actual murderer is another nephew also living with the uncle, resentful of his authority and anxious to inherit. Father figures are threatened and killed in this novel. However, despite its quite credible presentation of the relation between family hierarchy and family violence, and the reliance of its plot on a failure of the justice system, *The Trial* overtly argues for traditional power relations both in social institutions and in the family. Policemen, lawyers, and prison officers are all presented as just, sympathetic and helpful, and Leonard, his sisters, and the May family all come to regard the murder and its consequences in part as a lesson in the necessity for being "submissive and yielding" (*The Trial*, 243) to patriarchal figures. And all three novels, of course, end as comedies with family structures strengthened and restored for the new generations: Robert Audley is married and a father, Arthur Vincent begins to fall in love, Leonard Ward is exculpated, and his sister returns from her American exile married to Ethel May's brother.

A growing demand for action and reaction drove popular fiction in the late 1850s beyond the tranquillity of the home. The three popular novels from the beginning of the sensation decade examined here exploit the intense emotional power of public shame and disgrace in the culture of the period, and show the various degrees to which this shame is magnified by considerations of gender. All three employ the powerful image of the murder trial, whether real or imagined, to epitomize that shame. Braddon's Lady Audley must be both punished as a transgressive woman and protected from such public exposure because of her connection with the aristocracy. Oliphant's Susan Vincent is represented as a noble and virtuous woman whose family's status and income are threatened by the taint of a public trial. For Yonge in *The Trial* the whole issue of the feminine and the public gaze is so highly charged that a middle-class woman in the dock becomes an impossibility for her fiction. She invokes the emotional power of a murder which, within the context of the novel, is carefully removed from the feminine realm so that discord and disgrace touch on the female characters only indirectly. Yet—as I suggested at the beginning of this chapter—by repeated parallels with such a notorious contemporary murder, the Constance Kent case, in which a young, middle-class woman faced public exposure, *The Trial* exploits the added emotional power of such a narrative. The scene suggested by all three novels, but missing from each of them, the scene of the woman on trial, indicates the real point of anxiety. The newspapers could and did deal at length, in detail, and repeatedly with the cases of women like Madeleine Smith and Constance Kent. These women novelists refused to present such material directly. Their final avoidance of the scene of a middle-class woman in the ultimately public role of an accused murderer is silently eloquent.

Notes

1. Mary S. Hartman, in *Victorian Murderesses: A True History of Thirteen Respectable French and English Women Accused of Unspeakable Crimes*, (NY: Schocken Books, 1977), expresses some doubts about Kent's guilt, pointing out that her story is not consistent with the facts of the case, and suggesting that her father may have been guilty.
2. *Saturday Review*, 1860. Quoted by Anthea Trodd, in *Domestic Crime in the Victorian Novel*, (London: Macmillan, 1989). 22. Hartman refers to the 1861 account of the Kent case by Joseph W. Stapleton, 122.
3. Trodd 19-26.
4. Jonathan Loesberg, in "The Ideology of Narrative Form in Sensation Fiction". *Representations* 13 (1986). 115-38, bases important arguments on the distinguishing feature of the sensation novels—the powerful physical and emotional responses they represent and evoke. So does Ann Cvetkovich in *Mixed Feelings: Feminism, Mass Culture, and Victorian Sensationalism.* (New Brunswick, NJ: Rutgers University Press, 1992).
5. See Linda Colley, *Britons: Forging the Nation 1707-1837*, (New Haven: Yale University Press, 1992). 263, 241, 181.
6. Colley says that "if British women were being urged to remain at home more stridently in this period than ever before, it was largely because so many of them were finding an increasing amount to do outside the home" (281). Philippa Levine in *Victorian Feminism 1850-1900*. (London: Hutchinson Education, 1987), comments that "the ideal division between the domestic woman and the public man was never realised in many homes and never became the dominant reality. As an ideology, however, it was highly effective in ordering people's values according to its perspectives" (12). And she points out that for many women "manipulation of its fundamental values" (13) was more effective than rejecting this ideology.
7. In "Golden Age to Separate Spheres? Review of the Categories and Chronology of English Women's History". *The Historical Journal* 36 (1993), 390.
8. The case of Madeleine Smith is as important as that of Constance Kent in indicating British attitudes towards accused middle-class women at the period, but is less directly relevant to my present arguments.
9. For further discussion of the significance of this sequel to the history of popular fiction see my "Sequels, Series, and Sensation Novels: Charlotte Yonge and the Popular Fiction Market of the 1850s and 1860s" in *Part II: Reflections on the Sequel*, ed. Betty Schellenberg and Paul Budra, (Toronto: University of Toronto Press, 1998). 102-17.
10. Hartman 95. Charlotte Mary Yonge, *The Trial or, More Links in the Daisy Chain.* (London: Alan Sutton Publishing Limited, 1996). 29. Hereafter to be referenced parenthetically as "*Trial*".
11. John Rhode in *The Case of Constance Kent.* (New York: Scribner's, 1928). 92. *The Trial.* 170.
12. Thomas Boyle, in *Black Swine in the Sewers of Hampstead: Beneath the Surface*

of Victorian Sensationalism. (New York: Viking, 1989) argues that though there is no "really extended pattern of imitation of real life crime from the newspapers", all the same sensation fiction is "riddled with details which recall widely reported criminal occurrences of the time" (146). H.L. Mansel, in "Sensation Novels", *Quarterly Review 113* (1863), suggests that a recent novel, *Such Things Are*, was based on "the Road murder and the Glasgow poisoning"—that is the cases of Madeleine Smith and Constance Kent (262).

13. Margaret Oliphant, "Novels". *Blackwood's Magazine* 94 (1863), 168.
14. Both Trodd and D.A. Miller, in their discussions of sensation fiction, argue in different contexts concerning the intrusions into the private. See Miller's *The Novel and the Police*. (Berkeley: University of California Press, 1988). See also Patrick Brantlinger in "What is 'Sensational' about the 'Sensation' Novel?" *Nineteenth Century Fiction* 37 (1982), 1-28, for an essential account of the subgenre.
15. According to David Skilton, in his introduction to Mary Elizabeth Braddon's *Lady Audley's Secret*, (Oxford: Oxford University Press, 1987), "at no time were the techniques and subject-matter of fiction under more vigorous or more public debate". vii.
16. Charlotte Mary Yonge, *The Daisy Chain, or Aspirations: A Family Chronicle*, (London: Virago, 1988). xi-xii. Hereafter referenced parenthetically as "*DC*".
17. See "Novels". *Blackwood's Magazine* 102 (1867), 257-80.
18. *The Trial* employs a plot that Oliphant recognizes as one of the staples of that vogue: "the conduct and position of a man who finds himself or his friend unjustly suspected and who makes it the object of his life to bring the criminal to justice". As Oliphant (enviously?) points out this plot line operates in Braddon's *Aurora Floyd* and in *Lady Audley's Secret*, "those two remarkable instances of public favour". Oliphant 1863. 169.
19. Eneas Sweetland Dallas, in *The Gay Science*, (London: Chapman and Hall, 1866). 296-97.
20. Oliphant 1867. 275.
21. "Buried Alive" is the title of chapter 38 of *Lady Audley's Secret*. Lyn Pykett (in *The Sensation Novel: From The Woman in White to The Moonstone*. Plymouth: Northcote House, 1994, 47) and Brantlinger (5-6) both usefully discuss the relevance of contemporary interest in bigamy cases and the concern and anxiety aroused by reforms of divorce laws.
22. Georgina Battiscombe, *Charlotte Mary Yonge: The Story of an Uneventful Life*, (London: Constable, 1944), 14.
23. Yonge identified John Keble, the extreme Anglo-Catholic poet and priest, as "the greatest influence of my life" (*Musings over "The Christian Year" and "Lyra Innocentium", Together with a few Gleanings of Recollections of the Rev. J. Keble, Gathered by Several Friends*, London: Macmillan, 1871, iii) and described how he schooled her as a writer in "delicacy and reverence" (Battiscombe 72). Dallas explains the prevalence of sexual secrets in the sensation novel by the very fact that they feature women: "the most interesting side of a woman's character is her relation with the other sex and the errors of women that are most interesting spring out of this relation" (quoted Skilton vii). But Yonge does not share

Dallas's views of the character of women: See my *"Heaven and Home": Charlotte Yonge's Domestic Fiction and the Victorian Debate Over Women.* (Victoria: University of Victoria, 1995). passim.

24. Mansel. 255.
25. Dallas. 293.
26. Rhode. 106.
27. Rhode. 254.
28. Rhode. 212.
29. Rhode. 106, 223-24.
30. Charles Dickens *Our Mutual Friend*, (Harmondsworth: Penguin, 1985). 246.
31. Boyle, 129.
32. Alfred Austin, "Our Novels: The Sensation School". *Temple Bar* 29 (1870), 412.
33. Winifred Hughes, *The Maniac in the Cellar: Sensation Novels of the 1860s.* (Princeton: Princeton University Press, 1980). 3-37.
34. Oliphant actually relates fact to fiction to the extent of attributing the popularity of sensation fiction to the American Civil War. The domestic novel she sees as the product of an age "lost in self admiration", the age of the Great Exhibition, whereas in the sixties "on the other side of the Atlantic, a race blasé and lost in universal *ennui* has bethought itself of the grandest expedient for procuring a new sensation; and albeit we follow at a humble distance, we too begin to feel the need of a supply of new shocks and wonders…it is only natural that art and literature should, in an age which has turned out to be one of events, attempt a kindred depth of effect and shock of incident". "Sensation Novels". *Blackwood's Magazine* 91 (1862). 564-65.
35. *Punch* in September 1860 includes cartoons about the rainfall, showing a gondola in the streets of London.
36. The first of Yonge's novels to historicize its action in this way is *Dynevor Terrace* (1859), in which the French Revolution of 1848, and the opening to Atlantic-Pacific traffic of the isthmus of Panama both play an important role.
37. See Judith Butler. *Gender Trouble: Feminism and the Subversion of Identity*, (London: Routledge, 1990). 141.
38. *Hopes and Fears: Or, Scenes from the Life of a Spinster.* (London: Macmillan and Co., 1883). 424.
39. *The Clever Woman of the Family.* (London: Virago, 1986). 253. Herafter referenced as "*CW*".
40. Mary Elizabeth Braddon. *Lady Audley's Secret.* (Oxford: Oxford University Press, 1987). 122. Herafter referenced as "*LAS*".
41. Cvetkovich notes that "because detection occurs in its midst the family can no longer serve as refuge and instead becomes the scene of conflict and anxiety". 52.
42. Miller. 170, 169.
43. Jill L. Matus. *Unstable Bodies: Victorian Representations of Sexuality and Maternity.* (Manchester, Manchester University Press, 1995). 334.
44. Braddon's critics have noted the novel's pervasive emphasis on both secrecy and the curiosity that threatens it. Chiara Briganti, in "Gothic Maidens and Sensation Women: Lady Audley's Journey from the Ruined Mansion to the Madhouse",

Victorian Literature and Culture 19 (1991), sees the rambling family seat, Audley Court, with its secret passageways as "a suitable objective correlative of Lady Audley herself who, because of the necessity of rejecting her past, appears to be all surface, but who, like the house hides secrets" (192). The novel insists on the concealment of guilt: guilt can be hidden in landscape—the site of a rural murder, despite "the stain of that foul deed upon it", (*LAS*, 54) appears peaceful—or in the human face—Robert Audley says pointedly to the lovely Lady Audley that "I believe we may look into the smiling face of a murderer and admire its tranquil beauty" (*LAS*, 141). The concealments do not go unchallenged—Jennifer Uglow writes of Audley Court as infected "by a sense of probing and questioning" (Briganti 192) but the answers to the questions are revealed, only to be concealed once again.

45. Loesberg regards the genre as being "at least at first…as much a creation of the literary journals who grouped the novels together as it was of the novels themselves". He names the three seminal works as being *The Woman in White*, *East Lynne* and *Lady Audley's Secret*. 115.

46. Hughes speaks of Oliphant's "extended campaign in *Blackwood's* against the author of *Lady Audley's Secret*". 107.

47. *Salem Chapel* and *The Perpetual Curate* aimed for popular success to some effect. In a letter written while at work on *Salem Chapel*, Oliphant announces "I mean to make what one of the poor London painters despised by the Academy calls an 'it [a hit] if I can with this story". Mrs. Harry Coghill, *The Autobiography and Letters of Mrs. M.O.W. Oliphant*. (London: Blackwoods, 1909). 161. Her strategy worked, and she records that *Salem Chapel* did indeed make "a kind of commotion, the utmost I have ever attained to". *The Autobiography of Margaret Oliphant*. Ed. Elisabeth Jay. (Oxford: Clarendon, 1989). 102. However, some contemporaries, such as the *Quarterly Review* critic in 1866, regretted the "sensational portions" of these novels as being "rarely more out of keeping than in her pages", and suggested with distaste "that they would almost appear to have been inserted in deference to the prevailing taste". "Recent Novels: Their Moral and Religious Teaching". *Quarterly Review* 1866, 103—as indeed seems to have been the case.

48. Tamar Heller. *Dead Secrets: Wilkie Collins and the Female Gothic*. (New Haven: Yale University Press), 1992. 95.

49. *Salem Chapel*. (London: Virago, 1986). 285. Herafter "*SC*".

50. Pykett. 10.

51. Transgression is also dissociated from the professional-class May family, and associated with the upstart Wards. Similarly in *Lady Audley's Secret* insanity, sexual deviance, and attempted murder are associated not with the Audleys but with the "vulgar" family from which Lady Audley originates. In *Salem Chapel* the suspected murderess belongs not to an Anglican clergy family but to the inferior class from which non-conformist ministers are represented as originating—"a poor widow's son, educated at Homerton, and an English squire's son, public school and university bred, cannot begin on the same level" (2).

52. Trodd. 3.

Chapter 6

Anatomy of a "Nine Days' Wonder": Sensational Journalism in the Decade of the Sensation Novel

Dallas Liddle

> Let [the novelist] only keep an eye on the criminal reports of the daily newspapers, marking the cases which are honoured with the special notice of a leading article, and become a nine-days' wonder in the mouths of quidnuncs and gossips; and he has the outline of his story not only ready-made, but approved beforehand as of the true sensation cast.
> H.L. Mansel, *Quarterly Review*, April 1863.

The three major genres of writing labelled "sensational" in Great Britain in the 1860s—the sensation novel, the sensation drama, and sensational newspaper journalism—are now usually considered parallel and complementary projects, even as variations on the same cultural theme. Documenting a "direct relationship between the sensation novel and sensational journalism, from the extensive crime reporting in *The Times* and the *Daily Telegraph* to such early crime tabloids as the *Illustrated Police News*" (9), Patrick Brantlinger, for example, has shown how novelists including Charles Dickens, Wilkie Collins, and Charles Reade based characters, incidents, and whole plots on newspaper accounts (9-10). Two of the most frequently cited critical studies of mid-Victorian sensationalism argue that periodicals provided the themes as well as the plot material of sensation novels. In *Deadly Encounters: Two Victorian Sensations*, Richard Altick presses a theory that newspaper coverage of two remarkable crimes in 1861 "set the tone, if not the stage, for the Victorian Age of Sensation" (158), while Thomas Boyle's *Black Swine in the Sewers of Hampstead* advances the thesis that "newspapers were indeed the source (or *a* source) of the troubled and subversive tone of the Sensation novels" (4).

In critical writing about the sensation novel, however, readings of a close or even causal relationship between journalistic and literary "sensation" have to coexist with knowledge that it was hostile and offended journalists. From *Times* reviewers to the higher journalists of the *Quarterly Review, North British Review*, and *Blackwood's* (who first identified and named the "sensation novel" genre, coining the term as a criticism), the most characteristic response of periodical reviewers to the novels of Wilkie Collins, Mary Braddon, and Ellen Wood, considered as a genre, was to condemn them as a dangerous literary and cultural aberration.[1] For Victorian journalists to write "sensational" news stories even as they or their colleagues attacked sensation novels is not a logical contradiction, of course, but it has long been tempting—for some of the original sensation novelists as well as for modern scholars—to conclude that periodicals which printed highly-coloured crime coverage were guilty of either hypocrisy or a lamentable lack of self-awareness when they condemned sensation fiction. This was certainly the position of Charles Reade, who objected to a scathing *Times* review in 1871 on the grounds that *The Times* itself had always provided his best characters, plots, and themes.. "For 18 years, at least, the journal you conduct so ably has been my preceptor, and the main source of my works", Reade told *The Times*. It was "rabid egotism", he continued, for a journalist to claim that "he has any right to put into his leaded type and to amplify, discuss, and dwell upon any subject whatever, and that the poet or the novelist has not an equal right to deal with that subject in fiction" (31 August 1871, 4).[2]

In this much-quoted letter, however, Reade glosses over important differences between the practices of novelists and those of the mid-Victorian journalists who "amplify, discuss, and dwell upon" crime news. Like many other readers and critics who have accepted a simple equivalence between news and the novel, he overlooks the strong strain of anti-subversiveness, even anti-sensationalism, that characterized middle- and upper-class periodicals of the 1860s. Reade's letter to *The Times* is quoted by both Altick and Brantlinger. However, neither scholar mentions *The Times's* response, which was first to deny Reade's credentials as its student ("we cannot help thinking that if he really had stood in that position he would not only have written better novels but better letters") and then categorically to deny Reade's premise that newspapers and novels were discursive equals. "Ours are public, his private, duties. The columns of a newspaper necessarily contain 'facts' every day" which a mother might forbid her daughter to read, but "they do not contain *fictions* like Mr. Reade's" (31 August 1871, 4). Even if *The Times* resorts to sneers and pomposity here, there were crucial differences in the way Victorian news and novel writers approached the treatment of a "sensational" incident or character; differences which seem to me largely dictated by the conventions and generic goals of Victorian journalism.

In what follows, I hope to use a particularly striking example of "sensational" journalism from early 1868 to show that even the most flamboyant crime reports of the Age of Sensation may have been as opposed to the projects of the 1860s sensation novel as many journalists—including Reade's *Times* reviewer—claimed. Newspaper coverage of the six-week disappearance of the Reverend Benjamin Speke in January and February 1868 makes a good test text for comparison of newspaper and novel sensations, since the near-absence of real factual information in the case forced journalists to improvize their narratives and commentary onto the case, essentially creating its plot and characters to fit their own specifications. Unlike more familiar coverage of the Road murder, Palmer poisonings, and deadly Murray and Vidil encounters, the thousands of words of newspaper text produced during the Speke mystery are literally (though not intentionally) a fiction, crafted to match a specific set of generic requirements. This unusual "purity" of the Speke case makes it important and even unique as a document of mid-Victorian newspaper journalism—and an ideal text to compare with the work of the sensation novelists.

I) The Gentleman Vanishes

Benjamin Speke was alive and well, to begin with. Like Jacob Marley, his state of health must be clearly understood, or nothing wonderful can come of his strange story. No body, no bloodstain, no witness—no positive evidence at all—suggested that the Reverend Speke, M.A., of the Church of St. Andrew, Dowlish Wake, Somerset, had come to harm after his arrival in London on 8 January 1868. Yet by early February, the most respected daily and weekly newspapers were holding forth about his disappearance and presumed murder in spine-tingling detail; speculating about the means and opportunities exploited by his killers, and weighing the implications of the crime for public safety and the state of British civilization. Newspaper interest and public alarm quickly reached such a pitch that the disappearance was compared to both the Road murder and the Waterloo Bridge mystery. *The Times* called it a "public alarm", the *Leader* wrote of a national "epidemic of fear". Even a year later, the *Annual Register* for 1868 recorded that the Reverend Speke's mysterious disappearance had "occasioned an almost universal panic among the public".

Considering that this waylaying and murder occurred only in the imaginations of newspaper writers and readers, Richard Altick could hardly ask for a better illustration of his observation, that "murder had a part in [Victorians'] imaginative lives that was far out of proportion to its actual incidence" (281).[3] The case unfolded over six weeks in January and February 1868, reaching a peak of public interest in ten frantic days of press coverage (it is almost literally a "nine days' wonder") between 5 and 15 February. During this period *The Times* alone printed nineteen Speke items, while the *Spectator* estimated that "twenty or thirty thousand minds ... this week have been at work upon the case—minds including the whole body of police, the entire Bar, and the whole body of Clubmen—say, in brief, 5,000 of the quickest wits in Christendom" (8 February 1868, 157).

Before I consider the plot and themes which newspapers chose for this story, its few facts may be briefly summarized. On Wednesday, 8 January 1868, the thirty-eight-year-old Speke arrived in London at Waterloo Station on the 4.33 train from Islington, near his parish in the southwest of England. He was to officiate the next morning at the wedding of a friend, and then return home on a mid-afternoon train. The youngest brother of the celebrated African explorer John Hanning Speke, who had died three years earlier in an equally famous (and mysterious) hunting accident, Benjamin Speke had taken his M.A. in 1853 at Christ Church, Oxford. For the past eleven years he had been vicar of the Church of St. Andrew, Dowlish Wake, where (according to the 1861 *Kelly's Directory of Somerset*) he ministered to a rural flock of four hundred souls, and held a respectable living of four hundred pounds a year. Youthful-looking, with broad shoulders and an athletic build, he was dressed that evening in a black frock coat and overcoat, with a gray striped tie and high top hat with mourning band. He got into a four-wheeled cab at the train station, and was driven in twenty minutes, with his servant and a single piece of luggage, to the house of his brother-in-law at 79 Eccleston Square in West London.

Speke talked to the footman for about ten minutes, and then at about 5.10 p.m. he left the house, this time alone. He told his servant he was going to buy a hat and do some business in Westminster, but would be back to Eccleston Square by 6.30 for an appointment, and would afterwards dine in South Kensington. A hat shop in Warwick Street was just three minutes away, and Speke did indeed buy a hat there, ordering it to be sent to his brother-in-law's house no later than 6.45 p.m. so that he would be there to pay for it. At 5.30 p.m. he left the hat shop. At 7.30 p.m. a workman walking in Birdcage Walk, a promenade along the south of St. James' Park, half a mile to the north, found Speke's hat (the one he had been wearing, not the one he had bought) lying on the ground. When Speke did not return for his appointment or dinner engagement his family became alarmed and called in the Metropolitan police. But no one was found to say they had seen the Reverend Speke after 5.30 p.m. He had apparently vanished without a trace.

Within days the first public text about the Speke case appeared in *The Times*, and with it signs of the various emplotments that participants in the case had begun to consider. An advertisement in the agony column of *The Times* of 11 January offered a reward of three pounds "To Hotelkeepers, Tavernkeepers, and Proprietors of Lodging-Houses—Missing, since Wednesday last, a GENTLEMAN, of about 36 years of age, height 5 ft. 9 in, gray eyes, black hair and whiskers, no moustache or beard". In addressing the advertisement to "Tavernkeepers", this writer implied that Speke was considered to be in voluntary hiding. The text soon changed, however, to suggest that the family was looking for a body rather than a black sheep: by 15 January the advertisement was no longer directed to tavern keepers, and one of the items of information given was the initials on the missing man's linen. Meanwhile, the reward increased from three pounds to five, then to one hundred, and then on 27 January to five hundred pounds. Shortly after this, Speke's brother-in-law Charles Murdoch (signing himself "C.T.M.") sent a letter to *The Times* telling the story of the disappearance, including the date Speke had arrived in London, the time he had disappeared, and the discovery of the hat. Murdoch concluded on a note which made his own dark suspicions plain:

> [A]ny persons who noticed two or three people assembled [in Birdcage-walk] between 6 and half-past 7 o'clock ... or in the parts of Westminster adjacent; any persons who observed two or more dragging or apparently helping another man; in fact, any who saw anything suspicious that evening ... may possibly give the clue which will solve this distressing mystery (3 February 1868, 7).

Speke's own family thus gave the first hints of suspected foul play to journalists and their readers, and a *London Review* writer was later to remark drily that

Speke's relatives "from the commencement ... seem to have been inclined to grasp the difficulty of the situation in a dramatic style" (15 February 1868, 143). London's newspaper community, moreover, was not slow to take up the hint, and Murdoch's letter drew a flood of responses from both readers and professional journalists. Although amateur correspondents and the professionals shared many of the same concerns, differences in tone and purpose are immediately apparent between the letters, signed with initials or pseudonyms, and the anonymous leading articles and news accounts of staff writers.

For most of the amateurs, Speke's disappearance served as a pretext for discussion either of their own missing friends and relatives, or of their own brushes with urban danger. Under titles such as "Perils of the Streets / Another Mysterious Disappearance", *Times* readers learned of a young man who had vanished after arranging a passage for New Zealand, and of a twenty-year-old of "most exemplary character" who had disappeared from Regent Street at two o'clock in the afternoon in July 1863, while the *Western Morning Press* reprinted details of a Bristol disappearance case from December 1866.[4] Although four cases in five years would hardly seem to amount to an epidemic, *The Sunday Times*, among other papers, was ready to assume the worst: "Three or four cases [of disappearance] have been reported during the present week. Are these individuals murdered? Is there some secret association of assassins in London?" (9 February 1868, 2).

While amateur newspaper correspondents spun out the Speke mystery with mysteries of their own, however, other amateur and more professional journalists became concerned with bringing it to a definite resolution. The most characteristic texts of the Speke mystery, in fact, are those of newspaper writers who attempted to analyze and synthesize the few bare facts related by Murdoch into a firm conclusion about the missing man's fate. A remarkable number of writers were willing to take this unpromising detective role, and their letters and leading articles make compelling reading. Almost all of them begin with a plea for clear-headed logic in the weighing of evidence, and reach their grisly conclusions with all the satisfaction and finality of Q.E.D. The first, "An Amateur Detective" (*The Times*, 6 February 1868, 10), announces immediately that "the clue to the mystery must be sought in the character of the gentleman ... It may not be as perfect as 'C.T.M.' describes it, but domestic feelings had evidently a strong hold upon him". Assuming that Speke did not intend to disappear when he arrived in London, but genuinely meant to fulfill his engagements, "as it is almost impossible to disbelieve", it becomes obvious to the Amateur Detective that the case is one of murder for robbery. Speke had paid the cabman at his brother-in-law's door in Eccleston Square, and "it is natural to suppose that some person lurking near that door in the dark may have caught sight of the gold, may have followed Mr. Speke to the hatter's ... and may have tracked him in his further progress". Such a person might then have used a plea for help or charity to convince Speke to follow him into some "haunt" in Westminster, and killed him there. "A brave, athletic man, as the brother of Speke, the traveller, may be supposed to be, is not easily overcome—if attacked in the front; but in a narrow passage, in the dark, what avails strength against a treacherous blow from behind?" As for Speke's body, "[I]s not a dead man's body easily disposed of à la Mannings, under the flags of the cellar?"

On 8 February, however, *Times* correspondent "M.T." refused to accept even the small amount of ambiguity involved in not knowing which cellar Speke might be buried in. "M.T." agrees with "Amateur Detective" in assuming that "this gentleman, "described by his friends as a man in perfect health, of evenly-balanced mind, high religious character, and of a cheerful and amiable disposition … had no intention of going on secret expeditions in Pimlico, or to get drunk, or, in fact, to do anything but what he had said that he was going to do". M.T. finds the rest of the Amateur Detective's scenario unlikely, however. Speke's train to London had arrived late, and he was pressed for time; the odds are that he would not have walked to Westminster, but hailed a cab just after leaving the hat shop. Speke had a married sister living in Queen Square who was out of town at the time of his visit. This house was his most likely destination, M.T. argues, and also the place where he was almost certainly robbed and murdered. "It is no uncommon thing at such a time for servants to leave a house unguarded. Somebody having temporary access to the place may have received him". Not satisfied, perhaps, at the official response to his deductions, M.T. wrote again to *The Times* two days later to ask rather grumpily whether "this house, including its cellars and the shrubbery and offices at the back, has been thoroughly searched not only by Mr. Speke's relatives, but by those who are accustomed to investigate cases of this kind" (10 February 1868, 10).

Two even wilder theories surfaced that same week, the first when a writer in the *Pall Mall Gazette* suggested (no doubt on the basis of the photographs and woodcuts of Speke that had by this time become ubiquitous around London) that "Mr. Speke was very like Mr. Hardy, and might have been killed or kidnapped by Fenians in mistake for the Home Secretary. The likeness granted", commented *The Spectator*, "this seemed plausible; but Mr. Speke was twenty years younger than Mr. Hardy, and dressed in clerical costume" (15 February 1868, 185). A second possibility, even more lurid than Fenian terrorism, was suggested with a touch of Sweeney Todd by the *Manchester Guardian*, which reported (falsely) that the police searching for Speke had found a chopping block attached to the floor in one of the Westminster slums. "By accident one of the police touched a spring, and the top (found to be a lid) flew open, and it was discovered that the sham block was not only hollow, but that it communicated with the main sewer". *The Times* immediately debunked this story, adding that "[i]n the present state of public alarm occasioned by the disappearance, not only of Mr. Speke but of several other persons, such terrible inventions as chopping blocks communicating with main sewers might produce a panic" (13 February 1868, 9).

A much more ingenious and widely noticed[5] article in R.H. Hutton's *Spectator* of 8 February took all this speculation to a new height. Although the "natural presumption when any one disappears suddenly is that he has disappeared voluntarily", *The Spectator* dismissed this presumption in Speke's case as "violently improbable", again on the basis of Murdoch's statement about the missing man's character. "[H]is family hold,—and their evidence on such a point is practically eye testimony, quite as good as any testimony whatever,—he was totally incapable of any heartlessness of the kind". That meant, for *The Spectator*, "the only hypothesis admissable, the only theory, that is, which meets the facts, moral and physical, which have to be taken into the account, is murder, murder of a cool, deliberate kind, murder planned on system, carried out relentlessly, and dictated solely by the expectation of plunder". Speke must have been murdered by a well-organized gang, probably using a decoy hansom cab and chloroform, a gang who harvested victims in the city and drove the bodies to the countryside. These perpetrators were undoubtedly foreigners, since the crime was "too cool, too artistic, too complete, for the conception of the English criminal class" (8 February 1868, 158).

This remarkable article, reprinted in its entirety by *The Times* on 11 February, was in its turn embroidered and developed by other writers. Journalist William Hardman, in a letter to a friend in Australia, described one such elaboration:

> The latest of the many wild and improbable suggestions offered by newspaper correspondents is that [Speke] was polished off in a Hansom cab through the hole in the roof by means of a life-preserver or air-gun, or something quick in its action, silent and deadly. This is a diabolical notion, and will assuredly have the effect of injuring the trade of the Hansom cabs after dark (Hardman 314-15).[6]

While journalist-detectives were thus creating comprehensible and grimly complete narratives of Speke's death, leader-writers in *The Times*, *Sunday Times*, *Illustrated London News*, *Saturday Review*, and other periodicals were just as assiduous in extracting the lessons of the case, and translating it into either an indictment of modern law enforcement, or a call for more sweeping social or administrative change. "If there were nothing in the papers but the advertisements for the discovery of the Reverend B. Speke ... those announcements should be enough to set us all thinking, and to make us abstain from too much boast about our civilization", wrote the *Illustrated London News* on 6 February. "It is really a grave matter that a man can be thus 'spirited away' from the midst of us, and that all the skill of our officials cannot obtain the slightest clue" (143). The *Sunday Times* called for active investigation of the possible London assassination ring, the *Saturday Review* of 8 February went higher up the ladder, calling for a thorough reform of the police system, while *Punch* began to demand the resignation of Sir Richard Mayne, head of the Metropolitan Police. The *Illustrated London News* of 15 February considered the case serious enough to warrant suspension of traditional British liberties and broad new powers for the police, including powers to force social undesirables to emigrate. Even the *London Review*, which ridiculed the amateur detectives of the Speke case in a generally satirical article, entered into the same spirit when it warned of "the unquestionable risk involved in reminding our predatory classes that such things [as Speke's murder] may be done with comparative impunity, and in defiance of every organization of law" (15 February 1868, 143).

Enough threads of agreement run through these attempts at narrative and thematic closure to make the journalistic response to the Speke mystery quite coherent. There were clearly suspicions abroad (though few writers admitted to sharing them) that Speke had disappeared voluntarily, perhaps because of some sexual indiscretion—the *Illustrated London News* called these "the injurious surmizes which occur to the cynical when a country gentleman is missed in London" (15 February 1868). Within a little while, however, and on the basis of no additional information, these suspicions were disavowed almost everywhere, and something approaching a consensus had developed among professional journalists. The shared conclusions of the Speke commentators toward the end of the "nine days' wonder" may even be listed, giving the emplotment and themes chosen by newspaper journalists in a nutshell:

- Speke had not disappeared voluntarily.
- He was dead by violence in the course of a robbery.
- He was the victim of opportunistic professional criminals, who had probably never met or seen him before the crime.
- He had not courted his fate by seeking out a sexual liaison, or committing some other risky behaviour.
- The chief lesson of Speke's case was that some element of the London criminal classes had become ingeniously and ruthlessly predatory, or was now moving to exploit the vulnerability of the upper classes.

It is worth repeating that there was no factual—or even reasonable inferential—basis for any of these conclusions. The "facts" marshalled by the amateur detectives were all vague negatives, most of which did not originate even with the detective police, but with the statements of Speke's brother-in-law that Speke had not been seen, had not left signs of a struggle, had not seemed to be planning any secret escapade, had no known bad habits, and had no family history of insanity. That journalists could use such general premises to draw such particular conclusions about foreigners, Hansom cabs, and chloroform may seem to show primarily that all these writers' Occam's razors were badly in need of sharpening.

More importantly, however, the journalists' conclusions show clearly that for them the preferred choices of plot and theme were essentially different from those a Wilkie Collins or M.E. Braddon would have chosen for "sensational" effect. The random and predatory violence of the Speke "murder" as narrated in *The Times* and *Spectator* is certainly disturbing, but it is significant how tightly the issues the case is allowed to raise have been constrained, and how essentially conventional and conservative a plot has been chosen. Making the Speke case a robbery-murder, and Speke himself an unambiguously innocent victim, the newspapers deliberately excluded consideration of any plot which would have been genuinely "sensational" in sensation novel terms.

II) Making Sense of Sensation

As critics like Jonathan Loesburg have noted, the sensation novelists of the 1860s were dealing with much more challenging and vital issues than random urban violence.[7] It was these issues, in the form of a shared set of plots, themes, and character types, which seem to have made the sensation novel so noxious to so many periodical reviewers. Although the novels have been read and ranked by scholars in many different ways, a brief review of the most generally acknowledged characteristics of sensation fiction will show why the adjective most commonly applied to it is "subversive". First, many sensation novels implied that both personal and class identity in contemporary Britain were fluid and unstable rather than secure, and thus potentially subject to manipulation, misrepresentation, and outright theft.[8] The plots of the most exciting and characteristic sensation novels of the 1860s turn on precisely this issue. Both of the great criminal secrets in Wilkie Collins's *The Woman in White* are manipulations of identity: Sir Percival Glyde has "stolen" his aristocratic identity by concealing his illegitimate birth; to protect his secret, he and his partner Count Fosco steal another identity, that of Glyde's wife Laura. In both Mary Braddon's *Lady Audley's Secret* and Ellen Wood's *East Lynne* the main female characters deliberately disappear, changing their names and class identities in order to begin new lives. Braddon's Helen Talboys, shedding a working-class identity (and husband) eventually becomes Lady Audley, while as Andrew Maunder demonstrates in Chapter 4, Wood's Isabel Vane, moving in the opposite direction, steps down in rank to become the governess Madame Vine.

The second great preoccupation of 1860s sensation novels is the power of aberrant psychological states such as madness, addiction, or (especially) sexual desire to push personality and behaviour outside accepted social norms.[9] Hereditary insanity is the secret of the eponymous Lady Audley, and stands as her own explanation for the arson and attempted murders she commits. The theft of Laura, Lady Glyde's identity in *The Woman in White* is more convincing because her sufferings have caused mental impairment, rendering her still more like the half-sister whose identity has been forced upon her. In the novel Collins was writing in 1868 as the Speke mystery unfolded, *The Moonstone*, the hero Franklin Blake ultimately discovers that he himself (in an opium-altered state of consciousness) committed the crime he has been working to solve. Meanwhile, the edgy depiction of women motivated by sexual desire, always a potential "third rail" for novelists throughout the century, drew down furious critical attacks on novels such as Braddon's *Aurora Floyd*, whose heroine marries a handsome groom.

The third provocative move of the 1860s sensation novelist was to locate these daring treatments of identity, madness, and sexuality squarely in the (implied) reader's own world, the respectable ranks of the middle and upper classes. Henry James said of Wilkie Collins that he had "introduced into fiction those mysterious of mysteries, the mysteries which are at our own doors" (*Nation*, 9 November 1865). H.L. Mansel remarked upon the close identification of the novel's world to the reader's world as one of the most dangerously attractive moves of the sensation novelist:

> [A] tale which aims at electrifying the nerves of the reader is never thoroughly effective unless the scene be laid in our own days and among the people we are in the habit of meeting ....The man who shook our hand with a hearty English grasp half an hour ago—the woman whose beauty and grace were the charm of last night...—how exciting to think that under these pleasing outsides may be concealed some demon in human shape, a Count Fosco or a Lady Audley![10]

The final important thematic choice shared by many sensation novelists was to show the discontinuity and breakdown of established authority, both social and narrative. Francis Paget does not support his claim that sensation novels encourage their readers to "set all authority, parental, social, and political, at defiance" (301) with specific examples. However, Patrick Brantlinger has shown more convincingly how these novels, whether they employed Collins's technique of telling his story through several mystified participants in the plot, or Braddon's of using a coy "omniscient" narrator who withholds information from the reader, resulted in a general "undermining of the narrator's credibility" (15).

This group of shared characteristics seems to have made the sensation novel a remarkably offensive construct to the periodical reviewers of the 1860s. Even many reviewers who were also working novelists, including Margaret Oliphant and G.H. Lewes, generally agreed that use of these themes and techniques produced not only bad and immoral art, but inferior social criticism and incorrect psychology. Human nature and lived experience, they argued, are simply not like this—indeed, two critics of sensation fiction asserted the fundamental falseness of the genre even while the Speke affair was in progress. On 15 February the *Saturday Review* described sensation novels as "narrations of highly improbable events brought about by the agency of utterly impossible characters", while Paget, in an afterword to his polemical (but oddly charming) anti-sensation novel *Lucretia* (15 January 1868), devoutly hoped "that no such women as many of the heroines of the true sensational novel have been represented to be, have ever existed,—so unprincipled, so degraded, so wicked" (309).

Charles Reade had accused *The Times* of radical inconsistency for reporting sensational fact while criticizing sensational fiction, but in fact the preferred assumptions about contemporary society and human psychology made by these literary reviewers, and the assumptions driving contemporaneous crime reports, actually agree remarkably well. Far from sharing the sensation novelists' suspicions about class identity, for example, the journalists who covered the Speke case automatically endorsed the character of a man trebly class-marked as a beneficed clergyman, scion of an old county family, and brother of an heroic African explorer. The *London Review* might complain that the average newspaper correspondent "has little hesitation in theorizing that Mr. Speke was a man of any character that will suit his hypothesis". However, among professionals the spotlessness of Speke's scutcheon was earnestly defended, and his brother-in-law's vague encomium was accepted so completely that no one seems to have thought of asking why, if Speke were such a pattern of virtue, the first advertisements for him in *The Times* had been addressed to tavernkeepers.

In the newspaper writing about Speke the more truly transgressive plots were sometimes mentioned, but they were raised only to be regulated, controlled, and then dismissed. Even the most far-fetched robbery and murder scenarios—as "sensational" as they may seem—have much more in common with the anti-sensational philosophy of Paget and Mansel than with the projects of Collins, Braddon and Wood. Where the sensation novel challenged easy assumptions about class identity and character, reporters and leader-writers instead made Speke's character the primary and unassailable "fact" of the case. As the sensation novel pressed the boundaries of representation in matters of sexuality and morals, journalists asserted that sexual transgression for a man like Speke was practically unthinkable. Where the sensation novel called narrative authority into question, the journalist-detectives who wrote about Speke almost desperately asserted their own power to unravel and explain mysterious events. Finally, where the sensation novel introduced readers to misdeeds "at their own doors", committed by members of their own class, journalists (when, as in this case, they were given a choice) firmly asserted that crime was naturally the province of either foreigners or the British "criminal classes".

One of the richest ironies of the Speke case, therefore, is that at the end of February the newspapers were proven wrong in a way that showed the whole case more sensational—in the novelistic sense—than any journalist had publicly supposed. On 25 February *Times* readers were stunned to learn that Speke had been arrested at Padstow, in Cornwall, dressed as a cattle drover, with 200 pounds in cash and several disguises in his possession. He had been stopped on suspicion of being an escaped criminal from Hull for whom the police were searching. Though he quickly proved he was not that man, his upper-class accent and cattle drover dress were so obviously at odds that he was kept in custody—he had obviously done *something*, until someone thought of asking him if he were the Reverend Speke. He reportedly told police that he had been making a walking tour of southern England, waiting for the search to slacken, at which point he planned to go abroad, work for his living, and preach the Gospel to fellow-labourers. The *Western Morning News* immediately reported the new leading theories among Speke's friends to be: "excessive Biblical study, leading to religious monomania", or "that Mr. Speke had a morbid dread of marriage ... and he acted on the notion of flying from all inducement to commit so repugnant an act" (quoted in *The Times*, 28 February 1868, 10). By 4 March the family's public relations line had been chosen, however, and select physicians reported to *The Times* a diagnosis of "hypochondriasis", aggravated by unsound advice from quack doctors. In the Speke case, then, the sensation novelists enjoyed an appropriate revenge on the journalists.[11] Their favourite themes of unstable class identity and psychosexual transgression had driven a real-life drama, and the hero and victim of the Speke disappearance was revealed to be also its villain, in an appropriately *Moonstone*-ian twist. As for narrative authority, that of the newspapers, at least, was temporarily in tatters.

To the extent that the newspaper detectives had attempted to control and define the issues Speke's story could raise, it makes sense that its unexpected denouement was quickly disposed of by the writers whose hypotheses had proven to be so completely wrong, and that the most common reaction to the news was not gratitude for the life spared, but chagrin and disgust. *The Times,* whose fence-sitting approach had never quite ruled out a voluntary disappearance, could now afford to be smug. Yet the *Sunday Times* (which had called for investigation of a secret assassination ring) quickly claimed to have dismissed the whole issue long before, and wrapped up its coverage with a short paragraph in which the words "contempt" and "fool" figure prominently. Hardman, who had told the story of Speke's disappearance at length to his Australian correspondent, gave a bare two sentences to his reappearance: "You will see that Mr. Speke has been found in Cornwall, and seems to be out of his mind. Confound him, he has upset his own relatives and everyone else". In its final leading articles on the case, *The Times* argued that Speke, as the "author" of "his own mystery", had committed "not only an offence against morality but against the public peace". Moreover, it charged him to be guilty of criminal irresponsibility for "terrifying the more timid part of the population beyond measure" (25 February 1868, 6). *The Leader* asserted that it had been the British public in general (not journalists) who had overreacted to the case, thus making the entire affair another vague symptom of national decline: "amidst the history of national follies, surely the story of an eccentric clergyman who had chosen to hide himself, having alarmed a nation once mighty enough to win the battle of Waterloo, will stand pre-eminent and striking" (*Leader*, 29 February 1868, 378). An honourable exception was Hutton's *Spectator*, which both shared the laugh against itself and approved the erring clergyman's reported goal of leaving his wealthy family and class in order to work and preach as a labourer:

> We never heard of Mr. Speke in his life until Mr. Murdoch published his first letter, and shall be delighted never to hear of him again,—considering that he ought in common decency to have been murdered in a cab by foreigners,—but we would just ask Somersetshire to explain why, being Christian, and repeating litanies, and so on, it considers itself aggrieved? If Mr. Speke really thought, whether under the influence of mental disease or not, that he should be the better for not being Mr. Speke, why was it morally wrong for him to shake off his own identity? (29 February 1868, 253)

A great variety of final lessons for the Speke case were thus quickly chosen by discomfited journalists. Its clearest lesson for modern students of mid-Victorian sensationalism, it seems to me, is that the newspapers which printed voluminous crime coverage, yet repudiated charges of "sensational" writing, were not necessarily either hypocritical or blind to their own discursive practices. Mansel might coin the term "newspaper novels", and perceive the "true sensation cast" in newspaper leading articles, but the similarity of the novelist's and journalist's subject matter masks a crucial opposition of purposes. However outrageous its topics, the mid-Victorian quality press was at least consistent in its mission—

almost its generic imperative—to assert and defend traditional authority, minimize mystery, and dictate decisive action to those in power. The mid-Victorian higher journalist and press observer Fitzjames Stephen had remarked in 1862 on the essential social conservatism of even the most politically liberal papers: "It is easy to trace in every [leading article] proof of the fact that its author has a strong interest in the maintenance of all the chief principles and institutions of society, and a general conviction that alterations in these are rash" (Stephen, 57). Journalist J. Boyd Kinnear went so far as to reduce the mission of newspapers to a catechism: "What is the duty of the press? It is to inform, to advise, and to direct" (325). *The Times* might acknowledge that it reported the existence of immorality in modern society, and that "the wickedness of the age … is occasionally reflected in the columns of the press" (31 August 1871, 4). However, its intention in all this coverage was less to push the boundaries of acceptable representation than to guard them.

As it denied Charles Reade's imputation that it had been either "preceptor" or accessory to his novels, *The Times* argued that "in nothing does [Reade] more clearly show that he is not our pupil than in his impatience of well-merited reproof" (31 August 1871, 4). By the same token, nothing more clearly shows *The Times's* resistance to the subversive spirit of the Age of Sensation than its last comforting, conservative words[12] summing up the lesson and moral of the disappearance of Benjamin Speke: "Great crimes are rare in this metropolis, considering its enormous extent and population, and it may be said confidently that in no great city of the world are the streets more safe to one who goes about his business steadily and soberly" (25 February 1868, 6).

Notes

1. The virulence of anti-sensation novel reviewers has been remarked by many critics, and quoting the more outraged and outrageous passages is a favourite pastime among scholars who study sensation fiction. Commentaries on the Victorian critical furore over the sensation novel, with extended excerpts, are provided by Hughes *passim*, Leckie 112-153, and Altick (*Deadly Encounters* 145-58).
2. In what follows I will generally provide reference information from daily and weekly newspaper articles in the text, rather than referring the reader to a bibliography or endnote. Since virtually all of the newspaper articles about Speke were anonymous or pseudonymous, and many of them shared similar titles ("The Rev. B. Speke" was particularly popular), this method seems the only way to avoid confusion.
3. Altick does not notice the case, however, in any of his major works on sensationalism. Speke's disappearance has in fact become extremely obscure; the only secondary source I have found (outside the *Annual Register*) to discuss it is a popular collection called *Strange Disappearances*, by Elliott O'Donnell (New York: Dodd, Mead and Co., 1928) which recounts the story of the disappearance and reappearance, with imperfect accuracy, from the original London newspaper accounts.
4. "W.D.", "The Rev. B. Speke", *The Times* 7 February 1868. 5 ; "H.", "The Rev. B. Speke", *The Times* 13 February 1868, 7; "Perils of the Streets / Another Mysterious Disappearance". *Western Morning Press*, reprinted in the *The Times* 11 February 1868. 4.
5. The *London Review* said that the *Spectator* had done its detective work "cleverly and gracefully", and *The Times*, in addition to the compliment of reprinting the story, later noted that its theory accounted for the facts "very prettily". The *Pall Mall Gazette*, on the other hand, was critical of the piece.
6. I am indebted to Patrick Leary for discovering the passages about Speke in the Hardman papers, and generously sending me their entire text by email.
7. Loesberg points out that very little happens randomly in true sensation novels, and that their plots follow an almost deterministic "principle of inevitable sequence depicted alternatively as either a chain made of links or as a providential unfolding" (117).
8. A thorough and provocative discussion of the sensation novels' treatment of class fear and class identity is provided by Loesberg, who reads it in the context of the contemporary debate over the 1867 Reform Bill. Another angle is explored by Ronald Thomas, who discusses identity in the sensation novel in terms of the increasingly powerful Victorian professional discourses of law and medicine. Winifred Hughes (20-21) approaches the question of identity by pointing out consistent patterns of doubling among the main characters of sensation novels. In her reading of *Lady Audley's Secret*, Katherine Montweiler provocatively suggests that the book served almost as an instruction manual for women wishing to transgress class boundaries.

9. For a consideration of the significance of altered mental states in sensation fiction, see Patrick Brantlinger and Thomas 504-5. A thorough consideration of the metaphor of drug addiction both within sensation novels, and as it was applied by critics to the culture of novel-reading, is Leckie 112-153.

10. [H.L. Mansel]. "Sensation Novels". *The Quarterly Review.* Volume 115, 226, 1863. 488-489.

11. Unfortunately, the timing of the Speke case prevented some of them from appreciating this "sensation" and its outcome as they might otherwise have done. Charles Dickens was overseas on his last American tour during the whole of the Speke affair, though he must certainly have learned about it, from newspapers or friends, upon his return. It is at least interesting that the book he began immediately afterwards was *The Mystery of Edwin Drood.* Wilkie Collins, though ordinarily a close reader of newspaper sensations, seems to have been fully concerned during this time with writing *The Moonstone*, and with his mother's final illness; his published letters take no notice of Speke's disappearance.

12. The English language may narrowly have escaped a more permanent reminder of Speke's escapade in the form of a new verb. If the word had caught on, the OED would probably now cite the *London Journal* 42 (1 July 1868, 462):

    > SPEKED. – The following dialogue occurred between a lady and her husband, on the gentleman's returning home unusually late one night, and reproaching his wife with unnecessary anxiety at his absence:— "I was almost afraid that you had spoken".—"Spoken, my dear! What can you possibly mean?"—"Well, I suppose it is ungrammatical to say so; but it occurred to me, dearest Alfred, that you had *Speked*".

Chapter 7

The Inside Story: Crime, Convicts and Careers for Women

Barbara Onslow

The causes and consequences of crime have always been a staple subject for the journalist. In nineteenth-century periodicals these themes became enmeshed, on the one hand, within the provision of "entertaining information" for the consumption of an expanding reading public, and on the other within various agendas for social reform. My primary concern here is to examine how mid-century women activists and reformers, who engaged in journalism, harnessed the press to argue the cause of that sector of the prison population publicly regarded as particularly depraved—the female convict. In so doing they conflated the specific plea for changes in the treatment of women prisoners with their much larger demands for expansion of employment opportunities for women. But just as their ideas on prison reform were contextualized by their own wider political or feminist beliefs, so their articles and newspaper leaders drew upon a broader debate on the treatment of criminals generally, and were influenced by the dynamics of an expanding and diversified press.

Women journalists had to convince *male*, as well as female, readers of the justice of their views. It may be helpful, therefore, to offer an indication of the context in which they had to make their voices heard. This chapter, therefore, begins by indicating the variety of press treatments of crime, criminality and prison conditions, and the narrative structures developed to attract readers. The popularity of reports of crime, trials and executions in the Victorian press is well attested. Whilst some of this might justify itself as straightforward recounting of current events in the public interest, it also exploited personal fears and moral anxieties, and appealed to a more salacious taste for sensation. As Knelman has shown, women convicted of murder provided ready copy for lurid accounts of crimes and their, often grisly, resolutions.[1] Newspapers regaled the public not only with details of gruesome killings and court cases, but with vivid descriptions of the last hours and minutes of the condemned. Nor were such accounts of legal retribution restricted to hangings. Thus in the *Echo* of 6 January 1869 readers learnt of a flogging of three garotters who received 25 lashes in addition to penal servitude for life. "[M]ore dangerous prisoners" were "enabled" to witness the punishment as two of the men yelled for mercy whilst nineteen-year-old Solomon Robinson "bore his thrashing with a surprising amount of fortitude and endurance".

Such was the appetite for sensational crimes, it was presumed, that journalists used the trope of the poisoner to engage readers' interest in less publicized but more widespread horrors. Frances Power Cobbe once wrote a leader on bad cooks which was headlined "Female Poisoners of the Nineteenth Century" and Harriet Martineau ensured the agreement of her readership by opening one of her leaders with expressions of public shock at the prevalence of "the administration of narcotics" by working-class mothers to their babies. The thrust of this piece turned out to be the "more fearful and more shocking" revelation that "lack of a suitable milk supply" killed many more infants than maternal poisoners ever did (17 September 1864).

Alongside the sensational reports, serious responses to the problem of what to do with crime and the criminal surfaced regularly. Only a month after its report of the flogging, *The Echo* carried a leader by Frances Cobbe on "The Proper Treatment of Criminals" (6 February 1869).[2] Throughout the century the press debated questions of injustice within the legal system and argued for penal reform. Such suggestions for improvement were, however, often embedded in arguments for other social advances in particular those for more widespread education and training. The essays explored here, whether sensational narrative or serious polemic, exemplify these diffusions of the theme of the treatment of prisoners.

Though at one end of the spectrum, the higher journalism contributors might engage with issues of social reform in the reviews, and at the other hack reporters wallow in lurid details of murder in the penny press, it would be wrong to imagine that the sensation-mongers and the activists never met. Middle-brow journals could provide both titillation and debate. Essays on life in prisons at home and abroad, presented as the "inside story" or "exotic" real-life experience, proved popular right through the century. Some of these were informative on the penal system or the conditions in prisons, but entertainment was an equally important ingredient. Emphasis upon human interest, dramatic narrative structures, and the interview formula, with its gossipy tone, were characteristic of the "New Journalism"[3] of the final decades. Common formulæ were the journalist's guided tour by friendly police officers, pioneered by Charles Dickens, or the confessional tale where the narrator is exonerated from obloquy, having been mistakenly charged or convicted. Even when presented under the guise of authentic personal experience there was a frisson of horror and elements of the gruesome, or grotesque gallows humour in many of these narratives. *Cassell's Saturday Journal* enlightened and amused those who enjoyed reading about prison life with a stream of short "inside story" articles in which the documentary was fused with the sensational, the factual with the anecdotal and entertaining.[4] In their permutations of stories of crime and its penalties, journalists were almost as enterprising as the prisoners whose exploits they exposed. What these narratives share is the combination of amusement allied to the justifying claim of authenticity: the first-person narrative, the "insider's" viewpoint, secrets and revelations.

Even the highly respectable 1890s *Windsor Magazine*,[5] alongside insights into the Court of Queen Victoria and photographic glimpses of the young German emperor's sumptuous yacht, ran an illustrated two-part narrative "What Prison Life is Really Like By One Who has Tried It". The reader whose appetite for royal gossip is satisfied with details of the Kaiser's bedstead—"of aluminium; ... hung with dove-coloured satin"[6] will find "Prison Life" seeks to satisfy a similar, if more morbid, curiosity about the life among the "criminal riff-raff". Its narrator purports to be a man of the professional class embarking upon his experience on remand—and briefly as a convict—rather in the nature of an adventure. He details prison fare, cell furnishings, the embarrassment and degradation of prison routines, and the hardships of the treadmill and picking oakum. Since he is innocent, he appeals, securing simultaneously his rapid release and a happy ending. In that same volume a report on the remnants of thieves' dens in Paris draws upon the rhetoric of sensation fiction: the descent into the dark Parisian labyrinths "like Dante into the depths of misery and crime", in the company of "a distinguished member of the French detective police", redolent of those forays of Sherlock Holmes into the secret haunts of robbers and ruffians.[7]

However, recognition of the public's interest in "true" revelations, and journalistic experiments with interviews, had occurred much earlier. Forty years on, the London underworld Charles Dickens had visited with Inspector Field at the mid-century[8] was alleged to have vanished, but many of the *Windsor's* details of prison life echo *Household Words*' "Lodged in Newgate".[9] As "Conductor" of *Household Words* Dickens tried to ensure through vigorous editing that his journal's imaginative blend of instruction and entertainment maintained its hold over an often fickle readership.[10] *Household Words* both popularized serious pamphlets and carried dramatic stories about criminals. Dickens aimed to have his contributors attack such issues in as lively a manner as his own journalism did. Frederic Hill's "Crime: Its Amount, Causes and Remedies" was transmuted into "In and Out of Jail". In "Among the Shallows" the inequalities of sentencing policy, juxtaposing a long series of absurd divergences for seemingly similar offences, were drawn from official documentation, but the justices themselves were satirized as descended from Shallow himself—"seven years' transportation is the lowest figure at which he can be said to do business with any degree of pleasure...".[11]

In an account of a visit to a convict Stockade and prison ship in Australia the rhetoric of Richard H. Horne's "Convicts in the Gold Regions" might come from a novel. At night a "cold wind blows and drizzling rain falls... A jingling of chains is heard as the several gangs pass across the yard, then a sound of the drawing of bolts, then silence". The narrator's dramatic image of the "suppressed ferocity" in the faces of these "subdued human tigers" pent in their dormitories is destined to be disappointed; but when they appear at the muster the following morning "I am persuaded there is not one good face among them...Beneath that silent outwardly subdued air, there is the manifest lurking of fierce, depraved, remorseless spirits..." The sense of fear and alienation is thus reasserted.

Almost all the criminals "have originated in England. They had their chief experience and training at home". Former juvenile inmates of Parkhurst graduate to Pentonville, and are finally transported to Van Diemen's Land or Norfolk Island. "At each of these places, and in all their prisons, at home and abroad, the pet system of penal training and reform in use at the period has been tried, and all have failed". Though we are briefly told that many "do really reform, and lead decent lives" progressing over the years from solitary confinement in the hulks to a ticket of leave, there is little empathy with the convicts. At one level the article is informative about prison conditions. Despite some sense of the "painful and unresting" work of the Superintendent, Mr. Barrow, (apparently adept at providing monosyllabic answers to importuning journalists), the prevailing tone is atmospheric–the bleakness, cells "like clean dens for wild beasts", the imagery of iron-bolts, chains and the sounding of the Stockade bell which controls the prisoners' lives—"the spell of a sort of iron fate, a doom with an iron tongue" a world where the sudden arrival of a magpie in the prison yard is "the only relief" to the oppressive atmosphere. It is the stuff of the sensation novel.[12]

The shock tactics and polemics that characterize the journalism of *Household Words* provide a spectacular example of how mid-century magazines could successfully exploit the popular press to engage in the spectrum of debates around social reform and legislation. However, of course Dickens was not alone in recognizing the press as a channel for influence.[13] It was within this spirited climate that female activists and radicals found a platform for agitation over a specific issue—penal reform as it related to women. These women journalists may not have sought to entangle their subjects in the trappings of sensation fiction—though in some of her snappy leaders for the *Echo* Cobbe's drama comes near to it. They did, however, enmesh them in complex ways as they urged other reforms within a much larger social agenda on the position of women. Thus, feminist challenges to the inequitable treatment of women under the provisions of the Contagious Diseases Acts were overtly related to women's suffrage. Arguments about the dual standards these acts applied to female prostitutes and their male clients were linked to the equally double standards applied to husbands and wives joined in respectable matrimony.[14] In the late fifties and early sixties humanitarian concern for the female prison population was identified with yet another agenda—the campaign for increased employment opportunities for women. This issue, too, was at times linked to that of female influence through philanthropic enterprise, envisaged as incorporating the duty to forward feminist concerns and as self-fulfilment. Motives were often intertwined. Cobbe may have seen, as Barbara Caine suggests, her desire for change in the law relating to "young criminals as paupers" as arising directly from her voluntary work with Mary Carpenter, and leading to her support for Women's Rights,[15] yet when she promulgated such ideas as a professional journalist she expected to be paid professional rates. Mary Carpenter hoped that women attracted to work in reformatories for money would also gladly give "a zeal and devotion" not to be bought by gold alone; indeed she believed that the problem of female convicts was so deep-seated that this "foul understratum" could never be removed from society by law alone: it required the co-operation of government and the voluntary efforts of committed Christian women.[16]

Harriet Martineau came of an earlier generation than the activists of the *English Woman's Journal,* but her writings like those of the Langham Place women[17] were important catalysts in aiding the social shift to the acceptance of career women. Her long-standing involvement with the Unitarian periodical the *Monthly Repository* is itself a concrete illustration of the crying need for "remunerative" employment for women. Her first published essays appeared in it, the second "On Female Education" in 1823. She was a regular (unpaid) contributor during the late 1820s, but following the failure of their late father's business the Martineau daughters had to earn their daily bread. Harriet's deafness naturally precluded the most obvious genteel occupation—governessing—and, although she was an excellent needlewoman, writing must have seemed preferable on both financial and intellectual grounds.

Like Dickens and his staff, Martineau became adept at the journalistic strategy of taking some tract, society report or speech, or an article from another paper, and reworking the material as a peg for her own views. She had used this method early in her career for *Monthly Repository* pieces such as "Prison Discipline"[18] long before illness forced her to produce her work for the *Daily News* far from London, almost from her invalid's couch. By then, of course, this methodology was a necessity. An admirer of Elizabeth Fry's work,[19] crime, punishment and prison issues were amongst those causes she espoused in her prolific journalistic output (she produced over 1,600 leaders for the *Daily News* alone). Thus in 1853 she addressed the subject of reformatories and juvenile delinquency in four separate *Daily News* leaders. It turned up again in more leisurely style in the prestigious quarterly the *Edinburgh Review*, "Our Convict System" appearing in January 1863 and "Female Convicts" in 1865.

"Prison Discipline" appeared in 1832—the year of publication of the first volume of *Illustrations of Political Economy*. Given its appearance in a religious paper Martineau relates the justification for punishment by the State to Christian moral principles. It should not be gratuitously harsh, and it should be universal in its application. The length of time spent in jail before trial should not depend upon the part of the country in which the defendant lived.[20] She deplores the tendency of magistrates to avoid the responsibility of granting bail "so that stealers of hedge-stakes and boys guilty of street-rows are shut up in a school of corruption for weeks" because punishment should also have *reformation* as its aim. The main thrust of her paper is in fact to locate prison reform within the broader social argument for universal education in a civilized country. Prison reform is already here linked to questions of education and labour, though in relation to the *imprisoned.*

Martineau thought female prisoners had both the right and the duty to earn their keep, just as she believed that society should take responsibility for the punishment and reformation of its own offenders. She made this explicit in her leader on transportation (22 September 1864). Objecting to the practice of exporting criminals to Australia—"we cannot shift the charge of our criminals upon anybody else", she argued that "hard labour—the real thing and not the sham—" was the best discipline for criminals, claiming that female convicts, too, would benefit *if* the right kind of work could be found. "Useful, necessary, self-supporting public works" were what she had in mind, though what these might be are not specified. Martineau was later shocked by the reluctance of magistrates to use the provisions of the Reformatory Acts to help rehabilitate juvenile offenders, and welcomed Lord Stanley's endorsement of Manchester's new Discharged Prisoners' Aid Society. Yet she noted that women prisoners were not mentioned, and, recalling the recent closure of a refuge for discharged female prisoners, urged that, despite the perceived problems of women convicts, it was essential to try to attempt their rehabilitation. There was evidence from Ireland of success in their entering domestic service. Women convicts particularly needed help, since their "chances in life, if left to themselves, are incomparably inferior to those of men in any depth of disgrace".[21]

In drawing attention to the imperative need to help such women not in spite of, but *because of* their peculiar depravity, Martineau was reiterating Carpenter's views. Though the female sex was considered less criminal than the male, persistent female convicts were thought to be more hardened, depraved and, being prone to violent uncontrollable outbursts, more intractable than the men, Yet their baleful influence upon society was much greater since to their care was "exclusively committed the early nurture of the young" and the formation of the characters of the coming generation.[22]

Martineau's attitude to the management of criminals reflects her own strong sense of reciprocal rights and duties. Though she believed in women's right to earn an independent living, her sense of filial duty had caused her at the age of twenty-seven to return, at her mother's behest, from London to Norwich.[23] Martineau's polemicizing of the writings of others was symptomatic of the ways in which other women turned the periodical press into a platform for their causes. She became herself an inspiration to younger women like Barbara Bodichon and her friend Bessie Parkes.

Topics reiterated in the press captured the public imagination. As the staid *Quarterly* remarked in 1855, opening a review of five books and pamplets on juvenile delinquents, "There is hardly, perhaps, a subject, the war excepted, which occupies a larger share of attention at the present time than Reformatory Schools. To use a familiar expression, they are becoming quite the rage..."[24] Even Beeton's *Englishwoman's Domestic Magazine* took up the theme. Maria Rye, in an article "London Prisons and Female Prisoners", which drew upon work by Mayhew and Redgrave, publicized to middle-class women recent statistics showing an increase in female criminals, describing the "hardened and callous condition of these poor outcasts" considered to be "fifty times more troublesome to manage than men". Shocked though she is, Rye nevertheless attracts her readers to her subject by recounting, as *Cassell's* was to do decades later, anecdotes of of their ingenuity in devising stiffeners for their stays and whitening for their complexion; and, more seriously, by drawing attention to the social circumstances of young criminals—a high incidence of being orphaned or left with a step-parent. "Poor girls are not naturally more vicious than their richer sisters", but they enjoy less protection. Though expressing awareness of the complexity of the problem, she urges as a solution the extension of industrial schools, and (unlike Martineau) vehemently advocates emigration.[25] It was this possibility of a platform that led Bessie Rayner

Parkes and Barbara Bodichon to set up their own "Special Periodical" for women's issues. By the time Bodichon founded the *English Woman's Magazine* in 1858 she was committed to expanding women's education and work (as well as feminist causes such as suffrage and property law reform). A year later Parkes articulated one of their aims as reiterating ideas, systematically urging them via a monthly journal, until they filtered down into common currency. The middle class had to be convinced before reforms would come into being:

> Who controls the workhouses? the guardians of each parish; chiefly tradesmen and shopkeepers. Who manages hospitals? Boards of officials who are little likely to have leisure for perusing the "comparative physiology" of hospitals at home and abroad. Where does the power in prisons ultimately rest, except in the persons of members of the government and members of parliament, who are too busy to digest blue-books which do not bear on their own particular bill.[26]

Here she was targeting the *men* who had philanthropic and political power. Those who could effect change were too busy with other affairs to study questions outside their (very narrow) sphere. Shopkeepers, tradesmen and board officials, were largely, and Members of Parliament exclusively, male. It was left to women to present the case for reform. Women, however, were needed on the active, as well as the philosophical front, and this very provision of useful work, so Parkes argued, would in itself *prevent* crime. Bodichon's pamphlet of 1857, *Women and Work*, had argued:

> We hear cries that the world is going wrong for want of women...Work-houses, Prisons, Schools, Reformatories, Penitentiaries, Sanatoriums are going to rack and ruin for want of them ... One great corresponding cry rises for a suffering multitude of women, saying, "We want work" ...There is no way of aiding governesses or needlewomen, but by opening more ways of gaining livelihoods for women. It is the most efficacious way of preventing prostitution".[27]

In this context the idea of a new career for women, that of prison wardress, was conjectured. The word "career" in relation to work for educated women does not emerge as a common term in relation to women's work until much later in the century, but it was precisely what was being advocated in this identification of humanitarian concern for the female prison population with the campaign for increased training and remunerative employment for educated women.

The Times summed up the conflation of these two debates on November 17, 1859 when it referred to the "symptom of radical innovation" in the current argument, "that women in workhouses, women in prisons, women in reformatories, and women in sickness, do imperatively require female attendance and supervision; that for lack of this superintendence rising female generations are viciously disposed, and that *by excluding women from such places of trust and authority we not only deprive the sex of remunerative occupation, but work infinite damage to the whole social body*". (*The Times*, 17 November 1859. My italics)

Bodichon's paper had had an impact, as is indicated by *The Times*' view of the moral supervisory element as something striking. The connection between impoverished, unemployable governesses and prostitution links the female *criminal* with the need for steady employment, just as Martineau had done, and others continued to do. Mary Carpenter, for instance, argued in 1863 from the experience of the system in the Irish Mountjoy Female Prison and the follow-on refuges for discharged prisoners that a system of discipline, with staged promotions to more privileged regimes, education and industrial training, still needed an "after-care" system if reformed convicts were to obtain regular work and not sink back into former habits on their release.[28] But the *EWJ* went further. Under Anna Jameson's influence the journal had put its main emphasis on education and employment issues, rather than upon the highly contentious suffrage question which Bodichon originally favoured. Jameson, though an early advocate of education and employment for women, and by this time an established writer, was never a radical feminist, and though, in her rôle as "adopted aunt" and mentor to the young founders of the journal, she offered constant encouragement, she also counselled restraint.[29] From the journal's inception, articles linked the need for proper *training* for matrons and female officers not only to the more constructive management of female prisoners but equally to the desires of educated women for wider access to careers. The first of Parkes's articles "What Can Educated Women do?" published in the December 1859 issue, opened with the passage from *The Times*. The article was designed to make practical suggestions for potential new professional fields for women, and dealt with hospitals, prisons, reformatories, workhouses, education (for example, inspectors of girls schools), factories (as superintendents), and emigration (as ship-board matrons and land-based welcome superintendents.) As Parkes had no extensive personal knowledge of the "practical working" of such institutions she drew heavily on that of Anna Jameson, Florence Nightingale, Mary Carpenter,[30] Louisa Twining and Caroline Chisholm. Her section on Prisons relied largely upon Anna Jameson's published lectures on *Sisters of Charity* and the *Communion of Labour*[31] and included in a footnote her letter to Lord John Russell, referring in complimentary terms to the arrangements at Brixton and Fulham where the female prisons were entirely managed by women (apart from chaplains and medical officers). Parkes opens her section on prisons by pointing out that, despite legislation permitting the appointment of female matrons and officers, these positions did not attract, and therefore did not "produce the effects" of, *educated* labour because no provision had been made for proper training, and the qualifications for the jobs were not properly defined. This situation is contrasted unfavourably with Jameson's account of female prisons run by religious orders in Piedmont, where the managers were directly responsible to the government. There is no claim either by Jameson or Parkes to advocate any particular prison system, but only to urge the "due admixture of female influence and management". The quotations from official reports and Jameson's visits identify the success of the experiments in terms of the governance of the institutions and the relationship between male and female managers (chaplains and medics were again male). This was one of mutual aid, respect, and interchange of experience. Jameson noted that female managers were not subordinate to the men, and the prisoners benefited from the social and moral effects of an arrangement where soldiers and police officers were no longer needed to enforce discipline. Crucially the professional expertise of the religious is highlighted. One dispensary sister had two years of medical training and three years in the "general duties of her vocation". To this evidence Parkes adds a note on the success of the extensive use of female officials in the Irish prison system.

Parkes' article acknowledges that the involvement of religious orders might not appeal in a Protestant country (though her Hospital section attempts to dispel any sense of sectarian bias by reference to the work of Lutheran deaconesses in Germany and to the ladies of St John's House, Westminster). She justifies her use of these pioneering models by emphasizing that the topics are discussed not from a charitable, benevolent, standpoint but from an "*economical point of view*" (her italics). Religious communities "relieve the labour market"; women without a dowry to cover their life-long maintenance give the community their labour instead. Indeed many of these nuns "represent a class equivalent to our wretched superannuated governesses". Her concluding section on the essential need for organized training pushes for the acceptance by the powers-that-be for the professionalization of what she calls "social labour". She counters arguments that training for women is wasted because they will marry by referring to the success of the training of certificated female teachers, and by pointing out that social professions need, not young girls, but mature women—married, widowed or single—possessing "firmness, discretion and experience of life". It is, of course, the *men* in charge who need to recognize this.[32]

Parkes' own paper to the National Association for the Promotion of Social Science, published in the *EWJ* a year later, drew on something of which she did have direct experience, and bore eloquent testimony to this need for training. She described a year's experience with the *Journal's* Employment Register, intended as a modest gesture to place the occasional qualified reader as a teacher or matron, but resulting in the offices being inundated with ladies seeking work and advice. On one day alone they had twenty more-or-less educated "ladies" applying. They did *not* want to be governesses. They wanted to be something else—but what? Instead of a few hand-picked, trained women who might be found "places of trust" among subscribers (many of whom were acquaintances) Parkes was assailed by "hundreds of women neither well-trained nor picked, outnumbering any demand by 99 per cent". She reiterated the need to train women for "moral superintendence" and other kinds of social work, but saw no evidence of progress. Ladies whose natural abilities might make them competent holders of posts in penal institutions and reformatories could not be placed in such posts. Why not? They "do not ask for them, have little idea of the kind of work, and ... would probably fail in doing it if they tried; *because they have had no training*" (her italics).[33] Isabella Fyvie Mayo's recollection of her time working in that Employment Office endorses this depressing image of "feminine misfortune, misery and incapacity". Mainly middle-class and middle-aged with "a deadly gentility about them ... They were ready to do anything. They could do nothing".[34] Since she also saw many cast-off governesses it is not surprising that so few impoverished ladies fancied that profession.

Bessie Parkes' use of an anonymously published book purporting to be reminiscences of Brixton and Millbank jails by an experienced prison matron testifies to her dominant interest in women's employment.[35] She opens her article "Female Life in Prison" by connecting it to the lives of her readers through her own childhood memories of Millbank. She had played near it as a little girl and recalls the oddity of going to an elegant dinner-party in Victoria Street, and chancing to glance through a window at its "frowning walls, brooding like Nemesis over our gay and kindly social life". But her readers are not to indulge in the horrors of Newgate. Rather than dwell upon the book's anecdotes of prison life she reinforces the career aspect by concentrating on the wardress's conditions of service: A salary of £35 per annum on entry with a deduction of 3s.4d. a month for the uniform but a one pound a year rise, and promotion possibilities, eventually to principal matron, at £50 per annum with increases of one pound, ten shillings and a life pension after ten years' service, "far more favourable" she comments than most women's work, but particularly arduous in its duties—long hours averaging fourteen a day and the fourteen day annual holiday allowance eaten into by the not infrequent days off for sickness. Robustness and muscular power were necessary female attributes here. Perhaps aware that this might seem even less congenial than the miseries of governessing she urged readers interested in "the organisation of the higher and more responsible kinds of female labour" to read this chapter alongside the work of Mrs Jameson.

The *Journal* was way ahead of its time in suggesting the prison service as a career field for educated women.[36] In proposing that "social labour" be professionalized it was implying a more fundamental shift in women's rôle than the co-operative efforts of voluntary and paid workers which social activists like Carpenter advocated. However, if the dramatic changes Parkes hoped for did not materialize in the revolutionary way she envisaged, her journal nevertheless played an important and radical part in the re-formatting of the debate. Though on specific topics and in proposing solutions these Victorian women journalists naturally differed collectively they valorized the views of women in addressing key social issues, overt and repressed, facing their society,—questions of the moral health of the nation, the control of prostitution, the persistence of a criminal underclass, the management of the young unemployed, and the reformation of, to use Carpenter's term, "a pariah class" of female convicts—questions which tapped into fears of the destabilization of society. In popularizing official reports; in drawing on women's own investigations and voluntary experience; in questioning existing ways of both assisting the poor and punishing the criminal as virtually designed to reinforce the evils they attempted to redress they altered the nature of the debate.[37] In linking these issues to the submerged one of the *women* convicts with whom, Carpenter complained, "no one seems to concern himself", and embedding them within the larger question of employment for women, they made a significant contribution to the cause of women's rights.[38] Finally, in the very achievement of writing *about* and publicizing the condition of their fallen sisters, they exemplified the ideals they set for other women.

Notes

1. The level of interest and range of concerns may be gauged by reference to Palmegiano, E. M. *Crime in Victorian Britain: An annotated Bibliography from Nineteenth-Century British Magazines.* (Westport CT and London: Greenwood Press, 1993) which lists over 1, 600 articles culled from 45 periodicals from 1824-1900. Knelman, Judith. *Twisting in the Wind: The Murderess and the English Press.* (Toronto: University of Toronto Press, 1998).
2. Cobbe began leader-writing for the *Echo* at the end of 1868, continuing until 1875.
3. W.T. Stead and George Newnes were proponents of this style. For a succinct account of the "New Journalism" see Stokes, John. *In the Nineties.* (London: Harvester, 1989).
4. anon. "How Gaol-Birds Employ their Time: Work Done Behind Prison Walls". *Cassell's Saturday Journal* 6 March 1895. 486. ; anon. "When Prisoners are "Turned Over": Surprising Finds that Often Follow". *Cassell's Saturday Journal* 19 February 1896. 444.; anon. "Clever Work Done by Prisoners: Convict Labour, Seen and Unseen". *Cassell's Saturday Journal* 26 August 1896. 995. ; anon. Strange Doings in Prison Cells: Side-Lights on a Silent World". *Cassell's Saturday Journal* 4 September 1895. 1013.
5. Its co-founder was Flora Klickman who was eventually to edit another highly respectable magazine, the *Girls' Own Paper.*
6. Flora Klickmann. "At Sea with the German Emperor". *Windsor Magazine* II. July-December (1895), 499-503.
7. anon. "What Prison Life is Really Like by One Who Has Tried It: I 'Before Trial'". *Windsor Magazine* II. July-December (1895). 75-80. anon. "What Prison Life is Really Like by One Who Has Tried It: II 'One Month's Hard'". *Windsor Magazine* II. July-December (1895). 197-201. Major Arthur Griffiths. "Criminals in Private Life". *Windsor Magazine* II.July-December (1895). 293-9.
8. Charles Dickens. "On Duty with Inspector Field" *Household Words.* 1851.
9. anon. "Lodged in Newgate". *Household Words* VIII.3 September 1853 (1854). 1-6. Remand prisoners seemingly endured a tougher experience than in the provincial jail of the 1890s. Prisoners were locked in cages even in the chapel and bereft of the luxury of furniture in the cells. The food that could be purchased was more limited. Casts of the features of men who had been hanged adorned the Ordinary's room below the chapel. Some of the warders are, however, presented as considerate in performing their duties.
10. His letters to his assistant Wills are full of instructions to this end.
11. Charles Dickens, Henry Morley, and W.H. Wills. "In and Out of Jail". *Household Words* VII. 14 May (1853). 241-64. James Payn and Henry Morley. "Among the Shallows". *Household Words* VIII. 5 November (1853). 233-5.
12. Richard H. Horne "Convicts in the Gold Regions". *Household Words* VIII. Saturday September 17 (1853). 49-54. Many ticket-of-leave men apparently headed for the gold diggings, returning to crime when expectations failed. It is worth recalling that Margaret Oliphant viewed Dickens's *Great Expectations*,

with its horrific atmospheric visions of the 'hulks' and of convict life, as a sensation novel.

13. The radicalism of the *Daily News* survived its brief sortie with Dickens, running Martineau's vigorous leaders long after Dickens severed his connection.
14. See Philippa Levine. *Feminist Lives in Victorian England: Private Roles and Public Commitment*. (Oxford: Basil Blackwell, 1990) on the parallels between the Contagious Diseases Acts and the Matrimonial Causes Act. Levine cites examples of suffrage journals such as the *Women's Penny Paper* and the *Women's Suffrage Journals.*
15. Barbara Caine. *Victorian Feminists*. (Oxford: Oxford University Press, 1992). 106-7.
16. Mary Carpenter. "On the Treatment of Female Convicts". *Fraser's Magazine* 67 January (1863). 31-46.
17. For accounts of the Langham Place activities see Theodora Bostick. "The Press and the Launching of the Women's Suffrage Movement, 1866- 1867". *Victorian Periodicals Review* XIII.4 (1980). 125-131. S.R. Herstein. "The Langham Place Circle and Feminist Periodicals of the 1860s". *VPR* XXVI,1.Spring (1993). 24-28. Sheila R. Herstein. *A Mid-Victorian Feminist, Barbara Leigh Smith Bodichon*. (New Haven: Yale, 1985). Pam Hirsch. *Barbara Leigh Smith Bodichon, 1827-1891, Feminist, Artist and Rebel*. (London: Chatto & Windus, 1998).
18. "Prison Discipline" 1832 drew on the 8th *Report of the Committee of the Society for the Improvement of Prison Discipline* and a series of articles *Punishment of Death.*
19. Susan Hoecker-Drysdale. *Harriet Martineau: First Woman Sociologist*. (Oxford, New York: Berg, 1992).
20. For example, a year in one county, six weeks in London.
21. *Daily News* Jan 22, 1866. First leader.
22. Carpenter loc.cit. 36.31. Carpenter was by now drawing on her on experience with reformatory girls and prison visits, as well as official reports. See also Maria Rye cited below.
23. She thereby gave up the chance to earn £100 to £150 pa in proof-reading and other editorial work.
24. *Quarterly Review* December 1855. 32. Stafford Northcote, First Lord Iddesleigh. Two of the pamphlets were by Mary Carpenter. *Household Words* had also recently published "Instructive Comparisons" (Henry Morley and Geraldine Jewsbury) on the same topic.
25. *Englishwoman's Domestic Magazine*, Vol 6 January 1859, 298-302; 299, 301. A highly successful ladies' magazine noted for its fashion illustrations and the introduction of the paper pattern to Britain, it also carried some progressive articles. Rye virtually suggests compulsory emigration. She later became active in the cause of women's employment, establishing a law-copying office, and was a founder of the Female Middle Class Emigration Society. I am grateful to Marion Diamond for drawing my attention to this article.
26. "What Can Educated Women Do?" *EWJ* December 1859.
27. Barbara Bodichon. "Women and Work (1857)". *Barbara Leigh Smith Bodichon*

and the Langham Place Group. Ed. Candida Ann Lacey. (London: Routledge & Kegan Paul, 1987). 36-73 of *Women's Source Library*.

28. Carpenter loc.cit. Carpenter was, however, adamant that "gaol must not be made a more desirable place than the workhouse, provided with better food, and constructed with greater care for the well-being of the inmates". 34.

29. I cite examples from her letters in Barbara Onslow. *Women of the Press in Nineteenth-Century Britain*. (Basingstoke: Macmillan, 2000). For Jameson generally see Clara Thomas. *Love and Work Enough: the Life of Anna Jameson*. (London, Toronto: University of Toronto, Macdonald, 1967). Jameson is now recognised as an early and influential interpreter of the visual arts.

30. Carpenter's work was widely quoted. e.g. Martineau's first leader of January 22nd cited above.

31. Martineau in her *Autobiography* was dismissive of Jameson's achievements in the cause of women, but it is pertinent to note that during her visit to the ailing Martineau in 1842 Anna Jameson had read to the invalid an article on prison discipline in the *Examiner* and expressed her own horror to Lady Byron "[C]an such things be—*now*—under the awakened eye of humanity?—How can we know what things may be going on—behind stone walls—as under ground—but there is a comfort in the thought that we are making some progress—something is done when these things are dragged into light & published..." Mrs Steuart Erskine, ed. *Anna Jameson: Letters and Friendships*. (London: T Fisher Unwin, 1915). In her final years Anna Jameson became increasingly interested in social issues. "On Sisters of Charity Abroad and at Home" was first given privately in February 1855, "Communion of Labour" the following year.

32. Bessie Parkes. "What Can Educated Women Do?" *Barbara Leigh Smith Bodichon and the Langham Place Group*. Ed. Candida Ann Lacey. (London: Routledge & Kegan Paul, 1986). 150-62.

33. Bessie Parkes. "A Year's Experience in Woman's Work". *Barbara Leigh Smith Bodichon and the Langham Place Group*. Ed. Candida Ann Lacey. (London: Routledge & Kegan Paul, 1986). 180-9.

34. Isabella Fyvie Mayo. *Recollections—of what I saw, what I lived through, and what I learned, during more than fifty years of social and literary experience*. (London: John Murray, 1910).

35. I am grateful to Anne Wheeldon for the information that it was probably written by a male journalist, Frederick William Robinson, from interviews. It appears to have achieved some popularity. Carpenter also seems to refer to it. loc. cit. p. 34.

36. Even relatively recently the Prison Service has been cautious in its recruitment policy. In 1983 researching career changes for teachers I noted of direct appointment to Assistant Governorship Class II that "an increasing number of graduates is entering the service" but that a mature woman entrant with psychiatric nursing as well as a teaching qualifications had needed to work hard to convince the selection board of her suitability. By the 1987 edition of Barbara Onslow. *What Can a Teacher Do Except Teach?* (COIC, 1983). I noted that two-thirds of recruits to this scheme had higher education qualifications or training in a field such as social work or law.

37. For example, the treatment of juvenile offenders produced confirmed criminals; too lavish a prison diet made incarceration preferable to life outside; "long imprisonments defeat their own end". See *inter alia* Carpenter and Susannah Roe "A Convict's Views of Penal Discipline". *Cornhill Magazine* X (1864). 722-733.
38. Carpenter loc.cit. 33.

Chapter 8

"The Truth of Midnight" and "The Truth of Noonday": Sensation and Madness in James Thomson's *The City of Dreadful Night*

Dafydd Moore

In a development typical of the man and his life, just as he had begun to establish a reputation as a poet James Thomson died an undignified, painful and drink-hastened death in 1882. Born in Port Glasgow in 1834, Thomson, a sort of down-market Coleridge for his age, eked out a precarious existence, first as an army schoolmaster and then as jobbing writer. His output was split between radical writing for, for example, Bradlaugh's *National Reformer*, some acute literary criticism (he was an early admirer of Blake, Heine, Melville and Whitman), and articles in *Cope's Tobacco Magazine* devoted to the hitherto unsuspected importance of tobacco and tobacco products in the careers of great men.[1] The fact that at his death he had been recognized as a poet of some merit, and gained the admiration, for example, of George Eliot, George Meredith and William Rossetti, is down to one poem, *The City of Dreadful Night*, published initially in the *National Reformer* in three parts between March and May of 1874 under his usual pseudonym B.V., or Bysshe Vanolis (a tribute to his early masters Shelley and the German Romantic poet Novalis).

The City of Dreadful Night is in fact one of a number of morbid *fin-de-siècle* pieces Thomson wrote expressing cultural, spiritual and personal deracination, alienation and despair. The nature of this, his most memorable and distinctive verse, and a personal life crippled by poverty, alcoholism, and other less tangible woes (including, for example, bouts of terrible insomnia) led to Thomson's enthronement as, in Bertram Dobell's words, "the laureate of despair".[2] *The City* is indeed an extraordinary work, a Dante-esque vision of a half-ruined city of perpetual night, peopled by characters who have plumbed every depth of metaphysical, theological and personal despair. Guided by an anonymous narrator about whom we know nothing, the reader is addressed by, or overhears, the conversations of these nameless, faceless characters, entering into their personal hell before they slip away. All of this is presented to us in stately, titanic, and therefore at times overblown, verse that gives the poem and its people a dignity and authority, which seems to stretch back through time, as they lay bare the "bitter, old and wrinkled truth" as the proem has it. Both poem and people are the creation of a singular, possibly pathological mind.

However, readers have also responded to the way the poem manages "to achieve the transference of [Thomson's] private passion to the public poetic utterance".[3] Raymond Williams suggests that Thomson's lasting poetic achievement is the manner in which *The City* "is projected and is significantly total", speaking of a "projected city in which a particular mode of being, specifically the "dreadful strain of thought and consciousness", has been actualised", while William Thesing stresses the "social, connective, and total" perspective of *The City* with its "*social* commentary of suffering".[4] In other words a central critical question surrounding the poem is how Thomson manages to create an abyss of despair that appeals to and is understandable by those who have never experienced weeks of insomniac pacing through empty city streets, or who have not dwelled over-long in the spiritual and philosophical wastelands of modern existence. *The City* is sensational, it is quite possibly insane too, but it is rational, collected and "projected" for all that.

This issue is central not only because it is a pragmatic one of effective representation, but also because the poem explicitly broaches questions of the relationship between those who have experienced these extremes and those who are only reading about them, and because, in Thesing's words, "the social, connective" are a crucial part of message of *The City*. The poem opens by invoking a voice of reproach in precisely these terms:

> [...]why evoke the spectres of black night
>   To blot the sunshine of exultant years?
> Why disinter dead faith from mouldering hidden?
> Why break the seals of mute despair unbidden,
>   And wail life's discords into careless ears? (Proem, 3–7)[5]

In a move that, I will argue below, is typical of the poem, Thomson does not answer this question by denying "the sunshine of exultant years". Instead he acknowledges its existence and power and turns his attention to those who cannot feel it, those whose natures may lead them to dwell on the "bitter old and wrinkled truth" (Proem, 9). This early selective emphasis upon one of a number of subjective versions of reality implies a further question, made manifest at the climax of this opening section of *The City*:

> O sad Fraternity, do I unfold
>   Your dolorous mysteries shrouded from of yore?
> Nay, be assured: no secret can be told
>   To any who divined it not before:
> None uninitiate by many a presage
> Will comprehend the language of the message,
> Although proclaimed aloud for evermore. (Proem, 36–43)

The proem outlines what Paul Ricoeur has identified as a Romantic sense of hermeneutics:

> By "hermeneutic cycle", Romanticist thinkers meant the understanding of a text cannot be an objective procedure in the sense of scientific objectivity but necessarily involves a precomphrension which expresses the way in which the reader has already understood himself and his world.[6]

Thomson's mid-Victorian attitude towards Romantic aesthetics is crucial to the method and message of *The City*, and will be considered later. For the moment I merely want to note that Thomson reflected these doubts himself. Writing to Dobell as the poem was being published he claimed that the poem "is so alien from common thought and feeling that I knew well (as stated in the Proem) that scarcely any readers would care for it".[7]

This chapter explores the relationship between the poem and "common thought and feeling" and considers ways in which *The City*—despite the "confidence" of the proem and the doubts of the letter on this issue—circumvents the hermeneutic cycle inherent in the depiction of extreme states of mind, by locating Thomson's methods and goals within nineteenth-century ideas of madness and the city, and of the relation between the two. I will concentrate on Thomson's varied use of voice and dramatization or projection to convey his bleak vision of life bereft of cultural and spiritual salvation, intellectual and moral hope and, in the final analysis, of sanity itself. The first section concentrates on the way *The City* is constructed out of the voices the reader encounters, the qualities of those voices, and the dynamics that exist between them. Thomson's technique is contextualized with reference to the literary and imaginative discourse of the city, which developed throughout the nineteenth century, and to the century's understanding of the condition of insanity. The second section shifts attention to the literary voices deployed in *The City*, both to reinforce the comments made in the first section and to move towards an understanding of the deeper significance for Thomson of these techniques. In this section, nineteenth-century diagnoses of the symptoms of insanity and Romantic models of redemption (and how nineteenth-century attitudes to the latter are implicated in questions of the former) constitute vital contexts.[8]

I)

Ian Campbell draws attention to the deployment of different voices within the poem as a way of explaining its calm insanity.[9] There are, roughly, twenty voices present, and these have the result of reducing the role of the notional narrator of the poem, and of objectifying those extreme emotions Thomson wishes to convey. Campbell emphasizes the second of these effects, and aligns Thomson's technique with the protective displacement technique and understands it as a way of presenting subversive ideas about politics and religion to a potentially hostile audience. However, in taking my lead from Campbell, I am going to focus more on the first of the effects and will consider its significance less in ideological terms and more in terms of aesthetic and sociological factors.

The City is constructed out of the voices the narrator overhears or engages with as he wanders the streets of the city. Yet the speakers remain anonymous, appearing from and disappearing into the fabric of the poem without warning:

> Large elm-tress stood along that river-walk;
> Under one, a few steps from my seat,
> I heard strange voices join in stranger talk,
> Although I had not heard approaching feet:
> These bodiless voices in my waking dream
> Flowed dark words blending with the sombre stream:–
> And you have after all come back; come back.
> I was about to follow on your track.
> And you have failed: our spark of hope is black (VI: 7–15)

A second speaker goes on to relate how he tried to enter Hell, since "that positive eternity of pain" would have been better than "this insufferable inane" [sic], but had failed since he had no hope to abandon in Dantesque fashion: a grim joke, which sums up much of *The City*'s tone. Canto X, in which the narrator observes a young man mourning by the candle-lit coffin of his dead love, is representative, again not only of the general tenor and scenery of *The City* but of this technique. Thomson avoids using inverted commas to represent speech, so the grieving lover's words do not stand out visually from the body of the poem – they are the body of the poem. Speech is marked however, as above, in the unrhymed three line stanza form:

> Most beautiful were Death to end my grief,
> Most hateful to destroy the sight of thee,
> Dear vision better than all death or life (X, 58–60).[10]

There is then a close association between the constructing voices and the very fabric of the poem. The anonymous, disembodied voices that haunt what seem to be otherwise empty, echoing streets, go a long way to create the eerie, nightmarish atmosphere to the poem and its city. The notional narrator plays a minimal role in the descriptions of the places he visits, and one bridge, street or square, though carefully noted (described would be too strong a term) is exactly like the last one. What distinguishes the locations is the characters and stories we encounter, but there is no attempt to order these events or to arrange this impressionistic narrative into a cogent whole. The narrator himself seems something of a null category, "a screen on which other's perceptions are projected".[11] In XII he observes a series of characters telling a "shrouded figure" their background.[12] When it comes to the narrator himself, instead of hearing of his previous life and the implied cause of his disillusionment, we have to make do with "and in turn | I entered also, having given mine" (55-6). Yet there is little sense of being cheated here: by XII we are aware that the poem would seem to actively preclude such revelations from the everyman narrator. Even those cantos devoted to the narrator's reflections rarely evidence a confident voice. XIII and XVII are expressed in the first person plural, V in a kind of third person indirect, while VII begins with the enigmatic "some say that..." It is peculiarly fitting that the first event of the poem has the narrator following a figure for no more reason than that "he seemed to walk with an intent", which, this being *The City*, turns out to be compulsive morbidity, a "drear pilgrimage to ruined shrines" marking "dead Faith, dead Love, dead Hope" (I l.28, l.48). In short the narrator is observer of and our guide through this nether world, but lacks any of the authority or power such roles have the potential to confer.

This sort of literary imagining of the city and its inhabitants is at one with the "growing scepticism amongst men of letters (in the second half of the nineteenth century) about their capacity to read the city and to sustain a coherent vision of a structured public landscape".[13] For example, *The City* can be compared in these terms with George Sala's 1851 article for *Household Words* "The Key to the Street", in which a journalistic exposé of the plight of the urban homeless becomes tinged with an irrational, nightmarish air. Over the course of a night on the streets Sala's purpose and indeed his identity is revealed to be up for grabs: "I no longer walk, I prowl", he notes, and his being mistaken for a down-and-out himself is not so much amusing as a threatening invasion of character and social position, particularly in the context of a similar impulse in the opposite direction as he records his sudden fear of police officers. The article is disjointed: as in *The City*, crowds appear and melt away, there is no explanation for the events described and the night ends with the sudden "[I] find that it is broad daylight". Most significantly Sala's night on the streets has so drained him that he is unable to formulate his experience into any sort of coherent narrative or polemic. One might argue that it is a more effective piece of journalism for this, but that would be to miss the point of how an encounter with city night has revealed the instability of the social identity of its middle class observer, a narrator who can never quite manage to be the narrator he intended to be.[14] As Judith Walkowitz puts it with reference to Booth's *Life and Labour of the People of London* (1889):

> [E]fforts towards totalizing knowledge and self-creation also led to the exploration of multiple self-identities: to a desire to impersonate "the people", a masquerade that enabled him to gain command over his subject but that also articulated a questioning of his own class/gender position (1992, 33).

The narrator of Thomson's *The City*, and the narrative he produces, can be seen within this context of the fissuring of the confident flâneur tradition in the second half of the century.[15] The comprehensive representation of the city and its inhabitants involves the narrator becoming an empty signifier, lacking essential identity, an acted upon witness not a privileged observer. But if for Sala this threat to the autonomy of the individual personality is just that, a threat, *The City* exploits the devolution of narrative authority it implies by using different characters and episodes to fill out *The City*'s message of despair and disillusionment without ever becoming too hysterical. As Morgan suggests, *The City* represents "extreme and nightmarish states of mind [...] presented as vividly as possible" (18), but it is the episodic structure of the poem that pushes back the boundaries of what is possible by insuring that the demented ravings of cantos such as IV, VIII, X and XVIII (the last of which will be considered at length below) do not dominate the poem to the extent that readers flinch away.[16]

What I mean can be judged by a comparison with other poems by Thomson that demonstrate what happens without the distancing effects of *The City*. His 1878 poem "I had a Love" contains familiar Thomsonian themes: the solace of life nearly over and the myth of a lost redemptive love, expressed in a typical—a typically gothic—extended image of the desert:

> You would have kept me from the desert sands
> Bestrewn with bleeding bones,
> And led me through the friendly fertile lands, (73–5)[17]

Yet the poem does not convince in the way *The City* does: too over-wrought to be successful, the reader can get no purchase on its sensationalism. The apparent volte-face of the final sections, with the speaker refusing a hypothetical offer to turn back the clock, is hard to take as the final tragedy of a tormented soul, and reads as a contradiction in an unhinged mind. On the other hand *The City* separates out the various aspects of this poem and clears space for a full readerly engagement. Thus the desert is part of the schizophrenic vision of a pseudo Christ ("declaiming from the central grassy mound" to an imaginary crowd) in IV; the lost love motif appears, as we have seen, in X, while the idea of a welcome death near at hand is opposed to the enterprise of the figure in XVIII. Thus the episodic structure of the larger poem "permit[s] a greater variety and stimulate[s] a more intense emotion" while making sure that the pot does not boil over.[18] By replacing a single lyric "I" with multiple subjective perspectives Thomson not only reflects the breakdown of the single stable identity in the face of attempts to articulate the city, but also provides a functional breathing space within the text that—paradoxically—gives us nowhere to hide. Yet Thomson's use of voice is more essentially dramatic than this projection alone suggests, and he deploys other dramatic resources of distance and irony in order to create *The City*'s rational insanity.

A month after its three-part serialization had been completed George Eliot wrote to Thomson, praising *The City* but lamented that it lacked something of the "truth of noonday" to accompany the "truth of midnight". Thomson offered an oddly ambivalent defence of the poem:

> [*The City*] was the outcome of much sleepless hypochondria. I am aware that the truth of midnight does not exclude the truth of noonday, though one's nature may lead him to dwell in the former rather than the latter.[19]

This exchange, with its half-hearted defence is interesting because in it Thomson enacts a characteristic turn of *The City*, whereby multiple and mutually unimpeachable truths are set up, but truths which nevertheless may be grounded in personal pathologies: we might be talking about a hypochondriac insomniac here, but one who nevertheless has access to what is labelled the truth of midnight. This truth manifests itself in *The City* as an air of rationality, heightened by the way the speakers engage with the subjectivity of what they themselves are saying, however extreme that may be. They convince by both their passionate sincerity and fair-mindedness. Canto XVI is a reply to the preceding canto, in fact it is a contradiction of the previous canto's Thomsonian message of "solace" that "there is no God". What good does such solace do me, asks a speaker who laments the missed opportunities of his "breath | Of noble human life upon this earth" before listing, between lines 11 and 26, the various aspects of "gracious human life". The list is wide-ranging, including, for example, the thoroughly Wordsworthian "glories of the worlds of nature, lit | By large imagination's glowing heart", but for all that the speaker feels that his "sole chance" has been a disappointment, that his "wine of life is poison mixed with gall" (32). "Our life's a cheat" says the man in line 41, not because it is worthless but because it presents opportunities that have been denied him from his birth. That those opportunities exist is not denied however.

This is a trick repeated continuously by Thomson: his speakers, regardless of the pit of personal despair from which they hail the reader, have a striking ability to see life in a fully rounded sense. Rather than denying the existence of blessing they merely affirm the impossibility of partaking of it themselves. Furthermore, this ability to show both sides of the coin simultaneously, to hold a view without needing to silence its opposite, demonstrates a conviction which is, in is own way, convincing. Thomson deploys this device both in the speakers who, as here, usually allude to the other of a Coventry Patmore-esque home life, and in the narrator's more general speculations. XV sets out the narrator's conviction that the air is "charged with human feeling, human thought", that "each shout and cry and laugh, each curse and prayer" enters into it. The balance of positive and negative set up in these opening comments is maintained into the second stanza:

> [Man] nourishes warm life or hastens death
> With joys or sorrows, health and foul disease,
> Wisdom and folly, good and evil labours (10–12)

The balance is meticulous, and makes the twist in the third stanza all the more devastating as it begins "that City's atmosphere is dark and dense". Like the lit windows of canto X which promise a party but which only light a funeral bier, its simple power comes from the way the reader has been momentarily presented with an alternative possibility, a technique mirrored in the seven line stanza used by the poem:

> This recurrent, slow uncoiling, backward coiling stanza, with the overhanging rhymes towards the close only suggesting a freedom of movement in order that the close may be more ironically definite, is the pulse of the City.[20]

Of course nineteenth-century psychology recognized pathological conditions in which the subject could remain to all intents and purposes and on most subjects "sane". In 1835 James Pritchard described the condition of "moral insanity" as characterized by "the morbid perversion of the natural feelings, affections, inclinations, temper, habits, moral dispositions and natural impulses" but without ravings or hallucinations and indeed displaying the ability to deploy considerable ingenuity in arguing their eccentric ideas.[21] According to Pritchard the morally insane display "a tendency to gloom or sorrow" and drunkenness (254), while in the associated condition of monomania subjects are insane in relation to one thing only, and their disorder tends to manifest itself as "mental dejection or melancholy" (254), a "self-torturing imagination" and the "dark and gloomy anticipation of remorse" (255). As well as being a description of Thomson, such "partial insanity" begs a number of questions, the one of most relevance to us concerning the anxiety about the relationship between sanity and insanity this produced in the nineteenth century itself: if, as Vieda Skultans points out, moral insanity is "located in inappropriate emotions and feelings rather than in defective reasoning" then how easy is it to separate insanity from mere eccentricity?[22]

The City of Dreadful Night, with its rational insanity, its "geometry of delirium" in the words of an early reader, can be seen then as reflecting current thinking on the nature of insanity, but as also playing on doubts as to the possibility of establishing "sanity" in any absolute sense. Indeed the reasonableness of Thomson's speakers, however idiosyncratically—or pathologically—morbid they may be, plays less on the insanity of the sane but rather upon their sanity.[23] It is alarming enough to feel, as Andrew Wynter put it, that there exists a "vast army of undiscovered lunatics" in society, whose behaviour never quite topples into the openly insane, but it is even more disturbing that the insane may contain a vast army of sane people.[24] In other words, *The City's* speakers represent an extreme version of nineteenth-century psychology's doubts about the grounds on which one could determine absolute sanity, playing, as the novel of sensation does, on the anxieties about the nature of truth, reason and rationality that such doubts produce.[25] Thus the reasonableness of these speakers that strikes the modern reader was no less mad, but all the more disturbing for that, for the Victorian reader.

To return to the speaker of canto XVI, his speech is one of the many occasions where Thomson's verse is haunted by the voices of his literary forebears, here Shakespeare and, particularly, in the image of a poisoned chalice and the rhetorical question "can words make foul things fair" (but also I think in a number of more general ways) *Macbeth*. *Macbeth*, amongst other things, is a study of the human capacity to create a situation in which life is, or is perceived to be, blighted, a study of evil that creates the world in its own image. On this (not altogether straightforward) intertextual level too then, the canto, like so much of *The City* engages with ideas of subjectivity, expression and experience. It is also an example of Thomson's use of his literary forebears, and it is the influence of one of these forebears that I now wish to address in more detail.

II)

The City may be a proto-modernist text beloved, for example, by T.S. Eliot and exemplifying late nineteenth-century anxieties about metropolitan life, but we should not lose sight of the fact that Thomson's is also a thoroughly Romantic sensibility. While it is true that Thomson increasingly distanced himself from an early emphasis on the inspired prophet of high Romanticism to become an admirer of realism as he shifted from pantheism to pessimistic atheism (a relative shift from Novalis' *sturm und drang* to Heine's Byronic urbanity is, for example, one symptom of this), it is nonetheless true that Thomson's poetic debts are to the European Romantic movement in its widest sense, from Shelley and Blake to Leopardi, Novalis and especially Heine.[26] Thomson's affinities and debts are complicated, and in this section I shall explore Thomson's engagement with just one poet, William Blake, not only because it demonstrates another version of Thomson's use of irony and detachment, but it leads us towards a consideration of why such effects are so important to him. It also suggest to us ways in which the Romantic bequest relates to questions of inspiration, madness and sensation in the second half of the nineteenth century.[27]

Thomson's use of Blake in canto XVIII is by far the most striking (though far from unique) ironizing of Romantic tropes in *The City*. The narrator comes across "something crawling", a "wounded creature", dragging itself to its "den" to die:

> But coming level with it I discerned
> That it had been a man; for at my tread
> It stopped in its sore travail and half-turned,
> Leaning upon its right, and raised its head,
> And with the left hand twitched back as in ire
> Long grey unreverend locks befouled with mire.
> A haggard filthy face with bloodshot eyes, An infamy for manhood to behold. (XVIII, 19–26)

The specifics of this description reveal the figure as a rendering of Blake's engraving *Nebuchadnessar*; the "long-lost broken thread | Which unites my present with my past" which the figure searches for is an allusion to *Jerusalem* IV; while the idea of a return to childhood innocence finds its origins, according to G.M. Harper, in several of the "Songs of Experience".[28] Thomson turns the first of these images against the second two: the "infamy for mankind to behold" is the result of the Blakean search for "Eden innocence in Eden's clime", a condemnation of the search for the Romantic childhood. It is a powerful image: of all the lost and desperate souls who inhabit *The City*, this is the only one who has become somehow sub-human. Yet Harper points out that Thomson's 1864 essay "The Poems of William Blake" demonstrates an early enthusiasm for the least well known of the English Romantics, and as late as 1881 in "The Ring and the Book" he was placing "Blake undiseased" amongst his masters. Canto XIV's atheist preacher presents a dialectic vision of life of Blakean proportions (though typically, Thomson makes sure that such sentiments are in the mouth of an un-

Blakean atheist), complete with an echo of one of Blake's most famous poems:

> If toads and vultures obscene to sight
> If tigers burn with beauty and with might,
> Is it by favour or by wrath of Fate? (ll. 64–66)

The answer of course lies in that qualification "undiseased" and in the sort of poetry Thomson thought he was reading when he spoke of Blake. Blake was mediated to the mid-nineteenth century in two ways. Firstly, an edition of the *Songs of Innocence and Experience* produced in 1839 by James John Garth Wilkinson, an editor and biographer of Immanuel Swedenbourg (and, significantly for our purposes the author in 1857 of *Improvisations from the Spirit*, a collection of poems produced via a strain of automatic writing). Latterly, readers relied on Thomas Gilchrist's *Life of William Blake* (1863) for both a serious biography and selection of Blake. Gilchrist represented Blake exclusively as a mystic, a genius who had retreated into a visionary imagination to survive in an inamicable age; "a saint [...] who happened to be an artist".[29] When on Gilchrist's death Dante Gabriel Rossetti made the poetry selections for the volume he completed the misrepresentation by lyricizing Blake, "tend[ing] to Gothicise Gilchrist's already remote hero" (Dorfman, 81). Interestingly Rossetti also drew explicit parallels with Wilkinson's *Improvisations*, noting that the latter's works were "startlingly akin to Blake's writings—could pass, in fact, for no one's but his", an observation quoted in turn by Thomson in his own essay on Wilkinson, "A Strange Book".[30]

The links between Thomson, Blake and Wilkinson, and the commonplace association of the latter two, is suggestive: in the essay on Blake, Thomson recommends Gilchrist "to all good readers" before admitting that he had previously only known of Blake through Wilkinson. Thomson follows the logic of these associations when he characterizes Blake as "withdrawn from common life into mysticism".[31] However, in 1864 this comment does not stand as a criticism, indeed "simple mysticism" acts as a touchstone in the essay for the greatest of poetry. However Thomson is keen to assert a further dimension to the Blake of "seclusion" and "intense inner life":

> Blake has attempted what all profound poets and thinkers have ever most earnestly attempted – to seize a rude but striking image of some *sovereign truth*, and to stamp it with roughest vigour on the *commonest metal* for *universal circulation* (my emphasis 257).

It appears however that over the next ten years Thomson was unable to keep the balance between the inspired mystic and the public poet implied here. The conclusion to his essay on Wilkinson is fittingly instructive. Wilkinson, according to Thomson, has wasted his talent through a blind faith in inspiration which has "prevented him from using his natural faculties to correct and perfect conception and expression" (350). This is more than a question of aesthetic effectiveness: "can we help", he asks, "being angry, do we not well to be angry when, our poor race pining for illumination, some of the most fulgent spirits obstinately refuse to be effulgent?" (370). Ultimately Thomson, in a moment that characteristically combines ineffable sadness and gothic horror, talks of Wilkinson's "mournful frustrate life", frustrated in its "full development and happiness in usefulness":

> [He is] immolating his splendid powers on the altar built of dead men's bones, of a demented dogmatism more implacable than the old heathen altars of merely bodily human sacrifice (370).

Schaefer observes that the reformer Thomson's darkest despair grew not out of a loss of faith in God, or in Shelley, but out of a realization of the bounds of man's sympathy for man.[32] Thomson, for all his pioneering admiration for Blake, believed that he "never grasps or cares for the common world of reality" and for that he ultimately condemns him.[33] In other words Thomson's antipathy towards the solipsistic mystic life that denies the common—and useful—lot, brings us to the Nebuchadnessar figure of *The City*:

> Have pity on me! It is mine alone,
> If you could find it, it would avail you naught;
> Seek elsewhere on the pathway of your own; (XVIII, ll.38–40)

Thus the figure encountered in XVIII pays the price for being "Blake", for the Romantic refusal to interact with the world, and for his pre-emptive scorning of pity and solidarity. He also represents a by-now familiar manoeuvre on Thomson's part: just as the man condemns himself from his own mouth, so one Romantic image condemns another, a distancing manoeuvre that I have argued is essential to the air of rationality exuded by *The City*. At the same time the grounds upon which Thomson takes issue with Blake demonstrate the importance of the method. Thomson's view of the role of literature was at odds with the nineteenth-century's view of the Romantic model of highly personal—solipsistic, even—redemption. The importance of Thomson's determinedly inclusive vision of despair is further heightened by a sense of nineteenth-century depictions of the insane, with which it is appropriate to end.

III)

> [N]umbers without the slightest power of really combining for earthly purpose; a society of human creatures who have nothing in common but that they have all lost the power of being humanly social with one another.[34]

The inability to partake of social interaction was taken to be one of the major symptoms of madness in the nineteenth century. As Jean Étienne Esquirol put it, the asylum is a place where "social bonds are broken": "with no community of thoughts, each lives alone, and for himself. Egotism isolates all".[35] In his engagement with Blake (or at least what he took to be Blake), we see Thomson's troubled sense of the pitfalls inherent in Romantic transcendence, a condition of solipsistic absorption that may be just as insane as the spiritual and mental alienation it is calculated to redeem. Accordingly, *The City* also offers a counter-image to the Blakean isolationism, a response to life which is life-affirming: the thrilling evocation of the statue of Melencolia the people of the city have erected as an image of their plight with which the poem closes. Offering "renewed assurance | And confirmation of the old despair" (XXII, ll.83–4) the statue brings the poem full circle and casts us back to the proem, and its answer to the question as to why the poet should disinter the "bitter old and wrinkled truth":

> here and there some weary wanderer
> In that same city of tremendous night,
> Will understand the speech, and feel a stir
> Of fellowship in all-disastrous fight (proem, 29–32)

Thus the statue is an image of the poem itself, both gaining its strength and power from its clear-eyed confrontation with "the dreadful mysteries of time", from its refusal to descend permanently into melodrama and from its profoundly sociable–and humanist—mission. If alienation is one of the central features of modern life, symbolized by life in the city, then Thomson's attempt to set *The City* at a distance, to dramatize the effects of that alienation with the result that we can communicate with and understand each other, is perhaps a partial answer to the alienation. Some of Thomson's most desperate characters may "brood maddening inwardly" and "speak | To one another seldom" but we are also confronted with figures in some form of union of despair. Canto XI offers a vision of a city where the wealthy, gifted, poor and cowardly are "brothers | The saddest and weariest men on earth" (28–9), united in the strangely moving refrain repeated by all "I wake from daydreams to this real night". Our sorrows may be unique, but they place us in good company. Small consolation perhaps, but then the poem deals in, if not small consolations, then tenuous ones held onto in the face of despair.

There is then an intimate connection between these consolations and the business of understandable communication. Thesing, building on Sheaffer's analysis of the "two" *Cities*, the 1870 and 1873 versions of the poem, emphasizes the connective movement in Thomson's thought, from "individual self-absorption" to "a new *social* commentary of suffering" (1982, 143, his emphasis), from a poem "merely spinning around in a Wertherian whirlpool" to a poem which "leaves behind the personal hell in his mind and strikes an essentially Victorian note" (144), by which he has in mind, I think, the Carlylean note of "power and passion | In helpless impotence to try to fashion | Our woe in living words" (proem, 12–14). Thomson's attempts to project the desperation and alienation of the inhabitants of his city are an attempt to break out of the conditions of alienation itself, to allow communication. The poem's denial of its own premise—that "none uninitiate [...] will comprehend the language of the message"—is both profound and profoundly fitting since the very process of undermining given positions, of acknowledging subjectivism and the limits of perspective, is part of the technique whereby the denial occurs and whereby the poem achieves its universal utterance.

Jenny Bourne Taylor suggests that the sensation narrative can be read as "a collective nervous disorder, a morbid addiction within the middle class", a literary discourse not only interested in the pathological but in itself pathological (1988, 4), simultaneously a diagnosis and a symptom. *The City*, while sharing many features of the sensation narrative—most notably an interest in making problematical neat and stable distinctions between truth and illusion, sanity and insanity—is in the final analysis the opposite of this: the symptom which may also be a panacea. Thomson circumvents the hermeneutic cycle inherent in the literary depiction of extreme states of mind in *The City* through the dramatization and setting at ironic distance both the despair he wishes to portray and some of the Romantic models of redemption he sees as reinforcing the pathology of solipsistic despair. In doing so he not only essays a compelling vision of the emptiness and alienation of life but in doing so proposes a profound vision of humanist solidarity, Arnold's "eternal note of sadness" heard across time and space. This then is not just a matter of effective literary expression, but strikes to the heart of the role and function of the writer in an alienated and alienating world.

Notes

1. I am not approaching anything like a biographical sketch here. See Morgan's introduction. James Thomson. *City of Dreadful Night*. Introduction by Edwin Morgan. (Edinburgh: Canongate, 1993); Bertram Dobell. *The Laureate of Pessimism: A Sketch of the Life and Character of James Thomson ('B.V.')*. (London:1910); Tom Leonard. *Places of the Mind: The Life and Work of James Thomson (B.V.)*. (London: Cape, 1993); and, particularly, H.S. Salt, *The Life of James Thomson ('B.V.')*. (London: Reeves & Turner, 1889).
2. Dobell puts Thomson's woes down to his Scottish heritage, which he says made him susecptible to both alchohol and the 'poison' of Calvinist theology (1910, 60). Without doubt, Thomson's reputation suffered from the well-meaning biographical and editorial attentions of Dobell, whose canonization of B.V. as the dipsomaniac high prophet of doom does not do justice to a man with a sharp sense of humour, a keen eye for the absurd, and an appreciation of the fine things in life, and whose drunken episodes were at Hyde-like odds with his general character (see Morgan, 18, for Salt on Thomson's character transformations).
3. Ian Campbell, '"And I too burn": Thomson's *The City of Dreadful Night*', *Victorian Poetry*, 16 (1978), 123–33 (125).
4. Raymond Williams, *The Country and the City* (1973. London: Hogarth Press, 1993). 236, 238; William B. Thesing, *The London Muse: Victorian Responses to the City* (Athens, Georgia: University of Georgia Press, 1982), 143, 144.
5. James Thomson, *The City of Dreadful Night*, intro. by Edwin Morgan (Edinburgh, 1993). All future references are to this edition and appear in the text.
6. Paul Ricoeur, 'Metaphor and the Main Problem of Hermeneutics', *New Literary History*, 6 (1974), 95–110 (106).
7. Dobell, *The Laureate of Pessimism*, 24.
8. I want to say at this point that while this chapter contains appropriate use of citation and quotation, *The City* is a poem to be read.
9. Ian Campbell. "And I Too Burn".
10. This young man may be inspired Thomson's one-time hero Novalis. Compare this with 'unable to go forward or turn back. I hung on to my life's precious thread' "Hymns to the Night III", *Hymns to the Night*, trans. David Gasgoyne and Jeremy Reed. (London: Enitharmon Press, 1989). 21.
11. Jenny Bourne Taylor, *In the Secret Theatre of Home: Wilkie Collins, Sensation Narrative, and Nineteenth-Century Psychology*. (London: Routledge,1988). 63. She is, of course referring to Collins's novels, but it is an observation strikingly applicable to Thomson's narrator, revealing a kinship between *The City* and the narrative of sensation.
12. Campbell notes (128) that these figures would seem to include Milton, Coleridge and Tennyson.
13. Judith R. Walkowitz, *City of Dreadful Delight*. (London: Virago, 1992). 39.
14. See G.A. Sala, "The Key to the Street", *Household Words* no.76, 6th September 1851, vol.3 (1851), 565–72.
15. See Walkowitz, 16–39 for reasons for this.

16. Morgan also outlines some of the formal problems Thomson has to confront in the poem, in particular the question of "monotony": see page 16.
17. *Poems and Some Letters of James Thomson*, ed. by Anne Ridler. (Carbondale: Southern Illinois University Press, 1963). 205.
18. Imogene B. Walker, *James Thomson (B.V.): A Critical Study.* (Cornell University Press: Ithaca, 1950), 205. Of course, Thomson is not the only poet to fall into this trap. Tennyson's *Maud* (about which Thomson was amusingly rude—"young ladyish affectation" and "hysterics" were the phrases he used in his essay on Blake) also demonstrates the pitfalls of sensational poetry.
19. Letter dated 20th June 1874. Quoted in H.S. Salt, *The Life of James Thomson ('B.V.')*, 12.
20. *The City of Dreadful Night and Other Poems*, intro by Edmund Blunden. (London: Methuen & Co, 1932), 11.
21. *A Treatise on Insanity and Other Disorders Affecting the Mind,* in *Embodied Selves: An Anthology of Psychological Texts, 1830–1890.* Eds. Jenny Bourne Taylor and Sally Shuttleworth. (Oxford: Oxford University Press, 1998). 251–6, 252, 254.
22. Vieda Skultans, *English Madness: Ideas on Insanity 1580–1890.* (London: Routledge & Kegan Paul, 1979), 65, 67. Such social insanity also begs Foucaudian questions about the relationship between madness and ideological control, for example in Henry Maudsley's definition of moral insanity as a 'degeneration of social sentiments'—the inability to observe social and class conventions in his *The Physiology and Pathology of the Mind* (1867), in Bourne Taylor and Shuttleworth, 266–8.
23. The 'geometry of delerium' is a phrase of Paul Elmer More's, quoted by Robert Crawford in his *The Savage and the City in the Work of T.S. Eliot.* (Oxford: Oxford University Press, 1987). 45.
24. Wynter, *The Borderlands of Insanity and other Allied Papers* (1875), in Bourne Taylor and Shuttleworth (1998), 280–2, 281.
25. See Bourne Taylor (1988) for 'the absence of any stable reference point for defining insanity' in the novel of sensation (here Braddon's *Lady Audley's Secret*), 11.
26. See *The Speedy Extinction of Evil and Misery. The Selected Prose of James Thomson (B.V.)*, ed. by William David Schaefer. (Berkeley and Los Angeles: University of California Press, 1967), introduction 6 for an account of Thomson's shifting literary tastes. The relation with Heine is fascinating, but not strictly relevant here.
27. Shelley would offer an alternative case, given the Bysshe of B.V., and the similarities between Melancholia and Shelley's Medusa. For Thomson and Romanticism see Jerome McGann, 'James Thomson (B.V.): The Woven Hymns of Day and Night', *Studies in English Literature*, 3 (1963), 493–507. R.A. Foakes, *The Romantic Assertion.* (New York and London: Yale University Press, 1958). 169.
28. See G.M. Harper, 'Blake's *Nebuchadnessar* in "The City of Dreadful Night"', *Studies in Philology*, 50 (1953), 68–81 (72–3).
29. Deborah Dorfman, *Blake in the Nineteenth Century: His Reputation from*

Gilchrist to Yeats (New Haven, 1969), 92. For possible reasons for this critical move see 654–90.

30. See "A Strange Book" in James Thomson, *Biographical and Critical Studies*. Ed. Bertram Dobell (London, 1896), 298–371, 305.
31. "The Poems of William Blake" (1854) in Schaefer (ed), 229.
32. Schaefer, *James Thomson (B.V.): Beyond "The City"*. (Berkeley and Los Angeles: University of California Press, 1965). 98–99.
33. Quotation from Schaefer's headnote to "The Poems of William Blake" in Schaefer (ed.), 214. Schaefer advances a similar line in brief in this headnote. Of course, we can point the finger at Thomson's inadequate access to Blake, but in more general terms Thomson is reacting to the tension in Romantic thought between the humanist and the sublime or transcendental perspectives.
34. Wilkie Collins and Charles Dickens, "The Lazy Tour of Two Idle Apprentices", *Household Words*, 24th October 1857, 385. Quoted in Bourne Taylor (1988), 27.
35. Esquirol, *Mental Maladies: A Treatise on Insanity*, transl. E.J. Hunt (Philadephia, 1845), in Bourne Taylor and Shuttleworth (1998), 223–34, 234.

Chapter 9

Puffed Papers and Broken Promises: White-Collar Crime and Literary Justice in *The Way We Live Now*

Karen Odden

In 1838, an anonymous pamphlet, *The Ghost of John Bull; or, the Devil's Railroad: A Marvellously Strange Narrative*, offered a satirical commentary on an array of socio-economic problems that threatened to undermine Britain's notion of itself as morally upstanding and humane. Horrified by the corruption, greed and selfishness he sees around him, John Bull retires from society and dies; but one day an out-of-control railway train bolts from its tracks and brings a carriage with five men down into a valley where the Ghost of John Bull walks. The Ghost confronts the five men, each of whom represents one social group or issue: a railway director, an unscrupulous M.P., an assistant commissioner for the New Parish or Poor Law, a theatre manager who produces plays that have no literary merit, and an old, ill-tempered man called Blunt Humanity. The Ghost sharply questions the railway director first:

> 'So you are one of the heads of the railroad makers?' retorted John Bull.
> 'I am connected with one of those roads', said the director timidly.
> 'You have told me so', said John Bull fretfully. 'And pray for what particular purpose did you and your coadjutors undertake such a concern?'...
> 'It was done for the benefit of the Public', answered the director, trembling.
> 'It's a lie!' roared John Bull; 'it was done for the benefit of the directors' (51-52).

After John Bull completes his interrogation of the other men, the Devil appears to guard a gateway back to the real world. The director is allowed to reboard the train and re-enter normal life because he at least "make[s] a practice of providing for those that are hurt or worn out in your service"; but the M.P. and the commissioner confess that they act out of selfish greed ("[I] take care of myself"), and the Devil traps them in the valley of death.

If this satire had been written thirty-five years later, the railway director might not have escaped punishment so easily. Although the public's fear of demonic runaway engines had somewhat diminished, charges of hypocrisy with respect to railway directors had given way to charges of outright criminality. By 1873, when Anthony Trollope wrote his satire *The Way We Live Now* (published 1875), the

British public had witnessed two cycles of fraudulent railway promotion and manic speculation, a substantial financial crash in 1844-45, and smaller economic downturns in the 1860s. The railway schemes occupied an extraordinary place in the public imagination because they involved—and often ruined—thousands of investors, tradesmen, and directors; and because contemporary pamphlets, trade papers and newspapers offered an ongoing discussion of the schemes and their socio-economic implications. Trollope's villain, the railway director Augustus Melmotte, resembles several historical and fictional figures—particularly George Hudson, "the Railway King" of the 1840s—but he also represents corrupt railway promoters generally; and his demise suggests the anger Victorians felt toward these men. Unlike the 1838 pamphlet, which lets the railway director off with a slap on the hand, Trollope ruins Melmotte financially, humiliates him in Parliament, and has him commit suicide by drinking prussic acid.

The railway schemes had a profound and lasting impact on the way Victorians conceptualized crime itself, in great part because the schemes involved a wide array of aristocrats and what we would now call white-collar professionals in their conception, duration, and aftermath.[1] Every railway scheme required a lawyer to draw up the necessary papers for registration; lawyers also assembled fraudulent schemes on paper purely for their own gain. The provisional railway directorial boards drew their members from the white-collar professionals and upper classes because the public thought their names guaranteed the legitimacy of the scheme. Investors came from all levels of society but primarily the upper-middle and upper classes. A group of M.P.s, many of whom served on these boards, made up "the railway interest" in Parliament, which approved each individual railway scheme by an Act, and after the crashes, judges and legislators developed ways to adjudicate the charges of criminality that volleyed among railway promoters, tradesmen, and investors.

Trollope's novel provides a remarkable perspective upon what I consider the Victorian white-collar crime par excellence and upon the subsequent attempts to bring white-collar criminals to justice. *The Way We Live Now* is not only the longest and most developed narrative of a white-collar crime in Victorian literature but it deals with the commercial and legal issues both thematically and formally. The central plot of the novel is, of course, the railway promotion scheme which affects the lives of so many of the characters. More important, in his strategies of representation and emplotment, Trollope represents the painful effects of white-collar crime upon innocent individuals; and he produces a literary justice[2] that holds the place for the legal justice that could not be administered with complete success in the 1870s courts.

In order to understand the way this crime shapes the novel, we need to understand some of the details about the Victorian railway schemes.[3] In the 1830s, railways began to provide an alternative to stagecoach and canal transportation. Following the success of the early British railways, groups of railway engineers and investors began to assemble plans for extending the railway system to other parts of England. Although some promoters drafted and promoted railway plans in good faith, another class of men, whom we would now call white-collar criminals, began in the 1840s to create "bubble" railway schemes that generated revenue solely by circulating enormous amounts of "railway paper". These unscrupulous promoters had absolutely no intention of building a railway, which was the promise made to the investors; the sole purpose of filing the necessary registration papers was to generate revenue for the promoters. The Joint Stock Commission Act of 1844, spearheaded by Gladstone under Peel, was supposed to address the problem of bubble promotions that had surfaced by the early 1840s. It required that the promoters of railway schemes register the promoters' names, addresses, and occupations, along with the details for their proposed scheme, with an office in London. In other words, the JSC Act generated yet more paper to secure the value of the railway paper. But the mandatory registration did little to halt the development of fraudulent schemes. The promoters printed lavish advertisements for the planned railway, often "puffing" (or outright lying about) its virtues; then they invited applications for shares of scrip, issued letters of allotment specifying when money deposited on the shares was owed, and then sold scrip at prices that were driven up by (at least the appearance of) an enormous demand for the shares. Eventually, not only the scrip but the letters of allotment became traded commodities. Encouraged by the success of the early railways, the development of securities markets in towns outside London, the strong economy, and endorsements by eminent professionals and socially prominent people, novice investors flocked to purchase this paper in what some contemporaries termed a "mania".

The crash in October 1845 occasioned a crisis in legal thought and procedure. Hundreds of investors, tradesmen, and promoters accused each other of fraud, thievery, and corruption; and by December, the courts were overwhelmed with lawsuits. From laws that were developed before the new free market economy came into being, judges and legislators had to craft piecemeal a way of handling cases involving white-collar crime. Given the volume of cases that came before the courts and the public scrutiny devoted to every judge's charge or decision, this was a nearly impossible task. In invoking the railway scheme, Trollope references the historical moment when English law was completely incapable of responding to white-collar crime in a cogent fashion. For example, in the months immediately following the crash, judges held provisional directors personally responsible for the debts owed to tradesmen who had extended credit for the production of paper products—maps, brochures, advertisements, printed releases, and scrip—essential to the railway scheme. The following year, judges began to reverse these decisions: unless the tradesman had a direct contractual agreement with the individual director, the director could not be held liable. Similarly, in the initial fury and anxiety after the bubble schemes exploded, judges believed that individuals who bought scrip in fraudulent companies should be reimbursed; later, judges decided that if these investors bought scrip in a railway venture, they did so knowing that the venture might fail. By the 1850s, established precedents indemnified the railway board members and lawyers who assembled schemes that had failed—unless it could be proven that the scheme had been falsely advertised or fraudulent. This task was nearly impossible because the personal intentions of an individual working within a large board of directors were difficult to ascertain. In addition, even if the scheme could be proved fraudulent, the villains often had stashed their money, claimed bankruptcy, or fled to Europe. Paper made it possible to create the *appearance* of a railway company before even one foot of track had been laid; and railway law was in such a state of what one contemporary described as "incomprehensible balderdash"[4] that it gave investors very little recourse against promoters who broke their promises.

Many aspects of the railway scheme Trollope describes in *The Way We Live Now* accurately reflect the schemes proposed in the 1840s and 1860s. In the novel, an American investor named Fisker approaches Paul Montague, asking for an interview with Melmotte. Fisker wants to convince Melmotte to sign on as chairman to the board of directors because his name will lend credibility to the project. The narrator describes Fisker's idea, which Melmotte takes up: "The scheme in question was the grand proposal for a South Central Pacific and Mexican railway" (1.76.). Note that the "scheme" is not the railway itself but the written "proposal"; the narrator explains that, according to Fisker, "The object of Fisker, Montague, and Montague was not to make a railway to Vera Cruz, but to float a company. Paul thought that Mr. Fisker seemed to be indifferent whether the railway should ever be constructed or not" (1.77-78). The railway will be floated through the production of paper: "It was clearly [Fisker's] idea that fortunes were to be made out of the concern before a spadeful of earth had been moved. If brilliantly printed programmes might avail anything, with gorgeous maps, and beautiful little pictures of trains running into tunnels beneath snowy mountains and coming out of them on the margin of sunlit lakes, Mr. Fisker had certainly done much" (1.78).

Being a clever swindler, Melmotte recognizes the value of the scheme. The narrator explains Melmotte's character through gossip at first: "People said that Mr. Melmotte had a reputation throughout Europe as a gigantic swindler,—as one who in the dishonest and successful pursuit of wealth had stopped at nothing. People said of him that he had framed and carried out long premeditated and deeply laid schemes for the ruin of those who had trusted him" (1.68). Later, the narrator confirms Melmotte as "The bloated swindler, the vile city ruffian" (1.221). Meanwhile, he betrays the secrets of the railway boardroom:

> There was not one of them then present [of the Directors] who had not after some fashion been given to understand that his fortune was to be made, not by the construction of the railway, but by the floating of the railway shares...People out of doors were to be advertised into buying shares, and they who were so to say indoors were to have the privilege of manufacturing the shares thus to be sold. That was to be their work, and they all knew it. But now, as there were eight of them collected together, they talked of humanity at large and of the coming harmony of nations (1.89-90).

Here we see Trollope satirizing the hypocrisy that the pamphlet *The Ghost of John Bull* describes. In the name of bringing nations together and facilitating cooperation between them, these railway directors create an industry out of floating paper "shares" to unsuspecting investors. But of course Melmotte's crimes exceed mere hypocrisy. As chairman, Melmotte uses paper to produce the share-buying mania that will drive the share price up. By establishing the railway board and acting as though he plans to build a railway, he sets forth a promise that he has no intention of fulfilling. As historical accounts reflect and as this novel suggests, two key aspects of white-collar crime are puffery, or the exaggeration of value, which is facilitated by the use of paper; and the broken promise, whether the breach is wholly premeditated or not.

In his *Autobiography* (1883), Trollope suggests that Melmotte is the central character, whose vices seem to pervade the society—particularly the marriage market and literary circles: "[A]s I had ventured to take the whip of the satirist into my hand, I went *beyond* the iniquities of the great speculator who robs everybody, and made an onslaught also on *other vices*,—on the intrigues of the girls who want to get married, on the luxury of young men who prefer to remain single, and on the puffing propensities of authors who desire to cheat the public into buying their volumes" (355, my emphasis). This is a somewhat misleading statement, for, as Trollope's working notes reflect, this was first conceived as "the Carbury novel"; and Trollope suggests in the first sentence of the novel that Lady Carbury, not Melmotte, was originally the "chief character": "Let the reader be introduced to Lady Carbury, upon whose character and doings much will depend of whatever interest these pages may have" (Sutherland 475). She quickly becomes the object of satire, for later in the chapter, Lady Carbury explains that "[t]o puff and to get one's self puffed have become different branches of a new profession", and she must puff to advance her literary career (1.10). As an author, Trollope abhorred this type of "puffing"; so why did he shift his emphasis from Lady Carbury to Melmotte? I suggest that in the early stages of writing, Trollope recognized that if he made the Melmotte plot central, he could identify and explore the effects of a second form of dishonesty, in addition to the puffery that Lady Carbury uses: the broken promise. Melmotte and the railway scheme are introduced in chapter nine, halfway between Lady Carbury's puffery of her bad book *Criminal Queens* in chapter one and Sir Felix's promises of love to Ruby and Marie in chapters seventeen and eighteen. Melmotte's broken promises to investors are like Sir Felix's broken promises to Marie Melmotte and Ruby Ruggles; later and with a less premeditated quality, Paul breaks his promise to Mrs. Hurtle and Ruby breaks hers to John Crumb. In other words, the two aspects of white-collar crime that characterize Melmotte's railway scheme—puffery and broken promises—are redistributed over the two other main plots in the novel: Lady Carbury uses puffery to advance her literary ambition plot ("the puffing propensities of authors who desire to cheat the public into buying their volumes") and broken promises are a part of all the romance triangle plots ("the intrigues of the girls who want to get married, [and] the luxury of young men who prefer to remain single"). Because Trollope represents these two aspects of white-collar crime twice it helps us identify and understand these two aspects as the salient aspects of white-collar crime, deserving of—and, because they are now performed by individual characters rather than by a large railway scheme—capable of responding to punishment or reform.

The primary protagonist of the broken promise plots is Sir Felix. Sir Felix makes overtures to Marie Melmotte in chapter seventeen ("Marie Melmotte Hears a Love Tale") and to Ruby Ruggles in chapter eighteen ("Ruby Ruggles Hears a Love Tale"), but he never performs the role of hero in either romance "Tale". Like the promises of the fraudulent railway promoters, Sir Felix puts forth his promises with only, at best, a feeble intention of fulfilling them. As Ginger Frost suggests in *Promises Broken*, the broken promise plot was familiar to any novelist who read the newspaper, for breach-of-promise cases in the Victorian courts were not only melodramatic but highly publicized. As a result, they began to serve as topics in literature. In 1832, the comedy *Breach of Promise* was performed on the London stage; Charles Dickens represented a breach-of-promise case famously in *Pickwick Papers* (1836); and in 1845, the novel *The Breach of Promise* was published anonymously. Despite its title, the breach-of-promise case was actually a subplot in this novel, involving a villainess named Lucilla Undermine who plots with her working-class lover to fabricate evidence and sue the wealthy Sir Felix Archer for damages (Frost 1-5). Whether the name of the wealthy man is a coincidence or not, in *The Way We Live Now*, it is Sir Felix Carbury who breaks promises most flagrantly.

There are many instances of broken promise plots in Victorian novels, but Trollope adds a twist not found in these other novels: excessive triangulation. When Trollope claims in his *Autobiography* that the part of the novel that concerns "the young lady with her two lovers is weak and vapid", it is unclear which love triangle he means. A few sentences later, he claims that "Roger Carbury, Paul Montague, and Henrietta Carbury are uninteresting" (356), but his very delay in naming these three characters suggests some ambiguity. If we include Lady Carbury's divided loyalties, there are five love triangles in this novel containing a "young lady with her two lovers" and two more that consist of a young man with his two lovers: Sir Felix—Lady Carbury—Mr. Broune, Roger—Hetta—Paul, John Crumb—Ruby—Sir Felix, Sir Felix—Marie—Lord Nidderdale, and Mr. Brehgert—Georgiana Longestaffe—Mr. Batherbolt; Paul Montague—Mrs Hurtle—Hetta and Ruby—Sir Felix—Marie Melmotte. On one level, this triangulation enables plot complexity and delay of closure, for marriage between any two characters necessarily depends on at least one broken promise. More importantly, it enables Trollope to capture metaphorically the triangulated relationship between the railway promoters, the investors and the justice system, which was forced to choose between the first two, and to uphold either the promises made by the directors or the claims made by the investors. That is, Trollope uses the triangulated romance to represent the dilemma of the judges who had to discover personal intention and assign liability for debt.

In addition to exaggeration, Lady Carbury's literary ambition plot also suggests another aspect of the railway schemes: the schemes guaranteed the value of paper by generating more paper. In the first chapter, Lady Carbury writes three letters to three different editors, attempting to convince them of her history's value: she writes a letter verging on "another book" to describe the virtues of *Criminal*

Queens to Mr. Broune (1.2); she offers to write a good review for Mr. Booker's *New Tale of the Tub* if he will "repay the service by fulsome praise" of her book in his "Literary Chronicle" (1.6); and she extends a party invitation to Mr. Alf, in whose paper "the facts, if not true, were well invented; the arguments, if not logical, were seductive" (1.7). Lady Carbury generates paper (letters) in the hopes of securing good reviews (in newspapers) that will increase the perceived value of her book (a paper product).

By developing these two plots, Trollope suggests that white-collar crime depends not only upon puffery and broken promises but also upon the assumption that paper can adequately stand in for the object it represents. As a consequence, white-collar crime results in a nearly insoluble dilemma for the courts. Trollope's use of these plots to accomplish all this seems rather tidy and convenient, but one of the problems in this novel is the acute reflexivity between one of the objects of its satire and the method by which satire achieves its effects. I have shown that Lady Carbury's system of "puffing" is to exaggerate the good aspects of her novel and convince others to represent her novel in its best possible light, even if that means encouraging a dishonest review. However, satire, according to Trollope, necessarily involves exaggeration and dishonesty, which are the very traits that he satirizes through the Lady Carbury plot. He describes satire as he uses it in *The Way We Live Now*:

> The book has the fault which is to be attributed to almost all satires, whether in prose or verse. The accusations are exaggerated. The vices implied are coloured so as to make effect rather than to represent truth. Who, when the lash of objurgation is in his hands, can so moderate his arm as never to strike harder than justice would require? The spirit which produces the satire is honest enough, but the very desire which moves the satirist to do his work energetically makes him dishonest (*Autobiography*, 355).

For Trollope, there is a peculiar reflexiveness between the object of the satire (dishonesty) and the means used (dishonesty) to achieve the desired effect of the satire. By its very nature, satire requires dishonesty characterized by exaggeration; it separates the "made effect" from "represented truth". In a way, written satire is the most unsuitable mode for a novel that satirizes the widespread use of various forms of paper (IOUs, scrip, reviews, etc.) to produce an effect rather than resemble the truth. The difference, of course, between the two kinds of "puffery" that Lady Carbury and Trollope use is that Lady Carbury, like the M.P. and commissioner in the 1838 pamphlet, uses puffery "[t]o take care of [her]self"; Trollope, at least ostensibly, uses it to benefit society. But the reflexivity between puffery as the object of the satire and as the satirical method gestures toward the vigour with which Trollope pursues his narrative project and toward the formal problem at the heart of the novel. We can best understand this problem by turning once more to Trollope's commentary on *The Way We Live Now*.

Toward the end of *An Autobiography*, Trollope describes what he sees as the central concern of the novel: he intended to satirize "a certain class of dishonesty, dishonesty magnificent in its proportions" (354). However, while he believes "*The*

Way We Live Now [is], as a satire, powerful and good", he feels that the weakness of his novel is his inability to synthesize the satire with the romance: "the young lady with her two lovers is weak and vapid. I almost doubt whether it be not impossible to have two absolutely distinct parts in a novel, and to imbue them both with interest" (355-56). I suggest that we can rethink this criticism and recognize that, although these two "parts" may not fit neatly together, their friction is necessary to the project of this novel. In using the word "parts" to describe "satire" and the "young lady with her two lovers", Trollope effaces the difference between a narrative mode and a plot. We can begin to recognize the formal tension at the core of this novel if we reestablish the distinction between romance as a narrative *mode*, in opposition to satire; and the problematic romance as a *plot* distinct from the two other main plots he names: Lady Carbury's literary plot and the railway scheme.

The relationship between the two narrative modes and three plots is extraordinarily complex, as I suggest in my discussion of the reflexive puffery that characterizes both Lady Carbury's literary scheme and Trollope's satiric mode. But we can understand this complexity if we recognize that in writing this novel, Trollope has two overarching projects: to correct society's dishonesty and to entertain. Specifically, Trollope wanted to address the problems associated with white-collar crime, partly because he recognized the difficulties inherent in settling white-collar crime disputes in the courts. Many of the judges expressed disgust with both the men who designed the fraudulent schemes and the individuals who hoped to get rich quick without work by trading on the fraudulence. In addition, it was nearly impossible to reconstruct anything other than a paper trail to determine whether the railway scheme was fraudulent from the beginning, as Trollope depicts Melmotte's scheme, or merely a good-faith proposal that failed. Even in cases when white-collar criminals could be brought to trial, they could abscond or were penniless or could prolong court proceedings for years. In other words, the legal system could not always bring satisfactory closure to these cases. Trollope provides both the unambiguous censure and the closure that was often impossible to obtain in the Victorian courts by linking the two narrative modes. Satire has correction as its goal but by its very nature is somewhat lawless and formless because it lacks closure.[5] A satire such as the 1838 pamphlet, for example, castigates the villains ruthlessly; but the social reform the text desires, which would bring closure, does not occur within the text. Romance, on the other hand, is perhaps the most common nineteenth-century plot, with established conventions that include a hero and heroine, some stock impediments, and closure of the plot in marriage. Through marriages, novels can produce literary justice by bringing good and deserving characters together in wedded bliss and by punishing bad characters by refusing them the marital state, or by having them marry each other. By using satire and romance together, Trollope adjudicates white-collar crime using two different approaches: he energetically criticizes society; and he rewards the good characters and punishes the villains. I can show how the romance becomes the vehicle for closing the satire and bringing literary justice to white-collar criminals by tracing the outcome of Lady Carbury's plot and the broken-promise plot.

If we turn back to Trollope's working notes, we can begin to see the way he created a space for his version of literary justice. In chapter eighty-three, Melmotte commits suicide, which is described in two sentences and barely discussed afterwards. As P.D. Edwards noted in 1963, Trollope had originally planned to have Melmotte stand trial for his crimes, and quite late in the process of writing the novel, he opted to have Melmotte commit suicide instead. Critics have advanced various theories to account for this change in plot: that Trollope had used a trial in three of his last four novels and it was stale, that the suicide would preserve Melmotte's stature in the public imagination, or that Melmotte's suicide and silence reflect the way his language gives out once the forgery is detected.[6] I suggest, however, that the form of Melmotte's death uncannily recuperates his ingestion of the incriminating documents in the same room: "Mr. Melmotte on entering the room bolted the door and then, sitting at his own table, took certain papers out of the drawers...This one [document] he put bit by bit into his mouth, chewing the paper into a pulp till he swallowed it" (2.118-19). He destroys the evidence that would incriminate him at a trial. In foreclosing the possibility of a trial within the English justice system by destroying evidence and by destroying Melmotte, Trollope provides space for his own brand of literary justice, which is roughly forged between the two narrative modes in this novel.

The romance plot already operates within the satiric mode that predominates in this novel, two of whose several targets are "girls" who are scheming to marry and "young men" who are not marrying. In this novel, however, two men remain firm in their desire to marry: Roger Carbury and John Crumb. Significant twists in their two romance plots come in chapters seventy-one and seventy-two respectively. In "John Crumb Gets into Trouble", Sir Felix, the representative of the "young men who prefer to remain single", is beaten to a pulp by John Crumb. In beating Felix, John Crumb embodies the very spirit of satire. The narrator describes John Crumb's act as physical violence that adheres to the principles of justice as they are administered in Chancery, answering the question Trollope sets forth in his *Autobiography*: "Who, when the lash of objurgation is in his hands, can so moderate his arm as never to strike harder than justice would require?": "John Crumb raised [Sir Felix], and catching him round the neck with his left arm,—getting his head into chancery as we used to say when we fought at school,—struck the poor wretch some half-dozen times violently in the face, not knowing or caring exactly where he hit him, but at every blow obliterating a feature" (2.198). Just as the reflexivity between Lady Carbury's and Trollope's exaggeration signals the energy with which he pursues his narrative project, the resemblance between John Crumb and Trollope, both of whom use their "arm" to beat their victims, gestures toward Trollope's feeling of satisfaction when he metes out literary justice. Crumb is arrested by the police and thrown in jail for one night, but "he was buoyed up inwardly by the conviction that he had thoroughly thrashed his enemy" (2.200). Significantly, John Crumb's lower-class crime is enacted through the body rather than through words. John Crumb refuses the methods of white-collar crime altogether. In fact, Ruby's complaint about John Crumb is that he "hasn't ever a word to say". Roger replies, "Words to say! What do words matter? He loves you after that fashion that he wants to make you happy and respectable, not to make you a bye-word and a disgrace" (1.409). Rather than using words to make Ruby a "bye-word" herself (a verbal approximation of using paper to guarantee paper), John Crumb thrashes Sir Felix with his fists, lashing him like a satirist—but without words (the novelist of course does not have this choice). John Crumb marries Ruby and Sir Felix is banished to the continent in the company of a curate, who keeps "that gentleman as one of his Protestant population in the German town" (2.474)—a dire punishment for the dissipated Sir Felix.

Like Sir Felix, Lady Carbury is disciplined by the novel. Perhaps because she, unlike Melmotte and Sir Felix, has a redeeming quality—being willing to sacrifice anything for her son—the novel lets Lady Carbury off with a reprimand and reforms her. Towards the end of the novel, Lady Carbury proposes to write another book, *Wheel of Fortune*. The fact that she chooses this title, which alludes to the mythical wheel and the wheels of the railway engine, suggests that her book might tackle the same themes that Trollope's novel has. But Mr. Broune puts a stop to Lady Carbury's irresponsible writing. At the climax of the second proposal scene, Lady Carbury goes on her knees before Mr. Broune, who embodies literary ethics in so far as they can be upheld in this corrupt age. Through Lady Carbury's marriage to a man who is the editor of the *Morning Breakfast Table*, her puffery will be subordinated to responsible journalism. Lady Carbury finds happiness in her reformation and marriage: "Mrs Broune's Tuesday evenings were much more regarded by the literary world than had been those of Lady Carbury" (2.466).

Although the novel produces some literary justice by killing Melmotte, banishing Sir Felix and reforming Lady Carbury, Trollope also suggests how difficult it is to assign blame with fairness to all, through the fates of Paul Montague and Roger Carbury. Like Sir Felix, Paul serves on the provisional railway board of directors and breaks an engagement. According to the precedent established for Sir Felix, Paul might seem to deserve a worse fate that marrying the beautiful and virtuous Hetta Carbury. The novel lets Paul off with a reprimand and a warning: once Hetta finds out about Mrs Hurtle, she breaks their engagement and Paul endures several anxious chapters during which he is unsure whether he can win her back. By having Paul reclaim Hetta in the end, Trollope represents realistically the problems that the lawcourts faced when they attempted to assign responsibility in white-collar crime cases. White-collar crime, by its very nature, was more complex than the blue collar crime that resolved the issue between John Crumb and Sir Felix so satisfactorily. Paul's case has extenuating circumstances: although he serves on the railway board, he is the one member who approaches Melmotte and tries to discover whether the scheme is being conducted ethically. He breaks his promise to Mrs Hurtle but only after discovering that she may or may not still have a husband, whom she may or may not have murdered. By rewarding Paul with Hetta, this novel suggests that decent motives and honest mistakes in judgment such as these make white-collar crime a complex category of crime to punish.

On the other hand, the virtuous if somewhat priggish Roger Carbury loses Hetta. Unlike John Crumb, who seems able to cope with his rival, Roger refuses to avail himself of the means to dispose of his. The chapter following the scene in which John thrashes Sir Felix, describes Roger's refusal to lash Paul, even though he has the weapons with which to do it (72, "Ask Himself"). Even Hetta recognizes the parallel between Roger and John Crumb, for when Roger explains that John lashed Sir Felix because Sir Felix thought he could "be in love with two [women] at once", "Hetta as she heard the story hardly knew whether her cousin, in his manner of telling the story, was speaking of that other man…or of himself" (2.204). Rather than use what he knows of Paul's treachery with Mrs Hurtle against Hetta Carbury, and far from puffing it up to exceed even Paul's *appearance* of impropriety, Roger tells Hetta to ask Paul about Mrs Hurtle. Roger refuses to respond to Lady Carbury's letter of inquiry with more writing: "As he could not trust himself to write an answer to Lady Carbury's letter he determined that he would go to London. If he must tell the story he could tell it better face to face than by any written words" (2.202). Unlike Lady Carbury, Roger refuses to use writing to promote his own interests; unwilling to use his fists, he has no recourse but to grow old quickly so that he can leave his fortune to Paul and Hetta's child, to whom he will be like a grandfather. Trollope's ending for Paul and Roger stands in opposition to the literary justice he proposes for Melmotte, Lady Carbury and Sir Felix, for it suggests that dishonourable actions do not necessarily receive (or deserve) punishment; and honourable motives are not always rewarded. Trollope thus represents the final tragic outcome of the railway schemes that built nothing and destroyed people's lives: people lost faith in the justice system. In having Roger pass his inheritance to the next generation, symbolically skipping his own, Trollope perhaps expressed his hopes that the generation that lived later would have more answers than those who live the way we live now.

Notes

1. Edwin Sutherland first defined "white-collar crime" in 1949, "as a crime committed by a person of respectability and high social status in the course of his occupation" (7). This definition has been revised by some critics since then; see Croall 8-10. For a complete discussion of the various forms of white-collar crime in Victorian England, see Robb.
2. I use this phrase rather than the more common "poetic justice" to avoid confusion with Martha C. Nussbaum's argument in *Poetic Justice: The Literary Imagination and Public Life* (Boston: Beacon Press, 1995). I am less interested in the way reading literature enables people to make good policy decisions, for example, than the ways that Trollope responds to a legal crisis.
3. For treatments of this topic see Kostal 1-109, Robb 31-55, and Vaughan 102-148.
4. Kostal 361, quoting "Plunder of Railway Subscribers by Attornies", *Railway Gazette*, 23 June 1849.
5. Dustin Griffin explains that satire has two aspects historically: "*satyr* (the half man-half beast, suggesting that satire is lawless, wild, and threatening) and *lanx satura* (the "mixed" or "full platter"), suggesting that satire is a formless miscellany, and food for thought" (6).
6. P.D. Edwards "Trollope Changes his Mind: The Death of Melmotte in *The Way We Live Now*". *Nineteenth-Century Literature*. Volume 18, 1963. 89-91. Roger L. Slakey's argument in "Melmotte's Death: A Prism of Meaning in *The Way We Live Now*", *ELH* Volume 34, 1967. 248-59.

Chapter 10

Something to Hyde: The "Strange Preference" of Henry Jekyll[1]

Grace Moore

> "You think 'tis nothing. 'Tis a crime believe! A crime so great you scarcely can conceive".[2]
>
> "I have brought on myself a punishment and a danger that I cannot name. If I am the chief of sinners, I am the chief of sufferers also. I could not think that this earth contained a place for sufferings and terrors so unmanning..."[3]

The nineteenth century saw the continuation of a policing of sex and sexuality, which had originated in the seventeenth century and which coincided with the rise of the new middle class. Britain's transition to an industrial capitalist economy forced sexuality to retreat from the public to the private domestic sphere. With the commodification of labour power, the pleasure of the sexual act was negated to its utility and the value of its end product. Thus, non-reproductive forms of intercourse—which did not result in the production of a new labour force—were gradually devalued as self-indulgent and, because of their lack of issue, "unnatural".[4] As Foucault has suggested, "The couple imposed itself as a model, enforced the norm, safeguarded the truth, and reserved the right to speak while retaining the principle of secrecy".[5] It is a short step from labelling deviation from the norm as "unnatural" to the criminalization of the alternatives. As monogamous heterosexual activity within the confines of marriage was posited as the ideological norm, other expressions of sexuality developed an aura of the illicit, and such urges had either to be repressed or acted upon clandestinely.

The practising homosexual was undoubtedly marginalized and persecuted by a society which had come more and more to regard same-sex partnerships as depraved or sick. He, however, at least had the possibility of a partner with whom to share feelings of guilt and isolation as his sexual identity became increasingly criminalized, culminating in the Labouchère Amendment of 1885.[6] Even more marginalized than the homosexual, though, were the solitary offenders, the masturbators or onanists, whose explorations of their own bodies became subject to a regime of surveillance and suppression, leading to a cycle of guilt and fear.[7] Although forming an enormous group, the rhetoric aimed at deterring the deed led perpetrators to believe that they belonged to a small, and particularly repulsive sector of society. It is with the so-called "self-polluter" that this chapter is concerned, and I shall begin by examining the shift in perception which led to the construction of a discourse of criminality surrounding interest in one's own body.

I shall then demonstrate the influence of these discourses on one of the most frequently sexually allegorized texts of the *fin de siècle*, Robert Louis Stevenson's *Dr. Jekyll and Mr. Hyde*.

Although presumably practised since time immemorial, there is no evidence to suggest that the habit of masturbation was regarded as either dangerous or debilitating before the beginning of the eighteenth century. Tissot's publication of works such as *Onania; or, the Heinous Sin of Self-Pollution* (1707) and *An Essay on Onanism* (1772) unleashed (or generated) a torrent of anxieties about masturbation which were perpetuated until the beginning of the twentieth century. Tissot's tracts list a series of maladies that he believes will ensue from indulging in auto-eroticism, while to invest his warnings with the ultimate authority, he also invokes the biblical story of Onan to draw attention to divine prohibitions of the act. By the nineteenth century a positive torrent of anti-masturbation publications had flowed into the market place, most of them indebted to Tissot's work for their "facts". Essentially, there were two types of pamphlet in circulation, the first being the scholarly medical work, exemplified by Joseph Howe's *Excessive Venery* (1887), which sought to warn young men against the consequences of "secret sins" and "solitary indulgence".[8] The second kind comprised an accumulation of symptoms and dire warnings produced by quacks like R.J. Brodie & Co. in the hope of terrifying young people (usually boys) or those responsible for them into purchasing a variety of potions and contraptions to "cure" the onanist of the vice.[9] Frequently, there was little to choose between the two, with the charlatan's adoption of medical terminology to simultaneously frighten their readership and promote an air of professionalism, while men like William Acton (whose *The Functions and Disorders of the Reproductive Organs* [1857] was, as Steven Marcus points out, still being published in 1894) employed sensationalist language to grab the public attention.[10]

These warnings to young "self-polluters" are the product of a growing regulation—or policing—of the individual body, which mirrored the ever more rigid police structure of the body politic. Sexual desire was being channelled into "an allegorical choice between good and bad": healthy, or "natural" sexual impulses were equated with a high moral stature, while less conventional sexual practices were construed as evidence of incipient corruption.[11] As the locus of moral health, the body of the child thus became a site to be kept under vigilant surveillance. By the nineteenth century children had been divested of their sexuality and any curiosity they showed in their own bodies was regarded as abnormal and perverted. The rise of the public school system had led to concerted attempts to ensure that young middle-class men were unable to indulge in solitary sex. Manuals for youth groups, such as Baden-Powell's early twentieth-century *Scouting for Boys*, referred to masturbation euphemistically as "beastliness" and recommended to the young practitioners that they "cure" themselves of the habit through confessing it to their scout masters and following a strict regime of exercise and cold showers.[12] Baden-Powell's concern reflects the solicitude for the moral and physical health that gained in impetus from 1870 onwards. Young men had to be strong and healthy in order to serve their empire, and the superiority of the British race could not be undermined by such unmanly activities. The confession trope employed by Baden-Powell is illustrative of the way in which onanism had come to be perceived as a crime, and those in positions of authority, whether in schools, youth movements, or the medical profession had come to view themselves as guardians of a national morality. As Ed Cohen describes:

> [B]y weaving an ideological web of medical, pedagogical, religious, and familial practices around the adolescent male body, nineteenth-century British bourgeois culture transformed the ubiquitous potential for male autoeroticism into a set of physiological, psychological, and moral symptoms that revealed the execrable existence of "the masturbator". Moreover, this new pathological definition not only (re)produced a kind of male youth whose "self-abuse" legitimated the watchful gaze of those who devoted themselves to his governance, but it also inscribed the "material" experiences of all middle-class male children within a mode of embodiment that earnestly sought to transform their relationships to themselves.[13]

Paradoxically, though, these efforts to suppress and deny childhood (or as we would now term it, adolescent) sexuality resulted in a near-obsession with the pubescent body, not only through the legitimation of a constant adult gaze, but also through compelling the child to think about his body incessantly.

The taboos that were being constructed around self-abuse made the activity at once both desirable (as a transgression) and repugnant. Any engagement in the vice would lead to anxiety and self-censureship, and not simply in the short term. Young men were led to believe that the results of childhood masturbation could lie dormant for years and then suddenly manifest themselves in a startling and grotesque manner:

> It is well-known to physiologists that masturbation excites and agitates the system to a much greater degree than sexual intercourse, and in consequence of the facilities to repeat *the crime*, and the delusion it causes, makes rapid inroads upon the constitution, destroys the health, and produces disease. Those infatuated indulgences bring their own punishment, producing nervousness, hypochondriacism, depression of spirits, melancholy mania, epilepsy, hysteria, paralysis, dimness of sight, difficulty of hearing, & c. A person addicted to this vice is certain, *sooner or later*, to experience its ill effects; it weakens the functions of the reproductive organs, and produces temporary or permanent impotency.[14]

Self-pollution must therefore have been an omnipresent anxiety in the Victorian consciousness. It is safe to assume that virtually everyone would have indulged in the habit at one time or another, so that the slightest hint of any of the diverse illnesses that could be linked to onanism must have sparked multitudinous anxieties. William Acton outlined the belief that a regular self-abuser could never be the same again and was tainted for life, when he observed:

> If the struggle is severe for a youth to extricate himself from these vicious propensities, experience teaches me that it is very doubtful if, when the practice has been much indulged in, the physical frame will ever be wholly built up again; the haggard

expression, the sunken eye, the long, cadaverous-looking countenance, the downcast expression, which seems to arise from the dread of looking a fellow-creature in the face, may be carried to the grave.[15]

The young self-abuser was, then, the antithesis to every quality valued by his society. He was sickly, he was an outcast and he was good for nothing. The psychological impact of these documents was damaging in the extreme, and must have impacted dramatically on basic character formation. Boys who were led to believe that their physique would prevent them from being re-assimilated into society would thus regard themselves as outsiders, and by forming this attitude were likely to remain so.

As Lesley A Hall has so astutely commented, masturbation anxieties, while certainly focused on young boys, were definitely not restricted to this age group. With middle-class men often waiting until their thirties to marry, concerns extended to the continence of the bachelor.[16] It must also be registered that the ideas circulating in literature of this kind, in order to police young bodies, had themselves become Ideological State Apparatuses. What had begun as a sensationalist pamphlet in the early eighteenth century had gradually been incorporated into medical discourse as a given truth, until the adverse side-effects of such behaviour were universally believed. The possibilities that the symptoms displayed by masturbators could be attributed to general ill-health, or that they could have been the psychosomatic results of the fear instilled into the onanist through reading pamphlets do not seem to have been considered. A.A. Brill outlined the process at the beginning of the twentieth century when he remarked:

> The patients are terrified by reading quack literature...and, I regret to say by uninformed doctors. They are threatened with paralysis, paresis, consumption of the spine, insanity, etc., and as a result they become depressed, hypochondriacal, and self-conscious. But as soon as they become convinced that they are not doomed, and that masturbation cannot cause insanity or other dreadful maladies, they soon lose their symptoms.[17]

What Brill is essentially describing is an illness of hysteria, which was all too real for the sufferer. The self-abuser was a criminal and he would be punished through ill health. Such fears were not dispelled by initiation into adulthood, either; men read the tracts as children and were terrified by them, often imagining themselves to be exhibiting one of the multitudinous side effects that were attributed to the action. Thus as adults they retained the belief in the evils of masturbation and became complicit in fostering a regime of guilt, fear and surveillance over a new generation.

Sander L. Gilman's assertion that "By the 1880s the identification of masturbation as the major etiology of mental as well as physical illness had all but vanished from medical literature", whilst factually correct, belies the continued debate by non-specialists, which continued well into the twentieth century.[18] By the 1880s concerns surrounding onanism had widened to encompass not merely individual masturbators, but future generations. The habit, or "disease" as it was still termed gained prominence once more in the wake of anxieties evoked by the furore surrounding the Contagious Diseases Act (eventually repealed in 1886) and a growing concern for future racial vigour. In 1887, (*Dr. Jekyll and Mr. Hyde* having appeared in January of the previous year), Howe's *Excessive Venery* was published. The Social Purity Alliance also focused its efforts on those it perceived as young self-polluters in 1887, with the publication of Lyttelton's report on *The Causes and Prevention of Immorality in Schools*. While previous studies had stressed the consequences for the individual transgressor, the pamphlets of the 1880s played upon fears of hereditary weakness and illness, which had been evoked by Darwin's work on the process of natural selection.[19] It was asserted that excessive masturbation would lead to defective seminal fluid, resulting in weak children. The prophetic doom-laden rhetoric of the Old Testament invoked to emphasize the gravity of the danger:

> "The sins of the father shall be visited on the children, even unto the third and fourth generation". Nowhere in the category of disease is the truth of this saying so manifest as in the case of masturbation. The evil that they do lives long after them. Their vicious habits, continued as they are through the period when nature is endeavouring to create a vigorous condition which will resist the wear and tear of active adult life, leave an indelible impress on the whole structure. All tissues and secretions of the body are affected, and the seminal fluid partakes of the general deterioration.[20]

Here, we see a shift in the discourse surrounding masturbation. The act is transformed from an unpleasant self-indulgence endangering only the perpetrator, to a far broader social evil with the potential to undermine the future of the race. Stevenson had suffered from tuberculosis for most of his adult life, and was convinced that it would be selfish and irresponsible to run the risk of fathering a child to inherit his own ill health.[21] His attention would, therefore, have been caught by the claim that masturbation was the root cause of complaints as diverse as rickets and hereditary insanity or, more pertinently for him, consumption.[22] The (mis)deed of the individual could cause widespread misery and suffering and masturbation was reconfigured from mere hedonistic non-productive sex, to a dangerous and anti-social crime. The onanist became a perpetrator of evil, and a criminal that it was nigh impossible to detect.

It is this aura of unspecified, alienating wickedness that surrounds Henry Jekyll and his döppelgänger, Edward Hyde in Stevenson's novella. I would argue that whilst it is impossible to pin down the precise nature of Jekyll's misdeeds, his narcissism and the symptoms he manifests suggest that his problems may have begun with self-abuse. In an article which appeared in the *Journal of Mental Science,* and that is too rapidly dismissed by Robert Mighall, Edward Spitzka was struck by "the impression that the author of that ingeniously absurd romance, 'Dr. Jekyll and Mr. Hyde' had some such person as my patient in mind when he described the repulsive influence exerted by the latter on persons passing him in the street".[23] Spitzka's patient, it emerges, was none other than an "inveterate masturbator". However, Mighall responds to this idea by down-playing the breadth of the anti-masturbation tract's circulation, and pointing to what he calls

"Stevenson's (non-)description of Hyde",[24] arguing that Spitzka's reading is one that is limited to a small sector of the medical community. The fact that Jekyll's vice is never explicitly named is perfectly in keeping with the often obscure and vague language of the anti-self-pollution literature which must have left many young readers puzzled as to precisely what was being prohibited. Mighall focuses his argument upon Hyde's appearance, suggesting that Stevenson leaves too much to the reader's imagination to allow the reader to detect any conclusive evidence for Jekyll's "private vices" in his countenace.

However, as I shall demonstrate, many of the descriptions of Jekyll's *change* into Hyde mirror the depictions of the process and results of onanism as outlined in the tracts warning against it. Such representations would have been instantly recognizable to upper- and middle-class (male) readers, who would have been exposed to them in their youth. It was therefore unnecessary for Stevenson to identify a crime that could not be named. Dr. Jekyll's friend Utterson inadvertently aligns Jekyll with the self-abuser who has lapsed into old habits, or is suffering the consequences of them when he declares:

> Poor Harry Jekyll...my mind misgives me he is in deep waters! He was wild when he was young; a long while ago, to be sure; but in the law of God there is no stature of limitations. Ah, it must be that; the ghost of some old sin, the cancer of some concealed disgrace; punishment coming, *pede claudo*, years after memory has forgotten and self-love condoned the fault (*J&H* 43).

Utterson's language here not only resembles the Old Testament forebodings of Howe and his kind, it also draws attention to Jekyll's condition as a recurring problem. A misdemeanour involving other men or prostitutes is unlikely to have been buried in the depths of his memory. However, a fleeting moment of self-gratification, stemming from the "self-love" that Utterson invokes could easily have surfaced either through physical consequences or the resumption of the habit. The Victorians believed that masturbation was a degenerative process, which would corrupt the individual and lead to further crimes—usually violence inflicted upon the self or another—or sexual excesses involving homosexual encounters or prostitution. Acton asserted that:

> In some patients, rash and even criminal acts are the result of the idea that an atonement may thereby be made for the sin committed. The attempt to injure the genitals and similar extravagances often, I believe, arise from such insane fancy while, on the other hand, extravagant masturbation or the tendency to commit rapes or unnatural crimes may be in some cases traced to the not less insane desire the sufferer feels to test and to prove to himself or others that he is not impotent.[25]

Henry Jekyll's intemperances are largely left to the reader's imagination, and this very vagueness draws attention to the solitary nature of his crimes. Whilst Jenni Calder has suggested that "Jekyll's indiscretions would have involved drinking and women",[26] there is no textual evidence to support this supposition. Elaine Showalter, on the other hand, has pointed to the text's absence of women as an indicator that *Jekyll and Hyde* constitutes:

> [A] case study of male hysteria, not only that of Henry J., but also of the men in the community around him. It can most persuasively be read as a fable of *fin-de-siècle* panic, the discovery and resistance of the homosexual self.[27]

However, this assertion of Jekyll's illicit homosexuality conflicts with the deep-rooted sense of alienation pervading the narrative. The urban homosexual of the 1880s would, of course, have led an illicit existence, but he would still have been able to identify himself with an established and recognizable gay subculture. At the very least, he would have had a partner or fleeting encounters with other men. Jekyll, however, is noteworthy only for his isolation.

The pamphlets dealing with the act of self-pollution implicitly align the vice with egotism and ambition—traits for which Dr. Jekyll is noteworthy. Critics like Showalter have commented repeatedly on Jekyll's narcissism, but have failed to register the full implications of that term. According to Freud the narcissistic stage in children falls between autoeroticism and object-love. An individual who loves according to the narcissistic type will love in one of four ways:

> a) What he himself is (i.e. himself).
> b) What he himself was.
> c) What he himself would like to be.
> d) Someone who was once part of himself.[28]

I would argue that Jekyll's self-love corresponds to types a and c, and that it is not simply restricted to self-obsession, but also assumes physical dimensions too. His constant references to the "indignity" of his pleasures, combined with the fact that he partakes of them alone mark Jekyll out as an onanist. When he speaks of himself as someone who, "could thus plod in the public eye with a load of genial respectability, and in a moment, *like a schoolboy*, strip off these lendings and spring headlong into the sea of liberty" (*J&H* 80-1), he seems to be describing the resort to the traditional method of "schoolboy's relief". Indeed, an examination of his final struggles demonstrates that the evil with which he is grappling is an evil that emanates from his own frame. We are informed that:

> The resurgent horror was knit to him closer than a wife, closer than an eye; lay caged in his flesh, where he heard it mutter and felt it struggle to be born; and at every hour of weakness and in the confidences of slumber, prevailed against him and deposed him out of life" (*J&H* 89).

A horror clearly associated with bodily sensations that are "closer than a wife" can surely only stem from Jekyll's own body, as the only one that can come closer to him than that of a spouse. If we recall the narrator Utterson's own lifestyle we are reminded immediately that it is one of austerity and self-denial when alone. He is able to quell his needs and desires, while Dr. Jekyll is compelled to act upon his and cannot demonstrate the same self-discipline. It is revealing that although

Jekyll attributes his alteration to the rather unconvincing powders that Showalter has correctly identified as a major flaw in the plot, Lanyon charts Jekyll's decline to a much earlier period. He declares, "But it is more than ten years since Henry Jekyll became too fanciful for me. He began to go wrong, wrong in mind..." (*J&H* 38). Lanyon thus suggests that it is one of Jekyll's innate traits that has caused his downfall, a view that Jekyll endorses incessantly in his own narrative by frequently berating his own egotism and ambition.

Even more significant than his solitude, is the appearance of Edward Hyde, which bears a striking resemblance to that of the degenerate masturbator. Each protagonist who encounters Hyde feels an uncomfortable sense of foreboding when in his company, and the source of this discomfort cannot be directly attributed to any one characteristic. The reader learns that:

> Mr. Hyde was pale and dwarfish; he gave an impression of deformity without any namable malformation, he had a displeasing smile, he had borne himself...with a sort of murderous mixture of timidity and boldness, and he spoke with a husky, whispering and somewhat broken voice,—all these were points against him; but not all of these together could explain the hitherto unknown disgust, loathing and fear with which Mr. Utterson regarded him" (*J&H* 41).

The aura of unpleasantness that is loosely associated with Hyde's countenance marks him out as an onanist. William Acton has listed the physiognomical changes to be detected in the persistent offender as, "the haggard expression, the sunken eye, the long, cadaverous-looking countenance, the downcast expression, which seems to arise from the dread of looking a fellow-creature in the face".[29] Acton, who continues to suggest that even a reformed masturbator will never shed the signs of his offence, was certainly not alone in his belief. The stunted growth and discomfort generated by Mr. Hyde were, for the late-Victorians, clear evidence of self-pollution and constituted a signifier of his damnation. Hyde, of course, is so wrapped up in himself and the pursuit of his own pleasures that he spends most of the narrative in a state of oblivion to the presence of others. His trampling of the child at the beginning of the novella is not simply a rejection of reproductive sexual activity, it also highlights his inability to interact.

Like the "solitary offender" detailed in the anti-masturbation tracts then, Jekyll is both asexual and misanthropic. Joseph Brodie, among others, warns of the pariah existence that must be endured by the anti-social onanist:

> Oh! How delusive, selfish and prostrate, must be the spirit of him, who addicts himself to the habit of Onaism [sic]:—he banishes himself from his fellow-man,—he becomes an anti-social being; the tender sympathies, the ardent affection of the fairer portion of the species he eradicates from his heart, and instead of that heart being a shrine for those feelings which ennoble man, he becomes an outcast on earth; at the same time his impurities, his defilements, and his sins, unfit him from enjoying bliss hereafter, in those regions where there is no grief, woe, or tribulation, and where all is pure.[30]

Jekyll's true crime is, then, a total internalization and rejection of the society of others. The text constantly refers to the type of hand imagery that is, for obvious reasons, so central to the tracts on self-pollution. When Jekyll assures Utterson that Mr. Hyde will appear no more, he pledges, not by giving his word on the matter, but by giving his hand instead. Jekyll himself points to the centrality of this imagery when he delights in having become Hyde for the first time and stretches out his hands, "exulting in the freshness of these sensations" (*J&H* 78). More ominous still is the instance when the doctor, believing that he has succeeded in suppressing his dionysian alter-ego, having been free of him for two months, awakes with "somewhat odd sensations" (*J&H* 82) to discover that he has involuntarily become Hyde. Significantly, it is his hands that reveal the change to him:

> [M]y eye fell upon my hand. Now, the hand of Henry Jekyll…was professional in shape and size; it was large, firm, white amd comely. But the hand which I now saw, clearly enough in the yellow light of a mid-London morning, lying half shut on the bed-clothes, was lean, corded, knuckly, of a dusky pallor, and thickly shaded with a swart growth of hair. It was the hand of Edward Hyde (*J&H* 82).

Just as Acton warned of the dangers of involuntary auteroticism at night, so Jekyll finds that when he lowers his guard in sleep, the sensuous impulses that he can no longer control take hold of him once more. Jekyll's reaction here is akin to the type of response to "nocturnal emissions" recounted by Hoffman in which, "not only the powers are lost, the body falls away, and the face turns pale; but moreover the memory fails, a cold sensation seizes the limbs, the sight is clouded, and the voice becomes hoarse; all the body languishes by degrees; and disturbing dreams prevent sleep and administering any relief".[31] In his final days Jekyll may have been afraid that Hyde could manifest himself at any time, yet it is the act of sleeping that he fears most, as a time when he is unable to maintain his rigid self-control. Just as the persistent masturbator's body is figured as being unable to hold its "treasure" (a euphemism for nocturnal ejaculation), so we are informed that Jekyll's is a body, "that seemed not strong enough to contain the raging energies of life" and that if he "slept, or even dozed for a moment in [his] chair, it was always as Hyde that [he] awakened" (*J&H* 89). Herein lies one of the many dangers ascribed to the habit. Not only was masturbation addictive, it could also overwhelm the individual to the obliteration of all other concerns. Like the pleasure-seeking decadents of the *fin de siècle*, the onanist did not contribute anything to society in economic terms. However, more importantly, he ostracized himself in social terms, since he was reliant upon nobody for the source of his pleasure.[32]

As is all too frequently forgotten, Jekyll *is* Hyde, and the only body in which he shows any interest is his own. Jekyll himself frequently reiterates the fact that he and Hyde are one, not simply doubles. He is frequently imaged in front of mirrors, and Utterson and Poole's response to the looking glass in Jekyll's room, "into whose depth they looked with an involuntary horror" (*J&H* 67) is illustrative of a terror generated by something more significant than "the rosy glow playing on the roof, the fire sparkling in a hundred repetitions along the glazed front of the presses, and their own pale and fearful countenances stooping to look in" (*J&H* 67). The mirror itself is clearly the source of the men's fear, symbolizing as it does Jekyll's infatuation with himself. A comparison of the descriptions of Jekyll's metamorphosis into Hyde with the rhetoric of anti-onanism pamphlets reveals a striking resemblance between the two. Jekyll frequently makes explicit the fact that he and Hyde are one, not simply doubles. The account of his first successful transformation is couched in language remarkably similar to a detailing of a state of self-induced orgasmic rapture. Jekyll progresses from "deadly nausea" to a condition wherein:

> [T]hese agonies began swiftly to subside, and I came to myself as if out of a great sickness. There was something strange in my sensations, something indescribably new and, from its very novelty, incredibly sweet. I felt younger, lighter, happier in body; within I was conscious of a heady recklessness, a current of disordered sensual images running like a mill race in my fancy, a solution of the bonds of obligation, an unknown but not an innocent freedom of the soul (*J&H* 78).

This detailed depiction bears a remarkable resemblance to Rousseau's representation of the pleasures of sex for one in *Confessions*, as cited at length by William Acton in his dire warnings of the consequences of such acts:

> It might be said of me that my heart and my mind do not belong to the same person. My feelings, quicker than lightning, fill my soul; but instead of illuminating, they burn and dazzle me. I feel everything, I see nothing. I am excited, but stupid; I cannot think except in cool blood...My ideas arrange themselves in my brain with incredible difficulty; they circulate there dully, fermenting so as to excite me, heat me, give me palpitations; while in the midst of all this emotion I see nothing clearly, I could not write a single word—I must wait.[33]

Both Stevenson's and Rousseau's depictions highlight the subsumation and even obliteration of the self during the moment of climax—a condition which for Acton was threatening in the extreme. Having accepted Tissot's deduction that "orgasm is a form of seizure that is itself harmful to the brain leaving its functions 'necessarily deranged' and causing a harmful flow of blood away from other vital organs", Acton was convinced that self-abuse was not simply habit forming, but that it could become a necessity.[34]

By the time of his suicide (a fate frequently resorted to by the depressed and alienated masturbator, convinced that he has begun to display the signs of hereditary insanity), Jekyll's behaviour when he is *not* Hyde has deteriorated into that of a monomaniac. He has become totally obsessed with his misdeed and with Hyde, and he exhibits the same morbid depression and physical complaints detailed in many case studies of self-abusers. The parallels between Jekyll's account and the report below of a young boy from Beddoes' *Hygëia* are striking. Jekyll's narrative verges on the hysterical as he declares:

> Under the strain of this continually impending doom and by the sleeplessness to which I now condemned myself, ay, even beyond what I had thought possible to man, I became, in my own person, a creature eaten up and emptied by fever, languidly weak in both body and mind, and solely occupied by one thought: the horror of my other self. But when I slept, or when the virtue of the medicine wore off, I would leap almost without transition (for the pangs of transformation grew daily less marked) into the possession of a fancy brimming with images of terror, a soul boiling with causeless hatreds…(*J&H* 89).

By comparison, the excerpt from *Hygëia* seems positively restrained, but note that both sufferers complain of languor and weakness and also, like Jekyll/Hyde, the boy is convinced that he inspires terror:

> My present situation is as follows: My faculties are greatly impaired. My apprehension is become blunt: continued thinking is impracticable: my memory is weak, or rather entirely gone—my body is helpless, mere skin and bones. The sight of me excites horror...But not only am I disabled; I constantly feel the most violent pains, particularly where I have offended most—Add to this a restlessness and a melancholy, that exceeds every thing—Often should I have yielded to the temptations of putting an end to my wretched existence, if the motives of reason and the doctrines of the most beneficent reason—which is my only friend and treasure—had not restrained me.[35]

Of course, the young man projects his feelings of guilt onto those around him and imagines that his crime elicits a repulsion, which is completely separate from their reactions to his physical illness.

As a doctor, Henry Jekyll would have been all too familiar with the debates surrounding onanism, and would therefore have known exactly the type of symptoms that would be expected to emerge from systematic masturbation. It would therefore seem that Jekyll is a victim of the type of self-policing that arose as a result of Victorian society's acceptance of the dangers of onanism. It is impossible to determine whether Jekyll actually suffered from the various reactions he described, or whether his conscience led him to delude himself into believing that he might be going mad or physically deteriorating. As a wealthy and successful man who had evidently opted for a single life, Jekyll can certainly be charged with an assault on bourgeois propriety. Rather than taking a wife and breeding a generation of new consumers and conquerors of the globe, Jekyll chooses to remain alone and indulge only himself. Dr. Jekyll's sexual identity has retreated that little bit too far from the mainstream and had simply become too private. The sheer hedonism of his quest for self-fulfilment is incompatible with the basic moral code privileging bourgeois coupledom that had turned procreation into a utility. The struggle between Jekyll and Hyde is not merely a grappling between moralist and sensualist. Stevenson also employs his schizoid protagonist to demonstrate the conflict inherent in the increasingly introspective nature of Victorian middle-class life and the constraints that its rules and system of (self) policing placed on sexual identity and individuality.

Notes

1. The first version of this chapter was completed six weeks prior to the appearance of Robert Mighall's *The Geography of Victorian Gothic*, a superb re-evaluation of the gothic genre and a text I engage with in the pages that follow. Particular thanks are due to Chris Bongie of Queen's University, Ontario, who encouraged me to re-work the piece when I was at the point of abandoning it altogether. Chris Willis, with her customary generosity, read and commented upon an early draft. Laura Salisbury facilitated the post-Mighall reworking process by inviting me to deliver a paper at Birkbeck College, where I received useful and detailed feedback from the Graduate Research Group. My especial thanks go to Dr. Andrew King of Christ Church University College, Canterbury for his astute reminders on the Labouchère Amendment and other matters.
2. R.J. Brodie & Co. *The Secret Companion: A Medical Work on Onanism or Self-Pollution*. (London: 1845). 14.
3. Robert Louis Stevenson. *The Strange Case of Dr Jekyll and Mr Hyde*. (1886. Ed. Martin A. Danahay. Ontario: Broadview Press. 1999) 56. All subsequent references will be acknowledged parenthetically.
4. See Michel Foucault. *The History of Sexuality Volume One: The Will to Knowledge*. (1976. Trans. Robert Hurley. Middlesex: Penguin, 1990).
5. Foucault. *History of Sexuality Volume One*. 3.
6. Of course the outlawing of "gross indecency" between men was almost a by-product of the Criminal Law Amendment Act, which raised the age of consent for heterosexual relations as a means of protecting young girls against prostitution. The Act was a direct response to Stead's "Maiden Tribute" articles in the *Pall Mall Gazette*, and section II, which came to be known as the "blackmailer's charter", was appended only at the very last minute, and was not fully debated in parliament.
7. Although strictly the term "onanism" is incorrect as Onan's crime was coitus interruptus rather than masturbation [see *Genesis* 38, 4-11], since the authors of anti-masturbatory tracts frequently employed the term as a synonym for "self-abuse" I shall use the two terms inter-changeably.
8. Joseph W. Howe. *Excessive Venery: Masturbation and Continence: the etiology, pathology and treatment of the diseases resulting from venereal excesses, masturbation and continence*. (New York: 1887). 24.
9. Brodie's pamphlet, which is in fact an extended advertisement describes itself as a "Medical Work" (29). Fortunately help is at hand in the form of a "cordial balm of zeylanica", which just happens to be available at the bargain price of three large bottles at five pounds from none other than R.J. Brodie & Co. The price of the cure itself, along with the lengthy case-study style of the pamphlet demonstrates that the targets for this restorative were boys of the middle and upper classes.
10. Steven Marcus. *The Other Victorians: A Study of Sexuality and Pornography in Mid-Nineteenth-Century England*. (1974. New York: W.W. Norton & Company, 1985). 12.
11. Ralph Strachan. "That Familiar Feeling of Something Lost: Homosocial Desire in

David Copperfield". Conference paper. The Dickens Project Winter Conference. February 19-21, 1999.

12. Robert Baden-Powell. *Scouting for Boys: A Handbook for Instruction in Good Citizenship Through Woodcraft*. (1908. 13th Edition. London: C. Arthur Pearson Ltd. 1928). 210.
13. Ed Cohen. *Talk on the Wilde Side: Toward a Genealogy of a Discourse on Male Sexualities*. (New York & London: Routledge,1993). 36.
14. Brodie. *The Secret Companion*. 11.
15. William Acton. Quoted in Howe. *Excessive Venery*. 107.
16. Lesley A. Hall. "Forbidden By God, Despised by Men: Masturbation, Medical Warnings, Moral Panic, and Manhood in Great Britain, 1850-1950". In *Forbidden History: The State, Society, and the Regulation of Sexuality in Modern Europe*. Ed. John C. Fout. (1990. Chicago: University of Chicago Press, 1992). 299. As late as 1924 Meagher asserted that "masturbation while almost a normal phenomenon for the child and the adolescent is not to be so regarded in the adult. When persisted in by the latter, it shows a failure of psychosexual development. It is a bad way to meet sex cravings. It increases his selfishness, and interferes with his social progress". J.F.W. Meagher. *A Study of Masturbation and its Reputed Sequelae*. (London: Balliere, Tindall & Cox. 1924). 29.
17. Quoted in K. Menzies. *Autoerotic Phenomena in Adolescence: An Analytic Study of the Psychology and Psychopathy of Onanism*. (London: H.K. Lewis & Co. Ltd. 1919). 59.
18. Sander L. Gilman. *Difference and Pathology: Stereotypes of Sexuality, Race and Madness*. 1985. (Cornell University Press: Ithaca and London. 1988). 40.
19. As the step-parent of a boy who was going through adolescence in the 1880s (Lloyd Osbourne, b.1868), Stevenson is likely to have been familiar with at least some of the anti-masturbatory literature targeted at young men.
20. Howe. *Excessive Venery*. 92.
21. Jenni Calder. *Robert Louis Stevenson: A Life Study*. (Glasgow: Richard Drew Publishing. 1980). 322.
22. Howe. *Excessive Venery*. 93. The debate over responsibility for inherited disorders takes on gender implications with Howe's assertion that "Many cases of pulmonary consumption are directly traceable to the secret sin of the father. It is not so easy to detect the mother's share in the results, for the simple reasons that she cannot be questioned about the matter at all, and because many of the appearances which are found connected with old habits of masturbation are also seen in various forms of uterine disease".
23. E.C. Spitzka. "Cases of Masturbation". *Journal of Medical Science*. 34. April 1888. 52.
24. Robert Mighall. *A Geography of Victorian Gothic Fiction: Mapping History's Nightmares*. (Oxford: Oxford University Press, 1999). 193.
25. William Acton. Quoted in Howe. *Excessive Venery*. 107. Indeed, W.D. Morrison, the Chaplain of Pentonville Prison identified masturbation as a sign of weakness and repressed "deviant" impulses when he observed in 1895 of its most famous prisoner, Oscar Wilde:

> When he first came down here from Pentonville he was in an excited flurried condition, and seemed as if he wished to face his punishment without flinching. But all this has passed away. As soon as the excitement caused by the trial subsided and he had to encounter the daily routine of prison life his fortitude began to give way and rapidly collapsed altogether. He is now quite crushed and broken. This is unfortunate, as a prisoner who breaks down in one direction generally breaks down in several, and I fear from what I hear and see that perverse sexual practices are again getting the mastery over him. This is a common occurrence among prisoners of *his class* and is of course favoured by constant cellular isolation. The odour of his cell is now so bad that the officer in charge of him has to use carbolic acid in it every day…I need hardly tell you that he is a man of the most morbid disposition. See Richard Ellman. *Oscar Wilde*. (1987. Middlesex: Penguin. 1997). 464. My italics.

For Morrison—who was transferred to another position in the wake of his allegations—Wilde's self-abuse is symptomatic of a class-rooted decadence that, owing to the restrictions of solitary confinement, cannot be manifested in any other way. The accusations against Wilde demonstrate the way in which masturbation was still regarded as a signifier of a much deeper moral decay; the inate sickness of a criminal against nature.

26. Jenni Calder. Introduction to Robert Louis Stevenson. *Dr Jekyll and Mr Hyde and Other Stories*. (Middlesex: Penguin, 1979). 12.
27. Elaine Showalter. *Sexual Anarchy: Gender and Culture at the Fin de Siècle*. (London: Virago. 1992). 106.
28. Sigmund Freud. "On Narcissism: An Introduction". *The Freud Reader*. Ed. Peter Gay. (New York & London: Norton. 1989). 555.
29. William Acton. *Functions and Disorders of the Reproductive Organs* in Youth, in Adult Age, and in Advanced Life. (Sixth edition. London: J. & A. Churchill, 1875). 55.
30. Brodie. *The Secret Companion*. 14.
31. Quoted in R. & L. Perry & Co. *The Silent Friend: A Medical Work Treating on the Anatomyand Physiology of the Organs of Generation and their Diseases, with Observations on Onanism and its Baneful Results*. (London: 1847). 63. Recall that *Jekyll and Hyde* itself emerged from a "fine bogy tale" that Stevenson experienced as a nightmare. See Calder 220-221.
32. Of course, during the two months when Jekyll liberates himself from his indulgence and is free of Hyde, he is notable for his charitable conduct and the assistance he renders to others.
33. William Acton. *Functions and Disorders of the Reproductive Organs*. 56. See 55-57 for Acton's onslaught in its entirety. Interestingly, Rousseau continues his account by describing the effect of masturbatory activity on his handwriting, which he describes as "scratched, blotted, mixed up, undecipherable" (Acton 56). Recall that Stevenson pays particular attention to the changes to Jekyll's writing, which becomes an "odd, upright hand" when the Hyde persona takes over. (*J&H* 51)
34. Cohen. *Talk on the Wilde Side*. 45-6.

35. Quoted in Thomas Beddoes. *Hygëia or Essays Moral and Medical, on the Causes Affecting the Personal State of Our Middling and Affluent Classes*. Volume I. (Bristol: 1802). In three volumes.

Chapter 11

The Novelization of the Dreyfus Affair: Femininity and Sensation in *Fin-de-Siècle* France[1]

Christopher E. Forth

For French men and women of the 1890s, few political scandals were more sensational than the Dreyfus Affair. The controversy revolved around Captain Alfred Dreyfus, a Jewish artillery officer who in 1894 had been found guilty of selling military secrets to the Germans and was exiled for life on a penal colony in the South Pacific. Although this scandal gave rise to violent anti-Semitic agitation among those seeking confirmation of the inherently "treasonous" nature of Jews, for most observers the captain's treason was evident in an incriminating note that contained military information apparently written in his own hand. Yet, as friends and family of Dreyfus soon discovered, further investigation pointed to the work of another man–a certain Major Walsin-Esterhazy–whose handwriting was not only similar to that of Dreyfus, but whose sizeable gambling debts constituted a financial motive for treason. Buoyed with this information, from 1895 a campaign calling for a revision of the original trial steadily garnered the support of a few journalists and liberal politicians; yet what transformed the Dreyfus case into an "affair" was the intervention of the popular novelist Émile Zola, who, after writing a number of essays supporting the revisionist cause, in January 1898 published an explosive article that directly accused highly-placed government and military officials of covering up the truth. In addition to prompting the expected libel case that forced the Dreyfus issue into the open, the article, entitled "J'Accuse", facilitated a division of public opinion between pro-Dreyfus ("Dreyfusard") and anti-Dreyfus factions. As most historians agree, at this juncture the crisis had moved well beyond the fate of the innocent captain to the status of the Third Republic itself, which now seemed divided between defenders of traditional institutions like the Army and Church and those who championed a more liberal political order. It had also expanded far beyond France to become the talk of the Western world.

With the future of the French state apparently in the balance, one can see why the Dreyfus Affair created such a stir; yet the larger political question was all the more engaging given the dramatic twists and turns of the story behind it all. Indeed, the Dreyfus Affair had all the trappings of a popular novel. Not only was the provocative issue of espionage at the centre of all the commotion, but as the crisis unfolded it also featured disguises, military cover-ups, and secret meetings as well as mysterious women and midnight escapes from the country. There was moreover a compelling cast of characters, including a grieving wife and mother (Lucie Dreyfus), a devoted brother (Mathieu Dreyfus) who engineered the revisionist campaign, a dashing young officer (Colonel Georges Picquart) who discovered the identity of the true traitor, and an ensemble cast of "heroes" and "villains" who intervened either to see justice served or to defend the integrity of the army. The plot thickened further in 1899 with revelations that Colonel Hubert Henry, a member of the army's General Staff, had forged documents in an attempt to further implicate Dreyfus once a second trial had become inevitable. Henry's dramatic suicide (or was it murder?) not only added even more intrigue to this overheated plot, but helped strengthen the public image of the revisionist campaign. The retrial and subsequent pardon of Dreyfus in mid-1899 concluded the legal side of the scandal, but the political tensions exacerbated by the Affair fractured French politics well beyond the First World War.

If the intrinsically "novelesque" elements of this real-life drama were not enough, some claimed that the plot to frame Dreyfus had actually been *lifted* from a novel–not from one of the many espionage stories that circulated during this time, but from a *roman-feuilleton* entitled *Les deux frères*. Serialized in *Le Petit Journal* between January and July 1894, Louis Létang's novel recounts the story of a young woman who seeks to break her engagement to an army captain after falling in love with another man. Significantly, forged handwriting leading to the charge of treason are central to her strategy. After anonymously alerting her fiancé's superiors at the Ministry of War to a traitor in their midst, she arranges to have a letter forged in the man's handwriting promising to deliver secret documents to the chief of German intelligence. The similarities with the Dreyfus scenario were too striking to be ignored, which is why some charged that the General Staff had found in this novel a set of circumstances that would allow them to frame Dreyfus.[2] Literary and novelesque factors were also cited in the formation of public hostility to the campaign for a revision of the 1894 court case, where many Dreyfusards condemned the public's willingness to believe anti-Semitic propaganda, not to mention its addiction to popular novels that romanticized the military. For example, when Dreyfus returned to France in 1899, his withered and stoic figure in the courtroom did not elicit much sympathy. One sympathizer conceded that the public had, through the romantic military novels of Georges Ohnet and Jules Mary, come to expect certain conventions when conceiving of their ideal hero. "We would like [Dreyfus] to look like a hero, but this hero of the most frightful adventure only has the look of an impeccable functionary. Having come here as if to a theater, some are, without realizing it, disappointed that he should be himself and not play-act".[3]

Considered as a public sensation, one might say the entire Dreyfusard campaign was haunted by the novelesque, by the theatrical, and by "lies" in general. If the military plot to frame Dreyfus for treason was indeed literary in origin, it was also "literature" (in the form of yellow journalism and popular novels) that misled the public about the captain's innocence. Loosely united around the claim that "Truth is on the march!", Dreyfusards defended their campaign as the mission of rational minds carefully untangling the obfuscating web of lies, literature, and all that created in the public "sensation" rather than careful judgment. As this chapter will demonstrate, the battle of truth against lies in the Dreyfus Affair tapped into a deep pool of *fin-de-siècle* cultural concerns in which the problem of the sensational was often traced to the vagaries of physical sensation itself. During this time many physicians and social commentators were worried about the degree to which individuals and groups were vulnerable to external stimulations that, by exciting their nerves and appetites, might lead them into disorderly, even criminal behaviour. Explanations like these were central to discourses about the masses at this time, where social theorists like Gustave Le Bon and Gabriel Tarde interpreted collective behaviour according to models generated by the materialist psychology of the day. This is one reason why crowd psychologists often employed concepts like imitation, seduction, psychic automatism, hysteria and "moral contagion" when trying to make sense of the masses.[4] As Rae Beth Gordon explains, such models of the individual and collective mind referred repeatedly to what might be called the "corporeal unconscious", the substratum of nerves and pure sensation that, according to many physicians, seemed to generate "automatic" behaviour like hysterical fits, somnambulism, facial tics, gestural exaggeration, and hypnotic suggestion. Although there is ample evidence to suggest that many people relished popular entertainments that allowed them to temporarily lose control, such behaviour was also frequently damned by those for whom such distractions represented the more pernicious side of urban modernity.[5] Thus at the end of the nineteenth century, the problem of sensation was often approached through medical discourses that considered the "pathological" consequences of a wide range of phenomena, from the novel and the newspaper to religion and mass culture in general.

This chapter argues that the tendency to depict the Affair as sensational fiction reinscribed the crisis as a contest between truth and lying that, when viewed through the prism of medical discourses, allowed the pro-Dreyfus camp to depict their opponents as sick and effeminate, thus underscoring the pervasive (and often unacknowledged) role of gender and sexuality in the Affair. In so doing it inquires into how the language of truthfulness and a steadfast refusal of myth-making functioned within the polemical literature of the Dreyfusard camp itself. What did possessing knowledge of the "truth" *mean* at the *fin de siècle*? How did reason and truth relate to cultural understandings of irrationality, religion, lying, and fiction during this time? How did assertions of truthfulness contribute to bolstering the public image of unity, and even manliness, that many Dreyfusards endeavored to project?

I) Truth and Lies

Public opinion had been unkind to Alfred Dreyfus from the very beginning, which explains why until 1899 the captain's supporters often felt as if they were preaching in the wilderness. Animated in part by conservative and anti-Semitic newspapers, hostile mobs not only attacked Jews and their businesses, but went on to harass the most prominent and outspoken Dreyfusards, many of whom had their property destroyed, received death threats, or were physically attacked.[6] Against what they rightly described as the fabrications and fantasies of the military establishment and the anti-Semitic press, Dreyfusards typically emphasized their unity of purpose, and even social identity, as disinterested champions of truth. Given the heterogeneous social composition that comprised Dreyfusism, where lawyers and politicians rallied alongside professors, poets, physicians, and other bourgeois professionals, this sort of cultural network allowed this disparate group to project a united front to their opponents, at least in the public imagination. Although historiography on the Affair has since incorporated this sociological argument, less attention has been accorded to the gendered aspects of Dreyfusard unity.[7] Against the strictly physical courage apparently required by the military, Dreyfusards typically maintained the superiority of moral courage and personal sacrifice.[8] How fortuitous it was, then, when in 1899 Dreyfus's principal defence lawyer, Fernand Labori, was shot by an unknown assailant on the streets of Rennes. Despite the fact that Labori survived this assault, the Dreyfusards now had a hero who had literally risked his life for the cause. Outpourings of support congratulated the heroism of this new martyr, and Marcel Proust's letter to Labori gushed with admiration for this "invincible good giant" who "no longer even has to envy military glory the magnificent privilege of soldiers: Giving one's blood".[9] The fact that few of Dreyfus's champions would actually shed blood in his name did not diminish the presumed manliness of their campaign—even bold speeches and essays could be cited as proof of heroic action. "Finally!" exclaimed the journalist and politician Georges Clemenceau: "Here are Frenchmen who rise up and speak when to speak is to take action". Clemenceau even identified this newfound action as being transformative: "Men! There are men in France! So many weaklings who trembled before the barbarous threats of the Army and the Church are regaining their courage".[10] Zola had sown the seeds of heroism, and now heroes were cropping up everywhere. "Courage is contagious", declared the journalist Paul Brulat. "Under the mass of lies and calumnies, heroes are multiplying".[11]

This opposition between heroism and "lies" was central to the polemics of Dreyfusard journalists, and drew upon broader conventions about the relationship between manhood and truth. Ever since the early modern period, for instance, the accusation of lying was understood as a serious insult to any man of honour, an affront that was sure to provoke a challenge to a duel.[12] From another perspective, the capacity to discern truth from lies and the courage to proclaim it publicly was frequently represented as evidence of a superior man, one who was said to possess a keen intellect situated in a hardy physical constitution. The rhetorical sparring of the Dreyfus Affair was permeated by this overriding concern with the health or decay of the truth-telling body, thus lending credence to Robert Nye's claim that the closing decades of the nineteenth century were marked by an organicist discourse of national decline that was often presented as a crisis of manhood itself.[13] The Dreyfus Affair was thus in many important respects an affair of the body, for in the eyes of some it was precisely this unhealthy and feminine susceptibility to sensation that made the drama "sensational" in the first place.

Dreyfusard identity was thus in many respects defined by the "manly" struggle for truth, despite the fact that this ideal was represented in the traditional form of female allegory. Cartoonists like Henry-Gabriel Ibels and Hermann-Paul routinely depicted Truth as a beautiful naked woman trapped in a well by evil and cowardly denizens of the army and the church, only to be rescued by heroic revisionists. With her long flowing hair and mirror in hand, this nubile female was presented as the sole object of Dreyfusard desire. As many scholars have pointed out, however, the traditional *Nuda Veritas* image concealed an ambiguity common to the entire genre of female allegory: the ideal of truth was safely represented by an abstract woman because it was assumed that real women could not be relied on to tell the truth.[14] Given the masculinist trappings of Dreyfusard self-representations, the presumed femininity of lying conveniently transformed their opponents into another category of man altogether. Indeed, the Dreyfusard imagination saw lies everywhere at this time. Not only had the General Staff lied about the guilt of Esterhazy (who had also lied about his own involvement), but Colonel Henry had forged documents that further incriminated Dreyfus. Moreover, Dreyfusard graphic imagery often featured veritable seas of forged documents, all inscribed with the word "faux" (forgery, falsehood). As far as the Dreyfusards were concerned, the nation itself was swimming in lies.

Western culture's association between women and deception makes the presumed "femininity" of lying during the Affair much more understandable. Commentators sometimes argued that instances of female lying were due partly to the cultural demands imposed on women, requiring them to conceal certain bodily functions for the sake of preserving modesty and to use cosmetics, fashion, and culture to foster public impressions that might draw attention away from potentially less attractive features linked to their age, health, family wealth, or body shape. Most, however, were willing to connect the propensity to deceive with assumptions about female nature, concluding that women lied to compensate for physical weakness or did so out of their inherent suggestibility, which allowed them to believe sincerely in their own fabrications. Indeed, in her study of female criminality at the *fin de siècle*, Ann-Louise Shapiro demonstrates how discourses about the duplicity of "deviant" women were frequently shaped by durable assumptions about qualities possessed by "normal" women: "The criminal woman was like all women, only more so: she was suggestible, weak in the face of temptation, deceitful, prone to excess, intellectually limited, and morally stunted".[15]

Such stereotypes about female nature pervaded as well the developing science of legal testimony, which assumed that women counted among those unstable individuals who were most likely to be "false witnesses" and thus quite unreliable on the stand. Legal doctors who wished to underscore the female propensity to lie frequently invoked a sensational court case from the early nineteenth century known as the La Roncière Affair. In 1834 a cavalry cadet named Émile de la Roncière was accused of writing threatening letters to the adolescent daughter of his commander, General Baron de Morell. After being expelled from the École de Cavalerie he was later charged with assaulting the girl in her bedroom and sentenced to ten years' imprisonment. Nevertheless doubts lingered about the young man's guilt, and the La Roncière Affair would be cited in subsequent decades by sceptics convinced that the cadet had been condemned solely on the unreliable testimony of a girl. Here as in the Dreyfus case, everything had come down to analyzing the handwriting of an incriminating letter. While some concluded that La Roncière was indeed the author, others maintained the cadet had been framed by the daughter who forged the letter. The lesson that legal doctors drew from the case of La Roncière was clear: owing to a range of problems grounded in female nature, the testimony of women and girls ought to be treated with scepticism.[16]

Whereas women seemed marked by a pathological inability to tell the truth, worried observers also focused attention on spectacles, texts, and pastimes that might mislead women as well as impressionable men. For instance, a number of critics bemoaned the theatrical and novelesque elements that were integral to the functioning of French jurisprudence. Elegantly dressed spectators often filled the courtroom for particularly sensational cases, sometimes equipped with picnic baskets and champagne so as not to surrender their seats during lengthy recesses.[17] This public access to court proceedings, available since the Constitutional Charter of 1814, was criticized by those wary of the "contagious" effect that discussions of criminal activity could have upon impressionable individuals.[18] During the first step of the proceedings the clerk would read aloud the prosecutor's reconstruction of the crime, "a novelistic reconstruction of crime, motive and culpability" which could take up to an hour in certain cases.[19] Moreover, in so far as they represented "an individual in contest with a vast social body", defence attorneys were expected to be emotive and theatrical in order to sway the jury.[20] Taylor underscores the incongruence between such spectacular practices and the textual ideals of reason: "Insofar as the language employed in trials was an oral one informed by gesture and expression, which appealed to the imagination, that language . . . posed certain challenges to a persistent Enlightenment model of rational reflection".[21]

Legal doctors explicitly privileged the latter model when they condemned the negative effects of such theatricality and novelization upon highly suggestible individuals who, seeing criminality glamorized in the press, might even imitate the deeds themselves. Women were implicated here as well, not merely as those who told stories, but as those most likely to be inexorably swayed by the stories of others. Whereas lying had for centuries been considered an inherently feminine deed, many subscribed to parallel beliefs about the correspondingly "feminine" nature of those who were duped, a medical interpretation of credulity that encompassed at once religious adepts, readers of novels, and the masses generally. Within this framework the credulous were cast as possessing enfeebled and effeminate minds that, incapable of mastering themselves, were easy prey for the manipulations of others. The connection between the reading of novels and moral corruption leading to vice has been explored in a number of recent studies of French cultural life, most notably by Jann Matlock, Ann-Louise Shapiro, and

Vernon A. Rosario. The reading of novels was considered a most dangerous pastime that, by exciting the imagination, was thought capable of stimulating the genitals and leading impressionable minds to vice, something considered especially likely among what Matlock calls "endangered readers" like women, adolescents, proletarians, and the insane. Finally, Shapiro has revealed the continuing medical indictment of the journalistic convention of the *fait divers* for supposedly implanting in the minds of "naturally" mimetic females provocative models of criminal behaviour.[22]

Significantly, the critique of the novel reader was related to recent inquiries into hysteria and the psychopathology of religious belief. As Jan Goldstein's work suggests, the politicized nature of the hysteria diagnosis under the Third Republic provides a frame for the Dreyfusard association of lying and credulity with femininity, religiosity, literature, and nervous disorders. In the "retrospective diagnoses" performed by neurologist Jean-Martin Charcot and his colleagues at the Salpêtrière, historical cases of mysticism and demonic possession were re-interpreted as psychotic episodes that were at heart more about hysterical delusions than anything divine, thus undercutting in medical terms the supernatural basis of Catholic religiosity. Thanks to the veritable alliance forged between psychiatrists and the republican state during the 1880s, religious faith had become implicated in the very literary folly so often condemned by its adherents. The same imagination that, when left unchecked, allowed one to be duped by novels was revealed to be at work behind the religious spirit itself, thus positioning science as that which dispels the fabulations of both the novelist and the priest.[23]

Dreyfusards, as we will see below, made ample use of the above associations in order to better position themselves as the voice of masculine rationality in a culture overstimulated by fiction, religion, and downright lies. This placed female Dreyfusards in an interesting position. Given the emotionalism, piety, hysteria and suggestibility typically attributed to women, Dreyfusard women had to assert a capacity for journalistic detachment that was demanded of (but rarely practiced by) their male counterparts. For instance, in the case of the journalist Séverine (Caroline Rémy), who wrote for the newspaper *La Fronde*, an interview with Émile Zola offered an excellent opportunity to distance herself from such assumptions about women. Clearly aware of the charge that Zola's seductive power over female readers had lured them into the revisionist fold, Séverine launched a preemptive strike against any supposition that her convictions were colored by anything other than a clear-sighted search for the truth: "I am not blinded by an uncontrollable or limitless devotion", she asserted. "I remain very much the mistress of my judgment. I discuss, I evaluate–no fetishism hinders the exercise of my free will or the critical spirit that is always awake in me".[24]

Along with religiosity itself, the reading of novels represented a form of "seduction" or "infection" exercising a "contagious" influence over weaker minds that inevitably resulted in heightened suggestibility, hypnotic trances, and the loss of the will. Though women were implicated both among the seducers and the credulous, at the heart of this frightening narrative of decay was usually a problematic body which, either through morbid heredity or unhealthy milieu, was explicitly encoded as "feminine" regardless of the anatomical sex of the person in question. The strong presence of republicans and professors in the Dreyfusard camp meant the conflict between science and faith would necessarily mold the ways in which one's opponents were perceived. Noting the vocal presence of creative writers among the Dreyfusard ranks, for instance, Jean Ajalbert sardonically observed how the Ministry of War also seemed committed to imaginative works, referring to the patent lies told by "*les chroniqueurs* and habitual story-tellers" in their ranks.[25] Significantly, the La Roncière Affair was revisited during the Dreyfus Affair for the purposes of belittling anti-Dreyfusism and reinforcing the manly credentials of Dreyfusards. In a lengthy text that revealed in minute detail the circumstances of the accusation and the role of hysteria in Marie de Morell's lying, the writer Stéphane Arnoulin made a connection between this older case and the contemporary scene that would not have been lost on his readers. Just as scholars, artists, and men of letters rallied decades before around the falsely accused lieutenant against the "hysterical" fabrications of a woman and the "ignorant and stupid" crowd who believed such tales, so too did modern intellectuals struggle against "feminine" lies being told about Alfred Dreyfus.[26]

What was perhaps most alarming about "feminine" lying was that it raised the possibility that weak men might also be deceived. As we have seen, for a woman to lie was considered quite "normal", at least in so far as pathology was thought to be a constant feature of female nature; a male liar, on the other hand, signaled true deviance, the result of a malignancy which suggested a fall away from "honorable" masculinity. In short, men who succumbed to the sensual temptations of imaginative literature could easily be considered "feminized". Throughout the turn of the century numerous self-help manuals directed at young men warned of the dangers of novels, and often counseled against reading them in the prophylactic interest of proper "hygiene". The reading of novels, noted one concerned physician, "perverts the moral sense, can make one contract bad habits, and is capable of leading to a disorderly, even dissolute, life which often makes the most robust young men into 'old men' prematurely".[27] Jules Payot's popular book, *L'Éducation de la volonté*, was quite emphatic on this point, drawing clear parallels between literature and hypnotic suggestion that threatened to corrupt the fledgling volition of young men. Reading novels not only lured young men away from their duties, Payot charged, but encouraged them to reside in a fantasy world of their own making: "How many young people thus live out a novel, constructed piece by piece, over the course of several weeks . . . . Ah! how the passions of our novelists seem pale and faded alongside our own novels of the eighteenth year!"[28] The cultural critic Max Nordau also considered the reading of novels a most dangerous diversion for degenerates and hysterics, among whom he counted many males. Marked by excessive "emotionalism" that could not be controlled by their feeble wills, male hysterics manifested a tendency toward imitation that made it difficult for them to discern reality from fiction:

> A result of the susceptibility of the hysterical subject to suggestion is his irresistible

> passion for imitation, and the earnestness with which he yields to all the suggestions of writers and artists. When he sees a picture, he wants to become like it in attitude and dress; when he reads a book, he adopts its views blindly; he takes as a pattern the heroes of the novels which he has in his hand at the moment, and infuses himself into the characters moving before him on the stage.[29]

The feminizing degeneracy of individuals was easily inflated to collective proportions as a way of characterizing the reading public generally, those "crowds" of gullible people who seemed to swallow all the lies being told by the military and the anti-Semitic press. The habitual liar and the gullible dupe thus seemed to suffer from very similar disorders. Whether described as hysterical, neurasthenic, or degenerate, all were diagnosed with forms of pathological effeminacy that separated them from more "healthy" men who both recognized and told the truth.

II) Esterhazy's Novel

Dreyfusards seeking to project a credible image of healthy masculinity often found their plans thwarted by men in uniform, who, as cultural archetypes of active manhood, were frequently glorified in the press and in popular literature. One means of compensating for this problem was for Dreyfusards to belittle what they considered the feeble minds of military men, a deficiency that rendered soldiers capable of following orders like automata but ill-equipped for more valuable displays of moral courage. Moreover, as the case of the forger, Colonel Hubert Henry, seemed to suggest, this could be accomplished by investigating their reading habits. The son of rural parents who had clawed his way up the ranks of the military, Henry embodied the more traditional military ideal that had been recently challenged by the new breed of academically trained officer. As Armand Charpentier recalled, Henry naturally felt uncomfortable when appointed to his new bureaucratic post in Paris, and sought to compensate for his academic limitations. "After the agitated life of colonial expeditions and the placid existence of provincial garrisons, he found himself, at age forty-eight, called to duties whose exercise demanded a certain degree of intellectual culture. Desiring to complete his training, which he knew was incomplete, he flew indiscriminately from book to book". Beginning with fairly serious works, such as those of Marcus Aurelius, Henry allowed his penchant for police stories to take the upper hand, leading him to novels like *Les deux frères*, which, we have seen, arguably provided a narrative that would help frame Dreyfus.[30]

Yet Henry was not the sole target of Dreyfusard ire. If anti-Dreyfusards found their most rhetorically useful "foreigners" in the persons of the "German" Dreyfus and the "Italian" Zola, their opponents made very good use of the real traitor, Major Walsin-Esterhazy. Some scholars have proposed that, whereas Esterhazy indeed tried to sell artillery secrets to the Germans, he was actually a double agent seeking to tempt the enemy with bogus plans.[31] This might explain why, even after he fled to England once his involvement was discovered, Esterhazy insisted that he was in fact "a good soldier, a brave soldier. . . . I was moreover a soldier devoted to his superiors, a soldier disciplined to the point of heroism".[32] As many of Esterhazy's enemies pointed out, however, this sense of discipline did not extend to his personal life, where the major frequently indulged his passions for gambling and womanizing. Even more doubts, however, were cast upon his much vaunted loyalty. Further inquiries into his private life revealed that Esterhazy, who hailed from a noble Hungarian family, harboured some very definite opinions about France. In November 1897 the Dreyfusards published a letter the major had written thirteen years earlier disclosing his true feelings about the French: "If someone were to come tell me this evening that I would be killed tomorrow as a Uhlan captain running through Frenchmen with my saber, I would certainly be perfectly happy. . . . I would not hurt a puppy, but I would have a hundred thousand Frenchmen killed with pleasure".[33]

Just as the physiognomy of Dreyfus suggested to some his treasonous potential, so too did Esterhazy's body provide clues to his inner state. Séverine, for one, was quite taken aback by the physiognomy of the man (henceforth nicknamed "the Uhlan"), which in her description came close to the stock representations of the Jews she also despized. "A strange physiognomy . . . An animal of prey, certainly; he has a bird's head, with a great beak of a nose". The foreignness of the man, suggested in these readings of his body, assumed an even more racial tone as her analysis continued: "I have a living enigma before me . . . . Esterhazy surely seems to be of foreign origin, of a race that has naturalized a notorious and hereditary courage; not displeasing, but coming from farther away than Florence: from the *puzta*, from the Orient of scimitars, of bags sewn without much style, and of bad coffee".[34] Observations like these were fairly typical at the height of the Affair, and few Dreyfusards were persuaded either by Esterhazy's protests of innocence or by his references to the mysterious "Veiled Lady" who had supposedly warned him of a plot being hatched against him by the government. "The veil of the lady is already quite crumpled", quipped one unimpressed Dreyfusard; "we already perceive her moustache".[35]

To be sure, most prominent Dreyfusards took pot-shots at Esterhazy; yet credit for the most extensive account must go to Joseph Reinach, a noted republican politician who, given his Jewish background and outspoken defence of the exiled captain, was often the butt of anti-Semitic abuse. Reinach's seven-volume *Histoire de l'affaire Dreyfus*,[36] which is counted among the more authoritative contemporary accounts of the crisis, devotes well over 100 consecutive pages to the family history, character, and health of Esterhazy, all of which were scrutinized in terms of contemporary anxieties about physical decline and moral bankruptcy. Most important for our purposes is the fact that woven throughout these analyses is a concern about the relationship between Esterhazy's fraudulent self-fashioning and literature itself. For Reinach the intrigues and lies of Esterhazy were not merely deceptions, but veritable "novels" springing from the unhealthy ground of his feverish imagination and weakened body. In the person of Esterhazy, literature and lying were knotted together with a sick and even effeminate temperament that ended up deceiving a gullible populace. By placing Esterhazy under the microscope Reinach transformed every detail of the major's life into evidence that might explain his behaviour during the 1890s, a mode of inquiry that had much in common with the medical case histories of the time and which helped to render the anti-Dreyfusard cause "pathological" as well as wrong-headed. Above all, Reinach's case study of Esterhazy as an inveterate story-teller pointed to the diseased source of mass sensation and thus bolstered the Dreyfusards' view of themselves as healthy defenders of Truth.

Reinach shared with his republican colleagues a clear distrust of the power of religion and literature to obfuscate the truth, and frequently employed in his work literary metaphors to describe both lying and credulity. In Reinach's estimation, the many conservative novelists and literary critics who flocked to the anti-Dreyfus camp manifested all the excesses of aesthetes who lacked "the scientific spirit" and who were therefore unable "to reason any better than the ignorant and brutish crowd" (III: 248). It is therefore unsurprising that subtle connections between literature and lying recur in Reinach's analysis of Esterhazy and are used to explain how the Dreyfus Affair became a mass sensation. In an age when physical health to some extent meant descending from a healthy bloodline, it was significant that Esterhazy's whole family history and even his account of his own life were founded on lies: "this entire novel that he repeated one hundred times and embellished with details . . . is only a tissue of impostures" (II: 20). In Reinach's account this tendency to lie in accordance with literary models characterized both Esterhazy as well as his Hungarian ancestors, as if lying could be an inherited trait. Indeed, the last legitimate representative of the French Esterhazys had emigrated to Russia in the eighteenth century, while a "bastard line" remained to carry on the name. Yet even the name Walsin, which Esterhazy claimed was traceable either to a soldier or an actor, proved to be purely literary in origin, a derivation of "Valsin" that was frequently used by eighteenth century poets and novelists. By changing the name to "Walsin", Reinach concluded, "the novelesque nickname thus took on a fake Magyar air" (II: 13), an imposture further accentuated when the officer's father and uncle pretentiously attached the moniker to their family name.

In this age of escalating nationalism, pretending to be French proved even more scandalous than falsifying one's ancestry, and was redolent of many charges leveled by anti-Semites against Jews. The "Uhlan letter", we have seen, seemed to speak volumes about Esterhazy's true feelings about the French, and suggested to Reinach that the man had never truly overcome his Hungarian heritage, thus remaining "French in name only". Here too Reinach drew upon biological assumptions to clarify the strange case of Esterhazy, a man who, as the living result of "successive interbreeding", had been transformed into "the primitive type of the species" (II: 39). Although Esterhazy's mother had descended from a pure French bloodline, his father was the product of no less than sixteen Franco-Hungarian unions, and thus brought to his new family a tainted heredity. Had Esterhazy been of pure French stock, Reinach implied, he may not have been so compelled to betray his country and then conceal his crime in a cowardly manner with lies. Unfortunately for him, however, these "few drops of Magyar blood dominate the mixture, and impress upon it their stain" [*lui donnent leur teinte*]. All of this helped explain not only the moral failings of the traitor, but accounted as well for all that was "exotic" about the man's appearance. Esterhazy's body was not only "too thin for his massive head", but it betrayed a host of other unsavory features, including "the aquiline nose, truly the beak of a bird of prey, the small and sunken eyes of a marten, black, impenetrable, with a gaze always in motion, with something underhanded about it, the gestures, sometimes brusque, sometimes insinuating, the slight accent . . . and, above all, that thing in man which is truly his own, the faithful translation of the ego: his manner of speaking and writing" (II: 40). Not only are these features–a beak-like nose, sunken and shifty eyes, awkward gestures, and a foreign accent–similar to traits typically attributed to Jews, but they worked well with Reinach's earlier description of Esterhazy as possessing "a certain aptitude for speculation . . . he was a financier just as he was a soldier, a reneger of debts [*boursier-marron*], and a ruffian" (II: 28-29). So often the target of anti-Semitic abuse, Reinach struck back by displacing his own anxieties about Jewishness onto the true traitor.[37]

What Reinach found most telling about Esterhazy's personality was his unhealthy predilection for literature, a pastime that repeatedly intruded into the major's daily life: "With a feverish imagination, he improvised . . . novels in which he was the hero: he ended up believing in these fictions" (II: 24). As we have seen above, this inability to tell truth from lies signalled the presence of an imagination that exceeded the bounds of reason and common sense, a character flaw typically attributed to women, children, and those suffering from hereditary degeneration. Not surprisingly, Reinach revealed that the traitor too suffered from physical defects which in part explained his susceptibility to feminizing literature. Having been afflicted with tuberculosis, which may have been inherited from his Hungarian father, a "sick man" lurked behind Esterhazy's facade of heroic vitality: "there are certain links between afflictions of the lung and those of the brain" that were confirmed by modern medicine. "Contemporary science has established that tubercular intoxication...is often the determining cause of morbid overstimulation, of an extreme enervation of the intellectual or moral faculties, with or without surface lesions" (II: 25). Esterhazy's capacity for resistance and the exercise of willpower had been fatally undermined by his health problems, thus rendering him a plaything of external stimulations and inner passions. Unbalanced by his illness and by the accumulated defects of his bloodline, Esterhazy was a man in the process of coming apart: "The sickness was eating away at him; for a long time only one of his lungs functioned; he supported himself with alcohol, he ate too much, devouring his food. An inner fire slowly burned...mocking and tragic, pathetic and filthy, he peddled his novel" (III: 9).

Reinach's damning characterization of Esterhazy is thus performed subtly and proceeds through a series of significant details that connect his tainted blood and corrupted body to sensuality, the reading of novels, pathological lying, and outright cowardice. For instance, had Esterhazy been a true man of honour, by all accounts he should have backed up his soldierly image with deeds. We know a great deal about how crucial a factor duelling was in nineteenth-century codes of masculinity and, even when no one was harmed, the willingness to publicly defend personal honour through displays of violence was integral to the maintenance of one's reputation as a man of honour.[38] It was thus significant that Esterhazy, who was presented by the anti-Semitic press as an expert swordsman, "never had a single duel" (II: 91). If Esterhazy's sick body lent a certain inevitability to his treasonous machinations, it also paled next to the more robust physiques of his comrades. Whereas Colonel Henry was "tall, corpulent, giving the impression of health and force", Esterhazy seemed congenitally predisposed to betrayal, an observation that Reinach shared with many other Dreyfusards: even before he committed the deed itself, Esterhazy seemed to have had "'the physique for the job'" (II: 77). It would be no surprise that Esterhazy, "the tempter, the perverter" who seduced himself with his own lies, would end up corrupting his friend Henry, a man who up until then had been "a brave soldier . . . fearless under fire". Making much of Henry's rural background, Reinach was able to present him as a healthy son of the soil who, having grown up away from the seductions of modernity, had been led astray by the sensual distractions promised by Esterhazy: "This peasant, who had only known a life of hard labour and hardly any common diversions, glimpsed a new world of pleasures which had seemed hitherto inaccessible and which he could enter whenever he liked" (II: 80-81). Henry's death by his own hand after the discovery of his forgeries was a tragic end for a once honourable soldier who had been seduced and corrupted by the traitor: "of these two actors, one has carried his secret to the grave, the other lies as he breathes" (II: 82).

However reprehensible it may have been, Esterhazy's corruption of Henry was nothing compared to his masterful seduction of public opinion. Esterhazy's novel thus worked impeccably alongside the contagion of other lies and anti-Semitic abuse that had so profoundly polluted the body politic. "The microbes flying out of Drumont's inkwell had poisoned the whole atmosphere", Reinach declared; "everyone breathed this polluted air" (III: 261). Having been repeatedly accosted by anti-Semitic street mobs during Zola's libel trial, Reinach shared this conventional view of the crowd. Indeed, one of his most vivid memories conflated a fear of multitudes with a vision of devouring femininity bent on robbing him of his honour: "I still see a furious young woman who pursued me, who wanted to rip from me my ribbon of the Legion of Honour, while the crowd howled 'Death to the Jews! Death to the traitors!'" (III: 349). Moreover, fears about the crowd provided him with the means of connecting Esterhazy's novel about himself to its natural audience. "It acted, with a speed that surprised the hypnotist himself, as if upon a hysteric whose personality doubles itself in an induced slumber" (III: 28). Whereas isolated individuals may be capable of preserving their own reason and personalities, "the collective soul of the crowd is not the vehicle [*la moyenne*] of these diverse mentalities: it is something else, truly a different being, something quite new...." (III: 28). Such informal "fictions" worked effectively with a population steeped in novelistic conventions: "the episode of the Veiled Lady enchanted the public", something that would have been easily recognizable from "a hundred novels and melodramas" (III: 11). What was at stake in all of this was the imposture of honour and manhood that had been facilitated through literature. Of course Esterhazy maintained that he was a martyr suffering at the hands of cowards: "I have against me all human cowardice and hypocrisy, I will struggle [against them] to my last breath".[39] As Reinach maintained, however, fictions such as these convinced the multitudes that he was in fact a true man of honour despite the fact that the "only soldierly thing about Esterhazy was his language. The crowd took him for a true soldier unjustly accused" (III: 11).

Though Esterhazy was just one among many targets of Dreyfusard abuse at the end of the nineteenth century, he was certainly one of the most notorious. Much of the force of Reinach's characterization of the man was fuelled by the connections he made between femininity, lying, and the major's diseased body, all of which worked very well as a way of understanding how "the crowd" might be led astray. Indeed, it was the anti-Dreyfusard Gustave Le Bon who claimed in 1895 that the leaders of crowds are often themselves degenerates, a belief seconded by many Dreyfusards and apparently corroborated by Reinach's quasi-medical sketch of Esterhazy. In addition, Reinach's discourse provided an opportunity to contrast the manliness of Dreyfusard truth to the decrepit liars (and gullible dupes) who insisted upon the captain's guilt. Through its steadfast concern with health and vitality, Reinach's account of Esterhazy contributes to our understanding of the Dreyfus Affair as a pivotal moment in the *fin de siècle*'s obsession with manhood and pathology. It also reveals the complicated path that led from the frissons of the easily stimulated body to the experience of mass sensations in *fin-de-siècle* culture.

Notes

1. For a more detailed analysis of these issues, see Christopher E. Forth, *The Dreyfus Affair and the Crisis of French Manhood* (Baltimore: Johns Hopkins University Press, 2004).
2. Armand Charpentier, *Les côtés mystérieux de l'affaire Dreyfus* (Paris: Les Éditions Rieder, 1937), 208. This explanation has even been employed in recent historical studies; for instance, see Armand Israël, *Les Vérités cachées de l'affaire Dreyfus* (Paris: Albin Michel, 2000), 82.
3. Henri Varennes, 'Dreyfus devant ses juges', *L'Aurore*, 8 August 1899, 1.
4. Gustave Le Bon, *Psychologie des foules* (Paris: Alcan, 1895); Gabriel Tarde, *L'Opinion et la foule* (Paris: Alcan, 1901).
5. Rae Beth Gordon, *Why the French Love Jerry Lewis: From Cabaret to Early Cinema* (Stanford: Stanford University Press, 2001), 20-27.
6. Nancy Fitch, "Mass Culture, Mass Parliamentary Politics, and Modern Anti-Semitism: The Dreyfus Affair in Rural France", *American Historical Review* 97 (1992), 55-95.
7. In particular see Christophe Charle, *Naissance des "intellectuels", 1880-1900* (Paris: Minuit, 1990).
8. See John J. Cerullo, "Intellectuals and the Imagination of Heroism during the Dreyfus Affair", *Proceedings of the Western Society for French History* 1995 (23), 185-195; and Christopher E. Forth, "Bodies of Christ: Gender, Jewishness, and Religious Imagery in the Dreyfus Affair", *History Workshop Journal* Autumn 1999 (48), 18-38.
9. Marcel Proust to Fernand Labori, 15? August 1899, in Proust, *Correspondance, Tome II: 1896-1901* (Paris: Plon, 1976), 295.
10. Georges Clemenceau, "Des hommes!" in *Vers la réparation* (Paris: Stock, 1899), 58.
11. Paul Brulat, *Violence et raison* (Paris: Stock, 1898), 12.
12. Robert A. Nye, *Masculinity and Male Codes of Honor in Modern France* (New York: Oxford University Press, 1993), 177.
13. Robert A. Nye, *Crime, Madness and Politics in Modern France* (Princeton: Princeton University Press, 1984).
14. Marina Warner, *Monuments and Maidens: The Allegory of the Female Form* (New York: Atheneum, 1985). For a more detailed discussion of female allegory in the Dreyfus Affair, see Christopher E. Forth, "Adventures of the Naked Truth: The Dreyfus Affair and the Female Form", *French Cultural Studies* June 2001 (12:2), 123-147.
15. Ann-Louise Shapiro, *Breaking the Codes: Female Criminality in Fin-de-Siècle Paris* (Stanford: Stanford University Press, 1996), 66.
16. Matt K. Matsuda, *The Memory of the Modern* (New York: Oxford University Press, 1996), 113-114.
17. Katherine Fischer Taylor, *In the Theater of Criminal Justice: The Palais de Justice in Second Empire Paris* (Princeton: Princeton University Press, 1993), 28.
18. Jan Goldstein, "'Moral Contagion': A Professional Ideology of Medicine and Psychiatry in Eighteenth- and Nineteenth-Century France", in Gerald L. Geison, ed., *Professions and the French State, 1700-1900* (Philadelphia: University of Pennsylvania Press, 1984), 207-208.
19. Taylor, *In the Theater of Criminal Justice*, 42.

20. Taylor, 53.
21. Taylor, 27.
22. Jann Matlock, *Scenes of Seduction: Prostitution, Hysteria, and Reading Difference in Nineteenth-Century France* (New York: Columbia University Press, 1994); Vernon A. Rosario, *The Erotic Imagination: French Histories of Perversity* (New York: Oxford University Press, 1997); Shapiro, *Breaking the Codes.*
23. Jan Goldstein, "The Hysterical Diagnosis and the Politics of Anticlericalism in Late Nineteenth-Century France", *Journal of Modern History*, 1982 (54), 209-239.
24. Séverine, *Vers la lumière: impressions vécues* (Paris: Stock, 1900), 49. On the seductive power that Zola seemed to wield over female readers, see Georges Sorel, *La Révolution dreyfusienne* (Paris: Rivière, 1909), 9, 22-24, 27.
25. Jean Ajalbert, *Sous le sabre* (Paris: Éditions de La Revue blanche, 1898), 166.
26. Stéphane Arnoulin, *L'Affaire La Roncière: Une erreur judiciaire en 1835* (Paris: Librairie Paul Ollendorff, 1899), 365.
27. Dr Gustave Lauth, *Que l'on doit éviter, ce que l'on doit faire dans l'intérêt de sa santé* (Paris: Fischbacher, 1888), 36.
28. Jules Payot, *L'Éducation de la volonté* (Paris: Librairie Félix Alcan, 1912 [1893]), 192-193.
29. Max Nordau, *Degeneration* (Lincoln: University of Nebraska Press, [1892] 1993), 25-26.
30. Charpentier, 208.
31. Jean Doise, *Un secret bien gardé: Histoire militaire de l'affaire Dreyfus* (Paris: Seuil, 1994).
32. Esterhazy [sic], *Les dessous de l'affaire Dreyfus* (Paris: Fayard, 1898), 4.
33. Quoted in Bredin, 222.
34. Séverine, 7, 8-9.
35. Jacques Bahar, *Le traître* (Vincennes: Imprimerie L. Levy, 1898), 13.
36. Joseph Reinach, *Histoire de l'affaire Dreyfus. Vol. 1: Le Procès de 1894; Vol. 2: Esterhazy; Vol. 3: La Crise. Procès Esterhazy. Procès Zola; Vol. 4: Cavaignac et Félix Faure; Vol. 5: Rennes; Vol. 6: La Révision; Vol. 7: Index général* (Paris: Éditions de la Revue blanche, 1901-11).
37. Sander Gilman, *The Jew's Body* (New York: Routledge, 1991). For a contemporary anti-Semitic portrait of the Jew, see Édouard Drumont, *La France Juive* (Paris: Flammarion, 1912 [1886]), I: 35.
38. Nye, *Masculinity and Male Codes of Honor*; Kevin McAleer, *Dueling: The Cult of Honor in Fin-de-Siècle Germany* (Princeton: Princeton University Press, 1994).
39. Esterhazy, 226.

Chapter 12

"Furious Passions of the Celtic Race": Ireland, Madness and Wilkie Collins's *Blind Love*

Maria K. Bachman

> Madmen do not appear to have lost the faculty of reasoning; but having joined together some ideas very wrongly, they mistake them for truths, and they err, as men do that argue right from wrong principles.
> (John Locke, *An Essay Concerning Human Understanding*)

> The possibility of madness is therefore implicit in the very phenomenon of passion.
> (Michel Foucault, *Madness and Civilization*)

In the 1870s, Henry Maudsley and Andrew Wynter, two highly influential thinkers in the emerging field of psychiatry, popularized the notion of a Borderland of Insanity, "a vast army of undiscovered lunatics"[1] who existed on the fringes of society. Maudsley argued that:

> [I]t is of great importance then to recognize a borderland between sanity and insanity and of greater importance still . . . to study the doubtful cases of which it is peopled. There are a great many people, who without being insane, exhibit peculiarities of thought, feeling and character . . . they bear in their temperament the marks of their peculiar heritage.[2]

Independent of Maudsley's suggestion of a borderland between the sane and insane, Wilkie Collins was already charting this liminal psychic geography in his fiction. In fact, a reviewer of Collins's *Armadale* (1866) was outraged that the author chose "vermin as his subjects",[3] though Collins's fictional counter world, peopled as it is by the deviant, the degenerate, and the deranged, has enthralled both Victorian and modern readers. Unlike Dickens, who uses caricatured figures for comic or bizarre effect, Collins explores the inner psyches of his mental deviants, examining what it means to be cast as "other" and relegated to the margins of society in Victorian England. Jenny Bourne Taylor asserts that Collins's "use of insanity as a narrative strategy is more complex than that of any of his contemporaries, but he wrote in a context in which the fictional mediation of madness helped to shape its cultural meaning".[4] Indeed, a number of Wilkie Collins works (particularly *Basil*, *The Woman in White*, *Jezebel's Daughter*) offer lively and provocative engagements with Victorian discourses of insanity,[5] but it is Collins's final novel *Blind Love* that breaks out from the confines of the asylum to explore the ways in which madness operates not only as a psycho-medical malady, but as a political malady as well.

In the novel's provocation of the chaotic Irish scene during the Land War of 1879-1882, Collins boldly attempts to answer "The Irish Question", one of the most persistent and prominent political controversies confronting Britain throughout the nineteenth century. While Collins was working on a draft of *Blind Love* in 1887, he would have been inundated with hostile reports (classified under "Special Crimes") and angry editorials in English newspapers describing the Fenian terrorist activities that followed the defeat of Home Rule the previous year. Originally titled *The Lord Harry* (a title that was softened as the volume went to press to avoid offending readers—"Lord Harry" being a slang allusion to the devil), the novel begins in rural Ireland, focusing upon the "Irish blackguard" Lord Harry Norland and his lawless activities with the Invincibles, a secret society of political assassins. Iris Henley, a high-spirited English woman, rejects a proper and conventional English suitor and finds herself compulsively drawn toward the devilish Lord Harry, eventually marrying him. Harry's criminal behaviour throughout the novel, along with the inexplicable "blind love" that Iris Henley manifests for her reckless husband, "the wild Irish lord", synecdochichally represent the perceived madness behind the movements for Irish independence, as well as the apparent madness of English sympathizers who displayed a misplaced "blind love" for the Celts and their native culture. More generally, *Blind Love* reflects English anxieties about and prejudices towards the Irish and their supposedly innate propensity for criminality and madness. One character surmises that "if sober English people" saw the wild Irish lord, they "would almost think him a fit subject to be placed under restraint" (206).[6]

Writing during England's era of high imperialism, Collins exploits the irrational workings of Lord Harry's mind to reinforce normative hierarchies of nation and race. "Drive to the devil!" Harry tells his coachman, shortly before his botched suicide attempt. It is Lord Harry's fatal wilfulness that causes him to vacillate wildly from his fervent political commitments to the Invincibles, to his avowed vengeance against that secret society, to suicidal despair over losing both Iris and his money, to his desperate involvement in fraud, conspiracy, and murder, and finally, to his ultimate act of self-destruction whereby he ostensibly arranges his own murder by the Fenian terrorists, the brotherhood he betrayed. It is this "fatal purpose" or mania which also enables Lord Harry to falsely rationalize his participation in deceit, bloodshed, murder, and treachery, never quite acknowledging his actions, as Locke would imply, for what they are.

In order to understand Collins's treatment of insanity within a political context, we must first consider how *Blind Love* engages implicitly with contemporary debates and theories on the nature of insanity, particularly through the figure of the highly unstable Lord Harry. While the nineteenth century saw a progressive shift in attitudes toward the mentally ill marked by the construction and development of the asylum system and the emergence of medical professionals to treat and cure the "lunatic"[7]—defining the nature of "madness" remained a vexed issue. In *An Inquiry Concerning the Indications of Insanity, with Suggestions for the Better Protection and Care of the Insane* (1830), a classic text of nineteenth-century psychiatry, John Conolly defined madness as an unstable state of mind whereby passion impedes upon an individual's ability to reason:

> It is only when the passion so impairs one or more faculties of the mind as to prevent the exercise of comparison, that the reason is overturned; and then the man is mad. He is mad only whilst this state continues; but whilst it continues for a short or a long time, he is mad on the subject of his fear. He ceases to be mad when he can correct the erroneous judgment of his excited state; and not before. We see many madmen whose malady consists in their peculiar excitability to anger, and in the impossibility of correcting the judgments of their angry state: seeming to have become tranquil, the renewal of the subject of their anger renews the passion; and as they are never able to reason upon it, to compare and to judge, they continue to be mad on that subject.[8]

This inability to determine clear boundaries between sensible and insensible behaviour was corroborated in part by James Cowles Prichard in his *A Treatise on Insanity and Other Disorders Affecting the Mind* (1835). Prichard acknowledged that, following Locke,[9] madness is not the loss of reason, but rather a gross mis-association of ideas and morals: "it has been customary to observe that insane persons reason correctly from erroneous premises; and some instance of illusion, or some particular erroneous impression". But this tendency toward irrationality was only one form of madness in Prichard's view. That is, partial insanity, as Prichard labeled it, was distinctive from cases of "raving madness, in which the mind is totally deranged, and the individual affected talks nonsense, or expresses himself wildly and absurdly on every subject".[10]

Despite the difficulty or perhaps reluctance in delineating "a precise definition of madness",[11] at least in scientific medical terms, a common indicator for determining an individual's place on the continuum between sanity and insanity was not an inability to reason, but rather faulty reasoning or, in Foucauldian terms, "unreason".[12] J.G. Millingen explained that "every morbid state that influences our reflective, observant and imaginative faculties, disables an individual from conducting the processes of reasoning, or the sound and healthy exercise of his mental attributes, [and thus] constitutes insanity".[13] Similarly, in *On Man's Power over Himself to Prevent or Control Insanity* (1843), John Barlow suggested that sanity or insanity is determined by the "consequences of a greater or less resolution in exerting the power of reasoning still possessed". For Barlow what essentially distinguished the sane from the insane was self-control: "He who has given a proper direction to the intellectual force, and thus obtained an early command over the bodily organ by habituating it to processes of calm reasoning, remains sane amid all the vagaries of sense; while he who has been the slave, rather than the master of his animal nature, listens to its dictates without question . . . and is mad".[14] This view informed theories of insanity well into the century. Writing in 1874, Maudsley characterized insanity not only as "the dethronement of will, the loss of power of coordinating the ideas and feelings" but also as an hereditary condition, a symptom of an individual's "faulty heritage".[15]

Thus, the nature of insanity, despite these attempts to explain it, remained a somewhat opaque phenomenon, and it is this enigmatic nature that Collins evokes in the "Irish blackguard", Lord Harry. In the opening scene of the novel, Sir Giles Mountjoy, an Irish banker and magistrate, receives an unsigned letter warning him that a family member is in mortal danger. This strange missive, this "impenetrable mystery" (67), is our introduction (as we later discover) to the wild Irish lord, Harry Norland. In 1870, G. Mackenzie Bacon suggested that "the letters of the insane are worth study—as the most reliable evidence of the state of the patient's mind . . . . In ordinary cases of mania the patients' letters are odd and grotesque, exhibiting the same want of balance that their actions do".[16] With the unsigned letter, Collins cleverly and obliquely establishes the Irish Lord's mental instability: his "writing looked worthy of a madman. Sentences appeared in the wildest state of confusion, and words were so mutilated as to be unintelligible" (67). As it turns out, Sir Giles' nephew Arthur Mountjoy has been boycotted by the Land League for taking over an evicted farm after the last tenant "refused to pay his rent" (71) and now the Invincibles, a secret society of political assassins with whom Lord Harry had been associated, are lying in wait to exact their revenge. Lord Harry admits that his alliance with the "murderous conspirators" had been "inexcusably rash and wicked" and it might seem, if we apply Conolly's theory of madness, that Lord Harry's noble effort to save Arthur Mountjoy and "defeat, secretly the murderous designs of the brotherhood" is an effort to reassert his reason and "correct [his] erroneous judgement".[17] However, when the Invincibles succeed in assassinating Arthur, Lord Harry's anger prevents him from behaving rationally and he embarks on a mission "to exact the terrible penalty of blood for blood" (158). Such behaviour sets a pattern for Harry's actions throughout the novel. Though Harry does not necessarily exhibit what Prichard described as "raving madness"—complete and total mental derangement—Harry's impulsive, and at times manic behaviour is accentuated by an excessive and volatile emotionalism that vacillates wildly from anger and vengeance to jealousy and despair. In Lord Harry's temperament, Collins is clearly drawing on a popular stereotype of the Irish in order to reinforce the idea of English superiority and to advance the novel's broader argument for empire. In fact, in his study of anti-Irish prejudice in Victorian England, L.P. Curtis notes that is was the "Celt's reputation for emotionalism in particular that undermined Irish political aspirations".[18] For instance, the mere mention of Arthur's name, a man so "foully assassinated", provokes in Lord Harry a fierce resolution of revenge: he "was no longer the easy, gentle, joyous creature whom Iris had known and loved. The furious passions of the Celtic race glittered savagely in his eyes" (157). And just as quickly as his anger seizes hold of him, in the next instant, Harry bursts into a fit of hysteria and despair: "Oh, my temper, my temper!' he cried as Iris shrank from him . . . . He staggered away from her, and burst into a convulsive fit of crying, dreadful to hear" (157-158). Such dramatic mood swings for Lord Harry are the rule rather than the exception: "[t]he hot temper of an Irishman, in moments of excitement, is not infrequently a sweet temper in moments of calm" (152), while his manner can change "with the suddenness of a flash of light, from the extreme of coldness to the extreme of cordiality" (200).

To return briefly to Conolly's theory, we can see how his "indications of insanity" are applicable to Lord Harry: "it has been said that anger is a short madness; and it has been said, as truly, that no man can at once be in love and be wise; and, in like manner, we may observe each passion and emotion in excess disturbing the mind by a direct impairment of the comparing power, and consequently, the judgment".[19] To add to his mercurial temperament, another "tyranny of the passion[s]" under which Harry also suffers is his insane jealousy of Hugh Mountjoy, Iris's more proper and conventional English suitor. In one of the novel's many tense confrontations with Mountjoy, Harry is barely able to maintain any degree of self-control:

> The Irish lord's good-humour had completely disappeared by this time. His handsome face hardened, and his voice rose. The outbreak of jealous feeling, which motives honourable to himself had hitherto controlled, now seized on its freedom of expression. His language betrayed (as on some former occasions) that association with unworthy companions, which had been one of the evil results of his adventurous life. (230)

The contrast between the two suitors is most provocatively suggested in a chapter entitled "Saxon and Celt" in which the hostile and agitated Harry fails to "find a bond of union" with the civil and gentlemanly Mountjoy. "Mine's the Irish point of view", Harry declares, "as an Englishman you fail to understand it" (229). This confrontation, of course, brings into sharp focus a pattern discernible throughout the novel of stereotypical Celtic vices versus Anglo-Saxon virtues.

The highly speculative nature of defining and diagnosing madness had broad cultural implications in the Victorian period. The sliding boundary between sanity and insanity was crucial to reinforcing not only hierarchies of gender, as Elaine Showalter has demonstrated in her groundbreaking study *The Female Malady*,[20] but also hierarchies of nation and race. In the highly unstable personality of Lord Harry, Collins draws quite deliberately upon culturally-accepted stereotypes that the Irish were bloodthirsty, feckless, violent, lawless, savage, and irrational—quite simply, mad. In fact, under the "Dangerous Lunatics Act", a law that not only regulated Irish lunacy in the nineteenth century, but unequivocally linked insanity with criminality, Lord Harry could have easily headed the "Most Wanted" list. Under this law, first enacted in 1838, any individual who had allegedly threatened violence toward others[21] could be committed to an asylum simply "by two Justices of the Peace, acting on a sworn statement by a third party", usually a relative.[22] The fact that medical corroboration was admissible, but not mandatory, contributed to the highly subjective practice of alleging madness. Oonagh Walsh reports that in 1893 an individual was committed to the Connaught District Lunatic Asylum in Balinasloe, County Galway for his participation in the Land League protests against unfair rents. The "lunatic's family alleged that he refused to work after he had been evicted from his holding for non-payment of rent".[23] In fact, even when the act was reviewed and amended in 1867 to facilitate the transfer of "lunatics" from prison to the asylum,[24] those committed had no right to appeal their case. Beyond the obvious capriciousness of the law, the fact that that it did not extend to England or Scotland points to the broader political implications of diagnosing and registering cases of lunacy. Indeed, Walsh notes that to look at statistics alone, one might conclude that "madness had taken a firm grip on the Irish population"[25] during the second half of the nineteenth century, when the population of Ireland had been reduced by almost half, yet the number of "lunatics" committed to asylums grew four-fold, particularly in the economically disadvantaged and politically turbulent western part of Ireland.[26] By the end of the century, 0.5 percent of the Irish population was housed in district lunatic asylums.[27]

It is perhaps not entirely coincidental that 1867, the year in which the Dangerous Lunatics Act was amended (and, in a sense, reaffirmed), also bore witness to a string of terrorist activities by a group of Irish nationalists known as the Fenians,[28] occurring first in Ireland and then spilling over onto English soil.[29] While the fear and hysteria engendered by the Fenian outrages forced public awareness of Irish grievances, these acts of violence contributed to the widespread belief on the part of the English that Ireland's political disorder was symptomatic of an inherent mental disorder.[30] As the Fenian agitation in 1867-68 and the Land League and Home Rule movements in the 1880s coalesced,[31] an acute anti-Irish prejudice that had been festering in the English psyche for decades gained in strength and vitriol. According to L.P. Curtis, "The Irish Celt was [sic] condemned by most Anglo-Saxonists for being not only emotionally incontinent but a man of violent passions who indulged in unprovoked attacks on people or executed the vicious orders of secret societies. These traits were part of his nature, they were in his blood".[32]

Queen Victoria corroborated this view in 1867 with her declaration that "[t]hese Irish are really shocking, abominable people—not like any other civilized nation".[33] And certainly the currency of Darwin's theories in the 1860s seemed to provide further scientific "proof" of Celtic primitivism. At the same time, there were also a significant number of texts which attempted to prove the racial (and by extension, socio-political) inferiority of the Irish[34] in order to justify English colonial rule. Amidst the debates in newspapers, magazines, and journals about the relationship between primates and humans, a spate of vicious cartoons appeared in the comic weeklies which perpetuated the stereotyping of the Irish Celt as a dangerous madman or ape-like savage, not "fully civilized and not quite human".[35] At the height of the Land League War, a cartoon appeared in *Judy*—"The Congress of Revolutionists; Or Lunatics at Large"—which reaffirmed these stereotypes while also belying an anxiety about the anarchical state of Irish affairs. The image features a group of simianized revolutionaries gathered around a party table that is decorated with streamers imprinted with slogans such as "No Laws", "No Property", and "No Religion". In the middle of the table is a punchbowl filled with "respectable people's blood" around which the lunatic assassins have laid aside their pistols and daggers to make merry and celebrate their exploits. Indeed, while the Irish had long been considered barbarous and savage by the English, the outbreak of Fenian violence, coupled with a rising tide of "dangerous lunatics" being committed to asylums, lent further credence to the long-held belief that the Irish were "out of their wits" and needed to be put under "proper restraint".[36]

Blind Love's sensational representation of the unruly Irish and Ireland's anarchic movements for independence can be seen as symptomatic of the pervasive anti-Irish sentiment that reverberated throughout Victorian public opinion and as one of Collins's most explicit defences of English colonial rule.[37] In *The Location of Culture*, Homi K. Bhabha theorizes that "[t]he objective of colonial discourse is to construe the colonized as a population of degenerate types on the basis of racial origin, in order to justify conquest and to establish systems of administration and instruction".[38] The identification of the Celt as mad and animalistic dramatically reinforced the scapegoating of the Irish as degenerate "other". Following Bhabha, if lawlessness and violence were believed to be inherent Irish traits, then it was England's obligation to civilize and govern (or in psycho-medical terms, restrain and treat) the savage Celt. Collins's Lord Harry is a synecdoche for all those disruptive and disorderly impulses that must be contained in Ireland. Not only does Iris, the embodiment of an imperiled England,[39] "hope to exercise a salutary restraint" on Lord Harry's reckless behaviour, his capricious jealousy, and his desperate resolution of revenge to protect her "domestic interests" (236), but Hugh Mountjoy, the embodiment of English respectability and solidity, also seeks to "keep the hot-tempered Irish husband passive and harmless" (239). Lord Harry is unrelenting nevertheless. Not only has he "contemplated (and still cherished) his merciless resolution of revenge" (166) but, like a textbook example of Prichard's morally insane, Harry is able to "display great ingenuity in giving reasons for the eccentricities of [his] conduct, and in accounting for and justifying the state of moral feeling under which [he] appear[s] to exist".[40] Revelling in a state of *unreason*, Harry justifies his plan to Iris:

> Brutus killed a man; Charlotte Corday killed a man. One of the two victims was a fine tyrant, and the other a mean tyrant. Nobody blames those two historical assassins. Why then blame me for wishing to make a third? Is a mere modern murderer beneath my vengeance, by comparison with two classical tyrants who did *their* murders by deputy? The man who killed Arthur Mountjoy is (next to Cain alone) the most atrocious homicide that ever trod the miry way of this earth. There is my reply! (164-165)

Lord Harry's delusional state is apparent. The fact that he fancies himself another Brutus, who killed Julius Caesar, *and* Charlotte Corday, a French revolutionary who was beheaded in 1793 for murdering the leader of the Jacobin party, attests to delusions of self-grandeur and his inability to see his own intended actions in their proper moral proportions.

Harry's madness is even more pronounced in his complete disregard of his fallibility and mortality:

> What a prospect that was before that reckless man—what misery, what horror, might not be lying in wait in the dreadful future! If he failed in the act of vengeance, that violent death of which he had written so heedlessly might overtake him from another

> hand. If he succeeded, the law might discover his crime, and the infamy of expiation on the scaffold might be his dreadful end. (166)

It is the reckless endangerment of his life—his very fearlessness—wherein Barlow would locate Harry's madness or his "delusion of sense". The sane person, according to Barlow, possesses not only a certain degree of self-control, but is driven by fear to "avoid actions which would have unpleasant consequences to himself".[41] This delusional, almost nihilistic state manifests itself most sensationally in Harry's "desperate attempt at self-destruction" (181). Driven to despair after gambling away his money, he cuts his throat in a botched suicide attempt, the "reckless victim of his love for the woman who had desperately renounced him again and again" (184).

Though Harry's behaviour and actions throughout the novel are symptomatic of what many Victorian observers would describe as some form of mental or emotional imbalance—and indeed, an attempted suicide was a common reason for committal to an asylum in nineteenth-century Ireland[42]—in the chapter "My Lord's Mind", the wild lord himself confirms his own mental condition: "My Irish friend is mad—you will say. Your Irish friend, my dear fellow, does not dispute it" (244). In an almost stream-of-consciousness narrative directed to Dr. Vimpany we glimpse "the cry of a patient with a sick mind" as Harry beseeches the doctor to "get at [his] diseased mind, through [his] healthy body" (243). Harry claims that he is in "a bad way" because he "can't get over" the fact that Arthur Mountjoy's assassin has escaped him again. He also confesses that "the devil whose name is Jealousy has entered into me" and pleads with his medical friend to "deliver [him] from [him]self": "I hate a man who pretends to be my wife's friend, and who is secretly in love with her all the time" (244). In addition to these obsessions and his increasing anxiety about his dubious investment schemes, Harry admits to his predilection for reckless behaviour: "I wish to be lost among strangers. I should like to find myself in a state of danger meeting the risks that I used to run in my vagabond days. Now I think of it, I might enjoy this last excitement by going back to England, and giving the Invincibles a chance of shooting me as a traitor to the cause" (246).

It is from this point on in the novel where Harry, believing his "position has altered for the worst" (246), commits himself entirely to a path of self-destruction—including fraud, conspiracy, and murder—from which he will not be able to recover. In a desperate attempt to pull himself out of serious financial difficulties, Harry joins forces with the quack physician Dr. Vimpany and plots an elaborate scheme to fake his own death and defraud London insurance companies out of thousands of pounds.[43] Purporting to have developed a "new system of treatment in diseases of the lungs", Dr. Vimpany gains access to the hospitals in Paris to seek out someone who might be suffering from lung disease and who might also bear a "certain accidental likeness" (277) to Lord Harry. The "opportunity that he wanted" (276) is presented to him in a man named Oxbye, a Dane who had migrated to France and then had fallen ill. Since his health had not seen any marked improvement under the care of his French physician, Oxbye eagerly accepts Vimpany's offer to test out his experimental treatment and hopefully recover in Harry's cottage where the "air is more pure" and where he won't be surrounded by other sick persons. As Oxbye's health unexpectedly begins to improve, Vimpany and Harry "add murder to their other crimes" (343) by slowly poisoning the consumptive Dane. Their plan is to substitute Oxbye for Harry so that Iris, who is unwittingly drawn into the plot (she is led to believe while she was away in Paris, Oxbye had died of natural causes), can pose as his widow to collect the money from the life insurance policy that Harry has taken out on himself. Prior to Oxbye's death, Vimpany photographs the victim while he is sleeping so that they will have evidence of Lord Harry's "death"— a post-mortem portrait—to present to the insurance companies. Unlike the vast array of fascinating villains who populate Collins's fiction—Robert Mannion (*Basil*), Count Fosco (*The Woman in White*) Lydia Gwilt (*Armadale*), Captain Wragge (*No Name*), among others—criminal masterminds who openly defy conventional morality,[44] Collins is not enthralled with, nor empathetic towards, the anarchic lawlessness of the Irish lord. One contemporary reviewer, in fact, observed that "Lord Harry marks quite a new departure" for Collins".[45] Once Iris discovers the murder that lies behind the insurance fraud, she comes to her senses and leaves her husband forever. Remorseful, Lord Harry confesses his crime to the insurance companies and returns the money he has obtained, urging them not to prosecute his wife. Shortly thereafter however, Harry once again lapses into suicidal despair and determines to return to Ireland "to meet the death of one who is called a Traitor to the Cause" (385). Indeed, for Collins, self-destruction is the only fitting end for a degenerate criminal committed to such murder, mayhem, and madness.

Collins also psycho-sexualizes Anglo-Irish relations by placing Iris Henley in a problematic relationship with the wild and rebellious Lord Harry, the epitome of the militant Irish nationalist. Iris's romantic entanglement with the Irish blackguard—"the man [to] whom she was forbidden"—serves as a culturally telling analogue to the madness of those Britons who sympathized with the misguided desire for Irish independence, and by extension, to those who were blind to the inherent moral deficiencies of the Celtic race. The blind love that Iris apparently manifests for her reckless husband throughout the novel is difficult to comprehend, though, unless we understand it as a type of madness:

> But the one unassailable vital force in this world is the force of love. It may submit to the hard necessities of life; it may acknowledge the imperative claims of duty; it may be silent under reproach and submissive to privation—but suffer what it may, it is the master-passion still; subject to no artificial influences, owning no supremacy but the *law* of its own being (91)

Here Iris attests to what Foucault would describe as "the determinism of the passions", a form of madness whereby laws are "compromised, perverted, [and] distorted".[46] In much the same way that we observe in Lord Harry what Conolly would describe as "passion and emotion in excess disturbing the mind . . . [and] the judgment",[47] we see Iris similarly tyrannized by her passion, her "curse" (371). Iris

Henley does not understand the man she loves because she is not "in her right senses". She cannot account for his "monstrous inconsistency"—his "tendencies to evil . . . as well as [his] tendencies to good" (118). More alarming is that Iris does not understand herself: "I am a wretched, unreasonable creature; I don't know my own mind for two days together, and all through my husband—I am so fond of him" (219). In her madness, Iris refuses to listen to the rational entreaties of Hugh Mountjoy to break off her engagement with Lord Harry: "You are blind to your future life. Your talk as if you were resigned to suffer. Are you resigned to lose your sense of right and wrong? Are you resigned to lead the life of an outlaw—and worse still—not to feel the disgrace of it?" (194). Hugh's warning of Iris's "moral deterioration" (221) is, of course, prophetic, as she soon finds herself caught up as accomplice and co-conspirator in the madness of Harry's criminal activities.

Even though Iris admits that "no woman in her senses could let the bare idea of being his wife enter her mind" (166), she nonetheless gives in to her "master-passion". Against her father's wishes, she marries Lord Harry and is subsequently cut out of her inheritance. As an observer of the early days of their marriage, Mrs. Vimpany notes that Iris's "blind belief in her husband" betrayed "signs of self-delusion. It was indeed sad to see that bright intelligence rendered incapable of conceiving suspicions, which might have occurred to the mind of a child" (208). Yet, it is only when Iris learns of the conspiracy—the murder of the Dane and the subsequent insurance fraud—that she is able to acknowledge the unrelenting savagery of her Irish husband and her own temporary descent into madness:

> A horrible crime has been committed—a horrible, ghastly dreadful crime—such a thing as one reads of in the papers and wonders, reading it, what manner of wild beasts must be those who do such things. Perhaps one wonders, besides, what manner of women must be those who associate with those wild beasts . . . . I am one of the women who are the fit companions of these wild creatures (371).

Iris can finally see that in Harry's betrayal and deceit, her life has been "wrecked" in a "blind passion". In *Madness and Civilization*, Foucault says that blindness is the essence of madness, it is "reason dazzled": "Madness begins where the relation of man to truth is disturbed and darkened".[48] It is in such terms that we can best understand Iris's irrational behaviour throughout:

> Then, as one who had been wearing coloured glasses puts them off and sees things in their own true colours, she saw how she had been pulled down by a blind infatuation to the level of the man who had held her in his fascination; she saw him as he was—reckless, unstable, careless of name and honour. Then for the first time she realized the depths into which she was plunged and the life she was henceforth doomed to lead. The blind love fell from her—it was dead at last (363).

Interestingly, this observation echoes the rhetoric of blindness that resonates throughout those hostile reports and angry editorials that appeared in English newspapers describing "the state of Ireland" during the Land War. In a May 1882 letter to the *Sunday Times*, Gladstone and his ministers were severely rebuked for attempting to "bribe" the "Irish malcontents". Accusing the English government of a "policy of cowardice", the writer declared that "Ministers are still trying to blind our eyes to the position into which they have betrayed their country . . . . Every day that Ireland is left to anarchy and Gladstone, increases its present dangers and renders more certain and absolute its future ruin".[49] Indeed, the violence that took place the very next week—the Phoenix Park murders[50]—seemed to justify that sense of outrage. Adopting a similar vocabulary, a writer for *The Times* indignantly declared that "[t]here are none so blind as they who won't see" that the brutal murders of Lord Frederick Cavendish and Mr. Frederick Burke, and the subsequent escape of the "black-hearted assassins" are not an anomaly in Ireland; rather, "hardly a day [during the past two years] has passed that has not witnessed its deed of blood".[51] And, in an historical explanation for the ongoing "troubles in Ireland", one commentator pointed out that "[i]t is astonishing how blind we are to what is passing under our very eyes". According to the writer, if the English would only look back to the lessons of history, they would see that the Irish question was simply an enthnological issue, "a question of the supremacy of race":

> Which race shall be the dominant one in Ireland, the Anglo-Saxon or the Celtic? . . . . Who are to be the masters of Ireland, the English or the Irish? . . . Unless a change comes over the minds of our rulers, the very existence of our own country may be threatened. We know there are times when a judicial blindness overtakes both rulers and people which, in spite of all warnings and rules of prudence, leads them onward to their destruction. Such an impotent infatuation seems at present to be the *ruling spirit* in this country, and it is certain to bring with it nothing but disaster and misery"[52]

In *Blind Love*, Collins traverses the political and psychological borderlands of both colonizer and the colonized to contain that very "ruling spirit". As he fictively navigates these liminal territories, Collins does not leave the question of which race will prevail unanswered and, in doing so, deftly advances Victorian arguments for colonial rule. Indeed, in a narrative that provocatively weaves together boycotts and tenant uprisings with lurid murders and romance, Collins reinforces England's narrowly-defined ethnocentric outlook and boldly predicts in Lord Harry's violent death —"one more murder to load the soul of Ireland" (385)—that Ireland's violent desire for self-rule will lead inevitably to self-destruction.

Notes

1. Andrew Wynter, *The Borderlands of Insanity and other Allied Papers* (London: Robert Harwicke, 1875), in *Embodied Selves: An Anthology of Psychological Texts 1830-1890*, ed. Jenny Bourne Taylor and Sally Shuttleworth (Oxford: Clarendon Press, 1998), 280.
2. Henry Maudsley, *Responsibility in Mental Disease*, London 1874, 23.
3. Unsigned review (H. F. Chorley), *The Athenaeum*, 2 June 1866, 732-3, in *Wilkie Collins: The Critical Heritage*, ed. Norman Page (London and Boston: Routledge & Kegan Paul, 1974), 147.
4. Jenny Bourne Taylor, *In the Secret Theatre of Home: Wilkie Collins, Sensation Narrative, and Nineteenth Century Psychology* (Routledge: London and New York, 1988), 10.
5. Taylor argues that in *Basil* (1852) and "Mad Monkton" (1855) Collins employs images of madness (hereditary insanity) to "generate sensation and suspense", while in *The Woman in White* (1860) he goes further by using insanity to not simply produce anxiety and fear, but to engage with contemporary debates on false confinement as well (Taylor, 71-130). Following *The Woman in White*, Collins's short story "A Mad Marriage" (1875), is not so much an engagement with those debates, as it is an overt attack on the ease with which an individual might be wrongly committed to a lunatic asylum, while *Jezebel's Daughter* (1880) features an alleged lunatic, Jack Straw, who is "cured" outside the walls of the asylum.
6. Wilkie Collins, *Blind Love*, eds, Maria K. Bachman and Don Richard Cox (Peterborough, Ontario: Broadview Press, 2004). Though *Blind Love* was Collins's final novel, it was a novel that he did not live to complete. Prior to his death, an ailing Collins left a detailed outline (including portions of dialogue) of the last third of his book to be faithfully completed by his younger colleague, the popular author Walter Besant. Because part of *Blind Love* was published posthumously (it appeared in serial form in *The Illustrated London News* from July 1889 through December 1889; Collins died on September 23, 1889), contemporary reviews of the novel tend to be overshadowed by obituary notices and critical assessments of his literary career. While critics made no specific comment on Collins's apparent stance on the Irish question—most reviews simply offered a plot summary while also drawing comparisons with some of his earlier works—there was, however, a general consensus that the Irish lord, Harry Norland was an inveterate vagabond.
7. This has been well documented. See for instance, W.F. Bynum, Roy Porter, and Michael Shepherd, eds, *The Anatomy of Madness: Essays in the History of Psychiatry*, 3 vols. (London and New York: Tavistock Publications, 1985), Michel Foucault, *Madness and Civilization: A History of Insanity in the Age of Reason* (New York: Vintage Books, 1988), Joseph Melling and Bill Forsythe, eds, *Insanity, Institutions, and Society, 1800-1914* (London and New York: Routledge, 1999), Andrew Scull, *The Most Solitary of Afflictions: Madness and Society in Britain, 1700-1900* (New Haven and London: Yale University Press, 1993), Andrew Scull, ed., *Madhouses, Mad-Doctors, and Madmen: The Social History of*

Psychiatry in the Victorian Era (Philadelphia: University of Pennsylvania Press, 1981).

8. John Conolly, *An Inquiry Concerning the Indications of Insanity, with Suggestions for the Better Protection and Care of the Insane* (London: John Taylor, 1830), in *Embodied Selves: An Anthology of Psychological Texts 1830-1890*, ed. Jenny Bourne Taylor and Sally Shuttleworth (Oxford: Clarendon Press, 1998), 241.

9. In their collection of primary materials on Victorian psychological thought, Jenny Bourne Taylor and Sally Shuttleworth note that well into the nineteenth century, John Locke's *Essay on Human Understanding* remained a touchstone for discussions on the nature of insanity (*Embodied Selves: An Anthology of Psychological Texts 1830-1890* [Oxford: Clarendon Press, 1998), 251n.

10. James Cowles Prichard, *A Treatise on Insanity and Other Disorders Affecting the Mind* (London: Sherwood, Gilbert, and Piper, 1835), in *Embodied Selves: An Anthology of Psychological Texts 1830-1890*, ed. Jenny Bourne Taylor and Sally Shuttleworth (Oxford: Clarendon Press, 1998), 252.

11. J. G. Millingen, *Aphorisms on the Treatment and Management of the Insane* (London: Churchill, 1840), 3. 1. Quoted in Andrew Scull, *The Most Solitary of Afflictions: Madness and Society in Britain, 1700-1900* (New Haven and London: Yale University Press, 1993), 346.

12. In *Madness and Civilization*, Michel Foucault argues that the history of madness cannot be understood without interrogating the history of reason. Specifically, he employs the term "unreason" to describe those people who reason wrongly or are beyond reason: "it is not reason diseased, or as reason lost or alienated, but quite simply as *reason dazzled*" (108).

13. Millingen, 346.

14. John Barlow, *On Man's Power Over Himself to Prevent or Control Insanity* (London: William Pickering, 1843), in *Embodied Selves: An Anthology of Psychological Texts 1830-1890*, ed. Jenny Bourne Taylor and Sally Shuttleworth (Oxford: Clarendon Press, 1998), 244.

15. Taylor and Shuttleworth, 277.

16. G. Mackenzie Bacon, *On the Writing of the Insane* (London: Churchill, 1870), 15-17, in *Embodied Selves: An Anthology of Psychological Texts 1830-1890*, ed. Jenny Bourne Taylor and Sally Shuttleworth (Oxford: Clarendon Press, 1998), 249.

17. Taylor and Shuttleworth, 241.

18. L.P. Curtis, Jr. *Anglo-Saxons and Celts: A Study of Anti-Irish Prejudice in Victorian England* (Bridgeport, CT: The University of Bridgeport, 1968), 55. Hereafter cited as *Anglo-Saxons and Celts*.

19. Taylor and Shuttleworth, 241.

20. Elaine Showalter, *The Female Malady: Women, Madness and English Culture, 1850-1980* (New York: Pantheon, 1985).

21. Any person could be considered a dangerous lunatic if they were "apprehended under Circumstances denoting a Derangement of Mind, and a Purpose of committing some [indictable] Crime" (Quoted in Mark Finnane, *Insanity and the Insane in Post-Famine Ireland* [Totowa, NJ: Barnes & Noble Books, 1981], 90.

22. Oonagh Walsh, "Lunatic and Criminal Alliances in Nineteenth-Century Ireland" in *Outside the Walls of the Asylum: The History of Care in the Community 1750-2000*, ed. Peter Bartlett and David Wright (London and New Brunswick, NJ: The Athlone Press, 1999), 135-36. Hereafter cited as "Lunatic and Criminal Alliances".
23. Oonagh Walsh, "'The Designs of Providence': Race, Religion and Irish Insanity" in *Insanity, Institutions and Society, 1800-1914*, ed. Joseph Melling and Bill Forsythe (London and New York: Routledge, 1999), 238-39. Hereafter cited as "Designs of Providence".
24. Walsh reports that under the initial Dangerous Lunatic Act, individuals who were charged were sent first to prison where they might be detained for up to one year, before being transferred to an asylum ("Lunatic and Criminal Alliances", 135).
25. Oonagh Walsh, "Lunatic and Criminal Alliances", 139-40.
26. See Finnane, 130-36. While the development of the Irish asylum system in Ireland was contemporaneous with that of England, its expansion in Ireland was much more rapid and dramatic. Moreover, unlike England, the Poor Relief Act in Ireland offered no provision for insane. Rather, asylums and their patients remained under the jurisdiction of the Lord Lieutenant of Ireland who also controlled the prison system and whose priorities ultimately were not so much to the Irish people as they were to Parliament in London (Oonagh Walsh, "Lunatic and Criminal Alliances", 134).
27. "Designs of Providence", 227.
28. Dedicated to the establishment of an Irish republic by force of arms, the Fenians initially were composed of the so-called "dangerous classes"—radicalized émigrés, artisans, urban workers, all of whom existed on the fringes of Irish society. With the agricultural crises of the 1860s, however, the movement spread rapidly among labourers, shopkeepers and others who had been particularly hard hit by the harvest failures. See Alan O'Day, *Irish Home Rule 1867-1921* (Manchester and New York: Manchester University Press, 1998), 23.
29. Several thousand Fenians turned out for a general uprising in Ireland in March 1867, though they were dispersed by Irish authorities. The uprising had been preceded by a planned invasion of Canada by Irish émigrés, a plot against the military arsenal at Chester, and an armed expedition to Dublin. In September 1867, the armed rescue of two Fenians from a prison van in Manchester resulted in the accidental killing of an English prison guard. In December, anti-Irish sentiment in England reached fever pitch following the explosion of a bomb during a Fenian rescue at Clerkenwell prison which left dozens of innocent victims dead or seriously injured. The Clerkenwell incident—"a crime of unexampled atrocity"—had a tremendous impact on British public opinion *vis-à-vis* the Irish: "With traitors and assassins there can be but one course . . . . The Fenians have cast the glare of a great moral crime upon the debatable ground which separates us, and we can no longer hesitate in which direction to advance...We are confronted by a gang of reckless criminals, who respect no laws, human or divine. . . . (Quoted in Norman McCord, "The Fenians and Public Opinion", *Fenians and Fenianism*, ed. Maurice Harmon [Dublin: Scepter Books, 1970], 47).

30. Even Gladstone's declaration upon becoming British Prime Minister in 1868 sounds more like a medical curative than a statement of foreign policy: "My mission is to pacify Ireland . . . .those sympathies in Ireland which now hang and float bewildered between law and lawlessness [must] be brought into active alliance" with the law (Travis L. Crosby, *The Two Mr. Gladstones: A Study in Psychology and History* [New Haven and London: Yale University Press, 1997], 119, 121).
31. The Land War began in 1879 when large numbers of tenant farmers in the west of Ireland, suffering from an agricultural depression (caused by poor harvests and the importing of cheap corn from America) rebelled against their landlords by refusing to pay their normal rents. The response to the landlord's program eviction was a combination of boycotts, violence, intimidatation, and murder, led in part by the Invincibles, a group of extreme nationalists who pledged themselves to a policy of assassination.
32. *Anglo-Saxons and Celts*, 61.
33. Quoted in Patrick O'Farrell, *England and Ireland Since 1800* (London and New York: Oxford University Press, 1975), 49.
34. See for instance, John Beddoe, *The Races of Britain* (London, 1885; Washington, DC: The Cliveden Press, 1983) and James Bonwick, *Who Are the Irish?* (London, 1880). While England's expansion of its overseas empire was motivated by the competition for resources and markets, the country justified its imperial mission by the ethnocentric assumption that primitive peoples, including the Irish Celts, were uncivilized and thus incapable of self-government.
35. L.P. Curtis, Jr., *Apes and Angels: The Irishman in Victorian Caricature*, rev. ed. (Washington and London: Smithsonian Institution Press, 1997), xxxii. Hereafter cited as *Apes and Angels*. In *Madness and Civilization*, Foucault notes that in the classical age, a period roughly between 1660 and the end of the nineteenth century, an "obsession with animality [was] perceived as the natural locus of madness": "madness borrowed its face from the mask of the beast" (77, 72).
36. "Grand Discovery—Ireland's Real Disorder" *Punch* 14 (1848): 57.
37. For an overview of the ongoing critical debate on Collins's imperial politics, see Lillian Nayder, "Wilkie Collins Studies: 1983-1999", *Dickens Studies Annual 28* (1999): 298-303.
38. Homi K. Bhabha, *The Location of Culture* (London and New York: Routledge, 1991), 70.
39. James Buzard notes that as England consolidated its empire in the late nineteenth century and "attained unprecendented international clout . . . Englishness or Britishness was [sic] routinely allegorized . . . as a vulnerable woman, who must . . . defend herself by English pluck" ("'Then on the Shore of the Wide World': The Victorian Nation and its Others" in *A Companion to Victorian Literature and Culture*, ed. Herbert F. Tucker (Oxford: Blackwell Publishers, 1999), 445.
40. According to Prichard, "Persons labouring under this disorder are capable of reasoning or supporting an argument upon any subject within their sphere of knowledge that may be presented to them; and they often display great ingenuity in giving reasons for the eccentricities of their conduct, and in accounting for and justifying the state of moral feeling under which they appear to exist. In one sense,

indeed, their intellectual faculties may be termed unsound; they think and act under the influence of strongly-excited feelings" (Taylor and Shuttleworth, 254).

41. Barlow theorizes that "fear, one of the lowest, but also one of the most general of instinctive emotions" functions to "balance the delusions of sense" and in doing so "has been found sufficient to curb violence, and enforce a certain degree of peaceable demeanour towards the attendants" (Taylor and Shuttleworth, 244).

42. Mark Finnane points out that attempted suicide in nineteenth-century Ireland was "irrefutable evidence of a person's insanity". Even an individual who simply threatened to kill himself could be and often was committed to an asylum. (*Insanity and the Insane in Post-Famine Ireland* [Totowa, NJ: Barnes & Noble Books, 1981], 151).

43. Like so much of Collins's fiction, *Blind Love* is based on sensational events in the news, in this case the Von Scheurer Insurance Fraud of 1883-84, in which it was discovered that Baron Von Scheurer, "a German adventurer", had faked his own death by burying a look-alike corpse in order to defraud five London insurance companies out of a large insurance settlement.

44. Though their actions lead to their ultimate demise, these master-criminals are mainly in control of themselves and others throughout the novels.

45. Unsigned review, "New Publications. Novels and Tales. *Blind Love*", *New York Tribune*, 23 January 1890, 10.

46. Foucault, 89.

47. Taylor and Shuttleworth, 241.

48. Foucault, 108, 104.

49. Unsigned letter to the Editor (H.E.S.), *The Times*, 7 May 1882, 2. This letter was written in response to the negotiation between Prime Minister Gladstone and Charles Parnell, the imprisoned leader of the Irish Parliamentary party of the Kilmainham Treaty. With an early release from prison, Parnell agreed to cooperate with the Irish government and use his influence to prevent further agitation, while the government, in turn, would compensate evicted tenants. Public perception about the government's inability to "pacify" Ireland continued to sour. In June 1882, a *Times* editorial accused England's rulers of being "blind and deaf" in their failure to quell the ongoing discontent and violence in Ireland.

50. In May 1882, following the release of Parnell, the newly-installed Chief Secretary for Ireland, Lord Frederick Cavendish and his Under Secretary, Thomas Burke were slashed and mutilated by the Invincibles as they walked through a park in Dublin. The incident which became known as the Phoenix Park murders, shook political opinion throughout England and Ireland.

51. "Passing Events", *The Times*, 14 May 1882, 3.

52. Unsigned letter to the Editor, *The Times*, 4 June 1882, 2 (italics mine).

Chapter 13

Time's Hand: Fingerprints, Empire, and Victorian Narratives of Crime

Gita Panjabi Trelease

"Always look at the hands first, Watson".
Arthur Conan Doyle, "The Adventure of the Creeping Man"

Over the course of the nineteenth century, crime became a subject of debate in England in a way that it had never been before. In the eighteenth century, crime management consisted primarily of a severe penal code whose list of crimes constituting capital offenses increased so rapidly that it earned the nickname "the Bloody Code".[1] Although the law was harsh, its execution was often uneven and erratic, its enforcement lacklustre. Under Victoria's reign, however, sweeping criminal reform resulted in the reshaping of nearly every element of crime management, including criminal law, criminal administration, the police, prisons, transportation, and capital punishment.[2] The century witnessed the transformation of John and Henry Fielding's Bow Street Runners—which Dickens had called "a very slack institution"—into a city-wide police force through the legislation of the Metropolitan Police Act of 1829; a specialized detective division was added in 1842.[3] With the expansion and specialization of the police force, London was ostensibly watched with greater vigilance than ever before. The positive change that the development of institutionalized policing represented, however, was counteracted by shifts in London's criminal population. Before the middle of the nineteenth century, transportation of convicted criminals to Britain's colonies had been the primary substitute for execution or imprisonment at home; transportation in turn freed the British penal system from developing effective institutional control for violent offenders and habitual criminals. By the 1840s, however, colonies began to refuse to accept any more convicts, and by 1867 the great hulks that cast their shadows over Pip's life in *Great Expectations* were gone: transportation had come to an end. As a result, the criminal population had to be managed at home.

Despite the Penal Servitude Acts of 1853 and 1857, the Prison Act of 1865, and the Habitual Criminals Act of 1869, crime continued to flourish, contributing to a growing concern over what appeared to be one of the great and unfortunate drawbacks to a century of progress. In response to the continuing crime problem, theorists of crime shifted their focus from the study of punishment (penology), which had fueled mid-century reforms, to the study of the criminal himself, which resulted in the science of criminology, or as it was known to many of its adherents, criminal anthropology. Imported from Italy in the work of Cesare Lombroso and popularized in England by Havelock Ellis, criminal anthropology brought together disciplines such as psychology, anthropology, physiology, anthropometrics, and statistics to frame a solution to what Ellis saw as the "great question":

> What is a criminal? Is he—according to the old legal assumption on which our criminal law is still mainly built—a normal person who has willfully committed an abnormal act? Is he the victim of acquired disease, such as some form of epilepsy? Is he an atavistic reappearance of the savage in modern society? Is he a "degenerate"? What is the "criminal type"?[4]

This shift in emphasis from crime to criminal necessitated a new set of technologies designed to manage the individual criminal. Identification systems, such as that pioneered by Alphonse Bertillon, in which descriptions of the criminal's physical attributes (hair color, eye color, skin color) and measurements of his body were recorded in an index, allowed police officers to track offenders more effectively. In addition, law enforcement marshalled technologies such as fingerprinting, the "lie detector"—which Lombroso developed from earlier instruments like the plethysmograph and the sphygmograph—and the seemingly irrefutable evidence of photography in hopes of fixing the identity of criminals by making their bodies "tell the truth".[5]

Part of what characterized the criminal was the perception that he was unwilling or unable to tell the truth.[6] In the absence of trustworthy testimony, law enforcement turned to these scientific technologies as verifiable and accurate replacements for the criminal's word or for descriptions of his alleged actions. In 1888, the year of the Ripper murders, Sir Francis Galton, Darwin's second cousin and a dabbler in statistical analysis and anthropometry, saw in the embryonic study of fingerprinting the potential for an efficient system of criminal identification. It seemed to promise, he noted, the possibility of verifying identity in the most extraordinary circumstances, as in the case of

> [A] person who was insane, severely wounded, or of a dead body that had been partly destroyed, or so disfigured as to be hardly recognisable from a sudden or violent death due to crime, accident, shipwreck, or battle...when it is a question of identifying persons who are living at a great distance, and after the lapse of a considerable time, when the physiognomy, the features, and the physical habits may have changed from natural or artificial causes.[7]

The goal of this system of identification would be "to fix human personality, to give to each human being an identity, an individuality that can be depended upon with certainty, lasting, unchangeable, always recognizable and easily adduced" (169).

Nowhere did the need to be able to "easily adduce" identity arise more strongly than in Britain's imperial holdings. The imperial project as a whole depended upon an orderly and efficient bureaucracy to function, and fingerprinting first came into being as a practice designed to improve imperial government.

Crime management in India from 1858 through the 1870s not only serves as an excellent example of the development of criminal anthropological practice, but it also offers a valuable study of the way crime came to be a matter of individual identity. Finally, the Indian origins of fingerprinting reveal the emphasis on bodily identification and authentication of testimony that continued to shape the science of fingerprinting. I therefore turn to a consideration of the work of Sir William Herschel, an Indian civil servant and district administrator who wrote a book-length study as well as several articles on fingerprinting that drew Francis Galton's attention to the possibilities of dactyloscopy. A brief look at the origins of fingerprinting, as sketched out in Herschel's often disregarded work, sheds light on the assumptions that underlie the process of criminal identification Galton adopted, developed, and popularized in his ground-breaking work, *Finger Prints* (1892).[8] I then turn to look at the way detective fiction, in particular Arthur Conan Doyle's "The Norwood Builder", the only Sherlock Holmes story in which a fingerprints provide a crucial clue, adjudicates the problem of criminal identification through recourse to narrative structure.

In 1858, in Jungipoor, India, Herschel commissioned bids for a road-building project. He eventually came to terms with an Indian named Rajyadhar Konai over the cost of the project and drew up the contract. Just as Konai was about to sign the document, however, Herschel proposed an "experiment"—to ink Konai's hand and use the print of his hand on the back of the contract as a sign of the road-builder's commitment and thereby to "frighten Konai out of all thought of repudiating his signature".[9] Strangely, Herschel admits that Konai "of course, had never dreamt of such an attestation", implying that Herschel had no apparent reason to distrust him. This uneasy moment of ingrained and seemingly unjustified colonial suspicion marks the beginning of fingerprinting.

Recorded in Herschel's summary of his experience with fingerprinting called *The Origin of Fingerprinting* (1916), this brief episode embodies the suspicion that so often characterized British relationships to their Indian subjects in the wake of the Mutiny of 1857. As Herschel notes, after five years' service in the East India Company, his experience with the court system in India had forced him to "distrust all evidence tendered in Court"; he despaired "of any good coming from orders and decisions based on such slippery facts" (7). According to Herschel, disturbances in India, such as those following the Indigo riots of 1860 near Calcutta, produced a wave of forgery, perjury, and fraud exemplified by the false documents submitted to the British court by Indian landlords and their tenants, which Herschel notes "were frequently worth no more than the paper on which they were written" because their authenticity could not be guaranteed (11). But it was not until Herschel took a position as magistrate and collector, which gave him control of the criminal courts, the jail, and the department through which deeds were registered, that he began to take fingerprints as part of an attempt to reduce the incidence of fraud in his district.

Herschel was not alone in considering Indians to be "natural" criminals.[10] Galton, too, took for a fact the Indians' falseness in legal affairs. According to him, natives of the colonies were "characterised by a strange amount of litigiousness, wiliness, and unveracity" which necessitated a system of fingerprinting like the one Herschel was beginning to develop. In *Finger Prints*, Galton quotes a retired major from the India Staff Corps as saying that "Without going into the ethics of falsehood among Western and Eastern peoples, it would be impossible to explain how what is repugnant to the one as downright lying, is very frequently considered as no more than venial prevarication by the other" (151). Major Ferris believed that the need for "an official system of identification" in India was compounded by the mendacious character of the Indians and their in-born love of land which brought them into constant contact with the British court system. With no hint self-consciousness, Ferris remarks that

> The tenacity with which a native of India cleaves to his ancestral land, his innate desire to acquire more and more, and the obligation that accrues to him at birth of safeguarding that which has already been acquired, amounts to a religion, and passes the comprehension of the ordinary Western mind (150).

However ironic Major Ferris's comments may seem, they reinforce an important point of Herschel's: that fraud was an inevitable and "natural" consequence of England's governing the colonies and that in order for the vast bureaucratic machine of empire to function, some system of verifying signatures on legal documents had to be found.

Herschel believed that fingerprinting could solve this problem because of two characteristics particular to the print itself. First, every print was unique; although it might share certain characteristics with other prints, under close scrutiny it would always prove to be individual, even more so than the written signature of a man. As Galton pointed out in his later work, even a burn on the fingertip would only temporarily disfigure the fingerprint; the characteristic ridges which made up the whorls, arches, and loops that in turn composed the patterns of the print would eventually be "wholly restored" (59). Second, the print did not change over time; Herschel's records allowed for the comparison of prints taken at different times and based on minute observation of the individual prints, he concluded that the marks were persistent.

The individuality of the prints and their persistence over time made them well-suited to the problems Herschel confronted as administrator at Hoogly. Aside from the legal issues of fraudulent claims to land or other property and the frequent repudiation of signatures on legal documents, Herschel also needed to intervene in the problems that plagued the jail he oversaw. In this case, the primary issue for Herschel was to fix the prisoners' identity in the face of various impersonation schemes. It sometimes happened that prisoners, not content to serve out their sentences, invented elaborate schemes to avoid long-term incarceration; the "common device of hiring a substitute to serve out a term was not unknown, but it involved a long risk of detection. A safer but very costly, and therefore rare, device was sham death and a purchased corpse, affording comparative safety after escape" (21). To prevent this personation or switching/displacing of identities, Herschel instituted the practice of taking the prints of each prisoner in duplicate at the time of his incarceration so that they could be compared to prints taken at some later time, at the jailer's discretion. The prints were then collected in books for easy reference.

The problem of impersonation was aggravated by the administrator's inability to identify individual Indians by their physical appearance. Although Herschel does not state this directly, it seems clear that he experienced difficulty in telling a particular prisoner from another who might take his place; this implies that to his eye, Indians all looked the same. In *Finger Prints*, Galton expresses this difficulty directly: he notes that "their features are not easily distinguished by Europeans". Galton's eye-witness in India, Major Ferris, corroborates Galton's statement when he notes that

> The uniformity in the colour of the hair, eyes, and complexion of the Indian races renders identification far from easy, and the difficulty of recording the description of an individual, so that he may be afterwards recognized, is very great. Again, their handwriting, whether it be in Persian or Devanagri letters, is devoid of character and gives but little help towards identification (150).

While Bertillonage, the criminal identification system most widely used in Europe at the time, worked reasonably well on a population displaying a wide variety of colouring (red, blond, black, and brown hair, for example), in India it was less successful because the European eye could not distinguish more subtle differences among members of the Indian population. The description of physical features which had served law enforcement in the past did not help Herschel, for as he perceived it, the obvious outward signs of the body could be duplicated, falsified, or switched through the tricks of false personation and thereby erase what he perceived to be subtle differences in appearance. Further, even astute observations and descriptions were subject to interpretive mistakes or judgments on the part of the police officer or jailer.

Faced with impersonation schemes that impeded the criminal court's efficacy, Herschel employed fingerprinting as an imperial practice to bring order and stability to the "wily" and mendacious bodies of the Indians imprisoned in his jails. In 1877 Herschel says that he had recorded the fingerprints of all people who had registered documents in Hoogly, and he proposed the same measure be adopted in the jails. Such "sign-manuals", as Herschel called the sets of prints, would be "the means of verifying the identity of every man in jail with the man sentenced by the court, at any moment, day or night" (24). Regardless of time, the correspondence between sentenced man and prisoner, which previously had been disrupted by false personation, would be realigned here, and the marks in the sign-manual would correspond directly with what they signified, the fingers of the prisoner himself. The "indistinguishable features" of the Indian would in this way become irrelevant. Another feature—that of the fingerprint's pattern—would instead become important. Herschel's description of a hypothetical use of the sign-manual underscores its efficiency:

> Here is the means of verifying the identity of every man in jail with the man sentenced by the court, at any moment, day or night. Call the number up and make him sign. Is

> No. 1302 really dead, and is that his corpse or a sham one? The corpse has two fingers that will answer that question at once. Is this the man brought into jail the real Simon Pure sentenced by the magistrate? The sign-manual on the back of the magistrate's warrant is there to testify, &c. (24)

In this passage, Herschel has rectified the disruption caused by impersonation by substituting for the false witness of the Indian and his worthless documents the incontestable testimony of the corpse's fingers and the sign-manual. The corpse could now be made to speak—to "answer" the question that Herschel would pose—through an impression made from his lifeless fingers. In this way, the sign-manual could provide "testimony" through its reiteration of a bodily mark, as the examiner compared the first mark made upon entering the jail with the second, taken from the dead man. For Herschel, the sign manual functioned in lieu of a narrative of crime: two fingerprints that did not match created, in effect, the *simulacrum* of a narrative of the prisoner's escape, a story of crime. Criminal testimony could be disregarded since the book provided the effect of a person's words—in the criminal's absence, what Herschel called the "speaking book" spoke for the crminal as his fingerprint attested to his guilt or innocence.

For Herschel, the system of fingerprinting as established through the sign-manual had an added virtue: that of preventing future crime. The system was so difficult to subvert, Herschel intimates, that he thought "its general use would be a substantial contribution towards public morality. Now that it is pretty well known here, I do not believe the man lives who would dare to attempt personation before the Registrar [who was responsible for verifying identity]" (24). Herschel proved to be right, at least on one account. Although he does not specifically report a decrease in crimes of personation or in the false attestation of signatures, he does include an anecdote which records the gruesome deterrent of the sign-manual:

> [M]any years afterwards a man (in another district) who had given his fingerprint before a Registrar repudiated it. He was summoned to give his evidence on oath. It was found that he had cut off the joints of his fingers, hoping to defeat justice by corrupting the witnesses so as to prove that he was *not* the man they had recognized before the Registrar. The High Court rejected [the man's] sworn story of an accident…with the necessary consequences to the offender for his perjury. I do not know of any other repudiation having been pressed to this bitter end in India or elsewhere. (19-20)

In this instance, the fingerprint does not even need the finger from which it came in order to sentence the offender. In fact, the *absence* of the original seems paradoxically to confirm the veracity of the print, reversing the order implicit in the process of fingerprinting and overturning the primacy of signifier over sign. In other words, in this strange example, the print stands alone as a testimonial to the identity of the offender, and the missing body part confirms the print's presence. I will have reason to return below to the solitary, disembodied print since just such a print appears in Doyle's "The Norwood Builder", where it expresses most clearly the crisis of criminal identification that preoccupied the late Victorians.

Galton acknowledged Herschel as the progenitor of the science of dactyloscopy, and while he adopted many of Herschel's observations, he also expanded upon them. In developing a system by which fingerprint records could be organized and used for identification, it struck Galton that this method far surpassed Bertillon's, since the fingerprint—unlike bodily measurements or photography—did not change over time. In Galton's words, it was "persistent". In the details of the pattern, its minute lines, dots, and curves, lay its uniqueness, which did not change; with age, weight gain, usage, the dimensions might be altered, but the design itself remained the same. Under the influence of time, Galton explained, a fingerprint "like a piece of lace may be stretched in this way, or shrunk in that, and its outline altogether altered; nevertheless every one of the component threads, and every knot in every thread, can easily be traced and identified in both" (99).

Furthermore, the fingerprint was discrete. Galton described fingerprints as entities that "form patterns…whose boundaries can be firmly outlined, and which are little worlds in themselves" (2). The peculiarities of the individual pattern he called "bifurcations, origins, islands, and enclosures" which were "*almost beyond change*" (9). In these descriptions Galton figured the fingerprint as a world unto itself, a miniature landscape that could be surveyed, measured, and mapped like any other *terra incognita.* Crucially, the fingerprint was a world that existed outside time, a tiny Shangri-La that resisted change. Galton emphasized that fingerprints' patterns were "self-signatures, free from all possibility of faults in observation or of clerical error" (168). That is, the fingerprint represented the direct mark of the criminal, the impression of his body on paper that stood in a one-to-one correspondence with the criminal himself. Combined with the fingerprint's absolute trustworthiness in regards to the specific individual it identified, Galton believed that in criminal cases, "*By itself it is amply sufficient to convict*" (167, emphasis in the original).

Although the use of footprints to determine identity has a long history in the novel, from Defoe's *Robinson Crusoe* to Collins's *The Moonstone* to Doyle's *The Sign of Four*, fingerprinting as an identification technology first makes its way into literature in Mark Twain's *Pudd'nhead Wilson* (1894). By 1906, when Doyle uses a fingerprint as a clue in "The Norwood Builder", fingerprinting had become an accepted feature of police investigation—ripe, it seems, for a critical examination by Holmes himself. In this story, Holmes intervenes to clear a young solicitor suspected of murder. The solicitor, John Hector McFarlane, was a guest of the Norwood builder, Jonas Oldacre, the night he disappeared. Although the builder's body has not been found, circumstantial evidence—signs of a "murderous struggle", blood stains in Oldacre's rooms, a bloodied oaken walking stick belonging to McFarlane, and the charred remains of a body on the woodpile—implies Oldacre was murdered and his body burned. McFarlane appears at Baker Street to ask for help, insisting that he had nothing to do with the murder. The story he tells Holmes and Watson is nevertheless strange. An old acquaintance of McFarlane's parents who had been estranged from them, Oldacre contacted McFarlane under the pretence of making over his will to him. Surprised, the solicitor agreed to become his heir and helped Oldacre draw up the necessary papers. Oldacre insisted, however, that McFarlane mention nothing to his parents about the matter. Under these unusual circumstances, McFarlane becomes the prime suspect, since he stands to gain most by Oldacre's death.

When Holmes learns, however, that Oldacre was a jilted beau of Mrs. McFarlane—who calls him a "malignant and cunning ape"—the mystery becomes more complex.[11] As the investigation draws to an end, the police commissioner, Lestrade, finds the piece of evidence he needs to convict McFarlane. In the house where the murder was committed, Lestrade brings Holmes into a dark hallway, where, by the light of struck match, he points out to Holmes a "stain of blood upon the whitewashed wall". It was, however, Watson notes,

> [M]ore than a stain. It was the well-marked print of a thumb.
>
> "Look at that with your magnifying glass, Mr. Holmes".
>
> "Yes, I am doing so".
>
> "You are aware that no two thumb-marks are alike?"
>
> "I have heard something of the kind".
>
> "Well, then, will you please compare that print with this wax impression of young McFarlane's right thumb, taken by my orders this morning?"
>
> As he held the waxen print close to the blood-stain, it did not take a magnifying glass to see that the two were undoubtedly from the same thumb. It was evident that our unfortunate client was lost (506).

Yet Holmes does not echo Watson's dismay over what Lestrade called a "fresh" piece of evidence. Instead, Holmes asks Lestrade if he believes the mark was there yesterday, and Lestrade insists that it must have been, since McFarlane would not have left the jail in the middle of the night "in order to strengthen the evidence against himself". Lestrade questions whether any expert in the world would say that "that is not the mark of his thumb". To this, Holmes agrees: "It is unquestionably the mark of his thumb" (506). But when Lestrade strolls out, comically sure of himself, Holmes tells Watson that the mark was indeed "fresh", that is, it had not been on the wall the day before.

The mystery is solved when Holmes, eager to take the pompous Lestrade down a notch, lights a fire in the house. Out of a secret room runs Oldacre himself, who has manufactured all the evidence of the murder in a desperate attempt to revenge himself against McFarlane's mother, who would have seen her son hanged. Holmes suspects that Oldacre, waiting in his little room as the investigation dragged on, brooded over the crime and wished to implicate McFarlane even more clearly. Accordingly, Oldacre left his hiding place during the night and made an impression from the wax seals McFarlane had affixed to the legal documents with his thumb; with his own blood, Oldacre then made McFarlane's mark on the wall. In trying to incriminate an innocent man, he ended by incriminating himself.

In this interesting story, the fingerprint is tested as irrefutable evidence of identity. While both Lestrade and Holmes agree that the fingerprint on the wall is "final", they do so for different reasons. Lestrade sees in the bloody mark a unique sign of McFarlane's presence, what Galton had called a "self-signature...free from all possibility of faults in observation or of clerical error". That is, the fingerprint stands alone as a signifier of identity; it needs, as Herschel's studies pointed out, only a double taken at a later date to confirm the bearer's identity. Lestrade has adopted Galton's dictum that the fingerprint *by itself* is amply sufficient to convict; in fact, he takes it one step further by conflating identity and guilt. He reasons that if it is McFarlane's print in blood, then McFarlane is guilty—the nature of the one-to-one correspondence that characterizes fingerprints ("no two thumb-marks are alike") admits of no other possibility for Lestrade. When he confidently assumes that the mark must have been *made* by McFarlane since it is McFarlane's mark, he assumes that because a fingerprint is unique, it cannot be forged—that is, he does not acknowledge that while the fingerprint itself cannot be duplicated, the events resulting in the mark may be misleading. In turn, what Lestrade does not account for is the possibility of "faults in observation", which his less-than-keen eyes made. What he failed to observe is not the print itself—that he saw immediately, as the wily Oldacre had intended—but the *absence* of the print. In other words, he did not notice that the print had not been on the wall the day before. In a crucial sense, he failed to observe the passing of time.

It is precisely this attention to temporality that allows Holmes to identify the criminal correctly. In a passing reference to this story, Ronald Thomas suggests that Holmes's solution to the problem "reinforces his own expertise and the scientific training necessary for 'decipherment'" (218). I argue instead that it is not Holmes's scientific training—important as it might be—that helps him put the print in its proper place, but his training as a storyteller, as a assembler of narratives. As Carlo Ginzburg points out, Holmes's detective work participates in an epistemological framework that Ginzburg calls the "conjectural paradigm", one in which seemingly insignificant details—cigar ash, a mud smear, a scratch on a lock—provide information not available otherwise. Ginzburg suggests that in considering these details, the observer constructs, like a hunter tracking his prey, a "narrative sequence—at its simplest, 'someone passed this way'".[12] Like Ginzburg's hunter, Holmes's ability to reconstruct narratives allows him to refute or at least qualify the "testimony" of the bloody fingerprint because he reads the mark as belonging to a narrative, part of a sequence of events in time, and not as a sign that on its own is enough to convict. As in Herschel's case of the fingerless man convicted despite the absence of corroborating fingerprints, in the case of the Norwood Builder the fictional Lestrade eliminates narrative and overrides testimony through his assertion of the fingerprint's final incontestability.

In his essay, Ginzburg tracks the development of fingerprinting as a mobilization of the semiotic paradigm that pays attention to throw-away detail, suggesting a similarity between fingerprinting methods and the detective work of Holmes and Freud. But in doing so, Ginzburg blurs the differences between the *police* use of fingerprinting, as represented by Herschel's or Galton's work, and the *fictive* use of fingerprinting, as represented by Doyle's story. As Herschel, Galton, and Doyle's fictional policeman Lestrade make clear, a great benefit of fingerprinting is that it eliminates the need to construct a narrative—for them, the fingerprint is enough.

For Holmes, however, the fingerprint does not stand alone; it is always accompanied by a story. Unlike Herschel's use of the sign-manual, in which the repetition of a print takes the place of observed action or experience, Holmes's use of the fingerprint relies directly on observed particulars and details through which he (re)constructs an exonerating narrative. In doing so he firmly places the fingerprint within a larger corpus of evidentiary material of which it is only one of many; and as is always the case in the Holmes stories, the purpose of the evidence is to solve the crime through the reconstruction of a chain of events.

Written twelve years after the London police began taking fingerprints of criminals, this story proposes a different answer to the problem of criminal identity than that put forth by theorists of crime. Identity, the story suggests, is not written on the body and therefore is not available solely through identification systems or technologies such as dactyloscopy. Fingerprinting appealed to criminal anthropologists like Galton because it seemed so transparent and promised to eliminate observation and its attendant "faults". Further, it also allowed for easy classification and arrangement, eliminating the need for careful observation in the field; the archive organized the prints so that the information they contained was rendered easily accessible. If Galton's science of fingerprinting reduced the role of the observer to that of the clerk who indexed the prints according to their patterns, Doyle's literary identification system revived that observer in the figure of Holmes. In recording Holmes's adventures, Watson designs his stories to show off his friend's "peculiar qualities", often at his own expense, since Watson's faulty observations or misguided deductions provide the foil against which Holmes's powers shine. As a continuing motif in the stories, Watson's naive observations—and those of the police force—function as tiny moments of instruction, in which Holmes reveals his secrets. In an important sense, they also teach proper reading, proposing an epistemological model that combines careful observation of minute details with an attention to the bigger picture, that is, of narrative itself.

As we have seen, the science of fingerprinting rose out of a century's preoccupation with crime and the criminal. Its Indian origins attest to its use as a system of authentication that sought to dispense with what was perceived to be inherently untrustworthy testimony in favour of irrefutable imprints of the suspect's body. Further, an examination of its beginnings in India reveals a focus on the identification of the individual which would characterize modern criminal management as it developed in the late nineteenth century. Proponents like Galton and Herschel, saw in the print's persistence and individuality a means by which to fix criminal identity and thereby contribute to a vast but efficient archive through which criminals could be identified and managed.

I suggest, however, that literature constructed its own "technology" of crime. Not content to let fingerprinting eliminate the need for testimony and narrative—for the consideration of events in time—Doyle's story asserts the role narrative must play in determining guilt and innocence. In "The Norwood Builder", Holmes reasserts the position of the observer through the careful scrutiny and observation that are his trademarks, and by doing so he overthrows the primacy of the static fingerprint for the transformative aspect of narrative reconstruction. The epistemological mode through which criminal anthropology operated, one in which human behaviour was reduced to an index or sign-manual, is here overturned by an epistemological mode embodied in the literary drive of narrative: identity and meaning come out of reading and telling stories.

Notes

1. Ian Ousby, *Bloodhounds of Heaven: The Detective in English Fiction from Godwin to Doyle* (Cambridge: Harvard University Press, 1976) 5.
2. Philip Collins, *Dickens and Crime* (Bloomington, Indiana: Indiana University Press, 1968) 3.
3. Collins, 199.
4. Havelock Ellis, "Preface to the Third Edition (1900)", *The Criminal*, Fifth edition. (London: Walter Scott Publishing Co., Ltd., 1910) xxiii.
5. Ronald R. Thomas, *Detective Fiction and the Rise of Forensic Science* (Cambridge: Cambridge University Press, 1999) 22.
6. As criminal anthropology developed, greater emphasis was placed on the insane or "epileptic" quality of certain criminals, a characteristic believed to make it difficult, if not impossible, for them to tell the truth.
7. Herbette, quoted in Francis Galton, *Finger Prints* (1892; New York: Da Capo Press, 1965) 169.
8. Writings on the subject of fingerprinting, such as Ronald Thomas's *Detective Fiction and the Rise of Forensic Science* (Cambridge: Cambridge University Press, 1999) and Carlo Ginzburg's "Morelli, Freud, and Sherlock Holmes: Clues and Scientific Method". *The Sign of Three: Dupin, Holmes, Pierce,* ed. Umberto Eco and Thomas A. Sebeok (Bloomington and Indianapolis: Indiana University Press, 1983) tend only to discuss the work of Francis Galton. Further, their tendency is to refer to Herschel's work as Galton represents it in his writing, that is, second-hand.
9. William J. Herschel, *The Origin of Finger-Printing*, 1916 (New York: AMS Press, 1974) 8.
10. The rhetoric of the Indian as violent, untrustworthy, and without conscience has its origins in the British reaction to the Indian Mutiny of 1857. For further reading on this subject, see Patrick Brantlinger, *Rule of Darkness: British Literature and Imperialism, 1830-1914* (Ithaca: Cornell University Press, 1988); Pratul Chandra Gupta, *Nana Sahib and the Rising at Cawnpore* (Oxford: Clarendon Press, 1963); Christopher Hibbert, *The Great Mutiny: India in 1857* (New York: Viking, 1978); Jenny Sharpe, *Allegories of Empire: The Figure of the Woman in the Colonial Text* (Minneapolis: University of Minneapolis Press, 1993) as well as Charles Dickens's infamous letters in which he wrote that he wished the entire Indian race "exterminated from the face of the earth", collected in Kathleen Tillotson and Graham Storey, eds, *The Letters of Charles Dickens* (Oxford: Clarendon Press/Oxford University Press, 1995) Vol. 8. For a re-appriasal of Dickens's stance on the Mutiny see Grace Moore, *Dickens and Empire: Discourses of Class, Race and Colonialism in the Works of Charles Dickens*. Aldershot: Ashgate, 2004.
11. Arthur Conan Doyle, "The Story of the Norwood Builder". *The Complete Sherlock Holmes* (Garden City, New York: Doubleday & Company, Inc., 1930) 503.
12. Carlo Ginzburg, "Morelli, Freud, and Sherlock Holmes: Clues and Scientific Method". *The Sign of Three: Dupin, Holmes, Pierce*, ed. Umberto Eco and Thomas A. Sebeok (Bloomington and Indianapolis: Indiana University Press, 1983) 89.

Chapter 14

Vamping the Children: The "Bloofer Lady", the "London Minotaur" and Child-Victimization in Late Nineteenth-Century England

Leslie Ann Minot

I) Luring Away by Wiles

The "bloofer lady" section of *Dracula*, in which Lucy Westenra returns as a vampire to attack small children on Hampstead Heath, has received relatively little critical attention compared to the multiple, complex psychosexual analyses of other scenes of "vamping" in the novel. Perhaps this is not surprising, since to carry through the sexual logic which equates "vamping" with sexual passion and/or violence, we would have to envision the sweet Lucy sexually molesting toddlers. If we can admit to taking vicarious pleasure in the surfacing of other aspects of the text's supposedly "repressed" sexuality, we perhaps prefer to downplay this incident. The few discussions of this section have largely been within the context of readings of mothering and "bad mothers". Gail B. Griffin comments that Lucy "has become a demonic mother-parody, taking nourishment from children instead of giving it, as do the three women at the castle...she has lost all maternal feeling (143). Phyllis Roth argues that both Mina and Lucy represent "the mother" (62). Judith Weissman declares that "there is obviously a suggestion that [female vampires] become child molesters" (73), but doesn't pursue this reading.

Like Alan Johnson, I am sceptical of readings which insist that the sexual content of *Dracula* was necessarily covert, and I would echo Brian Murphy's apostrophic comment to Stoker, "What I find baffling is that anyone who has read your novel would conclude that you were unaware of the sexual implications of the story" (cited in Johnson 235). Foucault and a number of historians have shown, despite our myths of nineteenth-century reticence and prudery, how much the Victorians had invested in bringing sexuality into discourse or producing forms of sexuality through discourse. These discourses in fact included child sexual victimization. By locating a plausible historical context for a reading in which women are (or stand in for) sexual threats to children, I hope to draw attention to the broader issues raised by the representation of child victims in *Dracula*.

The child-victim—of both sexual and physical abuse—became an increasingly prominent figure in late nineteenth-century public discourse in England.[1] It began, to some degree, with increased interest in regulating the family life and children of the poorer classes. By the middle of the century, the situation of child labour and of children indentured under the Poor Laws had come under particular scrutiny, and children had begun to receive some legal protection in the workplace with the Factory Act of 1891. Anxiety was also expressed publicly about the children of the poor being done away with directly (by suffocation) or by neglect so that their parents could obtain the burial insurance, which usually left some available cash after funeral expenses were met. A few particularly vicious parents were prosecuted for abuse in the 1860s, and thanks to the concern of the medical community, the worst excesses of "baby farming" were brought to public attention and began to be seriously addressed in the 1870s. These changes took particular impetus from the case of Margaret Waters and her sister Sarah Ellis, who took in infants for a fee and fed them on "common lime mixed with water"—with predictably fatal results. Referred to as the "Brixton horrors", this case received significant publicity and was called "one of the most horrible...stories ever brought to light in a Court of Justice" by *The Times* (Behlmer 29).

The real emergence of a large-scale political movement for child protection began, however, in the 1880s with the founding of the Liverpool Society for the Prevention of Cruelty to Children (SPCC) in 1883. The Liverpool SPCC gained fame throughout England for its successes precisely because it only prosecuted the most extreme and spectacular cases, where the chance of losing was virtually nil. The London SPCC was founded a year later, and by 1888 SPCCs were springing up in cities throughout England, and the issue of cruelty to children had gained widespread and consistent national attention. In 1889, the London SPCC reconstituted itself as the National Society for the Prevention of Cruelty to Children.

Publicity was an important tool in the hands of the SPCC. Early on, Benjamin Waugh of the London SPCC gained the support of the *Pall Mall Gazette* (*PMG*) and its fiery and opinionated editor, W.T. Stead. Stead chronicled such lurid cases as the London SPCC's 1887 prosecution of Alice Clay, who ended up serving six months in prison with hard labour for applying a hot poker to her daughter's groin. This increasing public attention to the plight of physically and sexually abused children went hand in hand with heightened concern about child prostitution, brought about almost single-handedly by the *PMG*'s "Maiden Tribute" series. On Monday, July 6, 1885, the *PMG* published on its front page the first installment of a week-long series on the recruitment of girls under sixteen into the London prostitution racket. Described as the report of a "Secret Commission", the "Maiden Tribute" was in fact primarily Stead's work, although he did have others assisting him in his research. Written in an effort to secure the passage of stalled legislation raising the age of consent from thirteen to sixteen, the "Maiden Tribute" was an instant *succès de scandale*. Peppered with lurid titles, such as "Why the Cries of the Victim Are Not Heard" and "How Girls Are Bought and

Ruined", the series provoked rioting in the streets outside the *PMG*'s office, mutterings about prosecution for obscenity in Parliament, and exclusion from the news stands of W.H. Smith and Son, one of the largest distributors in England.

Stead was subsequently prosecuted for the abduction of 13-year-old Eliza Armstrong, a girl he arranged to have "bought" from her mother in order to prove that such things were possible. Stead was convicted of taking her from her home without the express permission of her father, and consequently served time in Holloway Prison, emerging as a martyr to the cause of sexual purity. The highly-publicized trial and the issues it raised about the accuracy of what Stead described in the "Maiden Tribute" are a crucial part of how historians understand this narrative today.

The earliest dated manuscript of *Dracula* sets its conception at least as far back as 1890,[2] following on the heels of the passage of the 1889 Act for the Prevention of Cruelty to Children, also known as the "Children's Charter". Moreover, Devendra P. Varma has suggested strong links between the conception of *Dracula* and specific events in Stoker's life from the 1870s and 1880s. Stoker was a friend of Stead's, and maintained connections with prominent members of the press. While I would hesitate to point to a direct link between any one of these particular press campaigns and the "bloofer lady" sequence in the novel, I think an understanding of the public discourses addressing violence against children at the time Stoker was gathering material for and beginning work on the novel help to explain the presence of this sequence and its function in the narrative.

Certainly, Stoker's use of pastiched newspaper clippings to introduce Lucy's ghastly return links it to the developing conventions of crime and sex-scandal reporting in the English press into which the "Maiden Tribute" campaign fit. Stoker's experience as a journalist in Dublin perhaps contributed to the authentic quality of the various "news articles" he produced for *Dracula.*[3] Anyone familiar with Stead's invention of the "universal interview" for the *Pall Mall Gazette* will find Stoker's *PMG* pastiche—concerning the escaped wolf—particularly apt. His *Westminster Gazette* articles on the "bloofer lady" explicitly locate themselves within a genre of mysterious crime reporting that could be found even in this most respectable Liberal publication.[4] The first one begins:

> The neighbourhood of Hampstead is just at present exercised with a series of events which seem to run on lines parallel to those of what was known to the writers of headlines as "The Kensington Horror", or "The Stabbing Woman", or "The Woman in Black" (161).

The second announces itself quite simply with the headline: "The Hampstead Horror: Another Child Injured: The 'Bloofer Lady'" (161).

The first article reveals a number of common aspects of Victorian journalism about the poor. As may frequently be seen in Henry Mayhew's earlier interviews, the "grubby-faced little children" are simultaneously appealed to and discredited as sources of information, "too young to give any properly intelligible account of themselves" (161). No adults actually associated with them have been allowed to speak in the article. The seriousness of the incidents is also obscured in the middle of the article by the attempts of "a correspondent" to render these children picturesque in their "favourite game of luring each other away by wiles" (161) as the "bloofer lady" is said to do. Indeed, the correspondent notes that "to see some of the tiny tots pretending to be the 'bloofer lady' is supremely funny" (161). The direct quotation of the children's pronunciation of "bloofer lady" for "beautiful lady" quickly becomes a proper name for the monstrous—but not fully believable—cause of their wounds.[5]

This game of "luring each other away by wiles" which supposedly mimics the allure of the "bloofer lady" can be understood in relation to Stead's description of the luring away of adolescent (and in some cases much younger) girls into prostitution in the "Maiden Tribute". One of the reformed procuresses he interviews notes,

> Every woman who has an eye to business is on the look out for likely girls. Pretty girls who are poor, and who have either no parents or are away from home, are easiest picked up. How is it done? You or your decoy find a likely girl, and then you track her down. I remember I once went a hundred miles and more to pick up a girl (*PMG*, July 6, 1885).

Another source, a sixteen-year-old prostitute named Annie, explained to Stead how she came into the profession:

> I was at that time, as I still am, in a situation as a nurse girl. I used to go out with the perambulator and the baby to St. James's Park every day. When wheeling the perambulator a nicely-dressed lady used to pass me nearly every day. She used to say "Good morning" and pass on. One day she stopped a little to talk about the baby (*PMG*, July 7, 1885).

The "nicely-dressed lady" turns out to be the infamous "Miss X" of a firm of procuresses specializing in providing their clients with virgins. According to Stead's account, "decoy girls"—usually lovely, well-dressed, and apparently respectable looking—lurked in railway stations, near churches and schools, and in the neighbourhood of nice shops:

> Children as they go to and from day school and Sunday school are noted by the keen eye of the professional decoy—waited for and watched, until the time has come for running them down. "Baker-street station", said a female missionary, "is regularly haunted by an old decoy, who entices little children to a place in Milton-street. Watch has been kept for weeks at a time, but she is wary, and when the watch is on the decoy goes elsewhere. As soon as the watch is removed we hear from children whom she had tempted that she is back at her old haunts". Most respectable little girls of the middle class are sometimes accosted when looking into shop windows by pleasant-spoken, well-dressed ladies, who offer to buy anything they take a fancy to in order to win their confidence and get them away. One fine child of fourteen in the Brompton-road was promised by "such a nice little lady" rides on her beautiful quiet pony as often as she liked, if she would only go home with her (*PMG*, July 8, 1885).

Stead's narrative requires the reader to imagine a vast, well-organized, professional system of duplicity behind the recruitment of young girls into London prostitution. As historian Judith Walkowitz has noted, the "Maiden Tribute" emphasizes (disproportionately) the role played by women in the corruption of young girls. The "nicely-dressed lady", "the pleasant-spoken, well-dressed ladies", the "nice little lady"—like the "bloofer lady"—lure their victims away, aided by a pleasant appearance which clearly also carries the implication of respectable, middle-class standing. A number of previously mentioned press accounts similarly highlight murderous women like Margaret Waters and Sarah Ellis, or cruel women like Alice Clay.

So, too, in *Dracula*, female vampires have a way of taking a spectacular centre stage. The three female vampires in Castle Dracula—described in great physical detail—are seductive and alluring to Jonathan Harker, and horrifically grotesque as they devour the infant brought to them by the Count. Lucy's nightmare life in death and violent staking are similarly caught up in specularity and spectacle. Mina too becomes a female instrument of Dracula's, and a marked female body. Dracula, in contrast, remains discreet and dissimulating, trying to blend in. No other male vampires exist.

Carol Fry, among other critics, recognizes the link between Dracula's conquests—particularly Lucy Westenra—and the typical Victorian fallen woman (35-7). Lucy's sexual menace to the children may be read both as a threat of sexual abuse and as a threat of sexual recruitment, since the bite of the vampire also has the quality of contagion or conversion—that is, turns the victim into a vampire. Admittedly, Lucy's victims are considerably younger than the majority of girls discussed in the "Maiden Tribute" series, and include both boys and girls.[6] What is important, however, is a recognizable public discourse about the sexual threat posed by strange, attractive women—particularly those who are, at least apparently, financially well-off.

II) Impersonating the Minotaur

Dissimulation, impersonation, and imposture all play a crucial role in Stead's "Maiden Tribute" campaign, which similarly foregrounds the role of a multiplicity of sinister women who serve a small number of wealthy men, among them the person described by Stead as the infamous "London Minotaur", for whom the virgins were supposedly procured. Stead himself obtained much of his information by pretending that he was seeking to purchase virgins for violation. Stead's imposture, particularly as it relates to the kidnapping of Eliza Armstrong, was much discussed by his contemporaries and has likewise received ample treatment from later historians. Walkowitz, for example, explains that the use of multiple narrative frames

> [A]llowed Stead to impersonate a range of characters: from "Chief Director" of the "Secret Commission", he metamorphosed into a voyeuristic explorer and shadowy

> villain; and then, as he sensed the danger of this identification, he retreated once more into the impersonal persona of the "Chief Director" (94-95).

Stead was quite clear and direct in discussing his imposture. In his own defence of his actions, published first in the *PMG* and then reprinted in pamphlet form, Stead wrote:

> If it was a cruel thing to play the part of a purchaser of innocent maidens for imaginary violation, was it not far more cruel to allow them to continue to be sold in real earnest into a life of shame? And so the very anguish that the playing of my assumed rôle occasioned me, spurred me on and nerved me to persevere. I bought Eliza Armstrong to save Eliza Armstrong, and not only that child, who was before you in court, but many thousand others as young and innocent as she, over whom, as the direct and immediate consequence of what I did for Eliza Armstrong, the law has now cast its protecting shield (2-3).[7]

While Havelock Ellis and others have turned to Stead's repressed sexual desires to account for his fascination with the impersonation of sexual villainy, I am less interested in the source of Stead's impersonation than in its narrative effects. The nature of the impersonation marks one of the important ways that Stead alters his mythical source story of Theseus and the Minotaur. It also differs markedly from certain structures in the popular melodramatic narratives of sexual danger that informed the "Maiden Tribute".

Although Stead compares his descent into the "strange inverted world" of "the streets and the brothel" to Theseus's descent into the Labyrinth in Crete, unlike Theseus, he does not pose as a victim—part of the offering to the Minotaur—but as a villain. This no doubt has something to do with Stead's erasure of the young men who constituted half of the tribute in the myth (and the possibility of male prostitution in London). Its effect was to produce a connection or a parallel, and even a possible identification between the figure of the hero and the villain, rather than emphasizing the connection between the victim and the hero. This did not have to be the case—at least not so thoroughly the case—in Stead's narrative, since young women were involved in the "Secret Commission". Two young women whose names have never been revealed, one a journalist, the other a member of the Salvation Army, are said to have participated in the "Secret Commission", and to have infiltrated a brothel and a house from which girls were shipped to Continental brothels (Terrot, 154-155). Stead's impersonations, however, not theirs, were narrated in the "Maiden Tribute".

The "Maiden Tribute" thus becomes a battle between Stead and the variety of villains who people the narrative, including the Minotaur he impersonates, the mothers who knowingly sell their children, the women who procure the supply of maidens, and the female friends who betray their companions into seduction. As Walkowitz has noted, the Minotaur tends to disappear from the narrative—perhaps, I would suggest, through Stead's "absorption" of the character—while the poor and working women remain as the most visible perpetrators of crimes against young girls. A key aspect of popular melodrama was the power granted to the villain, whose victims—male and female—tended to be passive and long-suffering, and to be rescued more by chance than their own initiative (Walkowitz 86). Stead, by contrast, appropriates to himself the power that would traditionally be associated with the villain. He will later, during his time in Holloway prison, take on the role of a martyr suffering for the cause, but the text of the "Maiden Tribute" bustles with a vision of Stead as a man of action.

Stoker, in addition to being a man of the theatre (in his professional capacity as assistant to the great actor and manager Henry Irving), had a tremendous fascination with cases of fraud and imposture. In 1910, he published a study of *Famous Imposters*—"impersonators, pretenders, swindlers, and humbugs of all kinds; those who have masqueraded in order to acquire wealth, position, or fame, and those who have done so merely for the love of the art" (v). Many of these impostors, notably the man he argues was Queen Elizabeth I, played for extremely high stakes in terms of political power and personal gain. *Dracula*, like the "Maiden Tribute", highlights some of the ambivalences of both villainous and heroic imposture. Through the narrative episode of the children on Hampstead Heath, Stoker raises specific questions about mimicry, fantasy, and play.

III) Impersonating the Bloofer Lady

The children's response to Lucy as the "bloofer lady" offers potential insight into the questions of class raised by some critics in relation to the Count's atavistic nobility and the largely bourgeois character of the Crew of Light which opposes him. While the newspaper account of the attacks doubts the existence of a woman at all in favour of "a rat or a small dog", based on the wounds on the children's necks, the children take up the idea of the "bloofer lady" with enthusiasm. They continue to tell their story about being asked to go for a walk with the "bloofer lady"—a story which readers recognize as true—and they continue to go off with her, even when their playfellows return injured.

What desire of theirs does the "bloofer lady" fulfill, what fantasies of adventure or a better life? In Stead's overall account of the "decoy girls", we know that they promise gifts, money, nice clothes, pony rides, and freedom. In the case of the "bloofer lady", we cannot tell from the *Westminster Gazette* accounts why the children go off with her, but the language of being "lured away" implies offers or promises of something, or pleasures given. Even the hospitalized child visited by Van Helsing and Seward, who was "terribly weak" and "quite emaciated" when found (162), asks the nurse if he can leave so that he can "play with the 'bloofer lady'" (176). This language of play in itself recalls the language repeatedly used by procuresses to refer euphemistically to sexual relations: "he will only have a game with you, and you will be none the worse for it …" and "…it is enough for us if the girl willingly consents to see or to meet or to have a game with a rich gentleman" (*PMG*, July 7, 1885). Games with the "bloofer lady", like play with rich gentlemen, offer different pleasures for the players who know the stakes and horrors for those who do not. In both kinds of narrative, the attractions of the well-dressed or beautiful woman also seem to provoke a kind of desiring admiration—a literal desire to *become* the object of attraction.

This desire to be, or to mimic or impersonate, the other (and one another) is emphasized in the account of the children's play. The *Westminster Gazette* writer, while doubting the existence of the "bloofer lady", assumes that the children's story comes from an inherent tendency to mimic one another, noting,

> It is generally supposed in the neighbourhood that, as the first child missed gave as his reason for being away that 'bloofer lady' had asked him to come for a walk, the others had picked up the phrase and used it as occasion served (161).

The problem of mimicry becomes more involved, however, since the children also pretend to be—or mimic—this "bloofer lady".

> This is the more natural, as the favourite game of the little ones at present is luring each other away by wiles. A correspondent writes us that to see some of the tiny tots pretending to be the "bloofer lady" is supremely funny. Some of our caricaturists might, he says, take a lesson in the irony of grotesque by comparing the reality and the picture. It is only in accordance with general principles of human nature that the "bloofer lady" should be the popular role at these *al fresco* performances. Our correspondent naively says that Ellen Terry could not be so winningly attractive as some of these grubby-faced little children pretend—or imagine themselves—to be (161).

We are later informed by Dr. Vincent, attending the latest child victim, that ten days before the attacks, when a wolf escaped from the Zoological Gardens, "the children were playing nothing but Red Riding Hood on the Heath and in every alley in the place until this "bloofer lady" scare came along" (176). This second account seems to undermine the idea that the coincidence of the game of "luring each other away by wiles" with the appearance of the "bloofer lady" is accidental. The two accounts together suggest a recognition of the ways in which play, particularly through imitation, can be used to master fears, and also how it may reveal the link between desire and fear. These are important questions throughout the narrative of *Dracula*, where to give in to the vampire's desire—to desire the vampire—is to risk *becoming* the vampire. They are also issues which are far from trivial in Stoker's other profession, the theatre, and his reference to the actress Ellen Terry, a good friend and business associate, makes this link explicit.

Not only do the children appear to enjoy their encounters with the "bloofer lady", they also enjoy playing at being the "bloofer lady", perhaps precisely because she is something they are not. She is grown-up, she is beautiful, she is probably clean, and as we know when we recognize her as Lucy, she is of the upper middle class, the kind of young woman who was hovered over and protected by her family, not running wild and disappearing in the night on Hampstead Heath. That the "grubby-faced" children should "pretend" or "imagine themselves to be" this mysterious, attractive, and perhaps dangerous figure is "grotesque" and "supremely funny" to the journalist writing for a middle-class audience. The distinction drawn between "pretending" and "imagining" is particularly interesting because it seems to offer a different type of liberating potential. To pretend to be something one is not is ultimately to recognize one's actual place in the order of things. To imagine that one is, or might be, something that one is not implies that one can envisage a different order of things entirely.

All this attention to the fantasies of children who appear as minor episodic characters might seem misplaced if the questions of imagination and mimicry or imposture were not central to the problems of defining (or failing to define) the difference between the Count and his mostly middle-class opponents. At the risk of exaggerated generalization, I would argue that none of the Count's opponents, with the exception of Van Helsing (and possibly Mina when possessed by the Count) values the imagination or exhibits imaginative potential. Van Helsing—a Dutch, Roman Catholic outsider—says as much to Dr. Seward:

> You do not let your eyes see nor your ears hear, and that which is outside your daily life is not of account to you. Do you no think that there are things which you cannot understand, and yet which are? But there are things old and new which must not be contemplated by men's eyes, because they know—or think they know some things which other men have told them. Ah, it is the fault of our science that it wants to explain all; and if it explain not, then it says there is nothing to explain (172-173).

Dracula, on the other hand, with what Van Helsing calls his "child-brain" (305), is both imaginative and given to mimicry. In the midst of his ruined Transylvanian splendour, he imagines overturning the order of things, modernizing himself, becoming ruler of a new world by beginning with the conquest of bustling, imperial London. In order to do so, he studies the English way of life meticulously, learning English, desiring to blend in. He tells Jonathan Harker,

> ...did I move and speak in your London, none there are who would not know me for a stranger. That is not enough for me...A stranger in a strange land, he is no one; men know him not—and to know not is to care not for. I am content if I am like the rest, so that no man stops if he sees me, or pause in his speaking if he hear my words, to say "Ha, ha! A stranger!" (26)

Mimicry is central to his strategy for mastery. In Transylvania, he also dresses in Harker's clothes in order to kidnap a child for the women of his castle to feed on, ensuring that if Harker escapes, he will be *persona non grata* in neighbouring villages. Yet the overall strategy of the Count's impersonation carries with it a curious reversal, an appetitive quality: He would mimic the English in order to be able to transform them into subservient imitations of himself.

Stephen Arata has argued forcefully that one of the central fears played out in the text of *Dracula* is the fear of "reverse colonization", the sense that "what has been represented as the 'civilized' world is on the point of being colonized by 'primitive' forces" (85). What makes Dracula unusual among late-Victorian manifestations of this fear, Arata observes, is that the Count is a rare—perhaps the only—fictional outsider who is successful in "passing" in London (95). This anxiety finds a parallel in the fears of "fallen" women "passing" as respectable in Stead's narratives of child prostitution. *Dracula* is fairly explicit in the representation of an external threat to England; however, it maintains remarkably clear delineations of class boundaries, and any threat to the existing order from within the working classes or "the residuum" appears in oblique moments like that on Hampstead Heath.

As in the "Maiden Tribute" series, the children's enthusiastic game of impersonating the "bloofer lady" draws attention to the difficulties of distinguishing—in spite of the apparently clearly delineated sides—the victim from the villain in the novel. *Dracula* is, after all, a text that depends to a great extent on strange doublings and split-consciousnesses. Lucy herself emblematizes these ambiguities; she is both a victim and a villain, a virtuous virgin and a sexual demon. Even Jonathan and Mina—who survive the narrative and produce the heir to unify its heroes and embody its struggles—experience moments of ambivalent desire for the vampire. On the one hand, the Count seems to require some sort of internal weakness—unacknowledged desire or other duplicity—in order to gain power over his victims. On the other, his opponents seem unable to fight him except by acknowledging what there is of him within themselves. The heroes are only able to locate and destroy Dracula by drawing on the split-consciousness of Mina—the fact that, once bitten, she can in effect "be" the Count, sharing his consciousness through the same telepathy that allows him to control her.

Moreover, the heroes are not free from the kind of imposture which seems to make the Count a particularly terrifying figure of reverse colonization. In order to track down the Count's boxes of sacred earth—necessary to his rest and continued existence—the Crew of Light is more than once forced to rely on criminal strategies, including imposture:

> "Now suppose that you were, in truth, the owner of that house, and could not still get [the key]; and think there was to you no conscience of the housebreaker, what would you do?"
> "I should get a respectable locksmith, and set him to work to pick the lock for me".
> "And your police, they would interfere, would they not?"
> "Oh, no! not if they knew the man was properly employed" (261).

This is exactly the strategy they adopt, without qualm, for burgling the Count's house in Piccadilly. Even this plan, however, lacks the extravagance of the Count's imagination. Lord Godalming will pose as nothing more interesting than himself: "My title will make it all right with the locksmith, and with any policeman that may come along" (266).

If the children on Hampstead Heath are linked to Dracula because his four-hundred-year-old "child-brain" employs similar strategies for learning about and coping with the world, they are also linked with the position of the reader. Their use of mimicry and play to master their fears and act out their desires suggests that the narrative of *Dracula* itself might be a form of play in which readers can vicariously experience forbidden desires and temporarily inhabit identities which they might otherwise fear. The shifting subject positions offered by the structure of the narrative, with its multiplicity of narrative perspectives and interspersed pastiches, might certainly be congenial to shifting reader identification.

Stoker's attitude toward the fraud of imposture—like his attitude toward the sensational and sexual material on which he draws—is difficult to disentangle fully. He notes in *Famous Impostors* that he has

> [M]ade no attempt to treat the subject ethically; yet from a study of these impostors, the objects they had in view, the means they adopted, the risks they ran, and the punishments which attended exposure, any reader can draw his own conclusions (v).

The ultimate inconclusiveness of this ethical pronouncement is striking. Yet bearing in mind the "successful" imposture of Queen Elizabeth I which concludes Stoker's collection of largely disastrous tales of impersonation, he might literally be undecided himself, leaving each reader to determine how he or she feels. The writing of *Famous Imposters*—or of the multiple voices and interspersed genres of *Dracula*—may well have been undertaken "merely for the love of the art" of imposture.

Through the representation of child victims in the Hampstead Heath scene, Stoker is able to tap into an ambivalent public discourse about victims, villains, and heroes that employs both fear of and proactive use of imposture, and that offers a model for gendering how sexual villainy is carried out. He is simultaneously able to use children to provide a more neutral space in which to explore the elements of play, fantasy and impersonation that are most attractive, but also highly dangerous.

Notes

1. George K. Behlmer chronicles the movement for increased protection for children in *Child Abuse and Moral Reform in England, 1870-1908* (Stanford University Press, 1982).
2. For more details, see Joseph S. Bierman, "The Genesis and Dating of *Dracula* from Bram Stoker's Working Notes" in Margaret L. Carter, ed., *Dracula: The Vampire and the Critics* (Ann Arbor: UMI Research Press, 1988) 51-55.
3. Stoker was a drama critic for the Dublin *Evening Mail* beginning in 1871. Within a few years, he was also, briefly, the editor of the *Irish Echo* (later *The Halfpenny Press*), and many have commented that his writing style—particularly his resistance to revision—resulted from the pace of journalistic writing. As Henry Irving's assistant, he was also in much contact with London journalists, particularly the drama critics, and kept files of newspaper clippings about himself and Irving.
4. The *Westminster Gazette* was founded as a major Liberal newspaper in the early 1890s, after the *Pall Mall Gazette*, no longer under Stead's editorship, has been sold to become a Tory publication. Koss, *The Rise and Fall of the Political Press in Britain* (London: Hamish Hamilton, 1981).
5. An earlier use of "boofer" for beautiful can be found in Dickens' *Our Mutual Friend*. Although "bloofer" may be a legitimate dialect, variation, I suspect the insertion of the "L" is meant to link the "bloofer lady" not only with the beautiful, but also with the "bloody" and with "Lucy".
6. In his courtroom testimony and his published defence, as well as in a limited portion of the "Maiden Tribute", Stead does discuss the sexual violation of very young children.
7. Cited from the pamphlet, the Stead Papers at Churchill College, Cambridge.

Chapter 15

Ballad of a Demon Barber: The Criminal Career of George Chapman

Nicholas Freeman

"[George] Chapman is one of those criminals about whom we know too little . . . We know absolutely nothing of his character, or the state of mind that made him poison three women". So begins Colin Wilson's account of Chapman's criminal career in his influential *Encyclopaedia of Murder* (1961).[1] Chapman is undoubtedly an enigmatic figure, although he is in many ways an unlikely member of the pantheon of English "classic" poisoners whose deeds so fascinated George Orwell in "Decline of the English Murder".[2] While most of the members of this group; Crippen for instance, or Thomas Wainewright; have about them a strangely appealing aura that makes students of popular criminology reluctant to dislike them, despite their murderous activities, George Chapman has never inspired such ambivalence. Neither has he passed into criminal or urban folklore in the manner of Sweeney Todd, the notorious demon barber. Hargrave Adam's summary of the Chapman case in the *Notable British Trials* series (1930) calls him "a universally detested criminal", and there has been no attempt to rehabilitate or reappraise him in the succeeding years.[3] His murders seem to have been entirely lacking in extenuating circumstances and his guilt so obvious that the judge's summing up at his trial was practically a continuation of the speech for the prosecution.

Yet, the Chapman case continues to attract criminal historians, with an account of the murders opening Brian Marriner's *Murder with Venom* as recently as 1993, and other writers continuing to pursue links between Chapman and Jack the Ripper.[4] Marriner draws attention to the hatred felt for Chapman at his trial and remarks on his apparently unattractive physical appearance, calling him "no matinee idol . . . an ugly man of meagre physique with a skin rough in texture and dull in colour, hair coarse and a moustache so long that it drooped some four or five inches below his mouth".[5] It would seem that Chapman continues to generate a disgust and anxiety that extends far beyond his actual offences, vicious as these may have been.

Chapman murdered three women, all of whom he had "married" bigamously. His victims were Mary Spink, who died on Christmas Day 1897, Bessie Taylor (February 1901) and Maud Marsh (October 1902). Chapman was arrested on 25 October 1902, the day of Edward VII's Coronation procession. He was tried at the Old Bailey from 16-19 March 1903 and executed on 7 April. Such is the bald outline of his criminal career. Of course, like all such summaries, it leaves much unsaid. Chapman has been suspected of murders in the United States and Poland, and is often suggested as a candidate for the Jack the Ripper Whitechapel outrages of 1888. In addition to being a serial poisoner, he was an arsonist and perjurer. He was also a foreigner, a fact that links him with a number of cultural discourses of the late nineteenth century, notably imperialism and degeneration.[6]

The purpose of the present chapter is not to reinvestigate Chapman's crimes, but to examine why such a man should have been so demonized by the Edwardian public. When his trial began, the courtroom was packed, with perhaps a hundred people standing outside, and his execution at Wandsworth prison in April 1903 attracted "a large crowd, principally women . . . loudly arguing that Chapman deserved every conceivable torture".[7] Clearly Chapman was an unpleasant and ruthless criminal, but this alone cannot explain why he went to the gallows amidst such public hysteria.

George Chapman may have shared his name with an Elizabethan dramatist but he was in fact a Pole, whose real name was Severin Antoniovich Klosowski.[8] Born in Nargornak in December 1865, he was apprenticed to a surgeon in 1880, training for six years before failing to obtain the post of junior surgeon.[9] In 1886, Klosowski was working as a "barber-surgeon" or *feldscher* in Praga hospital in Poland, carrying out blood-letting and other simple operations, as well as hairdressing. At some point during this time, he married. He abandoned his career as a *feldscher* and enlisted in the Russian army before moving to England in 1888.[10] Once there he worked as a hairdresser's assistant in Whitechapel, calling himself "Ludwig" Klosowski and living among refugees from Russian pogroms. In October 1889 he "married" a Polish woman, Lucy Baderski.[11] Their union was never a happy one, and cannot have been improved by the death of their baby son in March 1891. In the aftermath of their bereavement, the couple embarked for New York, eventually settling in Jersey City. Baderski returned to England alone in February 1892, apparently sickened by her husband's infidelities and violence towards her. Unfortunately, she was again pregnant, giving birth to a daughter in May 1892. Perhaps because of her condition, she made an attempt at reconciliation with her husband when he returned later that month, but the breach was not to be healed and the marriage broke up.

Klosowski never seems to have been without female company for very long, and was soon living with a woman called Annie Chapman, with whom he cohabited for about a year in 1893-4. Although she shared her name with the third of Jack the Ripper's victims, Chapman was more fortunate than her namesake, and escaped alive from her relationship with Klosowski. Nonetheless, she suffered frequent abuse at his hands, and even lived briefly in a *ménage à trois* with him and another lover (who may have been an earlier "wife"), before walking out on him towards the end of 1894. Like Baderski before her, she found she was pregnant, but when she told Klosowski the news in January or February 1895, he reacted with disinterest and she was forced to raise the baby without his assistance. He had, meanwhile, adopted her name as his own.[12] His reasons for choosing "George" are uncertain, but for a late nineteenth-century immigrant attempting to assimilate himself into English life, it is a sensible choice: solid, traditional, and with usefully regal and patriotic associations.

Using his new identity, George Chapman denied any knowledge of his past life and set about escaping from his marital and sexual obligations. He continued to work as a hairdresser's assistant in Leytonstone, before meeting the woman who would become his first victim, Mary Isabella Spink, *née* Renton. Mrs. Spink had been left by her husband as a consequence of her excessive drinking, but they were not divorced. It was not long before Chapman was able to add her to his growing list of conquests, "marrying" her in a bigamous ceremony in October 1895, in which he seems to have posed as a Jew. As her "husband" Chapman now managed to gain access to a legacy of nearly £600, left to her by her grandfather. Some of this money was invested in a barber's shop in Hastings, where Chapman shaved his customers to the accompaniment of his wife's piano playing. One of those who enjoyed the so-called "musical shaves" was William Henry Davidson, a Hastings chemist. He was impressed by Chapman's medical knowledge, and sold him the tartar emetic that would play such an important role in his murderous activities on 3 April 1897. Chapman had already begun to beat Spink, and was pursuing a domestic servant, Alice Penfold, whilst claiming to be a piano salesman. This particular intrigue seems to have come to naught, and Chapman and Spink left Hastings, resurfacing in London where Chapman took the lease of the Prince of Wales tavern in Bartholomew Square.

Mary Spink's health, previously robust despite her incipient alcoholism and Chapman's violence towards her, started to fail soon after the move to London. Tended by her husband, who prepared and administered all her medicines (though the prescriptions were in fact those of Dr. Rodgers, her G.P.), she quickly sickened and died. Chapman appeared grief-stricken, although drinkers were surprised to see the Prince of Wales open at the usual time on the day of Spink's death. Rodgers certified that Spink had died from "phthisis", perhaps because of her emaciated condition and she was buried in a common grave at Leyton. With Spink dead, Chapman waited a few months before advertising for a replacement barmaid. He engaged Elizabeth "Bessie" Taylor, a former domestic servant, whom he soon persuaded to "marry" him. Before long, she too was beginning to sicken and pine. Chapman left the Prince of Wales, taking a new tavern, The Grapes, in Bishop's Stortford. His treatment of Bessie had begun to worsen: to verbal abuse he added threats with a revolver. Meanwhile, Chapman's career as a publican was also failing. He was soon back in London, leasing another pub, the Monument Tavern in Union Street, Borough. All the time, Bessie Taylor's health was worsening, but Dr. James Stoker, the Chapmans' physician, was at a loss to explain her symptoms. He could only watch as she entered an apparently inexplicable final decline, dying in February 1901. The death was attributed to "exhaustion from vomiting and diarrhoea".

Although Chapman had abused her both mentally and physically, before finally poisoning her with his faithful tartar emetic, Bessie Taylor had remained loyal to him, praising him to her parents who visited her at the tavern. Chapman charmed both, Mrs. Taylor remarking that she "had never seen a better husband".[13] In view of the treatment her daughter had received, this seems a singularly unperceptive observation, but it perhaps suggests that Chapman possessed a charisma in defiance of his appearance. This charm was to feature strongly in the circumstances surrounding the killing of his final victim, Maud Marsh.

Maud Marsh answered Chapman's advertisement for bar staff in August 1901. A young woman of nineteen, she was living with her parents in Croydon when she applied for the position at the Monument, and they insisted on inspecting the premises before allowing their daughter to move there. To allay their suspicions concerning their daughter's welfare, Chapman told them that he was a bachelor and rented the top floor of the tavern to a family. Both of these statements were untrue, but they served their purpose and Maud Marsh was soon living in the Monument and had embarked upon a relationship with her employer, perhaps even colluding with him in his attempt to burn down the pub for the insurance money later that year.

A pattern had long since been established in Chapman's affairs. A bigamous marriage was followed by an unsuccessful business venture, sexual indiscretion (usually with barmaids), then a debilitating illness, followed by the death of the current "wife", and her rapid replacement in another bigamous union. Unfortunately for her, Maud Marsh was enmeshed in this cycle almost at once, although on this occasion, Chapman was unable to win over her parents. Mrs. Marsh never ceased to be suspicious of him, and her anxieties increased following a letter from her daughter stating that, "George says if I do not let him have what he wants he will give me 35lbs [£35] and send me home".[14] This letter was contradicted by a second almost immediately, and was then followed by Chapman visiting the Marsh family in person to assure them of his good intentions. They were unconvinced by his performance, and Mr. Marsh warned his daughter to be careful. However, when he was taken ill (not, it seems, as a result of Chapman's activities), Maud lost her chief protector. She visited her father in hospital soon afterwards, and he noticed a wedding ring on her finger. Maud had, it transpired, been married at what was termed a "Roman Catholic 'Room'" in Bishopgate Street. From this point on, her death seems to have been assured.

The inevitable illness began, with the now familiar symptoms of sickness, vomiting, diarrhoea, sore throat, and severe abdominal pain that developed quickly into gastro-enteritis. Dr. Stoker was called in, but he was as baffled as before. As his "wife" became increasingly stricken, the ever-solicitous Chapman insisted on preparing and serving all her food and drink. Each meal was accompanied by agonizing side effects, and much of the subsequent trial record was to be occupied with descriptions of Maud's gastric irregularities. On one occasion, Mrs. Marsh drank from a glass of brandy and soda prepared by Chapman and was herself violently ill. This, coupled with Mr. Marsh being discharged from hospital and his strong suspicion that his daughter was being poisoned, led to the Marshs calling in their family doctor, Francis Grapel. He was convinced that Maud Marsh was being dosed with arsenic, closely related in toxicology and chemistry to antimony, and indeed likely to appear in the impure tartar emetic. In a desperate telegram, Grapel told his less insightful colleague to check for arsenical poisoning, but it was too late. Confronted by Grapel's knowledge of toxins, Chapman panicked, and killed

Maud with a large dose of tartar emetic. Her last words were, "Goodbye George".[15] Stoker refused to sign a death certificate, causing Chapman to harangue him violently. As Hargrave Adam observes:

> Dr. Stoker more than held his own, as the following interesting colloquy will show: "Why?" asked Chapman, after the certificate had been refused. "I cannot find what is the cause of death", replied Dr. Stoker. "It was exhaustion", said Chapman, "caused by inflammation of the bowels". "What caused the inflammation?" asked the doctor. "Continual vomiting and diarrhoea", answered Chapman. "What caused the vomiting and diarrhoea?" persisted the doctor. There was no reply.[16]

Prompted by Grapel, Stoker sent Maud's stomach and contents to Richard Bodmer, consulting chemist to the Clinical Research Association. Bodmer's analysis detected both arsenic and antimony in the stomach. Stoker contacted the City and Southwark coroner, Dr. F.J. Waldo, and called in the police. Chapman's rooms were searched, and the police discovered numerous documents, some white powders, £155 in gold and £110 in bank notes.[17] They also uncovered conclusive evidence that Chapman was actually Severin Klosowski, and that night, 25 October 1902, Chapman was arrested.

Despite the presence of such a sum of money at the crime scene, it is difficult to believe that Chapman was significantly motivated by monetary considerations. Adam suggests instead that "his operations were characterised with remarkable recklessness and daring, having for their primary purpose and *idée fixe* the pursuit, the capture, and the destruction of women".[18] This reading of the case poses its own problems however, and any discussion of Chapman's possible motives must be a cautious one.

Chapman was outwitted by superior forensic knowledge, but his own arrogance is hard to ignore as a contributory factor in his downfall. The killing of Maud Marsh in particular was sheer foolhardiness, while his refusal to part with highly incriminating documents, notably the receipt for an ounce of tartar emetic, which contained enough antimony to kill over a dozen people but which cost only tuppence, not to mention material relating to his life as Severin Klosowski, is almost inexplicable.[19] He also retained, perhaps as macabre trophies, the undertakers' accounts and memorial cards from the funerals of his previous wives. Adam describes him as "a most remarkable example of the over-confident criminal . . . exceptionally clever at one moment and a hopeless blunderer the next", pointing out that his audacity, or imprudence was bolstered by "a long immunity from detection".[20] Once Chapman was in the hands of the police, a formidable case was marshalled against him, and his guilt was very quickly obvious. The open and shut nature of this case might lead one to wonder why Chapman's deeds are so often considered to be a "classic crime". After all, there is no complex puzzle to unravel, no astonishing detective work, no public ambivalence towards the malefactor and the overwhelming evidence of guilt. Chapman's trial lasted a mere four days: his execution took place within a month, unopposed by anyone. The answer lies in the way that the killings tapped into so many late-Victorian and early-Edwardian cultural anxieties, and the mechanism by which Chapman was established in the public imagination as a quasi-demonic figure.

Clive Bloom has noted of Jack the Ripper that, "Jack combines notions of evil, insanity and moral justice at the moment when the nineteenth century saw itself as the century of progress, enlightenment and escape from 'moral' prejudice. The Ripper's name denotes a certain consequent frontier for the human sciences at this time".[21] While Chapman cannot be seen as a problematic agent of "moral justice", since he killed "ordinary" women rather than prostitutes, much of Bloom's point applies to him, especially as he has been suggested as a suspect for the Ripper killings. Like the Ripper, Chapman represented a dark menace in the streets of the capital, yet in some ways, he is even more frightening. The Ripper prowled the alleys of Whitechapel, anonymous, armed, perhaps insane. Chapman inhabited instead the *locus classicus* of English hospitality, the public house. He was not Sweeney Todd, merely a hairdresser seeking to advance up the social scale.

To read the details of the Chapman case now, especially when they are filtered through contemporary news reports rather than trial documents, is to be given a sense of a secret and hidden London, concealed from bourgeois eyes and illuminated only briefly by the legal process.[22] The glimpses that they provide of a Slavic/Jewish metropolitan underclass, for instance, suggest the fiction of Israel Zangwill rewritten by George Gissing.[23] The news reports also hark back to Henry Mayhew and many other Victorian social explorers, delving into "the abyss" in order to provide their middle-class readership with a thrilling and yet shaming glimpse of an alternative society.[24] The reports suggest too the increasingly polyglot nature of London's citizenry, encapsulated in the figure of a Russian Pole with the name of an English dramatist, masquerading as an American.[25] In such instances, national and racial boundaries begin to blur: a highly discomforting process for those who followed the trial in 1903. The judge's sentence reflects this alarm. In passing it, Mr. Justice Grantham intoned:

> Severin Klosowski, for I decline to call you by the English name you have assumed, the only satisfactory feature in the case we have just completed is that I am able to address you as a foreigner and not as an Englishman.[26]

By such remarks, Grantham hoped to banish overseas the contagion that Chapman represented. He certainly won the support of the *Pall Mall Gazette*, which approved his "very intelligible sentiment" in refusing to employ the "borrowed English name" of the accused.[27]

However, just as the body of Maud Marsh was found to be, "literally saturated" with antimony—the post-mortem revealed 7.24 grains in her vital organs—so the body politic of London itself was being continually invaded by figures of complex and, to an Edwardian audience, "impure" origin. By concentrating upon "rogue" or "deviant" individuals such as Chapman, the Edwardian press (not to mention judiciary) was able to offer a convenient method of metropolitan moral purgation, flushing out the poison that such characters represented into prisons and nooses, rather than considering the extent to which established norms of "Englishness" were being questioned by the processes of immigration and "inter-marriage". Public feeling concerning these matters ran high, and had played an important role in the "Khaki Election" of 1900.[28] The *Illustrated Police News* ran numerous articles dealing with "the alien immigration question" that missed no opportunity to promote xenophobic attitudes and paranoia and these concerns were by no means confined to that paper's largely working-class readership.[29] During the Chapman trial, a governmental committee on Alien Immigration was sitting, chaired by Lord James of Hereford. The *Daily Telegraph* reported its findings on the number of aliens housed in British prisons, and quoted the testimony of Haden Corser, magistrate at Worship Street Magistrate's Court in London. Corser informed the committee that Worship Street had seen 775 criminal charges against aliens in 1897, and 1279 in 1902: a considerable increase and evidence of a worrying national trend, despite the fact that few of the offences themselves were of a serious nature.[30]

A key late Victorian text concerning alien immigration and its related anxieties is of course, Bram Stoker's *Dracula.* A sinister Eastern European arrives in England and begins to prey on English women, taking over their identities and lives, subjugating them to his will, before destroying them by mysterious means that cause them slowly to sicken and die while he watches their suffering from a position of pseudo-matrimony. Expressed in these terms, the structure of George Chapman's criminal career inescapably recalls the events of Stoker's novel, published in June 1897, a mere two months after Chapman made his fateful visit to Davidson's pharmacy. Chapman had little interest in literature and was probably unaware of *Dracula.* Nonetheless, he seems in some respects to be almost an embodiment, albeit a proletarian rather than aristocratic one, of what might be termed the "*Dracula* paradigm". In sharing so many of the elements that Stoker employed to terrify his readers (and perhaps himself), Chapman intriguingly merges fact and fiction, revealing a cultural sub-text of anxieties and alarms that pervades not simply the literary market-place, but also the criminal court and its media coverage.

It might also be noted that Chapman, as well as having affinities with Dracula, bears more than a slight physical resemblance to Mr. Hyde in Robert Louis Stevenson's novella of 1886. Discussing Hyde, Jekyll's friend Mr. Enfield remarks that he is "not easy to describe. There is something wrong with his appearance; something displeasing, something downright detestable". "I never saw a man I so disliked, and yet I scarce know why", he continues, adding, "He must be deformed somewhere; he gives a strong feeling of deformity although I couldn't specify the point. He's an extraordinary looking man, and yet I really can name nothing out of the way".[31] Chapman was similarly (extra)ordinary, and it is tempting to suggest that only his known career as a serial bigamist and poisoner causes commentators like Brian Marriner to have recourse to Stevensonian description. Judging from surviving photographs, there is something indefinably sinister about Chapman, but it is impossible either to say what or to view the images impartially.[32] The English public (and jury) that followed the Chapman trial may not have made a conscious connection between Chapman and the fictions of Stoker and Stevenson, but it may have been tempted to read Chapman as the embodiment of a certain type of literary-influenced (one may even suggest constructed) compulsive pathology. Like Count Dracula, Chapman had a "heavy moustache" and "massive eyebrows": in themselves hardly proof of degeneracy, but within the context of *fin-de-siècle* understandings of the idea, notably suspicious.[33] Add to these markers of degeneracy the theories of Lombroso's *Man of Genius* (1891) concerning "loss of moral sense" and "excessive mutism"—Chapman was largely silent at his trial and died without confessing to his deeds—and one can begin to construct him as a recognizable late-Victorian type, shaped partially by the period's successful horror fiction, partially by its attachment to the pseudo-scientific theories of Cesare Lombroso and Max Nordau, and partially by the prevailing racial attitudes at the heart of the British Empire.[34]

Commentators on the Chapman case, as well as the prosecution and press corps, have often remarked on Chapman's repellent physical appearance.[35] Yet, as Marriner observes, "the cruel Casanova . . . could apparently lure women into his bed at will".[36] Adam professes himself baffled as to why in particular Bessie Taylor should have been attracted to a man about whom she can have had few illusions, and who was, as he points out, "socially far below her, illiterate and of repulsive appearance".[37] He speculates that Chapman's sheer otherness may have made him attractive, and this, together with his semi-fabricated exotic past may have helped him to impress the unwary. On this point, the press was rather ambiguous. The *Daily Mail* observed that "Klosowski is not in appearance a typical Russian Pole. He is an undersized man, with small, sharp features, and in repose his face does not suggest a foreigner".[38] The *Illustrated Police News* shared this view. In recalling the trial in its issue of 28 March 1903, it described Chapman as "a small, active-looking, keen-faced man, whose appearance gives no indication of his alleged nationality", assuming that that "alleged nationality" is Polish, rather than British or American. Two months earlier however, it had referred to his "typically Polish face", leaving readers to wonder about the differing expectations and perceptions of its journalists.[39]

However, it could be asked whether there was a more sinister side to Chapman's ability to bedazzle the women he met. Working as a travelling *feldscher* and army surgeon in Russia and Poland, it might be presumed that his access to proper medical supplies and surgical areas was a rare luxury, and that much of his work was literally out in the field. In blood-letting and similar operations, the ability to reduce pain and control blood-flow without recourse to drugs would have been enormously beneficial. It may have been that Chapman was familiar with the basic techniques of mesmerism, as practised in Europe and in the United States, and, under a variety of other names, as a staple of many folk-healing traditions.[40]

There is no direct evidence that Chapman was acquainted with mesmerism in practice, but the testimony of Florence Rayner (a barmaid at the Monument whom Chapman pursued from June 1902), concerning her employer's amorous attentions is suggestive nonetheless. On one occasion, Rayner "fainted . . . from the stuff the accused had given me", implying that Chapman was quite prepared to effect his seductions with the aid of drugs. On other occasions, she told the prosecution, she was constantly kissed by Chapman and found herself unable to resist his advances even though they were undesired. "I do not know if I wanted him to go on kissing me . . . I did not object; I could not help myself", she told the court.[41] Chapman's photographs of himself with Bessie Taylor and Maud Marsh show the women staring almost spell-bound into his face, although this may be because of the fixed pose necessary for a slow photographic exposure. Chapman may have possessed this entrancing power, which may in turn have encouraged his victims to go through with marriage ceremonies that they knew to be bogus. Here, the spectre of "peasant vitality" raises its head, another constant anxiety for eugenicists and racial scientists. In sentencing Chapman, Grantham denounced his "vile lust" for women: one wonders whether he would have been so keen to condemn the promiscuity of his peers.

Stir in a generous helping of late-Victorian anti-Semitism and one begins to suspect that Chapman was, as well as being a criminal identified as the murderer of three women, a veritable incarnation of late-Victorian fears about "the other". Although he was not Jewish, he had worked within London's Jewish community during his period as a barber, posed as Jew on occasion, and a number of witnesses at his trial were Jews of Eastern European extraction. This fact perhaps led other witnesses or observers of the case to believe that Chapman was Jewish "by association", an unpleasant thought for an audience familiar not only with East London's housing crisis, usually blamed on the rising numbers of Jewish immigrants, but with George Du Maurier's Svengali, another scheming foreigner of Polish extraction.[42]

Worse still, Chapman embodied the degenerate alterity seemingly rife in the English capital, the "murky modern Babylon" of much journalistic and evangelical writing of the period.[43] Chapman was prosecuted by Sir Edward Carson, the Solicitor General, who had famously established himself in the legal profession with his devastating cross-examination of Oscar Wilde in 1895, and who was consequently well-versed in the discourses of degeneration. A staunch Protestant, and thus unlikely to have warmed to Chapman's Catholicism, even without its attendant bigamy, he denounced Chapman as an "evil wild beast" and remarked, "I have never seen such a villain".[44] That these fears of the degenerate other were not expressed openly until Chapman's trial says much for their semi-buried status during the final years of Victoria's reign.[45] No wonder Chapman's defence counsel, George Elliott, began his doomed (and very brief) speech with a reference to the "storm of prejudice which in any other country might have imperilled the calm administration of justice".[46] He referred too to "the feelings which at the present time are entertained generally against the immigration of aliens into this country".[47] Chapman maintained throughout that he was a victim of prejudice, although shortly before his death, his solicitor, H.J. Sydney, "pointed out the absurdity of his assertion that he was 'persecuted as an alien' and that the police had got witnesses to falsely identify him".[48] Although the English legal system and media were at pains to consider themselves above suspicion of prejudice, it would be surprising if they or the trial jury were completely unbiased. After all, as well as the parliamentary committee on Aliens sitting at this time, members of Parliament and judges alike were denouncing foreigners. "At present the dregs of foreign countries flows incessantly into hospitable England, and within a few days are engaged in committing all sorts of offences. The sooner Parliament frames laws to prohibit the landing of these undesirables the better", said Mr. Loveland-Loveland, sentencing an immigrant who had assumed the name "Jack Baker" in January 1903.[49] To cries of "hear, hear", S. Forde Ridley, M.P. for Bethnal Green told a meeting of the Junior Constitutional Club that Britain "was becoming the dumping ground for all the undesirable characters of Europe".[50] Such views were widely reported in the newspapers during the first few months of 1903, and would feed into the "Aliens Political Offences Bill" at the heart of Edgar Wallace's 1905 best-seller, *The Four Just Men.*[51]

Another reason for the hatred of Chapman concerned the method by which he dispatched his victims. Tartar emetic (potassium antimonyl tartrate) was frequently employed as a purgative during the Victorian period, inducing vomiting in order to cleanse the system. As such, it had a long history dating back to Roman banquets, at which goblets of specially prepared antimony-doctored wine, the *pocula emetica* or *calyces vomitorii* would be employed in order to facilitate repeated doses of gluttony. R. Ian McCallum has traced the element's use in such concoctions, and points out its widespread use in Victorian medicine.[52] Chapman was thus not simply employing a poison, in the way that other poisoners soaked fly-paper in order to extract its arsenic, for example, but deliberately perverting a nominally medicinal substance. This fact not only brought down the execrations which always accompany violations of the Hippocratic Oath, but drew attention to his status as *feldscher* rather than "genuine" doctor. Chapman was, for the Edwardian public, committing two serious offences. One was to use his medical knowledge for maleficent purposes, the other was to claim bogus medical status in the first place. The severity of his original crime was thus compounded by his imposture, and the offence was further magnified by his status as a foreigner.[53]

Chapman's imposture was complex and multi-faceted. His reinvention of himself following his return from the United States in 1892 led him to change not only his name but also his nationality. Although "George Chapman" sounded reassuringly English, Chapman insisted on describing himself as an American. This fiction he maintained in his prison letters, claiming to be "an American orphend [sic] of good family" and in the London public houses he owned—he displayed a tattered Stars-and-Stripes, hung upside-down behind the bar alongside an equally dishevelled and topsy-turvy Union Jack.[54] He denied all knowledge of Klosowski, telling the police who were convinced that he and Klosowski were one and the same, "I don't know anything about that fellow".[55]

Had psychiatry not been in its infancy in 1903, this self-division might have been explored to useful effect. Perhaps Chapman's crimes were subconsciously committed by "Klosowski", the murderous *feldscher*, whose satyrical and homicidal instincts constantly subverted "Chapman's" attempts to settle down and lead a productive life. Here, the Stevensonian conception of the divided self looms large. In such a case, "Chapman" might well have seemed the "good" immigrant, determined to knuckle down and make an honest living in his adopted country. He craved social acceptance, turning the Hastings barber shop into a venue for entertainment as well as hairdressing, and ran a series of public houses in order to enact the role of genial publican and host so dear to the English heart. He tried to reinforce his position as "respectable" through marriage, and then, as a "widower". He also assimilated himself into London life with remarkable skill—he spoke English with almost no accent, allowing "his alias of 'George Chapman' . . . to have passed muster easily enough".[56]

Unfortunately for "Chapman", he was either trapped in "Klosowski's" degenerate body, or "Klosowski" had corrupted his own. "Klosowski" systematically undermined "Chapman's" ambitions through his uncontrollable, even animalistic (for an Edwardian public at least) sexual drives and compulsive criminality. In such a reading, the final rushed killing of Maud Marsh recalls the fevered "Statement of the Case" by Henry Jekyll in Stevenson's novella. Jekyll is able to triumph over Hyde through his suicide, but "Klosowski" would not be vanquished and gained control of "Chapman" at a critical moment as the medical and police net closed in.[57] "Chapman" wept over the suffering of his victims; "Klosowski" gloried in it. "Chapman" denied responsibility for the killings, pleading Not Guilty at the trial and never ceasing to play the role of the tragically and inexplicably bereaved husband. "Klosowski" on the other hand revelled in his knowledge of poisons and the power that they gave him. As Graham Young (Hugh O'Connor) laments in the film *The Young Poisoner's Handbook* (1994), the role of successful poisoner and famous poisoner are mutually exclusive—as soon as one gravitates to one status, one sacrifices the other. "Koslowski" could not place a city under siege as Jack the Ripper, and later Peter Kürten and Peter Sutcliffe would do, but he could nonetheless savour his seemingly god-like ability to grant life or death to those whose paths he crossed.[58] It might be posited that Chapman's crimes were even acts of appeasement by "Chapman" towards "Klosowski", each giving him a "breathing space" of normal life before the reassertion of his alternate personality. As "Klosowski" became ever more powerful, so the killings occurred with greater frequency. The final killing of Maud Marsh is consequently interpretable either as the ultimate victory of "Klosowski" or "Chapman's" final call for help.

The case against Chapman was immeasurably strengthened by his own boastful admissions. Adam's discussion of "The Mentality of Chapman" notes that he was "an accomplished liar", the key-note of whose behaviour was "consistent mendacity".[59] He was also a "braggart", Adam adds, claiming to be a keen sailor, a one-time big-game hunter, a medical student at Jesus Hospital, Warsaw, an American citizen and so on. In terms of his detection however, his most serious boasts concerned his medical knowledge. Having already killed at least two women, he seems to have grown careless during the murder of Maud Marsh, first pursuing Florence Rayner, and then one of his dying wife's sisters. He told Rayner that he could free himself from his marriage quite easily by giving Maud a pinch of "that", while Maud's sister Louisa reported that Chapman claimed he "could give her a bit like that"—here he snapped his fingers— "and fifty doctors would not find out".[60] If Chapman had hoped to remain undetected, such remarks were unwise to say the least, although in his defence he might have fooled any number of Dr. Stokers. A failed surgeon reduced to simple operations such as blood-letting and pulling teeth, Chapman (or, if one accepts the dual personality theory, "Klosowski") may have relished taking on the English medical establishment. He certainly impressed Davidson with his knowledge, one reason why the pharmacist sold him such a quantity of tartar emetic.

It is ironic to note that Chapman was further emboldened by one of Victorian England's great publishing success stories, the self-diagnostic medical manual which transferred some relatively specialized knowledge from the professional practitioner to the general public. At his trial, Mrs. Harriet Greenaway, who had once lodged in the same house as the Chapmans in Hastings, reported that she had lent Mrs. Chapman [Mary Spink], "some volumes of *Cassell's Family Physician*" in 1897. These had never been returned, and it is more than likely that their contents contributed in some way to Mrs. Chapman's death.[61]

Chapman did not defeat the medical and forensic profession, but he did force a review of its practices. Following the case, private autopsies such as that performed by Bodmer at Stoker's bidding were declared illegal, while the experiments used to discover the presence of antimony in the victims became known as the Marsh Test. This not only memorialized Maud Marsh, but also made the lot of the potential antimony poisoner a most unhappy one. Chapman's audacity and his bullying of doctors Stoker and Rodgers may also have forced many complacent general practitioners to review their methods and knowledge. Reporting Grantham's summing up, the *Daily Telegraph* drew attention to his comments concerning Chapman's amateur status. "It was a sad reflection that a man who had only been a hairdresser's assistant should be able to defy the doctors of this country", the judge remarked.[62] The case also drew attention to inadequate medical provision even at Guy's Hospital, "one of the finest institutions in the world". During proceedings, it was revealed that Maud Marsh had never seen the doctor who first prescribed drugs for her: the doctor had simply taken the symptoms from a "sort of clerk" and acted accordingly.[63]

The arrogance of Chapman's challenge to the medical establishment is nowhere more obvious than in his choice of poison. Had his victims been cremated, the evidence against him would have been far less conclusive, but it is one of the ironies of antimony that while it kills those who consume it, it also serves to preserve their bodies from decay. Describing the examination of Bessie Taylor following her burial in a "dry elm coffin" almost twenty-one months earlier, Dr. Thomas Stevenson noted:

> The body was covered with a mouldy growth, but otherwise was fresh. There was no putrefaction and no odour. The tissues were fresh. . . . Generally when bodies decompose they become wet and slimy. This one was extremely well preserved except for the superficial skin.[64]

Had it not been for the realization of Dr. Grapel that some form of arsenical poison was involved in the death of Maud Marsh, Chapman's victims may have remained undisturbed, their remains a secret challenge to what Chapman may have regarded as establishment stupidity.

Certainly, the Chapman case fascinated the public. The *Illustrated Police News* called it "the most notable murder trial of modern times", while even more sober commentators such as *The Times* and the *Daily Telegraph* testified to its creating "no little public sensation".[65] In January 1903, Chapman had instructed his solicitor to take action against the proprietor of an Islington waxwork show who was exhibiting models of "Chapman and his victims". The publisher and printer of what the *Illustrated Police News* called "some doggerel rhymes headed 'The Southwark Poisoning Case'" were also prosecuted.[66] Once Chapman was executed, no such cases could be brought, and M. Elton and Company, "Publishers, wholesalers and export newsagents" cashed in with a true "penny dreadful", a thirty-two page account of Chapman's life and crimes containing "portraits of Chapman, the Detectives, and the Victims".[67] The *Illustrated Police News* treated its readers to a double-page spread showing drawings of Chapman's progress to the gallows, complete with a final sketch of the prisoner, pinioned and with a noose about his neck, staring wild-eyed as the hood was placed over his head prior to his hanging.[68]

The significance of the Chapman killings for the late-Victorian and Edwardian public extends far beyond the killings themselves. Chapman was a type, a representation of all that early twentieth-century English metropolitan society most feared. Sexually insatiable, amoral, highly mobile (he seems to have had no difficulty in finding work or leasing premises) and possessing a mass of alternative identities, it was almost as if he represented a one-man pestilence, infecting traditionally safe enclaves such as the barber shop or public house.[69] Although he was without doubt guilty, the haste of the jury to condemn him—they deliberated on their verdict for only eleven minutes—and the hissing directed at him from the gallery and street as he left the court following his sentence says much for the terror, as well as disgust, which he was able to inspire. While we may regret not knowing more about Chapman himself, we can uncover much about the cultural context of his trial. In its anxieties about immigration and the fear that "they" may walk among "us", the case directly anticipates something of the world of Joseph Conrad's *The Secret Agent* (1907), not to mention the xenophobic panics inspired by the siege of Sidney Street in January 1911. Its themes are likely to continue to loom large in a heavily metropolized twenty-first century.

Notes

1. Colin Wilson and Patricia Pitman, *Encyclopaedia of Murder* (1961: London: Pan, 1984) 159.
2. George Orwell, *Decline of the English Murder and Other Essays* (Harmondsworth: Penguin, 1965) 9-13. Originally published in *Tribune*, 1946.
3. Hargrave L. Adam, *The Trial of George Chapman*, (Edinburgh & London: William Hodge & Co., 1930) 30. Afterwards Adam.
4. Brian Marriner, *Murder with Venom* (London: Forum Press, 1993), reprinted in 1998. Afterwards Marriner. The pros and cons of the theory that Chapman may have been the Ripper are well summed up by Adam 45-52. For more recent considerations of the topic, see Philip Sugden, *The Complete History of Jack the Ripper* (London: Robinson, 2002), 439-466, and two works by R. Michael Gordon, *Alias Jack the Ripper: Beyond the Usual Whitechapel Suspects* (Jefferson, North Carolina: McFarland & Co., 2001) and *The Thames Torso Murders of Victorian London* (Jefferson: McFarland & Co., 2002).
5. Marriner 10.
6. For illuminating discussions of these ideas, see Daniel Pick, *Faces of Degeneration: A European Disorder c.1848 – c.1918* (Cambridge: Cambridge University Press, 1989) and William Greenslade, *Degeneration, Culture and the Novel* (Cambridge: Cambridge University Press, 1994). For an examination of the place of immigrants within *fin-de-siècle* London, see Jonathan Schneer, *London 1900: The Imperial Metropolis* (New Haven: Yale University Press, 1999).
7. *Illustrated Police News (IPN)*, 11 April 1903 7.
8. Although the *Pall Mall Gazette*, the *Illustrated Police News* and a number of other periodicals referred to him as Severino Klosowski during the trial. The *IPN* even referred to him as "Severino Kloshoffski" (10 January 1903 6), while Wolff Levisohn, a witness at the police court hearing, claimed he had known the accused as "Ludwig Zagewski" in Whitechapel in 1888-89 (*IPN*, 17 January 1903 6).
9. As Adam points out on the opening page of his account, it is not known whether Chapman ever gained his degree. He certainly amassed a number of certificates of good conduct that may have been fraudulent - Adam reprints those found by police during a search of his rooms following his arrest.
10. Tracing Chapman's movements with certainty is impossible, not least because of his tendency to lie about his past at every opportunity. Adam cites no evidence for the claim that Chapman had served in the Russian army, but he is known to have been in Poland until at least February 1887. After that, he emigrated to London, gaining his first post as an assistant hairdresser sometime in late 1887 or early 1888.
11. Richard Altick makes the tart observation, "Some sources allege that when he 'married' Lucy, he already had a legal wife in Poland whom subsequently, to his embarrassment, turned up in London. But in view of his habits in such matters, the issue of who was, in fact, his first and legal spouse is utterly pedantic". Richard D. Altick, "The Deaths at George's American Bar" *Victorian Studies in Scarlet* (London: J.M. Dent, 1972) 269.
12. Annie Chapman testified against Chapman at his trial, pointing out that they had

lived together as "Mr. and Mrs. Klosowski" from November 1893 to November or December 1894. At the trial, she reported that Chapman had never used her name while they were living together. Adam 101-102.

13. Adam 10.
14. Adam 12.
15. *The Times* report of the trial gives some insight into Chapman's lack of interest in the metaphysical consequences of his actions. It quotes Mrs. Marsh's account of her daughter's final moments:

    > About nine o'clock the witness [Mrs. Marsh] noticed a change coming over Maud. She had a kind of fit. The witness went for the prisoner, and he came upstairs. Maud said, "I am going". The prisoner said, "Where?" Maud said, "Good-bye George," and she died *The Times*, 18 March 1903 4.
16. Adam 16.
17. *The Times*, 18 March 1903 4.
18. Adam 5.
19. At his trial, Chapman claimed to have found the receipt in a borrowed medical book, and swore that he had never seen Davidson before. *IPN*, 18 April 1903 2.
20. *IPN*, 18 April 1903 36.
21. Clive Bloom, "The Ripper Writing", *Cult Fiction: Popular Reading and Cult Theory* (London: Macmillan, 1996) 171.
22. Adam was not allowed access to the actual trial documents, and reconstructs events from secondary sources. Seventy years later, many important documents concerning the case have been lost, notably the Metropolitan Police file on Chapman.
23. In 1881, 46,100 Jews lived in London. By 1900, Russian pogroms were largely responsible for increasing this figure to 135,000, the majority of whom were Russian Poles. See Schneer, *London 1900* 7-8.
24. For a fuller background to these ideas, see Peter Keating, ed., *Into Unknown England 1866-1913: Selections from the Social Explorers* (Manchester: Manchester University Press, 1976).
25. The American connection may have reminded some Edwardians of the murders of Dr. Thomas Neill Cream, who poisoned several London prostitutes with strychnine during the early 1890s. Executed in 1892, he claimed on the scaffold to have been Jack the Ripper, although his claim is easily discounted. Cream was born in Scotland, trained as a doctor in Canada, and returned to London posing as an American. For full details of Cream's extraordinary life and crimes, see Angus McLaren, *A Prescription for Murder: The Victorian Serial Killings of Dr. Thomas Neill Cream* (Chicago: Chicago University Press, 1993). Dr. Thomas Stevenson, Home Office pathologist, was an expert witness in this case as he was in the Chapman trial.
26. Adam 164-165.
27. *Pall Mall Gazette*, 20 March 1903 2.
28. For detailed discussion of this point, see Schneer, 229-263.
29. Despite its name, the *IPN* was in no way connected with the police, and was instead much more akin to today's tabloid press. During the period January—March 1903, which covered the Chapman hearing and trial, the *IPN* ran stories

such as "The Alien Question: Foreigners who come to England and commit crimes galore" (17 January 1903 12), "The Alien Immigration Question—The first in a series of sketches by our special artist" (31 January 1903 6, double page spread 12-13), "Alien Criminals—An Italian's Dastardly Crime" (31 January 1903 13), "How the Aliens live and work" (7 February 1903 2), "An evening in Alienland—How the Undesirables spend their time when they come to England" (28 February 1903 2, "A free fight is a frequent occurrence . . . They are born gamblers"), "Aliens in London: Some of the crimes for which Foreigners have been convicted lately" (7 March 1903 5). The period also saw a number of anti-gypsy stories, while the coverage of the Chapman case allowed many other digs at immigrants, especially Slavs and Jews.

30. *Daily Telegraph*, 20 March 1903 7.

31. R.L. Stevenson, *The Strange Case of Dr Jekyll and Mr. Hyde*, ed. Emma Letley (1886: Oxford: Oxford University Press, 1987) 12. Elsewhere, Hyde is described as giving "an impression of deformity without any nameable malformation, he had a displeasing smile, and he spoke with a husky, whispering and somewhat broken voice . . .the man seems hardly human . . . troglodytic . . .or is it the mere radiance of a foul soul that thus transpires through, and transfigures, its clay continent?" "If ever I read Satan's signature upon a face, it is on that of your new friend," concludes Mr. Utterson, (19).

32. Oscar Wilde may have castigated those who did *not* judge by appearances, but Chapman's physical appearance was frequently read as evidence of some more profound degeneracy. He was not the first Victorian criminal to be viewed in this way. Discussing the trial of Dr. William Palmer, the so-called "Rugeley Poisoner" in May 1856, Charles Dickens observed:

> In passing, we will express an opinion that nature never writes a bad hand. Her writing, as it may be read in the human countenance, is invariably legible, if we come at all trained to the reading of it. . . . The physiognomy and conformation of the Poisoner whose trial occasions these remarks, were exactly in accordance with his deeds; and ever guilty consciousness he had gone on storing up in his mind, had set its mark upon him. "The Demeanour of Murderers", *Household Words*, 14 June 1856. Charles Dickens, *Selected Journalism 1850-1870*, ed. David Pascoe (Harmondsworth: Penguin, 1997) 477.

33. Bram Stoker, *Dracula*, ed. Maurice Hindle (1897: London: Penguin, 1993) 28.

34. Cesare Lombroso, *The Man of Genius* (London: Walter Scott, 1891) 5.

35. Chapman's hair and moustache were trimmed before his trial. The drawings by the *IPN*'s artist (21 March 1903 3) make him look a lot less sinister than the photographic evidence.

36. Marriner 10.

37. Adam 40. A not entirely fair comment, as Chapman could read and write in four languages, English, Russian, Polish and Yiddish, although his written English was weak. He also seems to have known a smattering of German. His English was certainly good enough to see him bring a false prosecution against Alfred Clark in June 1902, alleging that Clark had swindled him out of £700. Clark received a

three-year prison sentence, and was only released when some of the supposedly "stolen" notes were found in Chapman's possession after his arrest for murder. The motive for this crime remains unknown.

38. *Daily Mail*, 20 March 1903 3.
39. *IPN*, 28 March 1903 2, 31 January 1903 5.
40. On the subject of "animal magnetism", mesmerism and its prevalence throughout nineteenth century Europe, see Joscelyn Godwin, *The Theosophical Enlightenment* (New York: New York State University Press, 1994) 151-167 and Alison Winter, *Mesmerized: Powers of Mind in Victorian Britain* (Chicago: Chicago University Press, 1998).
41. Adam 99. She was also keen to secure a reference from Chapman if she sought future employment, so was reluctant to offend him.
42. Du Maurier's *Trilby* was published, complete with illustrations by the author, in 1894. The following year, an immensely successful stage version was launched. Svengali is a German-Polish Jew: Du Maurier's drawings suggest a strong sense of anti-Semitic caricature at work. According to the *IPN*, Chapman "pretended to go through the Jewish form of marriage" with Spink (10 January 1903 6), but the paper pointed out later that month, "Chapman, who by the bye, is a Polish Roman Catholic and not a Jew" (31 January 1903 5).
43. Though this memorable version of the idea is in fact taken from Henry James's essay "London", first printed in *The Century* magazine in 1888 and later in his *Essays in London and Elsewhere* (1893) and *English Hours* (1905). The most well-known reference to the idea of London as Babylon is probably W.T Stead's famous series of articles dealing with the prostitution of children, "The Maiden Tribute of Modern Babylon", published in the *Pall Mall Gazette* in 1888.
44. Marriner 10. Stoker of course denounces Dracula as "a wild beast" during the Count's attack on Lucy Westenra. *Dracula* 363.
45. Though anti-Semitism was widely prevalent in Victorian society. Like the *IPN*, Adam points out that Chapman was a Roman Catholic though "it has often been wrongly stated that he was a Jew". Adam 13.
46. Adam 149.
47. Adam 150. It is blackly comic to consider the many literary namesakes involved in the case, which include: George Chapman, George Elliott, Dr. Stoker, Davidson (though William Henry rather than the poet, John), Stevenson (Dr. Thomas Stevenson, Home Office analyst) and Gilbert (Frank Gilbert, mortuary keeper).
48. *IPN*, 18 April 1903 7.
49. *IPN*, 17 January 1903 12.
50. *IPN*, 11 April 1903 5. Ridley was opposed to "anti-Jewish" immigration laws, perhaps because so many of his constituents were Jewish. He did however suggest all new arrivals to Britain be assessed financially, educationally and medically before being allowed to become resident.
51. For further discussion of this point, including the vexed question of asylum, see David Glover's introduction to *The Four Just Men* (Oxford: Oxford University Press, 1995), ix-xxiii.
52. R. Ian McCallum, *Antimony in Medical History* (Durham: Pentland Press, 1999) 48.

McCallum notes that tartar emetic was the main ingredient in a variety of 19 century popular medicines in Britain and America. A.E. Hiss's *Thesaurus of Propietary Preparations and Pharmaceutical Specialities* (Chicago, 1898) lists: Analeptic Pills; Ayer's Cherry Pectoral; Jayne's expectorant; Piso's Cure for Consumption; Wistar's Balsam of Wild Cherry; Ransom's Hive Syrup and Tobias's Derby Condition Powder. See McCallum 102. Chapman may have encountered some of these during his American travels.

53. That imposture was a crime that bewitched highly stratified late-Victorian and Edwardian society is testified by its frequent recurrence in fiction and drama during the period. The precedent was perhaps set by the long-running case of the Tichborne Claimant.

54. Adam 44. Chapman's photograph of himself and Bessie Taylor before these ramshackle banners is reprinted in Adam, facing page 33. The Union flag is in fact part of a nautical ensign.

55. Adam 4.

56. *IPN*, 18 April 1903 2.

57. It was feared that Chapman would commit suicide in prison, and he was constantly watched by warders. The *IPN* and others were delighted to stress Chapman's "cowardice" in the face of death – "When he had to Face Death he showed his True Cowardly Nature" ran its double-page spread, 18 April 1903 8-9.

58. It might be wondered how such a character could continue to function relatively normally within society when such titanic internecine forces were at work. Joan Smith has argued that the Yorkshire Ripper murderer Peter Sutcliffe was faced with a similar dilemma, one that he solved by killing. Those who wondered how Sutcliffe could kill and yet seem "normal" were, Smith suggests, approaching the situation from the wrong angle. It was only *because* Sutcliffe committed periodic murders that he could ever hope to reintegrate himself into society and be anything approaching an "ordinary" citizen and husband. Joan Smith, *Misogynies* (London: Faber, 1989).

59. Adam 37.

60. Adam 85.

61. Adam 124.

62. *Daily Telegraph*, 20 March 1903 7.

63. *IPN*, 28 March 1903 2.

64. Adam 144.

65. *IPN* 21 March 1903 3, *Daily Telegraph*, 17 March 1903 7.

66. *IPN*, 10 January 1903 6.

67. *IPN*, 11 April 1903 7. The booklet cost one penny (the same as the *IPN*) and the advert proclaimed, "ORDER AT ONCE".

68. *IPN*, 18 April 1903, "Our Illustrations—Chapman's End—How the Poisoner Passed His Last Moments on Earth" 8-9.

69. Klosowski's aliases included George Chapman, Ludwig Zagowski, Ludwig Klosowski, "Smith" and "Lipski", the last a typical East End term for Jews or those thought to be of Jewish appearance.

Bibliography

Acton, William. *Functions and Disorders of the Reproductive Organs*. London: John Churchill, 1857.

---. *Functions and Disorders of the Reproductive Organs*. Sixth edition. London: J. and A. Churchill, 1875.

Adam, Hargrave L. *The Trial of George Chapman*. Edinburgh and London: William Hodge and Co., 1930.

Adams, James Eli. "Victorian Sexualities". *A Companion to Victorian Literature and Culture*. Ed. Herbert F. Tucker. Oxford: Basil Blackwell, 1999.

Ajalbert, Jean. *Sous le Sabre*. Paris: Editions de la Revue Blanche, 1898.

Allen, Dennis. *Sexuality in Victorian Fiction*. Norman, Oklahoma: University of Oklahoma Press, 1993.

Altick, Richard D. *The English Common Reader: A Social History of the Mass Reading Public*. 1957. Columbus: Ohio State University Press, 1998.

---. *Victorian Studies in Scarlet*. New York: W.W. Norton and Co., 1970.

---. *Deadly Encounters: Two Victorian Sensations*. Philadelphia: University of Philadelphia Press, 1986.

---. *The Presence of the Present: Topics of the Day in the Victorian Novel*. Columbus, Ohio: Ohio University Press, 1991.

Arata, Stephen D. "The Occidental Tourist: Dracula and the Anxiety of Reverse Colonization". *Victorian Studies*, volume 33, number 4 Summer 1990.

---. *Fictions of Loss in the Victorian Fin de Siècle*. Cambridge: Cambridge University Press, 1996.

Arnoulin, Stéphane. *L'Affaire La Roncière: Une erreur judiciaire en 1835*. Paris: Librairie Paul Ollendorff, 1899.

Bacon, G. Mackenzie. *On the Writing of the Insane*. London: Churchill, 1870.

Bahar, Jacque. *Le traître*. Vincennes: Imprimerie L. Levy, 1898.

Barlow, John. *On Man's Power Over Himself to Prevent or Control Insanity*. London: William Pickering, 1843.

Barrows, Susanna. *Distorting Mirrors: Visions of the Crowd in Late Nineteenth-Century France*. New Haven: Yale University Press, 1981.

Bartlett, Peter and David Wright. Outside the Walls of the Asylum: The History of Care in the Community, 1750-2000. London and New Brunswick, NJ: The Athlone Press, 1999.

Battiscombe, Georgina. *Charlotte Mary Yonge: The Story of an Uneventful Life*. London: Constable, 1944.

Beddoe, John. *The Races of Britain*. 1885. Washington D.C.: The Cliveden Press, 1983.

Beddoes, Thomas. *Hygëia or Essays Moral and Medical, on the Causes Affecting the Personal State of Our Middling and Affluent Classes*. Three volumes. Bristol, 1802.

Beer, Gillian. *Darwin's Plots: Evolutionary Narrative in Darwin, George Eliot and Nineteenth-Century Fiction*. London: Routledge, 1983.

Behlmer, George K. *Child Abuse and Moral Reform in England, 1870-1908*. Stanford: Stanford University Press, 1982.

Bentinck, William Cavendish. *The Correspondence of Lord William Cavendish Bentinck.* Ed. C.H. Philips. Oxford: Oxford University Press, 1977 (two volumes).

Bernstein, Susan David. "Dirty Reading: Sensation Fiction, Women, and Primitivism". *Criticism*, 36, Spring 1994.

Bhabha, Homi K. *The Location of Culture.* London and New York: Routledge, 1991.

Bierman, Joseph S. "The Genesis and Dating of Dracula from Bram Stoker's Working Notes" in Margaret L. Carter, ed. *Dracula: The Vampire and the Critics.* Ann Arbor: UMI Research Press, 1988.

Bland, Lucy and Laura Doan, eds. *Sexology Uncensored: The Documents of Sexual Science.* Cambridge: Polity Press, 1998.

Bloom, Clive. *Cult Fiction: Popular Reading and Cult Theory.* London: Macmillan, 1996.

Bonwick, James. *Who are the Irish?.* London, 1880.

Bostick, Theodora. "The Press and the Launching of the Women's Suffrage Movement, 1866-1867". *Victorian Periodicals Review* XIII.4, 1980.

Boyle, Thomas. *Black Swine in the Sewers of Hampstead.* New York: Viking Penguin, 1989.

Braddon, Mary Elizabeth. *Lady Audley's Secret.* 1862. Ed. David Skilton. Oxford: Oxford University Press, 1987.

Brantlinger, Patrick. "What is 'Sensational' about the 'Sensation Novel'?". *Nineteenth Century Fiction*, volume 37, June 1982.

---. *Rule of Darkness: British Literature and Imperialism, 1830-1914.* Ithaca: Cornell University Press, 1988.

Bredin, Jean-Denis. *The Affair: The Case of Alfred Dreyfus*, trans. Jeffrey Mehlman. New York: Braziller, 1986.

Bridgwater, Patrick. *Nietzsche in Anglosaxony: A Study of Nietzsche's Impact on English and American Literature.* Leicester: Leicester University Press, 1972.

Brodie, R.J. and Co. *The Secret Companion: A Medical Work on Onanism or Self-Pollution.* London, 1845.

Brooks, Chris and Peter Faulkner. *The White Man's Burdens: An Anthology of British Poetry of the Empire.* Exeter: University of Exeter Press, 1996.

Bronfen, Elisabeth. *The Knotted Subject: Hysteria and Its Discontents.* Princeton: Princeton University Press, 1998.

Buckley, Jerome. *Triumph of Time.* Harvard: Harvard University Press, 1966.

Butler, Judith. *Gender Trouble: Feminism and the Subversion of Identity.* London: Routledge, 1990.

Bynum, W.F., Roy Porter and Michael Shepherd eds. *The Anatomy of Madness: Essays in the History of Psychiatry* (three volumes). London and New York: Tavistock Press, 1985.

Cahm, Eric. *The Dreyfus Affair in French Politics and Society.* London: Longman, 1996.

Caine, Barbara. *Victorian Feminists.* Oxford: Oxford University Press, 1992.

Calder, Jenni. *Robert Louis Stevenson: A Life Study.* Glasgow: Richard Drew Publishing, 1980.

Campbell, Ian. "'And I too burn': Thomson's *The City of Dreadful Night*". *Victorian Poetry*, volume 16, 1978.

Cerullo, John J. "Intellectuals and the Imagination of Heroism during the Dreyfus Affair". *Proceedings of the Western Society for French History.* 1995.

Chadwick, Edwin. *A Supplementary Report on the Results of a Special Inquiry into the Practice of Interment in Towns.* London: W. Clowes, 1843.

Chamberlain, J.E. and Sander L. Gilman, eds. *Degeneration: The Dark Side of Progress.* New York: Columbia University Press, 1985.

Chiara, Briganti. "Gothic Maidens and Sensation Women: Lady Audley's Journey from the Ruined Mansion to the Madhouse". *Victorian Literature and Culture*, volume 19, 1991.

Clark, Anna. "Queen Caroline and the Sexual Politics of Popular Culture in London, 1820". *Representations*, volume 31, summer 1990.

Coghill, Mrs Harry. *The Autobiography and Letters of Mrs. M.O.W. Oliphant*. London: Blackwoods, 1909.

Cohen, Ed. *Talk on the Wilde Side: Toward a Genealogy of a Discourse on Male Sexualities*. New York and London: Routledge, 1993.

Colley, Linda. *Britons: Forging the Nation 1707-1837*. New Haven: Yale University Press, 1992.

Collins, Philip. *Dickens and Crime*. Bloomington, Indiana: Indiana University Press, 1968.

Collins, Wilkie. *Armadale*. 1866. London: Penguin, 1995.

---. *Blind Love*. 1890. New York: Dover Publications, 1986.

Colls, Robert and Philip Dodd, eds. *Englishness: Politics and Culture, 1880-1920*. London: Croom Helm, 1986.

Combe, Andrew. *Treatise on the Physiological and Moral Management of Infancy*. Edinburgh: Maclachlan Stewart, 1854.

Crosby, Travis L. *The Two Mr. Gladstones: A Study in Psychology and History*. New Haven and London: Yale University Press, 1997.

Curtis, L.P., Jr. *Anglo-Saxons and Celts: A Study of Anti-Irish Prejudice in Victorian England*. Bridgeport, CT: The University of Bridgeport, 1968.

---. *Apes and Angels: The Irishman in Caricature*, revised edition. Washington D.C. and London: Smithsonian Institution Press, 1997.

Cvetkovich, Ann. *Mixed Feelings: Feminism, Mass Culture, and Victorian Sensationalism*. New Brunswick: Rutgers University Press, 1992.

Dallas, Eneas Sweetland. *The Gay Science*. London: Chapman and Hall, 1866.

DeMille, James. *Cord and Creese*. New York, 1869.

Dickens, Charles. *Oliver Twist*. 1837, ed. Kathleen Tillotson. Oxford: Clarendon Press, 1966.

---. *Dombey and Son*. 1847-1848, ed. Alan Horsman. Oxford: Oxford University Press, 1982.

---. *Bleak House*. 1852-1853. London: Penguin, 1994.

---. *Great Expectations*. 1860-1861, ed. Margaret Caldwell. Oxford: Clarendon Press, 1993.

---. *Our Mutual Friend*. 1864-1865. Harmondsworth: Penguin, 1985.

---. *The Letters of Charles Dickens 1840-1841*, ed. M. House and G. Storey, volume two. Oxford: Clarendon Press, 1969.

---. *The Letters of Charles Dickens*, ed. Kathleen Tillotson and Graham Storey, volume eight. Oxford: Clarendon Press, 1995.

Dowling, Linda. *Hellenism and Homosexuality in Victorian Oxford*. Ithaca: Cornell University Press, 1994.

Doyle, Arthur Conan. *The Complete Sherlock Holmes*. Garden City, New York: Doubleday and Company, Inc, 1930.

---. *The Penguin Complete Sherlock Holmes*. Middlesex: Penguin, 1981.

Drumont, Édouard. *La France Juive*. 1886. Paris: Flammarion, 1912.

Eco, Umberto and Thomas A. Sebeok. *The Sign of Three: Dupin, Holmes, Pierce*. Bloomington and Indianapolis: Indiana University Press, 1983.

Eddrup, Edward P. *The Thugs; or, Secret Murderers of India*. London, 1853.

Edwards, P.D. "Trollope Changes his Mind: The Death of Melmotte in The Way We Live Now". *Nineteenth-Century Literature*, volume 18, 1963. 89-91.

Ellis, Havelock. *The Criminal.* London: Walter Scott, 1890. Rpt. Montclair, New Jersey: Patterson Smith, 1973.

Ellis, Havelock and John Addington Symonds. *Sexual Inversion.* London: Wilson and Macmillan, 1897.

Ellman, Richard. *Oscar Wilde.* 1987. Middlesex: Penguin, 1997.

Elton, G.R. "Introduction: Crime and the Historian" in J.S. Cockburn (ed.) *Crime in England 1550-1800.* London: Methuen and Co, 1977.

Emsley, Clive. "The Criminal Past: Crime in Nineteenth-Century Britain". *History Today*, volume 38, April 1988.

Erskine, Mrs Steuart, ed. *Anna Jameson: Letters and Friendships.* London: T. Fisher Unwin, 1915.

Féré, Charles. *La Pathologie des Émotions.* Paris: Alcan, 1892.

Finkelstein, David. *A Study of the Works of Philip Meadows Taylor.* Unpublished PhD thesis, the University of Edinburgh, 1990.

Finnane, Mark. *Insanity and the Insane in Post-Famine Ireland.* Totowa, NJ: Barnes and Noble Books, 1981.

Forth, Christopher E. "Intellectuals, Crowds, and the Body Politics of the Dreyfus Affair". *Historical Reflections/Réflexions Historique*, volume 24, Spring 1998.

---. "Bodies of Christ: Gender, Jewishness, and Religious Imagery in the Dreyfus Affair". *History Workshop Journal*, volume 48, Autumn 1999.

Foucault, Michel. *The Birth of the Clinic: An Archaeology of Medical Perception*, trans. A.M. Sheridan Smith. New York: Vintage, 1976.

---. "About the Concept of the Dangerous Individual in 19th Century Legal Psychiatry". *International Journal of Law and Psychiatry*, 1978.

---. *The History of Sexuality*, Volume I: An Introduction. New York: Random House, 1978.

Fout, John C. *Forbidden History: The State, Society, and the Regulation of Sexuality in Modern Europe.* 1990. Chicago: Chicago University Press, 1992.

Fox, Celina. *Graphic Journalism in England During the 1830s and 1840s.* New York: Garland, 1988.

Freeman, Sarah. *Mutton and Oysters: The Victorians and their Food.* London: Victor Gollancz, 1989.

Freitag, Sandria B. "Crime in the Social Order of Colonial North India". *Modern Asian Studies*, volume 25, number 2, 1991.

Freud, Sigmund. "The Uncanny". *Standard Edition of the Complete Psychological Works.* Trans and ed. James Strachey.

---. "On Narcissism: An Introduction". *The Freud Reader.* Ed. Peter Gay. New York and London: Norton, 1989.

Galton, Francis. *Finger Prints.* 1892. New York: Da Capo Press, 1965.

Geison, Gerald L. ed. *Professions and the French State, 1700-1900.* Philadelphia: University of Pennsylvania Press, 1984.

Gilbert, Pamela. *Disease, Desire and the Body in Victorian Women's Popular Novels.* Cambridge: Cambridge University Press, 1997.

Gilman, Sander L. *Difference and Pathology: Stereotypes of Sexuality, Race and Madness.* 1985. Ithaca and London: Cornell University Press, 1988.

---. *The Jew's Body.* New York: Routledge, 1991.

Gitter, Elisabeth G. "The Power of Hair in the Victorian Imagination". *PMLA*, volume 99, number 5, October 1984. 936-954

Godwin, Joscelyn. *The Theosophical Enlightenment.* New York: New York State University Press, 1994.

Goldstein, Jan. "The hysterical diagnosis and the politics of anticlericalism in late nineteenth-century France". *Journal of Modern History*, volume 54, 1982.

Gordon, Stewart N. *Marathas, Marauders and State Formation in Eighteenth-Century India.* Delhi: Oxford University Press, 1994.

Graham, Thomas. *On the Management of Disorders of Infancy and Childhood.* London: Simpkin Marshall, 1853.

Greenslade, William. *Degeneration, Culture and the Novel.* Cambridge: Cambridge University Press, 1994.

Gupta, Hiralal. "A Critical Study of the Thugs and their Activities". *Journal of Indian History*, volume 37, 1959.

Gupta, Pratul Chandra. *Nana Sahib and the Rising at Cawnpore.* Oxford: Clarendon Press, 1963.

Haining, Peter. *The Mystery and Horrible Murders of Sweeney Todd, The Demon Barber of Fleet Street.* London: Frederick Muller, 1979.

---. Ed. *More Tales of Unknown Horror.* London: New English Library, 1979.

Halasz, Nicholas. *Captain Dreyfus: The Story of a Mass Hysteria.* New York: Simon and Schuster, 1955.

Hardman, Sir William. *The Hardman Papers, a further selection (1865-1868) from the letters and memoirs of Sir William Hardman.* Ed. S.M. Ellis. London: Constable, 1930.

Harmon, Maurice. *Fenians and Fenianism.* Dublin: Scepter Books, 1970.

Harris, Ruth. *Murders and Madness: Medicine, Law and Society in the Fin de Siècle.* Oxford: Clarendon Press, 1989.

Hartman, Mary S. *Victorian Murderesses: A True History of Thirteen Respectable French and English Women Accused of Unspeakable Crimes.* New York: Schocken Books, 1977.

Hawkes, Gail. *A Sociology of Sex and Sexuality.* Buckingham: Open University Press, 1996.

Heller, Tamar. *Dead Secrets: Wilkie Collins and the Female Gothic.* New Haven: Yale University Press, 1992.

Herschel, William J. *The Origin of Finger-Printing.* 1916. New York: AMS Press, 1974.

Herstein, S.R. *A Mid-Victorian Feminist: Barbara Leigh Smith Bodichon.* New Haven: Yale University Press, 1985.

---. "The Langham Place Circle and Feminist Periodicals of the 1860s". *Victorian Periodicals Review*, volume 26, 1, 1993.

Hibbert, Christopher. *The Great Mutiny: India in 1857.* New York: Viking, 1978.

Hindley, Charles. *Curiosities of Street Literature.* London: Reeves and Turner, 1871.

Hirsch, Pam. *Barbara Leigh Smith Bodichon, 1827-1891, Feminist, Artist and Rebel.* London: Chatto and Windus, 1998.

Hiss, A.E. *Thesaurus of Proprietary Preparations and Pharmaceutical Specialities.* Chicago: 1898.

Hoecker-Drysdale, Susan. *Harriet Martineau: First Woman Sociologist.* Oxford and New York: Berg, 1992.

Hollingshead, John. *Ragged London in 1861.* London: Smith Elder, 1861.

Howe, Joseph W. *Excessive Venery: Masturbation and Continence: the etiology, pathology and treatment of the diseases resulting from venereal excesses, masturbation and continence.* New York: 1887.

Hughes, Robert. *The Fatal Shore: A History of the Transportation of Convicts to Australia, 1787-1868*. London: Harvill Press, 1996.
Hughes, Winifred. *The Maniac in the Cellar: Sensation Novels of the 1860s*. Princeton, New Jersey: Princeton University Press, 1980.
Hurley, Kelly. *The Gothic Body: Sexuality, Materialism and Degeneration at the Fin de Siècle*. Cambridge: Cambridge University Press, 1997.
James, Louis. *Fiction for the Working Man 1830-1850*. London: Oxford University Press, 1963.
---. *Print and the People 1819-1851*. London: Allen Lane, 1976.
Kaye, John William. *The Suppression of Thuggee and Dacoity*. London and Madras: The Christian Literature Society for India, 1857.
Kayman, Martin A. *From Bow Street to Baker Street: Mystery, Detection and Narrative*. Basingstoke: Macmillan, 1992.
Keating, Peter, ed. *Into Unknown England 1866-1913: Selections from the Social Explorers*. Manchester: Manchester University Press, 1976.
Keble, John. *Musings over "The Christian Year" and "Lyra Innocentium", Together with a few Gleanings of Recollections of the Rev. J. Keble, Gathered by Several Friends*. London: Macmillan, 1871.
Kellner, Hans. *Language and Historical Representation: Getting the Story Crooked*. Madison: University of Wisconsin Press, 1989.
Kershner, R.B. "Degeneration: the Explanatory Nightmare". *Georgian Review*, volume 40, 1986.
Kinnear, J. Boyd. "Anonymous Journalism". *Contemporary Review*, volume 5, 1867.
Knelman, Judith. *Twisting in the Wind: The Murderess and the English Press*. Toronto: University of Toronto Press, 1998.
Knight, Stephen. "Radical Thrillers" in *Watching the Detectives: Essays on Crime Fiction*. Eds. Ian A. Bell and Graham Daldry. Basingstoke: Macmillan, 1990.
Koss, Stephen. *The Rise and Fall of the Political Press in Britain*. London: Hamish Hamilton, 1981.
Krafft-Ebing, Richard von. *Psychopathia Sexualis*. 12th edition. Philadelphia: F.A. Davis, 1903.
---. *Psychopathia Sexualis*. Trans. Franklin S. Klaf. New York: Stein and Day, 1965.
Kristeva, Julia. *Powers of Horror*. Trans Leon S. Roudiez. New York: Columbia University Press, 1982.
Lacquer, Thomas. "The Queen Caroline Affair: Politics as Art in the Reign of George IV". *The Journal of Modern History*, volume 54, 1982.
Lacey, Candida Ann, ed. *Barbara Leigh Smith Bodichon and the Langham Place Group*. London: Routledge and Kegan Paul, 1987.
Landon, Laetitia. *Flowers of Loveliness; Twelve Groups of Female Figures, Emblematic of Flowers: Designed by Various Artists; With Poetical Illustrations by L.E.L.* London: Ackerman and Co., 1838.
Lane, Christopher. *The Burden of intimacy: Psychoanalysis and Victorian Masculinity*. Chicago: University of Chicago Press, 1999.
Langbauer, Laurie. *Women and Romance: The Consolations of Gender in the English Novel*. Ithaca: Cornell University Press, 1990.
Lauth, Gustave. *Que l'on doit éviter, ce que l'on faire dans l'intérêt de sa santé*. Paris: Fischbacher, 1888.
Le Bon, Gustave. *The Crowd: A Study of the Popular Mind*. 1895. New York: Viking, 1960.

Leckie, Barbara. *Culture and Adultery: The Novel, the Newspaper, and the Law, 1857-1914*. Philadelphia: University of Pennsylvania Press, 1999.

Leps, Marie-Christine. *Apprehending the Criminal: The Production of Deviance in Nineteenth-Century Discourse*. Durham and London: Duke University Press, 1992.

Levine, Philippa. *Victorian Feminism 1850-1900*. London: Hutchinson Education, 1987.

---. *Feminist Lives in Victorian England: Private Roles and Public Commitment*. Oxford: Basil Blackwell, 1990.

Loesberg, Jonathan. "The Ideology of Narrative Form in Sensation Fiction". *Representations*, volume 13, 1986.

Lombroso, Cesare. *The Man of Genius*. London: Walter Scott, 1891.

Lombroso-Ferrero, Gina. *Criminal man, according to the classification of Cesare Lombroso, briefly summarised by his daughter Gina Lombroso-Ferrero*. New York: Putnam, 1911.

Mandel, Ernest. *Delightful Murder*. London: Pluto, 1984.

Mansel, H.L. "Sensation Novels". *Quarterly Review*, volume 113, April 1863.

Marcus, Steven. *The Other Victorians: A Study of Sexuality and Pornography in Mid-Nineteenth-Century England*. 1974. New York: W.W. Norton and Co., 1985.

Marriner, Brian. *Murder with Venom*. London: Forum Press, 1993.

Mason, Michael. *The Making of Victorian Sexuality*. 1994. Oxford: Oxford University Press, 1995.

Matlock, Jann. *Scenes of Seduction: Prostitution, Hysteria, and Reading Difference in Nineteenth-Century France*. New York: Columbia University Press, 1994.

Matsuda, Matt K. *The Memory of the Modern*. New York: Oxford University Press, 1996.

Matus, Jill L. *Unstable Bodies: Victorian Representations of Sexuality and Maternity*. Manchester: Manchester University Press, 1995.

Maudsley, Henry. "On the Correlation of Mental and Physical Force". *Journal of Medical Science*, volume 6, 1860.

---. *The Physiology of the Mind*. 2nd edition. London: Macmillan, 1868.

---. *Body and Mind*. New York: Appleton, 1874.

---. *Responsibility in Mental Disease*. London, 1874.

Mayhew, Henry. *London Labour and the London Poor*. Volume two. London: Frank Cass and Co., 1851.

---. London *Labour and the London Poor*. 1849-1850 and 1861-1862. New York: Dover, 1968 (four volumes).

Mayo, Isabella Fyvie. *Recollections—of what I saw, what I lived through, and what I learned, during more than fifty years of social and literary experience*. London: John Murray, 1910.

McCallum, R. Ian. *Antimony in Medical History*. Durham: Pentland Press, 1999.

McLaren, Angus. *A Prescription for Murder: The Victorian Serial Killings of Dr. Thomas Neill Cream*. Chicago: Chicago University Press, 1993.

Meagher, J.F.W. *A Study of Masturbation and its Reputed Sequelae*. London Balliere, Tindall and Cox, 1924.

Melling, Joseph and Bill Forsythe eds. *Insanity, Institutions, and Society, 1800-1914*. London and New York: Routledge, 1999.

Menzies, K. *Autoerotic Phenomena in Adolescence: An Analytic Study of the Psychology and Psychopathy of Onanism*. London: H.K. Lewis and Co. Ltd., 1919.

Mighall, Robert. *The Geography of Victorian Gothic: Mapping History's Nightmares*. Oxford: Oxford University Press, 1999.

Miller, D.A. *The Novel and the Police*. Berkeley: University of California Press, 1988.

Millingen, J.G. *Aphorisms on the Treatment and Management of the Insane*. London: Churchill, 1840.

Mitchell, Sally. *Introduction to East Lynne*. New Brunswick: Rutgers University Press, 1984.

Moore-Gilbert, Bart. *Writing India, 1757-1990*. Manchester: Manchester University Press, 1996.

Moore, Grace *Dickens and Empire: Discourses of Class, Race and Colonialism in the Works of Charles Dickens*. Aldershot: Ashgate, 2004.

Morretti, Franco. *Signs Taken for Wonders: Essays in the Sociology of Literary Forms*. Trans. Susan Fischer, David Forgacs and David Miller. London: Verso, 1983.

Myers, Frederick W.H. "Multiplex Personality". *Nineteenth Century*, volume 20, 1886.

Nayder, Lillian. "Wilkie Collins Studies: 1983-1999". *Dickens Studies Annual*, volume 28, 1999.

Nead, Lynda. *Myths of Sexuality: Representations of Women in Victorian Britain*. Oxford: Blackwell, 1988.

Nordau, Max. *Degeneration*. 1892. Lincoln: University of Nebraska Press, 1993.

Nye, Robert A. *Crime, Madness and Politics in Modern France*. Princeton: Princeton University Press, 1984.

---. *Masculinity and Male Codes of Honor in Modern France*. Princeton: Princeton University Press, 1993.

O'Day, Alan. *Irish Home Rule 1867-1921*. Manchester and New York: Manchester University Press, 1998.

O'Farrell, Patrick. *England and Ireland Since 1800*. London and New York: Oxford University Press, 1975.

Oliphant, Margaret. *The Autobiography of Margaret Oliphant*. Ed. Elisabeth Jay. Oxford: Clarendon, 1989.

Onslow, Barbara. *What Can a Teacher Do Except Teach?* London: COIC, 1983.

---. *Women of the Press in Nineteenth-Century Britain*. Basingstoke: Macmillan, 2000.

Orwell, George. *Decline of the English Murder and Other Essays*. 1946. Harmondsworth: Penguin, 1965.

Ousby, Ian. *Bloodhounds of Heaven: The Detective in English Fiction from Godwin to Doyle*. London and Cambridge, Mass.: Harvard University Press, 1976.

Page, Norman. *Wilkie Collins: The Critical Heritage*. London and Boston: Routledge and Kegan Paul, 1974.

Paget, Frances. *Lucretia; or, the Heroine of the Nineteenth Century*. London: Joseph Masters, 1868.

Palmegiano, E.M. *Crime in Victorian Britain: An Annotated Bibliography from Nineteenth-Century British Magazines*. Westport, Connecticut and London: Greenwood Press, 1993.

Payot, Jules. *L'Éducation de la volonté*. 1893. Paris: Librairie Félix Alcan, 1912.

Pearsall, Ronald. *The Table-Rappers*. London: Michael Joseph, 1972.

---. *The Worm in the Bud: The World of Victorian Sexuality*. New York and London: Penguin, 1983.

Perry, R and L and Co. *The Silent Friend: A Medical Work Treating on the Anatomy and Physiology of the Organs of Generation and their Diseases, with Observations on Onanism and its Baneful Results*. London: 1847.

Pick, Daniel. *Faces of Degeneration: A European Disorder c.1848-c.1918*. Cambridge: Cambridge University Press, 1989.

Plunkett, John. *Queen Victoria: The Monarchy and the Media 1837-1867*. Unpublished PhD thesis, The University of London, 2000.

---. *Queen Victoria: First Media Monarch*. Oxford: Oxford University Press, 2003.

Pont-Jest, René de. *Les Procès des Thugs*. Paris: Bunel, 1877.

Powell, Robert Baden. *Scouting for Boys: A Handbook for Instruction in Good Citizenship Through Woodcraft*. 1908. 13th Edition. London: C. Arthur Pearson Ltd., 1928.

Prest, T.P. *The String of Pearls; or, The Barber of Fleet Street. A Domestic Romance* (begun by George MacFarren). London: E. Lloyd, 1850.

Pykett, Lyn. *"The Improper Feminine": The Woman's Sensation Novel and the New Woman Writing*. London: Routledge, 1992.

---. *The Sensation Novel: From The Woman in White to The Moonstone*. Plymouth: Northcote House, 1994.

---. *Wilkie Collins*. New York: St. Martin's Press, 1998.

Reynolds, George W. M. *The Mysteries of London*, volume one. London: George Vickers, 1845.

---. *The Mysteries of London*, ed. Trefor Thomas. Keele: Keele University Press, 1996.

Rhode, John. *The Case of Constance Kent*. New York: Scribner's, 1928.

Richardson, Ruth. *Death, Dissection and the Destitute*. London and New York: Routledge and Kegan Paul, 1987.

Richetti, John et al., ed. *The Columbia History of the British Novel*. New York: Columbia University Press, 1994.

Rogers, Helen. "The Good are not Always Powerful, Nor the Powerful Always Good", *Victorian Studies*, volume 40, number 4, 1997.

Rosario, Vernon A. *The Erotic Imagination: French Histories of Perversity*. New York: Oxford University Press, 1997.

Schellenberg, Betty and Paul Budra, eds. *Part II: Reflections on the Sequel*. Toronto: University of Toronto Press, 1998.

Schroeder, Natalie. "A Book that is Daring Enough to Speak the Truth". *Wilkie Collins Society Journal*, volume 3, 1983.

Scull, Andrew. *The Most Solitary of Afflictions: Madness and Society in Britain, 1700-1900*. New Haven and London: Yale University Press, 1993.

Scull, Andrew, ed. *Madhouses, Mad-Doctors and Care of the Insane: The Social History of Psychiatry in the Victorian Era*. Philadelphia: University of Pennsylvania Press, 1981.

Secker, Martin, ed. *The Eighteen-Nineties: A Period Anthology in Prose and Verse*. London: The Richards Press, 1948.

Sedgwick, Eve. *Between Men: English Literature and Male Homosocial Desire*. New York: Columbia University Press, 1985.

Séverine. *Vers la lumière: impressions vécues*. Paris: Stock, 1900.

Shapiro, Ann-Louise. *Breaking the Codes: Female Criminality in Fin-de-Siècle Paris*. Stanford: Stanford University Press, 1996.

Sharpe, Jenny. *Allegories of Empire: The Figure of the Woman in the Colonial Text*. Minneapolis: University of Minnesota Press, 1993.

Showalter, Elaine. *A Literature of Their Own: British Women Novelists from Brontë to Lessing*. Princeton: Princeton University Press, 1977.

---. *Sexual Anarchy: Gender and Culture at the Fin de Siècle*. London: Bloomsbury, 1991.

Shuttleworth, Sally. "Demonic Mothers: Ideologies of Bourgeois Motherhood in the Mid-Victorian Era". In Linda M. Shires. *Rewriting the Victorians: Theory, History and the Politics of Gender*. New York: Routledge, 1992.

Shuttleworth, Sally and Jenny Bourne Taylor, eds. *Embodied Selves: An Anthology of Psychological Texts, 1830-1890*. Oxford: Clarendon, 1997.

Simmel, Georg. *On Individuality and Social Forms*. Chicago: University of Chicago Press, 1971.

Singha, Radhika. *A Despotism of Law: Crime and Justice in Early Colonial India*. Delhi: Oxford University Press, 1998.

Skilton, David, ed. *The Early and Mid-Victorian Novel*. London and New York: Routledge, 1993.

Slakey, Roger L. "Melmotte's Death: A Prism of Meaning in The Way We Live Now", *ELH*, volume 34, 1967. 248-59.

Sleeman, W.H. *Ramaseeana*. Calcutta, 1836 (two volumes).

---. *The Thugs or Phansigars of India*. Philadelphia: Cary and Hart, 1839.

---. *Depredations Committed by the Thug Gangs*. Calcutta, 1840.

Smart, Carol. *Regulating Womanhood: Historical Essays on Marriage, Motherhood and Sexuality*. London: Routledge, 1993.

Smith, Joan. *Misogynies*. London: Faber, 1989.

Smith, Nelson and R.C. Terry, eds. *Wilkie Collins to the Forefront: Some Reassessments*. New York: AMS Press, 1995.

Smith, W. Anderson. *Shepherd Smith the Universalist*. London: Sampson Low, Master and Co., 1892.

Sorel, Georges. *La Révolution Dreyfusienne*. Paris: Rivière, 1909.

Spencer, Herbert. *Education: Intellectual, Moral and Physical*. London: G. Manwaring, 1861.

Springhall, John. "'Pernicious Reading?' The Penny Dreadful as Scapegoat for late-Victorian Juvenile Crime'". *Victorian Periodicals Review*, volume 27, number 4. Winter 1994.

St. Aubyn, Giles. *Queen Victoria: A Portrait*. 1991. London: Scepter, 1992.

Stearns, Peter N. *Fat History: Bodies and Beauty in the Modern West*. New York: NYU Press, 1997.

Stevenson, Robert Louis. *The Strange Case of Dr Jekyll and Mr Hyde*. 1886. Ed. Martin A. Danahay. Ontario: Broadview Press, 1999.

---. *The Strange Case of Dr Jekyll and Mr. Hyde*, ed. Emma Letley (1886): Oxford: Oxford University Press, 1987.

Stoker, Bram. *Dracula*, ed. Maurice Hindle. 1897. Middlesex: Penguin, 1993.

Stokes, John. *In the Nineties*. London: Harvester, 1989.

Strachan, Ralph. "That Familiar Feeling of Something Lost: Homosocial Desire in David Copperfield". The Dickens Project Winter Conference, U.C. Davis, California, February 19-21, 1999.

Strickland, Agnes. *Queen Victoria: From Her Birth to Her Bridal*. London: Henry Colbourn, 1840.

Sturrock, June. *"Heaven and Home": Charlotte Yonge's Domestic Fiction and the Victorian Debate Over Women*. Victoria: University of Victoria, 1995.

Sue, Eugène. *The Wandering Jew*. London, 1845.

Sweet, Matthew. *Inventing the Victorians*. London: Faber and Faber, 2001.

Taylor, Jenny Bourne. *In the Secret Theatre of the Home*. London and New York: Routledge, 1988.

Taylor, Jenny Bourne and Sally Shuttleworth. *Embodied Selves: An Anthology of Psychological Texts 1830-1890*. Oxford: Clarendon Press, 1998.

Taylor, Katherine Fischer. *In the Theater of Criminal Justice: The Palais de Justice in Second Empire Paris*. Princeton: Princeton University Press, 1993.

Taylor, Philip Meadows. *Confessions of a Thug*. 1839. Ed. Patrick Brantlinger. Oxford: Oxford University Press, 1998.

---. "State of Thuggee in India". *British and Foreign Review*, 15.29, 1843.

---. *Story of My Life*. 1878. Intro. Dennis Walder. London: Pluto, 1989.

T.D.L. *Narrative of a Journey Through India.* Westminster: Thomas Brettell, 1857.
Thomas, Clara. *Love and Work Enough: the Life of Anna Jameson.* London and Toronto: University of Toronto, Macdonald, 1967.
Thomas, Ronald R. *Detective Fiction and the Rise of Forensic Science.* Cambridge: Cambridge University Press, 1999.
Thornley, Henry. *Life in London.* London: E. Dipple, 1846.
Trodd, Anthea. *Domestic Crime in the Victorian Novel.* London: Macmillan, 1989.
Tromp, Marlene, Pamela K. Gilbert and Aeron Haynie, eds. *Beyond Sensation: Mary Elizabeth Braddon in Context.* Albany: State University of New York Press, 2000.
Tucker, Herbert F. ed. *A Companion to Victorian Literature and Culture.* Oxford: Blackwell Publishers, 1999.
Turner, E.S. *Boys Will Be Boys: The Story of Sweeney Todd, Deadwood Dick, Sexton Blake, Billy Bunter, et al.* 1948. London: Michael Joseph, 1975.
Van Wœrkens, Martine. *Le Voyageur Étranglé.* Paris: Albin Michel, 1995.
Verne, Jules. *Around the World in Eighty Days.* 1873. Ed. William Butcher. Oxford: Oxford University Press, 1995.
Vernon, James. *Politics and the People: A Study in English Political Culture, c. 1815-1867.* Cambridge: Cambridge University Press, 1993.
Walkowitz, Judith. *City of Dreadful Delight: Narratives of Sexual Danger in Late-Victorian London.* London: Virago, 1992.
Warner, Marina. *Monuments and Maidens: The Allegory of the Female Form.* New York: Atheneum, 1985.
Weeks, Jeffrey. *Sex, Politics and Society.* London and New York: Longman, 1981.
The Wild Boys of London; or, The Children of Night. Volume two. London: Newsagents' Publishing Co., 1866.
Williams, Raymond. *The Country and the City.* 1973. London: The Hogarth Press, 1993.
Williams, Richard, *The Contentious Crown: Public Discussion of the British Monarchy 1837-1901.* Aldershot and Burlington: Ashgate, 1997.
Wilson, Colin and Patricia Pitman. *Encyclopaedia of Murder.* 1961. London: Pan, 1984.
Wood, Charles. *Memorials of Mrs Henry Wood.* London: Bentley and Son, 1894.
Wood, Ellen. *East Lynne.* In *The New Monthly Magazine*, number 119, May 1860.
---. *East Lynne*, ed. Andrew Maunder. Ontario: Broadview Press, 2000.
Wynne, Deborah. *The Sensation Novel and the Victorian Family Magazine.* London: Palgrave, 2001.
Yang, Anand A. *Crime and Criminality in British India.* Tucson: University of Arizona Press, 1985.
Yonge, Charlotte M. *The Daisy Chain, or Aspirations: A Family Chronicle.* 1856. London: Virago, 1988.
---. *Hopes and Fears: Or, Scenes from the Life of a Spinster.* 1860. London: Macmillan and Co., 1883.
---. *The Trial or, More Links in the Daisy Chain.* 1864. London: Alan Sutton Publishing Ltd., 1996.
---. *The Clever Woman of the Family.* London: Virago, 1986.

Periodicals and Newspapers

The Atlas
The Athenaeum
Blackwood's Magazine

Cassell's Saturday Journal
The Century Magazine
The Christian Remembrancer
The Cornhill
The Daily News
The Daily Telegraph
The Englishwoman's Domestic Magazine
The Englishwoman's Journal
Figaro in London.
Fortnightly Review
Fraser's Magazine
Harper's Weekly
Household Words
The Illustrated London News.
The Illustrated Police News
Journal of Medical Science
The Lancet
Literary World
Medical Circular
Medical Critic and Psychological Journal
New Monthly Magazine
The New York Tribune
Overland
Pall Mall Gazette
The Penny Satirist
Le Petit journal
Punch
Quarterly Review
The Reader
Saturday Review
The Spectator
The Sunday Times
Temple Bar
Windsor Magazine
The Satirist.
The Spectator.
The Sun
The Times
The Westminster Gazette

Index